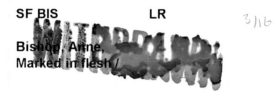
Donated by
Friends of the Nature Coast
Lakes Region Library

MARKED IN FLESH

MARKED IN FLESH

A NOVEL OF THE OTHERS

ANNE BISHOP

A ROC BOOK

ROC
Published by New American Library,
an imprint of Penguin Random House LLC
375 Hudson Street, New York, New York 10014

This book is an original publication of New American Library.

First Printing, March 2016

For more information about Penguin Random House, visit penguin.com.

LIBRARY OF CONGRESS CATALOGING-IN-PUBLICATION DATA:

Names: Bishop, Anne, author.
Title: Marked in flesh/Anne Bishop.
Description: New York City: ROC, [2016] | Series: A novel of the Others; 4
Identifiers: LCCN 2015041574 (print) | LCCN 2015044812 (ebook) |
ISBN 9780451474476 (hardcover) | ISBN 9780698190429 (ebook)
Subjects: LCSH: Women prophets—Fiction. | Shape-shifting—Fiction. |
Werewolves—Fiction. | Vampires—Fiction. | BISAC: FICTION / Fantasy/
Urban Life. | FICTION/Alternative History. | GSAFD:
Fantasy fiction. | Occult fiction.
Classification: LCC PS3552.I7594 M37 2016 (print) |
LCC PS3552.I7594 (ebook) | DDC 813/.54—dc23
LC record available at http://lccn.loc.gov/2015041574

Printed in the United States of America
10 9 8 7 6 5 4 3 2 1

Penguin
Random
House

For
Julie and Roger
and for
Nadine and Michael

ACKNOWLEDGMENTS

My thanks to Blair Boone for continuing to be my first reader and for all the information about animals, weapons, and many other things that I absorbed and transformed to suit the Others' world; to Debra Dixon for being second reader; to Doranna Durgin for maintaining the Web site and for information about housing for horses; to Adrienne Roehrich for running the official fan page on Facebook; to Nadine Fallacaro for information about things medical; to Jennifer Crow for insights about mom stuff; to Anne Sowards and Jennifer Jackson for the feedback that helps me write a better story; and to Pat Feidner for always being supportive and encouraging.

A special thanks to the following people who loaned their names to characters, knowing that the name would be the only connection between reality and fiction: Bobbie Barber, Elizabeth Bennefeld, Blair Boone, Kelley Burch, Douglas Burke, Starr Corcoran, Jennifer Crow, Lorna MacDonald Czarnota, Julie Czerneda, Roger Czerneda, Merri Lee Debany, Michael Debany, Mary Claire Eamer, Sarah Jane Elliott, Chris Fallacaro, Dan Fallacaro, Mike Fallacaro, Nadine Fallacaro, James Alan Gardner, Mantovani "Monty" Gay, Julie Green, Lois Gresh, Ann Hergott, Lara Herrera, Robert Herrera, Danielle Hilborn, Heather Houghton, Pamela Ireland, Lorne Kates, Allison King, Jana Paniccia, Jennifer Margaret Seely, Denby "Skip" Stowe, Ruth Stuart, and John Wulf.

GEOGRAPHY

NAMID—THE WORLD

CONTINENTS/LANDMASSES
Afrikah

Australis

Brittania/Wild Brittania

Cel-Romano/Cel-Romano Alliance of Nations

Felidae

Fingerbone Islands

Storm Islands

Thaisia

Tokhar-Chin

Zelande

Great Lakes—Superior, Tala, Honon, Etu, and Tahki

Other lakes—Feather Lakes/Finger Lakes

River—Talulah/Talulah Falls

Mountains—Addirondak, Rocky

Cities and villages—Bennett, Endurance, Ferryman's
    Landing, Hubb NE (aka Hubbney), Jerzy, Lakeside,
    Podunk, Prairie Gold, Shikago, Sparkletown, Sweetwater,
    Talulah Falls, Toland, Walnut Grove, Wheatfield

DAYS OF THE WEEK
Earthday

Moonsday

Sunday

Windsday

Thaisday

Firesday

Watersday

LAKESIDE

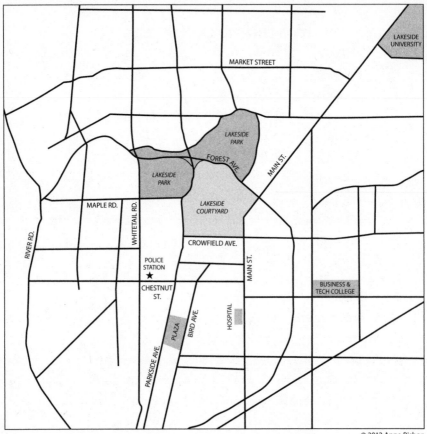

LAKESIDE UNIVERSITY

MARKET STREET

LAKESIDE PARK

FOREST AVE.

MAIN ST.

LAKESIDE PARK

MAPLE RD.

WHITETAIL RD.

LAKESIDE COURTYARD

RIVER RD.

CROWFIELD AVE.

MAIN ST.

POLICE STATION

★

CHESTNUT ST.

BUSINESS & TECH COLLEGE

PARKSIDE AVE.

PLAZA

BIRD AVE.

HOSPITAL

© 2012 Anne Bishop

This map was created by a geographically challenged author who put in only the bits she needed for the story.

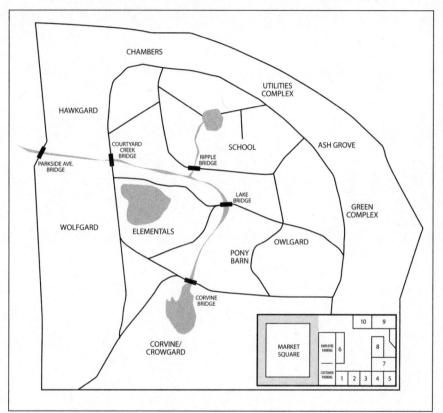

© 2012 Anne Bishop

1. Seamstress/Tailor & efficiency apartments
2. A Little Bite
3. Howling Good Reads
4. Run & Thump
5. Social Center
6. Garages
7. Earth Native & Henry's Studio
8. Liaison's Office
9. Consulate
10. Three Ps

MARKED
IN FLESH

A Brief History of the World

Long ago, Namid gave birth to all kinds of life, including the beings known as humans. She gave the humans fertile pieces of herself, and she gave them good water. Understanding their nature and the nature of her other offspring, she also gave them enough isolation that they would have a chance to survive and grow. And they did.

They learned to build fires and shelters. They learned to farm and build cities. They built boats and fished in the Mediterran and Black seas. They bred and spread throughout their pieces of the world until they pushed into the wild places. That's when they discovered that Namid's other offspring already claimed the rest of the world.

The Others looked at humans and did not see conquerors. They saw a new kind of meat.

Wars were fought to possess the wild places. Sometimes the humans won and spread their seed a little farther. More often, pieces of civilization disappeared, and fearful survivors tried not to shiver when a howl went up in the night or a man, wandering too far from the safety of stout doors and light, was found the next morning drained of blood.

Centuries passed, and the humans built larger ships and sailed across the Atlantik Ocean. When they found virgin land, they built a settlement near the shore. Then they discovered that this land was also claimed by the *terra indigene*, the earth natives. The Others.

The *terra indigene* who ruled the continent called Thaisia became angry when the humans cut down trees and put a plow to land that was not theirs. So the Others ate the settlers and learned the shape of this particular meat, just as they had done many times in the past.

The second wave of explorers and settlers found the abandoned settlement and, once more, tried to claim the land as their own.

The Others ate them too.

The third wave of settlers had a leader who was smarter than his predecessors. He offered the Others warm blankets and lengths of cloth for clothes and interesting bits of shiny in exchange for being allowed to live in the settlement and have enough land to grow crops. The Others thought this was a fair exchange and walked off the boundaries of the land that the humans could use. More gifts were exchanged for hunting and fishing privileges. This arrangement satisfied both sides, even if one side regarded its new neighbors with snarling tolerance and the other side swallowed fear and made sure its people were safely inside the settlement's walls before nightfall.

Years passed and more settlers arrived. Many died, but enough humans prospered. Settlements grew into villages, which grew into towns, which grew into cities. Little by little, humans moved across Thaisia, spreading out as much as they could on the land they were allowed to use.

Centuries passed. Humans were smart. So were the Others. Humans invented electricity and plumbing. The Others controlled all the rivers that could power the generators and all the lakes that supplied fresh drinking water. Humans invented steam engines and central heating. The Others controlled all the fuel needed to run the engines and heat the buildings. Humans invented and manufactured products. The Others controlled all the natural resources, thereby deciding what would and wouldn't be made in their part of the world.

There were collisions, of course, and some places became dark memorials for the dead. Those memorials finally made it clear to human government that the *terra indigene* ruled Thaisia, and nothing short of the end of the world would change that.

So it comes to this current age. Small human villages exist within vast tracts of land that belong to the Others. And in larger human cities, there are fenced parks called Courtyards that are inhabited by the Others who have the task of keeping watch over the city's residents and enforcing the agreements the humans made with the *terra indigene*.

There is still sharp-toothed tolerance on one side and fear of what walks in the dark on the other. But if they are careful, the humans survive.

Sometimes, they survive.

As humans it is our right, our destiny, to claim the world for ourselves. We must display the fortitude needed to wrest the land away from animals who hoard water and land, who have no use for resources such as timber and oil, who make no contributions to art or science or better living conditions for anyone. We cannot become the supreme beings we were meant to be as long as we allow animals to frighten us into believing we have to submit to the boundaries they set. The human race has no boundaries. If we stand together, we will be invincible. We will be the masters, and the world will belong to us first, last, and forever.

—*Nicholas Scratch, speaker for the Humans First and Last movement*

It's always about territory. It's about taking care of your pack, about having food and good water. It's about having enough of those things so your pack can survive and your pups can grow up. Other or human, it's what we all want. And when one kind of animal overruns an area to the point where many kinds of animal begin to starve, it's up to the predators to thin out the herds before there's nothing left for anyone. That's a simple truth whether you're talking about deer or humans.

—*Simon Wolfgard, leader of the Lakeside Courtyard*

N,

We must strike soon to achieve a swift and victorious result. Rally our allies and begin the diversions that will keep eyes focused away from Thaisia's ports. Ship whatever you can, however you can. A hungry army cannot fight the enemy we face. As soon as those last ships are secured in our ports, we will claim what rightfully belongs to the Cel-Romano people and wipe out the vermin currently overrunning the virgin farmland.

—Pater

To: All HFL Plains Chapters, Thaisia

Proceed with stage one of the land reclamation project.

—NS

CHAPTER 1

Sunday, Juin 5

*T*he sweet blood has changed things. You have changed because of her. We are intrigued by the humans who have gathered around your Courtyard, so we will give you some time to decide how much human the terra indigene will keep.

Simon Wolfgard, leader of the Lakeside Courtyard, stared at his bedroom ceiling, the words of warning, of threat, chasing away sleep, as they had for the past few nights.

The words weren't the only thing chasing away sleep. Procrastination was a human trait, and in this past week, he'd discovered that it had its own kind of bite. Wolves didn't procrastinate. When the pack needed food, they went hunting. They didn't make excuses or find some unimportant thing that didn't need doing at that very minute. They got on with the business of taking care of the things that in turn took care of them.

I wanted Meg to heal from the cut she made last week. I wanted to give her time before asking her to carry some of the weight of these decisions. She's the Trailblazer who is finding ways for other cassandra sangue to survive. She didn't make decisions for herself or anyone else for twenty-four years, and now she's supposed to make all these important decisions that could mean life or death for . . . who? The other blood prophets? All the humans living in Thaisia?

Growling, as if that would scare his thoughts into hiding, Simon rolled over, closed his eyes, and pushed his face into his pillow, determined to get a little more sleep. But the thoughts were excellent hunters and devoured sleep.

We will give you some time to decide how much human the terra indigene *will keep.*

For the past week, he'd made excuses to himself and the rest of the Courtyard's Business Association, and they had let him make those excuses because none of them—not Vlad or Henry or Tess—wanted to tell Meg what was truly at stake now. But time, like Meg's strange, fragile skin, was not something he could afford to waste.

Rolling the other way, Simon stared at the window. As he raised his head, his ears shifted to Wolf shape, pricking to better catch the sounds outside.

Sparrows. Those first sleepy chirps that announced the dawn when the sky began its change from black to gray.

Morning.

Pushing aside the tangled sheet, Simon hustled into the bathroom to pee. As he washed his hands, he glanced over his shoulder. Did he need to shower? He bent his head and gave himself a sniff. He smelled like a healthy Wolf. So he would shower later when he'd have to deal with more than the one human who was his special friend. Besides, she wouldn't be taking a shower either.

He took a step away from the sink, then stopped. Skipping a shower was one thing, but the human mouth in the morning produced scents strong enough to discourage close contact.

Loading toothpaste onto his toothbrush, Simon studied his reflection while he cleaned his teeth. Dark hair that was getting shaggy—he'd need to do something about that before the Courtyard's guests arrived. Skin that had browned a bit from working outside without a shirt on. And the amber eyes of a Wolf. Human skin or Wolf form, the eyes didn't change.

He rinsed out his mouth and started to put the toothbrush back in the medicine chest above the sink. Then he looked at his reflection and lifted his lips to reveal his teeth.

No, the eyes didn't change when he shifted to Wolf, but . . .

Shifting his head to Wolf form, he loaded the toothbrush with toothpaste a second time and brushed the other, *better*, set of teeth. Then he growled because a Wolf's mouth wasn't designed to rinse and spit. He ended up leaning over the sink and pouring cups of water over his teeth and tongue so no one would think he was foaming at the mouth.

"Next time I'm just chewing a twig as usual," he grumbled when he shifted back to fully human.

Returning to the bedroom, he pulled on jeans and a T-shirt. Then he stepped to the window and put his face close to the screen. Cool enough outside for socks and sneakers—and a sweatshirt since they would be walking at Meg's speed, not his.

He finished dressing, then grabbed his keys out of the dish on his dresser and went out the door in his apartment that opened onto the back hallway he shared with Meg. He unlocked her kitchen door and opened it carefully. Sometimes she used the slide lock as extra security, and breaking her door by accident would just cause trouble.

He'd caused enough trouble the time he'd broken the door on purpose.

No slide lock. Good.

Simon slipped into Meg's kitchen and quietly closed the door. Then he headed for her bedroom.

A light breeze coming through the partially opened window played with the summer curtains the female pack—Meg's human friends—had helped her purchase and hang. The morning light also came through the window, giving him a clear look at the woman curled up under the covers.

Was she cold? If he'd stayed with her last night, she wouldn't be cold.

"Meg?" Cautious, because she could kick like a moose when she was scared, he gave her shoulder a little push. "Time to wake up, Meg."

She grunted and burrowed under the covers until only the top of her head showed.

Wrong response.

Holding out one hand to block a potential kick, Simon laid the other hand on her hip and bounced her against the mattress a couple of times.

"What? What?" Meg struggled to sit up, so he obligingly grabbed her arm and pulled.

"Time to wake up."

"Simon?" She turned her head and blinked at the window. "It's still dark." She flopped down on the bed and tried to pull up the covers.

He grabbed the covers, and the brief game of tug had her sitting upright again.

"It's not dark; it's just early," he said. "Come on, Meg. We'll take a walk."

"It's not morning. The alarm clock didn't go off."

"You don't need an alarm clock. You've got sparrows, and they say it's morning."

When she didn't respond, Simon hauled her to her feet and steered her out the bedroom door and down the hallway to the bathroom.

"Are you awake enough to pee and brush your teeth?"

She closed the door in his face.

Taking that as a *yes*, Simon returned to Meg's bedroom and pulled out the clothes she would need. Most of the clothes. Apparently a male wasn't supposed to take a female's underclothes out of a drawer unless he was mated to that female. And males weren't supposed to *see* the underclothes unless females wanted the underclothes to be seen.

He didn't understand why everyone fussed about taking clean clothes out of a drawer. Underclothes smelled a lot more interesting *after* the female wore them.

Probably not something human females wanted to know.

While he waited, he made up the bed, more to discourage Meg from falling back into it than because he wanted to tidy the room. Besides, running his hands over the sheets and breathing in her scent made him happy.

Why had he thought sleeping in his human form last night was a good idea, especially when it meant sleeping alone? If he had shifted to his Wolf form as he usually did, he could have stayed with Meg, could have curled up next to her in her bed.

All right, he hadn't thought staying in human form overnight was a *good* idea, just a necessary exercise. Six Wolves from the Addirondak packs were coming to the Lakeside Courtyard next week to experience interacting with humans in ways they couldn't in their own territory. Three were adults who were already dealing with the humans who lived in towns located in and around the Addirondak Mountains. The other three were juveniles who had completed their first year of the human-centric education that would train them to keep watch over the humans living in Thaisia.

Keeping watch to make sure humans kept to the agreements their ancestors had made with the *terra indigene* was dangerous work. The Others might refer to humans as clever meat—and they were—but they were also invading predators who grabbed territory whenever they could. And despite what their government officials said, humans weren't really concerned with the overall well-being of their kind. Humans belonging to the Humans First and Last movement had howled about a food shortage in Thaisia and said the *terra indigene* had caused it. But it was the HFL humans who had sold the surplus stores of food to the Cel-Romano Alliance of Nations for profit and then lied about it. Those lies had spurred a fight in Lakeside that resulted in the deaths of police officer Lawrence MacDonald and Crystal Crowgard. By doing those things, humans had drawn the attention of *terra indigene* who usually stayed away from human-controlled places while their intentions were benevolent.

Those earth natives, who lived deep in the wild country, had decided that the humans living in Thaisia had committed a breach of trust, and all agreements between humans and the Others might be rescinded. Probably *would* be rescinded. Already there were restrictions on what kind of cargo could be carried by ships traveling on the Great Lakes. There were restrictions on what kind of human could travel from one human city to another. The human governments that oversaw human concerns on a regional level were reeling from the sanctions. If ships couldn't carry food and merchandise from one region to another, if trains couldn't carry food and fuel to cities that needed both, what would happen to all the humans living on the continent?

If the humans who were supposed to be in charge had paid any attention to Thaisia's history, they would know what would happen to the humans. The invasive, two-legged predators would be eliminated, and the land would be reclaimed by the earth natives, the *terra indigene*, the Others.

But that wouldn't be as easy to do as it had been a few centuries ago. Then, there was little that the humans built or used that would harm the land if left to decay on its own. Now there were refineries that processed the crude oil being drawn out of the earth. Now there were places that stored fuel. Now there were industries that might damage the land if left untended. How much would be harmed if those things were destroyed or abandoned?

Simon had no answers, and the *terra indigene* who watched over the wild country—the dangerous, primal beings who cloaked their true *terra indigene* nature in forms so old those shapes had no names—would not be concerned with answers. Even if everything else disappeared from the world to make room for the new that would be born from destruction and change, *they* would still exist.

The *terra indigene* shifters like the Wolves and Bears, the Hawks and Crows, referred to those forms as the Elders, a benevolent-sounding word for the beings who were Namid's teeth and claws.

Meg returned from the bathroom, looking a little more awake and a lot less happy to see him. She was going to be more unhappy when she found out why he wanted to take this walk.

"Get dressed, Meg. We need to talk."

She pointed at the bedroom door.

He was the leader of the Courtyard and she was an employee of the Courtyard, so she shouldn't be allowed to give him orders, even nonverbal ones. But he was learning that, when dealing with humans, pack order wasn't always maintained inside the den. Which meant Meg was dominant in her den and could disregard that he was dominant everywhere else.

He left the room and closed the door, then pressed his ear against the wood. Drawers opening, drawers closing. Movement.

"Stop hovering, Simon."

She sounded annoyed instead of sleepy. Having sufficiently poked the porcupine, so to speak, he went back to her kitchen and checked out her cupboards and fridge to make sure she had enough people food. Half a quart of milk; a couple of bites of cheese—maybe more in terms of human bites; a small bowl of strawberries—her share of the berries she and Henry Beargard had picked yesterday; a wrapped half sandwich from A Little Bite, the Courtyard's coffee shop.

Her cupboard had a canning jar of peaches, a jar of spaghetti sauce, and a box of spaghetti.

"If you're poking around for leftover pizza, I ate it last night," Meg said, entering the kitchen.

Simon closed the cupboard. Was this a typical amount of food for humans to store in the warmer months? He didn't have more than this in his kitchen, but he usually chased down his meal and ate it fresh, so other foods were just supplements that he enjoyed for taste and were good for the human form.

"Did you want something to eat?" Meg asked.

"Later." Leaving her kitchen, he went down the back stairs that led to the outer door, confident that she would follow him. Once outside, he took her hand, linking his fingers with hers, a form of contact and connection they'd started a week ago after she'd spoken prophecy about the River Road Community.

"The grass is wet," Meg said. "Shouldn't we walk on the road?"

Simon shook his head. This morning the road, which was wide enough for a vehicle and formed a circle inside the Courtyard, felt too human.

How to start? What to say?

They passed the expanded kitchen garden for the Green Complex, the only multispecies complex in the Courtyard. As a way to help the humans who were working for the Courtyard, the Others had agreed to let those humans share in the harvest if they did their share of the work. There was at least one human checking the garden every day, making sure the plants had enough water—and the females especially had eyes like a Hawk's when it came to spotting a weed.

He spotted a scrap of fur at the edge of the garden but didn't point it out to Meg. Something had come by to nibble on the seedlings and had ended up being someone's dinner.

"You wanted to talk," Meg said. "Is this about the sanctions? The *Lakeside News* has printed a lot of articles about the restrictions humans have to obey now."

"A lot of howling for trouble they brought on themselves," Simon growled.

"People are scared. They don't know what the sanctions mean for their families."

"Trust humans to try to build a beaver dam out of a couple of twigs. The sanctions are simple enough. Any human who belongs to the Humans First and Last movement is not allowed to travel on any right-of-way through the wild country. That means no roads, no trains."

"Boat?"

Simon shook his head. "All the water in Thaisia belongs to the *terra indigene*. Ships on the lakes and rivers travel on sufferance. Always have." And the Elementals known as the Five Sisters had already said that any ship that traveled the Great Lakes without their consent wouldn't reach port. Well, the ship might, but the crew wouldn't. After all, sinking the ship would soil the lake with all that fuel and debris. More likely, the ship would be set adrift after the easily transferred cargo had been removed. And the crew would become meals for the *terra indigene* doing the work of taking a human annoyance off the water.

"What about food?" Meg asked. "The newspapers and television reports said food can't be transported from one region to another."

"Either they're lying to cause trouble or they were too busy yelling about it to listen." As far as the Others were concerned, not listening was a big reason why humans, as a species, ended up needing harsh lessons: they refused to understand the warning nips. "Look, Meg, the buying and selling of foods and merchandise among the Simple Life folk, the Intuits, and the *terra indigene* isn't going to change,

and that includes all human settlements that are controlled by us. Any food coming from human-controlled farms has to be approved by Intuit and *terra indigene*
inspectors before it's allowed to cross from one region to another. We're doing
that to make sure humans can't lie again about food shortages here while they're
selling that food to humans in another part of the world." He huffed out a breath.
"But that's not what we need to talk about. This Courtyard—actually, a select
group within this Courtyard—has been given a duty by the Elders, the earth
natives who watch over the wild country. And that select group includes you
because you're the one who changed things."

"Me?" Meg's legs stuttered. "What did I do?"

Simon smiled. "You're you."

Meg Corbyn, Human Liaison for the Lakeside Courtyard, was a *cassandra
sangue*, a blood prophet who saw visions when her skin was cut. She had stumbled
into Howling Good Reads during a snowstorm, looking for work, on the run
from the man who had owned her and had cut her for profit. As vulnerable and
inexperienced as a puppy, she had worked hard to learn her job as Human Liaison
and also worked just as hard to learn how to live. Some of the humans who worked
for the Courtyard rallied around her, helping her, teaching her, even protecting
her. And that changed the relationship those humans had with the Others.

Simon's smiled faded. "How much human will the *terra indigene* keep? That's
what we have to figure out."

Meg stopped walking. "What does that mean?"

"That's the other thing we have to figure out." He tugged on her hand to get
her moving again, but she just stared at him, her gray eyes the same color as the
morning sky.

"How much human will you keep? What are you supposed to decide? If the
terra indigene in human form get to keep things like fingers and thumbs? Because
fingers and thumbs are really useful. Henry is a sculptor. He wouldn't want to do
without them. Neither would you."

Simon studied her. Maybe human brains really did take longer to wake up
than *terra indigene* brains. When he woke up, he was awake. He yawned, he
stretched, and he was ready to play or hunt or even deal with the human work
generated by the Business Association and Howling Good Reads, the bookstore
he ran with Vladimir Sanguinati. Even though Meg was a special breed of human,
apparently her brain didn't have a speedy wake-up button.

But he slept with her most nights, and he knew she wasn't usually *this* slow. So maybe sparrows were a sufficient call to morning for the body but the brain *needed* the mechanical alarm clock? Or maybe it was a difference between human males and females? He'd have to ask Karl Kowalski, who was Ruthie Stuart's mate as well as one of the police officers assigned to working with the Courtyard.

He started walking again and pulled Meg along for a couple of steps before she moved on her own.

"It's not about the shell." Simon thumped his chest with the fingers of one hand. Then, because this was Meg and they were learning together about a lot of things that involved humans, he told her more than he would have told another human—he told her his own fears. "In a way, it *is* about the shell. Namid shaped the earth natives to be her dominant predators, and we continue to be dominant because we learn from the other predators who walk in our world. We take their forms to blend in and watch them, learn how they hunt, how they live. We absorb a lot of their nature just by living in that form. Not everything. We are first, and always, earth natives. But because the animal forms have become a part of what is passed down to our young, a *terra indigene* Wolf isn't the same anymore as a *terra indigene* Bear or Hawk or Crow. Those forms have been around for a long time—and forms like the Sharkgard have been around even longer."

They walked in silence for a minute.

"Are you afraid of becoming too human?" Meg asked.

"Yes."

"Well, you won't," she said fiercely, squeezing his fingers. "You're a Wolf, and even when you're not a wolfy-looking Wolf, you're still a Wolf. You've said so. Looking human or running a bookstore won't change that."

Simon thought about what she was saying *under* what she was saying.

Meg didn't want him to be more human. She *needed* him to remain a Wolf. Because Meg trusted the Wolf in ways she didn't trust a human male.

He felt a lightness inside him that hadn't been there a minute ago. Working in a Courtyard, especially for the *terra indigene* who had to spend so much time around humans, was a danger because there was always the risk of absorbing too much of the human form and no longer fitting in with your own kind. That had worried him, more so lately as his exposure to humans became personal. But Meg wouldn't allow him to become *too* human because she needed him to retain the nature and heart of a Wolf.

He slanted a glance at her, with her clear gray eyes, and fair skin with those rose-tinted cheeks, and that thick black hair that was cropped so short it felt like puppy fuzz. Short and slim, and gaining some visible muscle beneath that fragile skin.

How much human would be too human for Meg?

Simon shook off the thought. He had enough challenges at the moment.

"You don't have to be afraid of what you might absorb from our human friends," Meg said quietly. "They're good people."

"How do you know?"

"I've known the bad kind of people." A grim reminder of the place where she'd been raised and trained and cut for profit.

He nodded to let her know he'd heard her. "We should consider what we'd like to keep, what we would be willing to make for ourselves if humans weren't around."

She gave him a sharp look, and her voice trembled when she said, "Are humans going to go away?"

"Maybe." He didn't say *extinct*. Meg was smart enough to hear the word anyway. And he didn't tell her that the Lakeside Courtyard was the reason the Elders hadn't already made that decision about the humans living on the continent of Thaisia.

"Can I talk to Ruth and Merri Lee and Theral about this?"

"They're human, Meg. They're going to want to keep everything."

"There are a lot of things humans need that I don't know about. I spent twenty-four years living in a compound as property, living in a cell once I was old enough to be by myself, and I don't remember how the girls lived before being old enough to begin training. And you know what the Courtyard needs, but surely that isn't everything either."

"By the agreements with humans, a Courtyard is supposed to have whatever the humans in that city have, so if it's not in the Courtyard, humans don't really need it." That was a thin-ice kind of truth that wouldn't hold any weight if put to the test, and they both knew it. "Besides, if you tell the female pack, Ruthie and Merri Lee will tell their mates, who are police."

"Who are around a lot and are helpful," Meg countered.

He couldn't argue with that. Karl Kowalski and Michael Debany were making an effort to understand the *terra indigene* and were likable males, even if they were human. And Lawrence MacDonald, another police officer and Theral's cousin, had died recently when a group of humans and Others went to a stall market in Lakeside to give the Crowgard a chance to buy some shinies and little treasures. That field trip ended when their group was attacked by members of the Humans First and Last movement. Almost everyone except Vlad had been wounded during the fight, and MacDonald and Crystal Crowgard had died.

"You should also ask Steve Ferryman for his suggestions," Meg said.

"Meg . . ."

"Those Elders didn't tell you that you *couldn't* ask humans, did they?"

He sighed. "No, they didn't, but we have to be careful about how many humans know about this. The humans who belong to the HFL are our enemies. They're burrowed in towns all across Thaisia, and they're the reason the Elders are looking at *all* the humans on the continent rather than eliminating the badness in one town and reclaiming the land."

Of course, he'd already told three humans what was now at stake. He believed Captain Burke and Lieutenant Montgomery could be trusted, but he hadn't known the third man who had been at the meeting when he told them about the sanctions. Greg O'Sullivan worked for the governor of the Northeast Region, so it was possible that there were already enemies of the *terra indigene* who were plotting to cause the final bit of trouble that would tip the scales.

If that happened, it wouldn't be the first time humans disappeared from a part of the world, and Simon doubted it would be the last.

And because that possibility was a rockslide waiting to come down on all of them, it became more imperative to figure out how much human the *terra indigene* should keep.

"All right," he said. "Talk to the female pack. But make sure they know this is dangerous information."

"I will." Meg stopped suddenly and whispered, "Bunny."

Bunny? Simon's mouth watered. Not that he had a good chance of catching one in his human form. He looked around. Smelled the bunny but couldn't see one. Then he realized Meg was staring at a brown lump in the grass a long step away from them. Could have been a rock or a bit of tree root poking out of the ground—but those things didn't have ears.

He sighed, disappointed. Just a one-bite bunny.

Meg backed away, pulling him with her.

"Isn't he cute?" she whispered, heading back toward the Green Complex.

"You won't think he's so cute if he eats all your broccoli," Simon said.

"He wouldn't do that. Would he?"

"Broccoli is green, and he's a bunny."

Meg huffed as she picked up the pace. "Well, he's still cute."

And probably would be allowed to grow since he wasn't much of a meal for anyone right now.

Simon didn't mention that since he suspected Meg preferred to think of the bunny as cute rather than crunchy.

CHAPTER 2

Sunday, Juin 5

Meg stared at those gathered in the sorting room at the Human Liaison's Office—Ruth Stuart, Merri Lee, and Theral MacDonald—and they stared back at her.

"You've already heard about this." The muffins Meg had picked up at A Little Bite sat on the table, untouched.

"Not about this," Ruth said. "But Karl headed to Captain Burke's house for a special, secret meeting—at least that's the opinion I got from what he couldn't say. And he thinks Captain Burke and Lieutenant Montgomery were told more about the sanctions than was made public. If they were told about this . . ."

"Michael was called in for that meeting too," Merri Lee said. She took a deep breath and let it out slowly. "Meg, we can't be responsible for something this . . . *big*. How can we make a decision about how much human the *terra indigene* will keep?"

"I don't think we're the ones making the decision," Meg replied. "We're providing information, maybe prioritizing, so that if . . ." She pressed her hands against the table, trying to ignore the painful pins-and-needles feeling that had started in her arms and was now prickling her entire torso under the skin.

The three girls snapped to attention.

"Meg?" Merri Lee's voice turned sharp with understanding.

Meg tried to ignore the pain, tried not to think about how the euphoria that came from speaking prophecy after she made a cut would make her feel *so* good. She'd made a cut last week; she didn't want to make another so soon. She didn't know if it was true that a *cassandra sangue* had only a thousand cuts before the one that would kill her or drive her insane, but if she wanted to live another decade or more, she needed to extend the time between cuts.

"Tell me about this morning," Merri Lee said. "What did you do this morning? Meg!"

Ruth and Theral hustled to the office's back room and closed the door—but not all the way.

"The sparrows were awake, so Simon was awake, so he woke me up because he wanted to take a walk. Poophead."

Merri Lee snorted a laugh. "Meg! That's not a nice thing to say."

"Didn't say it when he could hear me." And would have to be careful not to say it around the puppies, especially Simon's nephew Sam. Since she'd learned the bad word from the human boy Robert Denby, she was pretty sure young males of any species would find the term an appealing insult—and no doubt end up getting nipped by one of the adult Wolves, who would *not* find it as appealing.

Sam no longer lived with Simon on the weekdays. While she missed the pup when he stayed at the Wolfgard Complex instead of being right next door, maybe it was a good thing that Sam spent more time playing with other Wolves than he did playing with human children.

"We saw a little bunny," Meg continued. "He was cute. Simon said he would eat the broccoli."

"Possible." Merri Lee paused. "How do you feel?"

Meg rubbed one arm and then the other. "Better. The prickling is almost gone."

Ruth and Theral returned to the sorting room.

"You don't have to do this," Meg said. "Simon asked for my help."

"Of course we'll help," Merri Lee said. "It sounds like this is a double question: how much of what we call human nature do the Others want to assume for themselves, which is something none of us can answer, and how much of what humans use do the Others want to keep, or need to keep for the people who live in Thaisia?"

"If we're talking about products, we should start with the personal and work outward," Ruth said. "Make lists of the things we own and the consumable things we use. And the things we'd really like to keep, like indoor plumbing and ways to heat the house in the winter."

"We could tear out the business section of one of the phone books," Theral said. "The businesses wouldn't exist if someone didn't need the product or service."

"Simple Life folk don't use a lot of things other humans use." Meg started scratching her right arm, then forced herself to stop.

"It might be to our advantage to find out what they *do* use," Merri Lee said.

"We can compare lists tomorrow, and whatever is on *all* our lists will go on a master 'Really Want to Keep This' list," Ruth said.

"How specific do we need to be?" Theral asked.

Meg closed her eyes and pictured a piece of paper with the word "Tools." Then she imagined a piece of paper with a list of tools: hammer, screwdriver, saw, pliers.

She opened her eyes, fairly certain she had the correct answer. "General categories. I'm not sure how much time Simon has to provide input before a decision is made, so let's start with general categories. Tools instead of specific tools. Books instead of specific authors."

"We're all working across the street today," Ruth said. "Mrs. Tremaine moved out last Firesday, so Eve Denby wants to give the two-family house a good cleaning upstairs and down. She said we can paint the upstairs apartment first since Karl is currently bunking with Michael and I'm sleeping on the floor of Merri Lee's efficiency apartment here."

Meg almost asked why Karl and Ruth weren't staying with their families, but she remembered in time that both families were mad at them for being Wolf lovers—a slur given to humans who wanted to work in cooperation with the *terra indigene*.

"We won't say anything to Eve," Ruth said. "Not until we're told that we can."

"Will you be all right?" Merri Lee leaned to one side to see through the Private doorway that provided access to the counter in the front room. Then she whispered, "The front door just opened, but I didn't see—"

A *terra indigene* Wolf rose on his hind legs and plopped his forelegs on the counter. "*Arroo?*"

"Good morning, Nathan," they chorused.

The watch Wolf had arrived. Time to go to work.

Wrapping their muffins in paper towels, the female pack went out the office's back door, after assuring Meg that they would see her this evening at the Quiet Mind class.

Meg stepped up to the counter. Nathan was one of the Courtyard's enforcers and, as such, was one of the largest Wolves in the Lakeside pack. He'd also been with Simon when their group was attacked at the stall market, and some of the deeper wounds on his face were still scabbed over.

"We just got together to chat before work," she said.

Nathan stared at her.

"About things that are none of your business."

He stared at her.

"*Girl* things."

He pushed away from the counter and trotted over to the Wolf bed positioned beneath one of the big front windows.

Meg retreated to the sorting room to eat her muffin.

Used too often, it would lose its effect, but if you told a male Wolf something was a "girl thing," he would head in the opposite direction. As far as they were concerned, girl things were like porcupines—if you poked at them, you'd end up with a sore nose.

Figuring she had a little time before Nathan tried again to find out what was going on, Meg took a pad of lined paper and a pen out of one of the drawers.

How much human did the *terra indigene* want to keep?

The lists would be useful. Of course they would. But she wondered if Merri Lee was right and the question really had more to do with mind and heart. If that was the case, she had to hope that making lists would help the Elders see the real answer to the question.

Lieutenant Crispin James Montgomery paid the cabdriver, then turned to study the duplex that belonged to Captain Douglas Burke. Nothing to distinguish it from its neighbors, which had neatly kept yards and other signs that the people living there were what his mother called house proud—a compliment when Twyla Montgomery said it.

He hadn't been to his captain's home in the six months he'd lived in Lakeside. What little he knew about Burke outside of the office made him think the man didn't do much entertaining—and any entertaining he did do was handled in a public venue. This wasn't a social gathering either, not when they were meeting before their shift at the Chestnut Street Police Station to discuss things Burke wanted kept outside the station.

As he reached the front door and rang the bell, a car pulled into the driveway. Officers Karl Kowalski and Michael Debany, two members of his team, got out and hurried to join him just as the door opened.

"Lieutenant," Kowalski said, giving Monty a nod before looking at the man filling the doorway. "Captain."

Douglas Burke was a big man, an imposing figure with blue eyes that usually held a fierce kind of friendliness. His clothes were always pressed, and the dark hair below his bald pate was always neatly trimmed. Never having seen him outside of the job, Monty couldn't picture the man in anything but a suit, couldn't see him wearing jeans and a ratty pullover to mow the lawn or dig in the flower beds. In fact, the lack of the suit coat and the rolled-up sleeves were as close to casual dress as Monty had ever seen.

"Come in, gentlemen." Burke stepped aside, allowing them to enter. "We're in the dining room. Help yourself to coffee and pastries."

Monty glanced at the living room as he followed Burke. It looked masculine, comfortable, and minimal. He wouldn't be surprised if the furniture, what there was of it, was high quality, maybe even antiques.

Not a room that welcomed children.

Not so odd a thought since Monty's seven-year-old daughter, Lizzy, had arrived in Lakeside last month and was now living with him. All the secrets Lizzy had brought with her to Toland had been revealed, and she was safe from whoever had killed her mother. But that still put him in the position of having to figure out how to be a single parent and a police officer. For now, Eve Denby, the new property manager for the Lakeside Courtyard, was willing to look after Lizzy along with her own two children.

Monty walked into the dining room and hesitated when he spotted Louis Gresh and Pete Denby sitting at the dining room table, filling small plates with pastries and fresh strawberries. He wasn't surprised that they had become part of Burke's trusted circle.

The real surprise was the other man sitting at the table.

A toilet flushed, water ran, and then another man joined them. Shorter, leaner, and younger than Burke, the man had a full head of slightly curly, medium brown hair—but the fierce-friendly look in the blue eyes was similar enough to say *family*.

"Gentlemen, this is Shamus David Burke, a relative of mine who's visiting from Brittania. He's in law enforcement over there, so I thought his insights might be useful. Shady, this is Lieutenant Crispin James Montgomery and his officers, Karl Kowalski and Michael Debany. They handle most of the interaction with the Lakeside Courtyard. The man carefully inspecting that pastry is Commander Louis Gresh, who's in charge of the bomb squad. The pastries are fresh, Commander. Nothing for you to worry about."

"That you don't check food for unwelcome surprises just proves you've never had children," Louis replied. He bit into the pastry and chewed with care.

"The other man poking at his food is Pete Denby, an attorney who recently relocated from the Midwest Region."

"Who also has children," Pete said, smiling.

"And the only man unconnected to law enforcement is Dr. Dominic Lorenzo, who is currently working on the governor's task force to assist the *cassandra sangue* in this part of the Northeast Region." Burke waited until they were all seated. Then he folded his hands and rested them on the dining room table. "Lieutenant Montgomery already knows what's at stake. Before we discuss anything, you all need to understand that you can't share this information with anyone, for any reason. Not friends, not family, not colleagues. If you can't agree to that, walk away now because . . ."

"Because everyone in Lakeside will be at risk," Lorenzo said, sounding irritable. "Same song, different day."

"Actually, every human on the continent of Thaisia will be at risk," Burke said, the mild voice at odds with the bright fierceness in his eyes.

Silence. Then, matching Burke's mild tone, Shady said, "Are we talking about extinction, Douglas?"

Burke nodded.

Lorenzo swallowed hard. Pete pushed aside the plate with the pastry.

Louis let out a shuddering breath. "Gods above and below, talk about a bomb. What are the odds that we're going to lose control of this?"

"About even," Burke replied. "Maybe less."

Monty looked at his men. "This isn't a surprise to you."

"Not really," Kowalski said. "We've noticed—"

Burke raised a hand. "Let's be clear about who is staying before we get into this." He looked at Lorenzo.

Lorenzo thought for a moment, then pushed his chair back and stood. "I'm carrying enough secrets. You need to keep what you know within a tight circle, and I'm no longer sure when someone asks me questions about the Lakeside Courtyard or about blood prophets if they're asking out of curiosity, out of professional necessity, or because they're a member of the Humans First and Last movement trying to ferret out information that can be used against the Others. When I have to travel for the task force, I'm traveling alone. It would be too easy to be waylaid and . . . interrogated."

Monty wanted someone to make a joke, to say that Lorenzo was building a plot worthy of a thriller with talk of interrogations. But no one made a joke—mostly because Pete Denby had been run off the road, presumably by members of the HFL, when he'd packed up his family and bolted for Lakeside after helping Burke uncover information about a man called the Controller.

"Understood." Burke hesitated. "Ask Simon Wolfgard for a free pass through the wild country. I think he'll know what that means. Roads that you'll find on a map are roads humans can use. But there are unmarked roads that lead to places humans should not go. If you think you're being followed, turn down one of those unmarked roads, roll down a window and start shouting, honk the horn, do anything to gain the attention of the *terra indigene* before other humans catch up to you. Under those circumstances, you have a better chance of surviving an encounter with the Others than with humans."

Lorenzo nodded. "Good luck." He started to walk out of the room, then stopped. "If any of you should need discreet medical attention, you can count on me to not ask questions."

"Appreciate that," Burke said.

They waited until Lorenzo closed the front door. Waited a little longer, listening to the car start in the driveway attached to the other half of the duplex.

"Anyone else?" Burke asked. They all shook their heads. "Then let's start local and work up to the end of the world as we know it. Lieutenant? You have anything to report?"

Monty poured coffee he didn't want in order to give himself a little time. "The Courtyard took possession of the two-family house on Crowfield Avenue. The deal is done, the previous owner has been paid, and the Denbys will be moving in soon. So will Karl and Ruthie."

Pete nodded. "Yesterday the owner of the stone apartment buildings on either side of the double accepted the Courtyard's offer for those dwellings. Since the Business Association is planning to pay cash for those buildings, I expect we'll be able to expedite the paperwork and take possession by the end of the month. The apartments in those buildings have two bedrooms, Lieutenant. Something to think about with Lizzy being here for good."

Monty had considered whether he'd take one of the apartments if Simon Wolf-gard offered it. Lots of practical reasons to accept—and reasons to keep some distance from the Others. For one thing, there wouldn't be much division between work and home if he lived across the street from the Courtyard and had Kowalski and Denby—and probably Debany as well—for next-door neighbors.

But they would be good neighbors, he thought. *And police living so close to the Court-yard might be a deterrent to trouble. But none of us are talking about where the children will go to school next year—assuming they'll be safe going to a city-run school, or even a private one run by humans. After all, anyone living in a building owned by the Others will be con-sidered a Wolf lover, and prejudice is mounting against anyone who supports working with the* terra indigene *in any way.*

He and Lizzy needed a different place to live, and he would have to weigh the pros and cons carefully before making a decision. But that would have to wait.

"Next?" Burke asked.

"The Courtyard's first guests are arriving next week," Kowalski said. "Some Wolves from the Addirondak Mountain packs. No one mentioned other kinds of *terra indigene* coming in at the same time. Michael and I got the impression that we were expected to be visible in the stores and around the Market Square, at least for a little while each day."

"They're coming to interact with humans," Monty said. "It makes sense Wolfgard would want to have you around."

"Is this an invitation-only sort of thing?" Shady asked. "I've never seen a Court-yard or had a casual interaction with one of the *terra indigene*. I'd like the oppor-tunity. The dealings I had with a few of the Others when some of the *cassandra sangue* were . . . channeled . . . to Brittania were tense experiences for all the humans who were helping with the rescue. Except for the people who live along the border or the coast, most of Brittania's citizens have never come in contact with the Others. Considering what is going on in the world right now, I'd like some firsthand experience in a less life-and-death situation."

Catching Burke's look, Monty said, "I'll ask Simon Wolfgard about allowing us to bring in guests."

"Anything of concern about the folks on Great Island or information about the River Road Community?" Burke asked.

"No, sir," Monty replied. Shady would be the only person at the table who didn't notice the omission of Talulah Falls, a town that was no longer under human control after a bomb killed several Crows and a Sanguinati was killed while hunting for the humans responsible for the explosion.

"Then let's talk about the main event since Shady gave away the punch line," Burke said quietly.

"Extinction." Pete looked grim. "The Others are serious about this?"

"Because of the recent troubles, the earth natives in the wild country are considering extinction as a way to rid Thaisia of a menace to the land and a threat to the rest of the beings that were here before our ancestors set foot on this continent."

"But we've tried to help," Louis protested. "Monty and his team have been sticking their necks out every day to interact with the Others in the Courtyard. Gods, one of our own was killed during that attack at the stall market. Doesn't that count for something?"

"It counts," Monty said. "The time we spend in the Courtyard, the help we've provided . . . We're the reason the humans in Thaisia aren't going to be erased from this continent."

"Not yet anyway," Burke added. "One Courtyard and some police officers and civilians to balance out whatever stupidity the HFL movement is planning next. And let's be clear about who will be erased, as the lieutenant put it. I think Intuit villages will be spared. So will Simple Life farmers and craftsmen. As much as possible, they keep themselves separated from the humans living in human-controlled towns and cities, and they've been careful in their dealings with the terra indigene. And I think the Others will still need some humans—if nothing else, to provide labor for the products they want to have."

"That leaves the rest of us," Pete said.

"That leaves the rest of us," Burke agreed.

"If you'll pardon me for saying it, you're all screwed," Shady said. He poured cream into his cup and then filled it with coffee from the pot sitting on a thick cloth pad. "You should start laying in supplies while you can and start thinking about how to survive."

"Is it definite?" Burke asked. "Is the Cel-Romano Alliance of Nations going to war?"

"They are. And not among themselves, which, frankly, is what the people of Brittania were hoping they would do. They've been stockpiling food and weapons and supplies for a while, but now the signs are out in the open, with troops being transported around the Mediterran. They don't have enough land to grow the food they need to feed all their people. That's the truth of it. So the question we've been asking is this: is Cel-Romano going to try to grab the human part of Brittania, since we're the closest piece of human land to them, or are they going to try to annex some of the wild country, gambling that they have the kind of weaponry now that will eliminate the shifters who currently inhabit that land?"

"The shifters wouldn't be the only earth natives living on that land," Monty said.

Shady nodded. "I know that. Most people in Brittania may not have dealings with them, but we are taught the history of our land, so we know why very few humans go past the low stone wall that runs the width of the island and separates the land the world itself gifted to us from Wild Brittania. Just like we know that the tales told by the traders who do venture beyond that wall and return alive aren't embellished."

"If Cel-Romano is trying for a land grab, why cause trouble on this side of the Atlantik?" Kowalski asked. "Cel-Romano can't bring an army across the ocean."

"No, indeed," Shady said. "Even a fishing boat is carefully watched. Troop ships would never be allowed to reach land."

"Food was smuggled out of Thaisia," Burke said. "Troops could be smuggled in. If offered enough money, ship captains will try to slip past whatever is watching."

"None of this addresses the threat of extinction," Monty said.

"There's nothing we can do about that, Lieutenant," Burke said gently. "We just keep the lines of communication open. We provide assistance where and when we can. And we hope that we continue to balance whatever foolishness other humans instigate." He looked around the table. "Anything else?"

Michael Debany shifted in his chair. "Captain, you said the information shouldn't leave this room. Does that mean not saying anything to the girls, because"—he looked at Kowalski—"*they're* meeting with Meg this morning, so they might know about this anyway."

"I don't think Wolfgard told Ms. Corbyn about the earth natives' decision," Monty said. "But he may have shared something else with her that he didn't share with us."

"Need to know, gentlemen," Burke said. "For now, that excludes the girls. Next week, the Courtyard will have guests, and the girls don't need to be wondering about every word or gesture, afraid that it will be the thing that tips the scales against us."

"So business as usual," Louis said.

"Yes." Burke pushed away from the table. "If that's all . . ."

A dismissal.

Monty caught a ride with Louis to the station, which allowed Kowalski and Debany to talk between themselves on the way back to the Courtyard, where Debany would put in a few hours helping Eve Denby and the girls before reporting to work.

"Have you talked to Officer Debany about a new partner?" Louis asked.

"Not yet," Monty replied. "Even with the hazard pay that comes with working on this team, no one has made a request to be the fourth man."

"Well, it's not just dealing with humans who want to start trouble, is it? Anyone on your team is expected to interact and spend time in the Courtyard during off-duty hours. Even officers who won't hesitate to back you up are going to think long and hard about that."

"About being branded as Wolf lovers."

"It's not just the man who gets branded," Louis said quietly. "And it's not just people who interact with the Others on a daily basis. My wife and a neighbor—a woman she's been friends with for years—went shopping the other day. Carpooled to save gas. They parked in the general area of the shops. Two butcher shops, two blocks apart. One was showing an HFL sign in the window; the other shop doesn't support the movement. My wife's friend went to the shop with the HFL sign—a place where you have to show your HFL membership in order to be served. My wife went to the other shop because we've agreed that we aren't going to be a part of the HFL in any way."

"What happened?" Monty asked.

"The friend didn't say anything, but the car was gone when my wife finished her shopping and returned to where they'd parked. The woman, friend and neighbor, just left without her and hasn't spoken to her since. Gods, they used to watch each other's kids, used to have a night out once in a while—dinner and a movie that the husbands and kids didn't want to see. And now . . ."

"The lines are being drawn."

"Yes. I just hope there are enough of us standing on this side when the time comes to hold that line."

Monty looked out the window and didn't reply.

CHAPTER 3

Windsday, Juin 6

Just before daybreak, they drove south on the dirt road that led to Prairie Gold, silent men filling the cabs and beds of three pickup trucks. They knew this road well, and driving it today filled them with fear and elation. Finally they, and dozens of men like them from towns throughout the Midwest and Northwest, would strike the first blow that would free humans from the furred and fanged tyrants that were keeping them away from *everything* that this land had to offer.

When they reached the crossroads, they reduced speed, moving slowly toward the herds that had settled down on both sides of the road. On one side were thirty head of cattle from a human-controlled ranch. On the other side were three hundred bison that grazed on land that belonged to the *terra indigene*. The bison had been drawn to a salt lick the ranch hands had put out a couple of days ago. The cattle had been cut from the main herd and brought to this part of the ranch's fenced range—the necessary sacrifice in this dangerous, secret warfare.

The men had put out the salt openly, *a neighborly gesture*, they'd told the *terra indigene* Wolves who had trotted up to see what they were doing on land that wasn't leased to humans.

Now those same men climbed out of the trucks and checked their rifles. Once things got started there wouldn't be time or room for mistakes.

"Company A with me," the leader said quietly. "Companies B and C . . ." He pointed to indicate that their job was on the other side of the road. "Remember, it doesn't matter if it's a clean kill or a killing wound. Just put 'em down, as many as you can. My whistle is the signal."

Company A moved away from the road and quietly approached the cattle, while the other men crept within firing range of the bison.

All the men raised their weapons and waited.

Bait the Wolves by killing animals they needed for food. That was stage one of the land reclamation project. After all, fewer bison meant more land for cattle.

Bait the Wolves. Stir things up. And most important, don't get caught.

The leader whistled. The men opened fire and kept firing until they emptied their rifles. Then they ran back to the trucks and drove away, speeding up the dirt road to get back to the bunkhouse or their homes before anyone thought to look for them or wonder where they had been.

They had struck the first blow. Now secrecy was truly a matter of life and death.

Thaisia could be the breadbasket for the world. There are thousands and thousands of acres of land going to waste, providing nothing instead of growing the food the human race needs. One way or another the terra indigene must be persuaded to release some of the land they hold with such selfish disregard for the desperate needs of other species in the world. If the Others don't want to be bothered with such concerns, let the human race do the work of providing food for those who need it. Let us utilize some of this empty land instead of forcing us to watch our children starve.

—Nicholas Scratch during a speech at an HFL rally in Toland

There is no wasted, empty land in Thaisia. Every place on this continent is full of residents who need what the land already provides. Even the deserts have residents who live on what is available in those places. Even the coldest, remotest areas are not empty of life. When Mr. Scratch talks about the needs of other species, he is really talking about one species, the human species. He and his followers care for nothing else, which is why the terra indigene must care about all the rest.

—Elliot Wolfgard, when asked to respond to Nicholas Scratch's speech

CHAPTER 4

Windsday, Juin 6

White walls, white furniture, white clothes.

"Please, I need colors. I see the colors."

"You don't need colors, cs821. You just need a cut. You'll feel better after you're cut."

"Please."

"Stubborn little bitch, obsessed with colors. We recommend finger cuts as much as possible. Might as well use up that skin in case we have to remove the fingers to keep her from making drawings that dilute the prophecies."

The feel of the razor slicing through skin. And then . . . Color. That shade of red that looked like nothing else, at least to her eyes. Floating on the euphoria that came with a cut after she began speaking, she looked at the white walls, at the dark straps that held her to the chair.

"You don't need colors, cs821. You just need a cut."

White walls, white ceiling, white furniture, white clothes. As she stared at the wall, part of it darkened, becoming a shape. Four legs. A tail. Massive head with horns. Another dark patch on the wall began forming another animal. And another, until there was a herd of shapes on the wall.

Then she noticed dots forming on the wall just above the herd—that shade of red unlike any other. The dots grew and began to flow down the wall, covering the herd with bloody tears.

Panting, her heart pounding, Hope scrambled out of bed and staggered to the screened window in her room, sucking in cool, early morning air as she pressed her hands against the wood windowsill.

She wasn't in the compound anymore. The walls of her room weren't white. The cabin used by the Wolfgard in the *terra indigene* settlement at Sweetwater had walls made of wood, had floors made of wood. Everything was simple and wood except for the toilet and sink in the little bathroom attached to this bedroom. But some of the drawings she had made since coming to live with Jackson and Grace and the rest of the pack were pinned to the walls. A few were even framed.

Some were just drawings of the pack, of the land, of everything that lived in the Sweetwater territory that came within the boundaries of where she was allowed to wander.

"My name is Hope Wolfsong," she whispered. "I am *not cs821*. Not anymore. Never again."

But the dream. There was more, and the *more* settled over her skin like a smothering film. Had to get it down on paper to show Jackson and Grace. The dream image of the animal had already faded from memory too much for her to describe with words.

She closed the shutters over the window and carefully felt her way back to her bed and the lamp on the bedside table. She clicked on the lamp and waited. Jackson and Grace sometimes slept on the porch with some of the other Wolves. Sometimes they slept in the cabin's main room where they could hear her.

No one scratched at her door or growled. No male voice, rough from sleep and vocal chords that hadn't fully shifted from Wolf to human, demanded to know what was wrong.

Moving as quietly as she could, she gathered her big drawing pad and the colored pencils and pastels that Jackson had bought for her. She started to turn the top page of the pad. Then she stopped and looked at the drawing she'd made just before going to bed last night. She didn't know if it meant anything, but the last thing she'd added before blinking out of the trance she fell into sometimes when she drew pictures were the words "For Meg."

She removed the drawing and placed the paper on the desk in her room. Returning to the bed, she sat cross-legged and set the drawing pad in front of her. But the patchwork quilt, which usually delighted her with its shapes and colors, was a distraction now. Pushing it aside, she pulled off the top sheet—white because the Others didn't feel the need for colors in things that wouldn't be seen once you turned off the light—and placed it on the floor. Then she settled down, picked up her pencils, and began to draw.

The shapes. Yes, she remembered the shapes. And the sky. And . . .

She searched through her pencils and pastels. Nothing! How could she not have the necessary shade?

She sprang up, pulled open a drawer in the desk, and removed the silver folding razor that had been used exclusively on her when she had lived in the Controller's compound. Jackson had been told to let her keep the razor because, if she felt compelled to cut, using the razor was safer than all the other things that could be used to slice through fragile skin. Jackson and Grace had bought her paper and pencils, had allowed her to draw, so she had tried so very hard to be good and not cut, but . . .

"Need it," she muttered, all her thoughts focused on the drawing taking shape on the paper. "Need that shade."

When the color began to flow, she tossed the razor aside, dipped her fingers into the color, and continued drawing.

The scent of blood snapped Jackson Wolfgard out of a sound sleep moments before Hope screamed. Scrambling to his feet, he leaped for the bedroom door, aware that his mate, Grace, was right behind him. The Wolves who had slept on the porch or on the ground surrounding the cabin were awake and howling an alarm—or getting the pups away from potential danger.

Still shifting to human as he shoved the door open and stepped into the room, Jackson vaguely remembered some rule about adult males in human form not appearing unclothed in front of female puppies or juveniles, but he wasn't concerned about human rules, not when Hope was staring at the drawing pad on the floor and blood from a deep slice in her left forearm dripped onto the paper and the sheet bunched up beneath it.

"Oh, Hope." Grace sounded heartbroken.

Jackson wasn't heartbroken; he was furious. And very frightened. The blood of the *cassandra sangue* was a danger to Others and humans alike. After taking in Hope, he'd heard that some of the *terra indigene* called the girls Namid's creation, both wondrous and terrible.

Until now, he hadn't thought of Hope as something terrible.

<Jackson?> several Wolves called, using the *terra indigene*'s form of communication.

<Stay out!> he ordered.

The girl herself didn't smell like prey. None of the blood prophets did. But Hope's blood! He'd never smelled anything quite like it, and he craved a taste of it.

Fear fueled his fury as he covered the distance between the doorway and the swaying girl. He swept up the razor she'd tossed aside. He was about to drop it on the desk when he noticed another drawing with Meg Corbyn's name written in the bottom right corner. He set the razor away from the drawing, then turned to the girl.

Grace pulled off Hope's nightshirt and pressed the wadded cloth against the wound, leaving the girl wearing nothing but panties.

"I needed the color," Hope said, staring at the floor. "I needed . . ."

Jackson smacked the top of Hope's head, eliciting a snarl from Grace. It wasn't a hard smack, but it snapped the girl back from whatever she was seeing enough to focus on him.

"You have big teeth," Hope whispered.

"They're big so you'll feel them when I bite you," he growled, leaning closer. He wasn't sure if there were other parts of him that wouldn't pass for human. He didn't care.

"Jackson," Grace warned. <We need to get her to the human bodywalker at the Intuit village. The wound is still bleeding, and we can't lick it to help it heal.> She hesitated. <And this is my first time dealing with an injury to a real human.>

<All right. Take her into the bathroom and put enough clothes on her that the humans won't howl about it. I'll clean up as much of the blood as I can.> He waited until Grace hustled Hope into the bathroom. Then he went to the window and opened the shutters, relieved to breathe in untainted air. Wolf faces peered at him through the screen.

<Jackson? Is the human pup hurt?>

<Yes. We need the small wagon to take her down to the Intuit village. She can't walk that far.>

The faces disappeared. This *terra indigene* settlement didn't own any horses or burros. When the Others needed such creatures, they rented them, along with the humans who would handle them. But they did have a small wagon that could be pulled by up to three individuals in human form and was mostly used when the Others went down to purchase human-made merchandise. It was big enough to hold Grace and Hope.

Taking a last deep breath, Jackson turned back to the room. Some blood on the sheet, but not as much as he'd thought when he first saw Hope standing there with blood dripping down her arm. Most of the blood was on the drawing, although he would check all the pages carefully to make sure there wasn't a speck of blood on the rest of the paper.

She'd been doing so well since she'd come to live with them. She'd *said* she wanted to live. Hadn't they done everything they could to help her do exactly that? So why . . . ?

Jackson sucked in a breath as he stared at the drawing. A mound of bison, clearly dead. Bloody Wolf prints on all the carcasses. That didn't make sense. Wolves wouldn't drag their prey into a mound like that, and killing one bison was hard work and provided several days of food for the entire pack—for the whole *terra indigene* settlement. So why did Hope draw a slaughter? No recognizable landmarks. Was this going to happen around Sweetwater? Somewhere else?

Meg Corbyn—Meg, the Trailblazer—tended to see prophecies about the Lakeside Courtyard. But that hadn't always been true. It seemed her abilities, her sensitivity, became refined to Lakeside and the nearby communities that were connected with her Courtyard after she'd been living in Lakeside for a few weeks. But Hope's vision drawings ranged across the land.

He glanced at the drawing on the desk. Could these girls, these blood prophets, make connections that linked places because of their own connections to the people? Meg and Hope had known each other in the compound where they had been caged and cut so that wealthy humans could know about the future.

Meg was still struggling with her own addiction to cutting, but she was the Trailblazer for the rest of the *cassandra sangue*, and she might have the answers he needed right now.

Shifting his human hands into Wolf paws that had useful claws, Jackson tore the sheet, making a pad out of the clean linen. He placed the drawing pad on the linen. When the blood scent overwhelmed him to the point that he started salivating, he realized that the paper was more saturated with blood than he'd first thought.

More than a cut, he thought uneasily as he rolled up the part of the sheet that had blood on it. *She'd been drawing with her own blood . . . because she needed that color.*

The bathroom door opened. Grace led Hope into the bedroom, then stopped when she saw him.

<Jackson?> Grace said.

<We need help,> he said. <More than the human bodywalker.>

The pup looked scared. Did she think he would drive her out of the pack for this? He could. Maybe he should. But connections weren't always about place, and several of Hope's past drawings made it clear that there was a link between Sweetwater and Lakeside.

He and Simon, friends since they were juveniles, were the link.

And looking at the picture of dead bison, he thought of another Wolf linked to him and Simon through friendship.

Balling up the part of the sheet that had blood on it, Jackson walked out of the bedroom and put the sheet into a metal bucket half-full of fresh water. Then he got dressed and handed Grace the summer dress she'd been wearing yesterday before they'd shifted to Wolf form and gone to sleep.

Yes, they needed more help than the human bodywalker if they were going to keep the pup alive.

CHAPTER 5

Windsday, Juin 6

Joe Wolfgard narrowed his eyes against the sun and road dust. He was the newly chosen leader of the *terra indigene* settlement located at the southern end of the Elder Hills and an unknown commodity for the Intuits living in Prairie Gold, the human town connected to the settlement. So he tried not to growl at the Intuit who was driving the pickup. It wasn't Tobias's fault that some humans had gone rabid and killed many bison.

"You'll need to post guards at the town," Joe said. "Maybe put up a barricade across the road to stop strangers before they get too close to your mates and pups." And he would talk to the Hawks, Eagles, and Ravens about keeping watch and reporting *any* human or vehicle heading for the town.

Tobias Walker, the foreman of Prairie Gold's ranch, tightened his hands on the steering wheel. "You think we're in danger?"

"Don't you?"

Tobias didn't answer.

"Just because the humans who did this started with four-legged animals doesn't mean they won't go after targets that look like themselves."

"You'd have to ask my mother about that," Tobias said. "She's the one among us who's most sensitive to other people."

Jesse Walker, Tobias's mother, was an older, vigorous, gray-haired female and the leader of the Intuits in Prairie Gold—at least, she seemed to be since the rest of the humans referred him to her for answers to his questions about the town. She ran the general store and knew everything about everyone—including the *terra indigene* who had begun to venture in to purchase human-made items instead of receiving twice-monthly boxes of supplies that were left at the edge of their settlement. She had a Crow's curiosity, always asking questions and poking into people's lives, but she was so friendly when she did it, no one seemed to mind, especially when the next time you came to her store, she'd have just the thing you needed but didn't even know you wanted.

Despite the difference in the ages of the two females, Jesse's friendly, genuine interest in other beings reminded Joe of Meg Corbyn. In fact, he'd been chosen to be Prairie Gold's new leader because he'd met Meg during his visit to the Lakeside Courtyard and had seen how humans and Others *could* work together. Since his arrival a couple of weeks ago, he'd made an effort to visit the general store once or twice a week just to interact with Jesse Walker while a couple of other *terra indigene* who could pass for human hung back and observed. This was a first step in learning more about the Intuits who had received permission to build a community within *terra indigene* land three human generations ago. Along with the businesses in town, the Intuits ran a farm for produce, a dairy farm, and the ranch that raised the horses they needed as well as cattle for meat.

"Looks like we're not the only ones who got word of this," Tobias said.

Some of the Ravens, Hawks, and Eagles had spotted the carcasses early that morning and sounded the alarm, and Joe, in turn, had gone to the Prairie Gold ranch to fetch Tobias and his men, as well as the equipment needed to deal with the available meat. But the men who worked on the human-owned ranch adjacent to the *terra indigene*'s land must have been warned as well, because Joe saw three trucks and a dozen men standing near dead cattle.

"Pull up here," Joe said. "We don't want to be muzzle to muzzle with them."

Tobias pulled over and stopped the pickup. Joe got out and lowered the tailgate for the three Wolves who had been riding in the back. They jumped out and immediately began checking the area for scents. So did the Coyotes who were in the back of the second pickup. Their third vehicle was the town's hauler because it had a winch and could carry heavy loads—like big carcasses. And the last truck had a two-horse trailer attached to it, carrying the horses that would help them drag some of the meat to the hauler.

"Damn," Tobias said when he and Joe studied the dead bison. "Has to be a hundred of them. That much meat would have fed the town and settlement for a year or more."

"More," Wyatt Beargard said, joining them. "Even with someone like me feeding off the available meat now."

The Grizzly was also a newcomer to the settlement. His scent was enough to dissuade human-owned cattle from "getting lost" on the Others' land, and his presence was now a fair warning to the human ranchers that any cattle that "escaped" through a break in the fence and were found grazing on land not leased to humans were considered edible game.

Of course, the Grizzly wasn't the largest predator in the area who held that opinion. Despite the handful of human-controlled ranches in the area and the human-controlled town of Bennett, which was a way station for trains bringing supplies, this was the wild country, and shifters like Joe were the liaisons between anything human and the primal Elders whose size and appetite helped maintain the number of animals grazing on the grasslands. They were also the guardians of the water that flowed through the hills and provided a constant source for Prairie Gold's residents and crops.

Sure, the human ranchers had some water on their land, but the water that supplied Prairie Gold flowed with a surety that the ranchers envied. And as the HFL movement became more strident about what humans were entitled to claim, the ranchers weren't bothering to hide that envy anymore—an observation Jesse had shared yesterday when Joe went to the general store.

Blowing out a breath, Joe looked at the Wolves who were still sniffing around the bison carcasses nearest the road. <Anything?>

<Most of the scents are old and new, and match the humans milling around on the other side of the road,> they said. <Three scents we don't recognize. Maybe from town, maybe strangers.>

Could three hunters have done so much killing? Why hadn't more bison run after the first couple of shots?

Humans aren't allowed to hunt on our land without permission, so the bison didn't recognize them as a predator and wouldn't have been alarmed by a two-legged animal holding a stick—at least not until some of the bison started dying.

Joe looked at the salt lick that the neighboring rancher had left for the bison— supposedly a friendly gesture. Could someone have put that drug, feel-good, on the salt lick to make the animals passive? He'd been told that the drugs gone over wolf and feel-good hadn't caused any trouble in this part of the Midwest Region, but that didn't mean the drugs couldn't find their way here now. Just because the Controller, the man who had made the drugs, was dead didn't mean the supply had dried up completely. But how many humans beyond select police officers knew the drugs had been made from the blood of the *cassandra sangue*? Some of those girls were still being cared for by humans. Some were still living in the compounds, more than willing to trade a cut on their skin for having someone else take care of them. So the danger the two drugs posed wasn't gone, just covered with a bit of dirt.

<You smell anything wrong with the meat?> Joe asked. <Sickness? Or those bad drugs I told you about?>

Wolves and Coyotes all paused, then began sniffing again. <Smells like good meat.>

A Wolf tore into a smaller bison. After eating a couple of mouthfuls, he waited. They all waited.

<Just meat,> the Wolf reported. <I don't feel weak or angry; just hungry.>

"How many of these can your meat freezers hold?" Joe asked Tobias, waving a hand at the carcasses.

"A few, but not enough," Tobias said. "Floyd Tanner would know, since he's the town's butcher and has the big freezer. The ranch house is supposed to hold supplies for a month for everyone living there, but I don't know if we've picked up this month's supply of meat yet."

"We have a springhouse where we cache some meat. That might hold one of the smaller bison if we cut up the carcass. And Floyd Tanner can cut up another carcass and distribute the meat to all the families in the town." And maybe he could send some of the meat to Simon, trade it for things Simon could acquire more easily in Lakeside than he could here.

Tobias looked grim. "This was a third of the Prairie Gold bison herd. Even after we take what meat we can, most of it is going to rot where the animals fell."

Joe caught a wild, dangerous scent in the air. So did the rest of the Wolves and Coyotes.

There won't be as much meat left to rot as you think. The Elders are gathering for a feast.
Joe looked at Wyatt. Like the rest of the shifters, the Grizzly was looking at the land beyond the dead bison.

"Let's make use of what we can and get away from the kills," Wyatt said in a quiet rumble.

Joe nodded. There were plenty of Ravens, Hawks, and Eagles circling overhead, waiting to descend for their share of the feast. They would keep an eye on what the humans were doing across the road.

"Let's take the half-grown bison that were killed," he said. "Easier for us to haul since we're trying to use as much meat as we can." Then he looked at Tobias. "Tell Truman to hitch up the horses."

Tobias glanced over his shoulder, then turned away from the road and said softly, "The man standing a little apart from the others? That's Daniel Black. He owns that ranch. If he offers you any meat from the cattle, don't take it."

Joe cocked his head. "You have a feeling?" Intuits reacted to things around them—weather, animals, humans—and when one of them was uneasy about something, it was best to pay attention.

"Not about the meat, but about us taking some."

Tobias walked away at the same time Daniel Black crossed the road.

"Bad business," Black said. "You have any thoughts about who did this?"

"Humans with guns," Joe replied, although it should have been obvious to everyone that nothing with teeth and claws had killed the bison—or would want to waste so much food.

A change in the human's scent. A lack of something that had been there a moment before. Fear. A lack of fear now. Which meant the rancher was glad the *terra indigene* didn't know who had shot the bison.

"Look, we've both got the same problem—too much meat that's going to rot. There's no profit in that." Black removed his hat, scratched his head, then resettled the hat. "You want any of those cattle?"

Something wrong with the man's eyes. The words sounded friendly enough, but the eyes were hard and watchful. They reminded Joe of a rattlesnake—except a rattler had the courtesy of warning you of its intentions before it tried to bite you.

"Thank you for the offer, but we have plenty of meat." He gestured to the bison. "I've read in your newspaper that some human places don't have enough food. Maybe you could send the meat to them?"

The hardness sharpened in Black's eyes. "They don't have grains or flour. They need *bread*, not *meat*."

"When you're hungry, food is food." Apparently that wasn't as true for humans as it was for the Others, since his reply made Black angry, even if the man tried to hide the desire to bite.

"Suit yourself." Black walked back to his men. After a few snarled words, he got into one of the trucks. So did the rest of the men.

They drove away, leaving the cattle where they had fallen.

Tobias returned. "We found a few calves that had been killed."

"Take them; it's tasty meat," Joe replied, watching the men drive away.

"Mr. Wolfgard?"

Joe turned to the foreman, who suddenly smelled odd. "You can call me Joe."

Tobias nodded. "Why is Wyatt . . . ?" He pointed discreetly.

Joe followed the finger to where the Grizzly, who had shifted his hands to accommodate the useful claws, was moving among the carcasses, tearing open the bellies of a few bison. "That's the second reason why other animals wait for their share of a bison kill. Wolves and Grizzlies can open up the body and get to the meat. Makes it easier for everyone else to grab a bit for themselves and their young."

They filled the hauler's bed with as much as the vehicle could carry, then sent the vehicle back to Prairie Gold, where it would be unloaded in order to return as quickly as possible.

The Wolves and Coyotes wandered among the downed bison, searching for the younger meat. Some carcasses were roped for the horses to haul to the road. The smallest meat was hauled by men pulling together—or Wyatt pulling alone.

Then, while they waited for the hauler to return and the men were watering the horses, Truman Skye, one of the ranch hands, blanched and whispered, "Gods above and below, what is *that*?"

A half-grown bison seemed to float above the grass, its back hooves brushing the ground as it moved away from them. The air shimmered like heat rising, but the shimmer also had the vague shape of something very large.

"You didn't see that," Joe said, his voice dangerously quiet.

Tobias swallowed hard. "What could lift several hundred pounds like it was nothing more than a deer fawn?"

Joe glanced at the Wolves and Coyotes. Half of them were paying attention to the Intuits. The rest were keeping careful watch over what now moved among the carcasses, selecting a meal.

Grabbing Truman's and Tobias's arms, he turned them toward the road and growled, "If you want the people in your town to remain safe, *you didn't see that.*"

Tobias met Joe's eyes—almost, but not quite, a challenge for dominance. "We tend the ranch's livestock; we camp out away from the ranch when we need to. A lot of times, one of us is riding out alone. If the Intuits and the *terra indigene* are going to work together now, we should be allowed to know some of the things you know. Like what's out there."

The man had a point. One of the reasons Intuits and Others began these agreements generations ago was because they recognized a common enemy: the other kind of human.

"What's out there has been out there long before your people asked to settle around these hills," Joe said. "This is wild country with little pockets of land that have been . . . altered . . . by human presence. The ones who come down from the hills to hunt bison . . . Their kind of *terra indigene* have been around a long time."

"But what are they?" Tobias asked in a hushed voice.

"They are Namid's teeth and claws." Joe tapped his chest. "The *terra indigene* like me call them the Elders. They seldom shift out of their true form, and when they do . . ." He shrugged, uncomfortable about saying more.

"So now they're aware of us."

"They've always been aware of you. Today they allowed you a glimpse of what watches"—*and judges*—"humans when you step beyond your towns and cities. In a way, those hills are the Elders' city in this part of Thaisia. We located our settlement closest to your town in order to act as a buffer between them and you. It allows you to have some access, through us, to the timber, to the water, and to the prey that also lives in the hills."

"So you pretend they aren't out there," Tobias said.

Joe shook his head. "My form of *terra indigene* is small compared to them. Even a large pack of Wolves couldn't survive an attack by one of the Elders. You are a small predator compared to us, so being respectful is your best chance of surviving an encounter with one of them."

Wyatt joined them, carefully licking blood off his claws.

<It disturbs them to see you do that when you look mostly human,> Joe said, glancing at Tobias and Truman.

The Grizzly gave Joe a long look, then lowered his paw. "The hauler is back. Once we load what it can carry, we'll have enough meat."

"We'll want the meat of one more bison to trade," Joe said.

Wyatt growled, making Tobias and Truman flinch. "With the humans? They've left good meat to spoil in the heat; they aren't going to want any of ours."

"Not with the humans. I want to find out if we can ship some of this meat to the Lakeside Courtyard."

Wyatt finally nodded. "We'll come back for one more."

After they'd dragged one more half-grown bison close enough that the men would be able to winch it onto the hauler when it returned again, the horses were loaded into the trailer and returned to the ranch. The hauler slowly drove off with its cargo. The Wolves and Coyotes, having eaten enough, jumped into the pickup beds, happy to nap on the way back to the *terra indigene* settlement.

Tobias started the truck, then looked at Joe. "You want me to drop you off close to your place?"

Joe shook his head. "I need to talk to Jesse Walker and use the telephone." He waited for Tobias to put the truck in gear. "Something else?"

"The Elders. Do they mean us harm, Joe? I guess humans have done plenty to piss them off lately, so I have to ask."

He considered his words carefully. "If you honor the agreements you made with the *terra indigene*, there is no reason for the Elders to do more than watch you as they go about their own lives. But, Tobias? If they had wanted to do you and your community any harm, you wouldn't have survived long enough to ask the question."

Tobias put the truck in gear and headed back to Prairie Gold.

Their footsteps filled the land with a terrible silence. They moved among the carcasses, breathing in the mingled scents of Wolves, Coyotes, horses, and the two-legged beasts called humans.

They moved up to the road, where the scents were not mingled. A different smell here, a sourness in the air that displeased them—and reminded them of the human beasts who had entered their hills without their consent. Those beasts had snuck in, as if that would keep them hidden from the *terra indigene*, and scurried to one of the creeks to collect some of the yellow pebbles. Wondering if the new Wolf had given permission, they had allowed the beasts to take the pebbles and leave. But the new Wolf had not given permission, so the next time the beasts came for the yellow pebbles, they became meat, and the pebbles were returned to the creek where the smaller *terra indigene* would find them.

Humans were still new to this part of Thaisia, still something to watch. The new Wolf was also something to watch, something interesting—something connected to the Wolf who lived near Etu, the Wolf who was being watched by many while the Elders in the east considered if the little predators called humans were needed by the world.

They tore open the bodies of the prairie thunder and ate their fill. Then they tore off large pieces of the meat and returned to the hills to feed their young, to rest—and to keep watch.

CHAPTER 6

Windsday, Juin 6

Vlad leaned against the doorway of HGR's upstairs office. "Could you stop waking up Meg so early in the morning? Some of us would like to sleep a bit longer."

Simon bared his teeth. "I *didn't* wake her up this morning. *She* woke *me*." He turned on the computer. Everyone who lived in the Green Complex was getting an early start this morning—and everyone was so quick to blame *him*.

It *wasn't* his fault. One moment he was happily asleep; the next, Meg screamed and threw herself on top of him, startling him enough that he yelped. Loudly. And since the windows were open, and since *terra indigene* all had excellent hearing, the scream and yelp had brought the rest of the Green Complex's residents running to find out what was wrong.

Vlad approached the desk. "She just had a dream? You're sure she wasn't cut, even by accident?"

"No cuts. No broken skin."

"You're sure?"

Simon nodded. Before Henry Beargard pounded on Meg's front door and Vlad, in the Sanguinati's smoke form, flowed through the screened bedroom window, Simon had planted a paw on Meg's back and given her a quick but thorough sniff to make sure there wasn't any blood.

Not that he was going to mention that to anyone.

"You're not starting the day that much earlier," Simon growled. "And you were the one who said we needed to get our book orders in today to make sure the store was fully stocked when the Addirondak Wolves arrived next week."

"Fine. I'll start on those, and you can . . ."

The phone rang. Simon grabbed the receiver on the second ring. "Howling Good Reads."

"Simon? It's Jackson. We need to talk to Meg."

Simon looked at Vlad. <Get Meg. *Now.*>

Vlad opened the office's back window, shifted to smoke form, and flowed down the side of the building—the fastest way to reach the back of the Liaison's Office.

"Vlad is fetching her," Simon said. "Is the pack all right? Are you?"

"Yes. Look, we have the phone on the speaker thing. Grace and Hope are with me." Since Jackson had finished the sentence with a snarl and needed to talk to Meg, it was easy to figure out who had caused trouble for the Sweetwater pack.

Footsteps on the stairs. Then Meg rushed into the office.

"Simon?" She sounded a little breathless. He was going to have to chase her more to build up her lungs. "Vlad said—"

Simon waved her toward the desk. When she hesitated, Vlad gently gripped her shoulders and steered her behind the desk.

"Jackson?" Simon said. "I'm going to put you on speaker now that Meg is here."

"Meg?" A timid female voice.

Meg sat in the chair, so Simon leaned a hip on the desk while Vlad stood to one side.

"Yes, this is Meg."

"Tell her why she was a bad puppy!"

Hearing anguish beneath Jackson's anger, Simon's canines lengthened in sympathy. He poked Meg's shoulder. "Yeah, Meg. Tell her why she was a bad puppy."

Vlad gave him a sharp look.

"I just needed the color!" A wail.

"I remember you," Meg said, pretending she hadn't heard his comment. "You were called *cs821*."

"Yes."

"Did you choose a name for yourself?"

"Hope." A sniffle. "Hope Wolfsong."

"That's a wonderful name."

<After being snarled at today, I wonder if that will be her name tomorrow,> Vlad said, sounding amused.

But not really amused, Simon decided after studying the Sanguinati. There was nothing amusing about a *cassandra sangue* using a razor.

"You liked colors, liked to draw," Meg continued.

"Yes. I'm allowed to draw now. Or I was."

Poor puppy, Simon thought. She sounded scared. But he would still take Jackson's side because the Wolf was probably scared too.

"You drew a picture," Meg prompted.

"Yes."

"And then you cut yourself, using the razor?"

"Yes. No. I wasn't trying to *cut*; I just needed that shade of red."

Simon poked Meg's shoulder again. "Tell her the rules." He raised his voice, even though Jackson could hear him just fine. "There are rules."

Meg stared at him and bared her teeth.

Vlad muffled a laugh.

Meg leaned toward the phone. "Hope? Is this the first time you've cut since you left the compound?"

"Not exactly."

"The first time with the razor?"

"Yes."

"Well, Simon is right; there are rules."

"Told you," he said quietly.

Meg huffed. "Hope, sooner or later, cutting will kill you. You know that, don't you?"

A whispered, "Yes."

"Cutting is about revealing prophecy, and the euphoria that we feel when we cut is our bodies' way of protecting our minds from what we see. The only way *we* can remember the visions is to swallow prophecy—if we don't speak, if we don't describe what we see, we'll remember it."

"I can see my drawings," Hope said.

Meg nodded even though Hope couldn't see her. "It's different for you. But your drawings also mean you don't *have* to cut to release the visions of prophecy."

"I made a drawing for you."

Meg leaned back. *"About me?"*

"No. Yes."

"There is a shop in the Intuit's part of Sweetwater," Jackson interrupted. "They have a camera that will take a picture that can be sent through e-mail. We'll have a picture made for Meg and send it to you, Simon."

"That's fine."

"I'll create an e-mail account for Meg, adding it to the ones we have for Howling Good Reads," Vlad said. "She'll be able to receive mail for herself in a day or two."

<She can share my e-mail,> Simon said.

Vlad smiled. <She'll be more honest if she thinks her messages are private.>

Simon considered that. For a while anyway, Meg would know only what Vlad taught her about e-mail. <Are you the one who sets the passwords?>

<Of course.>

<That's sneaky.>

<I prefer to think of it as protective.>

No argument from him.

"The drawing you made for me frightened you enough to cut?" Meg asked.

"No! I wasn't frightened, and it wasn't the drawing I made for you! It was the *other* drawing. I made the other drawing." Hope sucked in a breath. "And then I saw . . ."

"What?" Simon asked when the only sound coming from the phone was uneven breathing.

"Dead bison," Jackson replied grimly. "A mound of dead bison."

"Mound?" Simon frowned, puzzled. "Bison are *big*. Who would put them in a mound? Who would kill so many?"

A phone began ringing downstairs. HGR's other line.

"I'll get that," Vlad said, rushing out of the office and down the stairs.

"Can you send that drawing too?" Simon asked.

Hesitation. "All right," Jackson replied. Then his voice turned urgent. "We need to know what to do about the cutting."

No one interrupted while Meg explained about cutting just deep enough to leave a scar but not so deep to cause serious injury; about setting the back of the razor's blade against an old scar, then turning the hand so the razor was in the correct place to cut new skin. Simon nodded when Meg emphasized the need to have someone there *before* Hope made the cut, that someone needed to be there to listen—and to help if something went wrong.

"Do you have a piece of paper?" Meg asked. "I'll give you the phone number of the Liaison's Office. You can call me if you have other questions."

"It's long-distance, Meg," Simon said. "The telephone companies charge a lot of money for long-distance. Besides, you'll have the e-mail."

"Hope? If it's urgent, you call me. Otherwise, you can use e-mail." Meg brightened. "Or we can exchange letters. Where can I send a letter?"

Grace joined the conversation, giving Meg the Sweetwater mailing designation for the *terra indigene*'s settlement.

"Are you feeling better?" Meg asked.

Simon wasn't sure who was supposed to answer the question, but Hope said, "Yes."

"Simon?" Jackson said. "We still need to talk."

Simon looked at Meg. "Shoo."

She blinked at him.

"Shoo," he said again.

He was pretty sure Meg wasn't *trying* to run the chair's wheels over his foot as she pushed away from the desk.

He waited until he heard her heading downstairs. Then he picked up the receiver and disengaged the speaker. "What else?"

"Have you heard from Joe?"

"I know he was resettling. All the Wolves who helped destroy the Controller and that compound decided to resettle, and a new pack formed to watch the humans in the town. Joe said he would let me know where to find him as soon as he could." Simon paused. "Why?"

"Dead bison. The Hawks, Eagles, and Ravens are checking the Sweetwater territory this morning. We do have a herd of bison that graze around here, but our prophet pup draws pictures that are connected to us but not always about us. I don't think we're going to find human-killed bison around here."

"If there is that much meat, it might not have been humans that killed the bison."

"Maybe."

"I think Joe's still in the northern half of the Midwest," Simon said after a moment. "He might have heard something about dead bison."

"Hope painted Wolf prints on all the bison. She painted them in her blood. And then she screamed."

Simon shivered. What had the pup seen beyond her drawing? Not Wolves, but maybe that was as close as she could get to what she *had* seen in some way?

"Stay in touch," he said. "I'll talk to Steve Ferryman. His people are sending out the e-mails to Intuit settlements, relaying information about blood prophets and how to help them stay alive. I'll have him include you on the Lakeside list. And I'll ask him to find out if any Intuit settlements have heard about bison being killed." And he would call Lieutenant Montgomery. It wasn't likely that the police would hear about dead bison, but Montgomery and his captain, Burke, heard about a surprising number of things that happened beyond their territory.

Finishing up the call with Jackson, Simon made his calls to Steve Ferryman and Lieutenant Montgomery.

Then he went downstairs to find out who was on the other line.

CHAPTER 7

Windsday, Juin 6

J esse Walker pushed at a lock of gray hair that had escaped the hairclip and looked up from her list as Shelley Bookman, the community's librarian, rushed into the general store.

"I contacted everyone I could think of, either to help Floyd deal with the meat or offer up a bit of freezer space," Shelley said. "And I brought over the discussion list, in case we have a chance to talk about more than meat."

"I wouldn't push for more discussion," Jesse warned. "At least, not until we have a better idea how upset Joe Wolfgard is about the bison being killed like that."

"I know, I know, but he's the first one of them to initiate contact with us since some of our ancestors pitched a few tents here and bargained for some land. He came into the library last week."

"Did he take out any books?"

"No, he shied away as soon as he saw me, but he came in."

Jesse looked at her list. "I've put in calls to the dairy farm, the produce farm, and the ranch. A couple of women from the farms are on their way to help, and Tom and Ellen Garcia are heading in from the ranch. For now, that's all we can do."

She watched the younger woman go to the door and look out. Like Tobias, Shelley was thirty years old and a child of Prairie Gold, having lived in this small community all her life except for the years she'd gone to school for her degree to become a librarian. The outside world wasn't an easy place for Intuits, and while Shelley never talked about her years away, Jesse had the feeling that the woman's heart had been betrayed and broken. Whatever had happened, Shelley liked men just fine as long as they wanted to be friends, but she wouldn't consider being more.

A shame, really, because, in Jesse's experience, a lot of enjoyment could be had with the right man.

Shelley hurried back to the counter. "Tobias is driving up, and Joe Wolfgard is with him."

"Don't crowd him." Jesse opened the small glass cooler behind her and pulled out the pitcher of lemonade she'd made that morning. She took out four plastic tumblers from her personal cupboard, put them on the counter, and poured the lemonade just as the door opened and Tobias walked in with the new leader of the *terra indigene* who kept watch over Prairie Gold and the handful of human-owned ranches whose fences bordered the rest of the land, which was claimed by the Others.

"Figured you could use something to drink," Jesse said, giving the males a smile. "You've been out there awhile." She handed glasses to Tobias and Joe, then to Shelley, before she picked up the last one.

"My mother makes great lemonade," Tobias said, taking a couple of long swallows.

Joe sniffed the liquid in the glass before taking a cautious sip. Looking surprised, he took another sip. "This is lemonade?"

Jesse nodded, watching the Wolf.

"I had something called lemonade once. It tasted like this but not like this." Joe sipped again. "This lemonade is better."

"I'll take that as a compliment."

"Yes." Joe drained his glass and carefully set it on the counter.

"Would you like more?" Jesse asked.

"No. Thank you."

Doesn't trust us. Not sure how to deal with us. But knowledgeable about human ways, at least to some degree.

"I need to use a telephone," Joe said, eyeing the phone that sat on the end of the counter near the cash register. "To call the Lakeside Courtyard. In the Northeast."

"All right." Jesse tried not to wince at the cost of a long-distance call. "Could we put the phone on speaker so we can all hear?"

Joe met her eyes, and she could feel the weight of the Wolf's stare as he considered her request. She wasn't being nosy—not too much, anyway. She just had a feeling that *this* conversation would change a lot of things in Prairie Gold, for good or ill, and she wanted to know what was said.

"All right," Joe said. "It is your phone, so that is fair."

Tobias gave her a *"Mother"* warning look, which she ignored as she turned the phone to make it easier for Joe to dial.

"It's still pretty early in the Northeast," Tobias said.

Jesse looked at the little clock on the wall behind her counter. "It's within the start of business hours."

Joe just shrugged and carefully pushed the numbers on the phone.

It rang. And rang. And . . .

"Howling Good Reads."

A voice with a slight accent. A voice that, while sounding polite and businesslike, made Jesse shiver—and made fur sprout on the back of Joe Wolfgard's hands.

"Vladimir?" Joe said. "This is Joe Wolfgard."

"Joe." The voice warmed enough that Joe leaned toward the phone.

"I need to speak to Simon."

"Simon and Meg are on another call with Jackson. There was an . . . incident . . . with Hope this morning."

"Jackson's prophet pup?"

Jesse made an effort not to react. Prophet pup. Was Joe talking about one of the *cassandra sangue* that she'd read about in the newspaper? Girls who could speak prophecy? News about them had been a blip, there and gone, leaving her wondering what had actually happened.

We need to be part of this, she thought. *I don't know how or why, but we need to have a connection to these girls.*

Silence. Then Vlad said, "Why does your voice sound distant?"

"I am using Jesse Walker's phone. It is on speaker so we can all hear."

"Who, exactly, is *we*?" No longer any warmth in Vlad's voice.

Jesse watched Joe's ears change from human-shaped to Wolf ears, caught a glimpse of a fang she was sure didn't belong in a human mouth. Vladimir, whoever he was, made their new Wolf leader wary.

"I'm Jesse Walker," she said. "With me are Shelley Bookman, the town's librarian, and my son, Tobias. We've had an incident here too, which is why we asked Mr. Wolfgard if we could participate in this conversation."

"I am Vladimir Sanguinati, comanager of Howling Good Reads, a bookstore in the Lakeside Courtyard."

Shelley turned deathly pale upon hearing Vlad's last name. She hadn't reacted to his voice or his first name, which meant she didn't know him personally. And *that* meant the Sanguinati as a group were something to be feared. Jesse would find out why later.

"Joe?" Vlad said. "Does your incident have anything to do with dead bison?"

Joe growled. "Yes. A hundred bison were shot this morning."

"What did they look like?"

Joe stared at the phone. "They looked dead. They dropped where they were killed."

"So you wouldn't describe them as a mound of bison?"

"Mound? Bison are *big*. You don't drag them into a mound. Although full-grown bulls are big enough that you might think one was a mound." Joe continued to stare at the phone. "You know something about our bison? How? I'm just calling now to tell Simon."

"That's why Jackson is on the phone. Hope drew a picture of dead bison, and something about the picture upset her so much, she cut herself. It's the first time she's made a cut since Jackson and Grace brought her to the Sweetwater settlement to live with the pack. They're understandably upset, which is why they, and Hope, are on the phone with Simon and Meg."

"The pup will be all right?"

"If Jackson doesn't bite her out of frustration—a feeling Simon sympathizes with."

"Meg and the exploding fluffballs won't sympathize."

Jesse blinked. What were exploding fluffballs? Rabbits that blew up when attacked? No, that was silly. They had to be connected with the blood prophets somehow.

Vlad chuckled. "Fortunately, our human female employees haven't reported for work yet. At least, I haven't seen any of them in the bookstore." A pause. "Do you want Simon to call you back, or should I relay the message about the bison being killed?"

"A hundred bison is a lot of meat," Joe replied. "I wondered if Simon and Henry would like some. It is not a meat you have in the Lakeside Courtyard."

"I think they'd be pleased to have some. Do you have a way to ship it?"

"We can package up the meat and get it on the evening train," Jesse said, inserting herself into the conversation. "Or on the first train tomorrow. There's always one refrigerator car to transport foods that need to be kept cool."

"No food coming to the *terra indigene* travels without an escort," Vlad said.

"Someone will have to go to Lakeside?" Tobias sounded interested.

"You would need fur to travel in a cold car," Joe said. "A Wolf, Bear, or Panther would need to travel with the meat."

"The escort doesn't have to travel the whole way with the packages," Vlad said. "The *terra indigene* have set up a relay of guards from our various settlements so that no one has to travel that far from home right now, but the provisions are still guarded."

Joe nodded. "We can make small packages of meat for the escorts, as thanks."

"They would be happy with that. So what would you like in exchange for the meat you're sending to Lakeside?"

"We don't need . . ."

Jesse raised a hand. Joe frowned at her, making her feel as if she had misbehaved. But they couldn't pass up this opportunity.

"You want something in exchange?" Joe asked her.

Jesse glanced at Shelley, who handed her the list. "Mostly, we would like connection, communication."

"I don't understand," Vlad said after a moment.

"Bennett is the nearest human-controlled town. It's our connection to other places because it has the train station, and the highway for the big trucks runs through there. We're as self-sufficient as we can be here in Prairie Gold, but we're dependent on the trains and trucks for the supplies that we can't produce." She waited. Apparently, Vlad was also waiting. "We have a library, and Shelley does her best to keep it running and bring in new books. And we have a small bookstore—well, I have a couple of shelves in my store where folks can buy new and used books. The point is, I used to be able to order a mixed box of books from publishers for my store, and Shelley was on e-mail lists that announced the new books that were available. Now we're being shut out, dropped from the lists, told we have to buy quantities of each title that we can't use. For the past couple of months, we've gone to the bookstore in Bennett and purchased books for the library, but last week, the bookstore was closed when we got to town. Funny thing for a business to be closed midmorning, but Shelley and I both had a feeling that the change in hours had something to do with the new decal displayed in a corner of the bookstore's window."

"HFL?"

Vladimir Sanguinati sounded friendly when he asked the question. Jesse hoped she was never around him in person when he was friendly in that way. Whatever he was, Vladimir was more of a predator than the Wolf standing on the other side of the counter.

"Yes," she said. "Those were the letters."

"So, the Humans First and Last movement has spread that far west." A thoughtful silence. "They aren't going to sell books to anyone from your town. Not for a while."

"That's just an example. I—well, all of us who have gone into Bennett in the past month—have the feeling that the town's people are trying to squeeze us out."

"You're an Intuit," Vlad said.

"Yes." No point denying it, since she figured he knew it already. "And these girls, these prophets, that were in the news briefly. I would like to know more about them. Maybe we could help. I'm not sure how, but I have a feeling we can help." She heard anger in her voice and tried to temper it. But she *knew* this was the moment that would make a difference.

"Mom!" Tobias said at the same time Joe said, "They're a lot of work. More than other kinds of puppies."

Silence.

"Vlad?" Joe finally said. "You still there?"

"This isn't a decision I can make alone," Vlad said. "Too many things need to be considered. But I think it would be wise to have some kind of connection between Lakeside, Prairie Gold, and Sweetwater, if for no other reason than our *cassandra sangue* are seeing visions of a connection. Joe, do you have an e-mail address?"

Joe moved away from the counter, as if the phone had turned into a rattlesnake. "No."

"I can set one up for him at the library," Shelley said, sounding so bright her voice was brittle. "Jesse checks her e-mail there too."

"All right," Vlad said. "Give me one where I can send information, and then you can send back the information we'll need. Also provide a couple of phone numbers so that we can reach you quickly if we need to. I'll make sure Jackson also has the numbers and e-mail addresses."

"Fair enough." Jesse gave him her e-mail address and the phone number for her store. "We'll let you know what train will be carrying the meat."

"Fine." A hesitation. "When did the bison die?"

"Around first light; maybe a little earlier," Joe replied. "Why?"

"And you didn't call Jackson or say anything to him about the bison?"

"No. Why?"

"Nothing yet. Jesse Walker? With your consent, I'll send your contact information to Steve Ferryman on Great Island."

Who was Steve Ferryman? "All right."

It must have been the correct answer, because Vlad wrapped up the call with a promise to send information. But just before she disconnected the call, he said, "Is there anyplace in your town where travelers can stay?"

"There's a motel at the edge of town, connected to the truck stop and diner. Most folks who come here are guests of a family and stay with them."

"Good to know. We'll be in touch. I'll tell Simon about the bison meat." Vlad hung up.

"We should help with the meat." Joe looked around, turned on his heel, and walked out of the store.

With a nod to her, Tobias turned to follow Joe.

"You be careful, son," Jesse said.

He looked back at her as he reached for the door. "Always. You do the same."

Jesse poured another glass of lemonade for herself and Shelley. "When you heard the name Sanguinati, you spooked like cattle in a storm. Why?"

Shelley drank half the glass before replying. "A form of *terra indigene* that drinks blood. There were rumors around the town where I went to school that the university was a hunting ground for a few of the Sanguinati. No deaths could be linked to them. In fact, a few girls would show off hickies they claimed were a 'special' kind of love bite. No one could prove that either. But there were a few young men around the campus who were very good-looking, and I heard they were quite skilled in making a girl feel very, very good."

"So you didn't actually talk to one of these young men?"

Shelley's smile held the bitterness of old wounds. "No. I wasn't anyone's type—not even a vampire's." She set the glass down. "I'll see you later. Thanks for the lemonade."

Jesse put the pitcher back in the cooler and cleared the counter of the other three glasses. Then she looked around her store. What did Joe Wolfgard see when he and the other *terra indigene* came in here? What did he and the Others want or need that she could supply? And Vladimir Sanguinati, so very far away. Maybe not far enough?

No way to know yet. But she had a feeling they were all going to find out soon enough.

Vlad idly looked at the books on the display table and front shelves. Were the two bookstores and libraries in Ferryman's Landing having the same problem ordering stock as Prairie Gold? And they had the rolling library too, a bus that went to the Simple Life community on Great Island as well as stopping in the spots where the Others on the island had built basic structures that were needed when they were in human form. They wanted books too. Maybe Meg could be in charge of handling book requests from Ferryman's Landing and Prairie Gold. They might as well include Sweetwater while they were at it. He and Simon would continue ordering for HGR and the *terra indigene* in the land surrounding Lakeside, while Meg handled the other places and gave them a list.

Something to think about. For now . . .

Vlad went to the stock room and returned with an empty cart. Doubtful the humans in Prairie Gold had read any books written by *terra indigene*. He'd talk to Simon before boxing up a selection. After all, he didn't want to cause trouble for Joe Wolfgard by terrifying the Intuits.

They still had a number of kissy books that he and Simon had pulled off the shelves. He could throw in a few of those and let Librarian Shelley tell him what kinds of books were popular with her people.

The timing didn't fit. That's what bothered him. The *cassandra sangue* spoke prophecy; their visions were warnings about something that *could* happen, not something that *had* happened. Except when something past provided context or reference for something coming.

Had Hope been making a vision drawing of dead bison at the same time the animals were being shot? Or had she seen something else, and Joe's dead bison weren't the same as the bison Hope had drawn? And why had the girl been so frightened that she'd cut herself? No, she said she'd cut because she needed the color. She'd needed to paint blood. But once she made the cut, what else did she see?

No, the timing didn't fit. And there were questions that needed to be asked—and answered.

"What are you doing?" Simon asked as he walked into the front part of Howling Good Reads.

"Pulling a book request."

Simon looked at the books on the top shelf of the cart. "Who's buying that many books?"

"More like bartering than buying. Everyone all right at Sweetwater?"

"Everyone is fine. Meg talked to Hope; I talked to Jackson. No one is going to bite anyone. Yet." Simon watched Vlad select a couple more books. "Who isn't fine?"

"Joe Wolfgard called while you were talking to Jackson."

"Joe? Did he leave a telephone number or an address?"

"Joe is fine. But, Simon?" Vlad looked at his friend and comanager. "We need to talk. We all need to talk."

CHAPTER 8

Windsday, Juin 6

"**M**ore disputes are heating up in the aftermath of the storm that swept up the East Coast yesterday. Some boat owners, whose vessels were damaged during the storm, are claiming the damage was done by members of the HFL movement because the boat owners refused to let the HFL use their vessels for 'questionable activities.' Representatives of the accused HFL chapters vehemently denied the allegations, saying the boat owners were targeting them because 'You can't sue the damn ocean for damaging your property.'

"Here in Lakeside, a number of businesses were vandalized last night. The police have no leads as yet on the person or persons who broke windows and painted obscene suggestions on the buildings. One store owner said he was going to leave a dictionary on a public bench so the vandals could at least spell the obscenities correctly. It was noted that none of the vandalized businesses displayed an HFL logo in the window. Police Commissioner Kurt Wallace, who recently admitted to being a member of the Humans First and Last movement, was not available for comment. This is Ann Hergott at WZAS, bringing you the news . . ."

Monty turned away from the break room doorway, having heard enough.

"Lieutenant?" Kowalski hurried out of the break room. "You ready to go?"

"Not yet. Did you hear anything on the news about bison being killed?"

Kowalski blinked. "Bison? Around here?"

"No, not around here. Anywhere in Thaisia."

"Didn't hear anything like that." Kowalski leaned closer and lowered his voice. "Is that a concern?"

"Could be. I need a minute with Captain Burke; then we'll go." Monty went to

Burke's office and knocked on the doorframe—and wondered what Burke's cousin Shady was really doing in Lakeside, since the man spent most of his time at the police station. "Captain? Can you spare a minute?"

"I can spare two," Burke replied.

Monty wasn't sure if that was literal or a joke. "Simon Wolfgard called. A hundred bison were shot in Joe Wolfgard's territory this morning. Simon wanted to know if we'd heard of any other incidents."

"Bison?" Shady asked.

"Large grazing animals that travel in herds," Burke said. "They're mostly in the Midwest and parts of the Northwest Region, although I think they can also be found in the High North. Some farming and ranching organizations feel that the bison are the impediment to opening up land humans need to grow crops and graze livestock."

"And if the bison are eliminated?"

"If you eliminate the bison, elk, deer, and everything else the *terra indigene* hunt for food now, the Others will end up eating the cattle, sheep, goats, and, most likely, the pesky humans who made a land grab."

"If it's an isolated incident caused by a few troublemakers in one Midwest town, that's one thing," Monty said. "If there are more incidents . . ."

"Then it could be a concerted effort by the HFL to antagonize the Others," Burke finished for him. "Or by another group altogether, but the HFL would be my first choice. I'll make some calls, see if I get any answers. You heading for the Courtyard?"

"Not yet. I heard on the news that some buildings were vandalized last night, so I want to check on Nadine Fallacaro. She's been supplying food for the Court-yard's coffee shop. She could be a target because of that."

"Nothing reported in our precinct, thank the gods." Burke leaned back in his chair. "All right, Lieutenant. You check on Ms. Fallacaro. I'll see if I can find out anything about bison."

Monty turned to Shady. "I will be at the Courtyard sometime today, and I'll ask Simon Wolfgard about human guests."

"Appreciate it," Shady said.

Of course he would be at the Courtyard sometime today. Monty was splitting his time between the one-bedroom apartment he'd rented when he'd first arrived in Lakeside and the efficiency apartment in the Courtyard that he was using as a place where Lizzy could stay while he was at work. Both places had disadvantages, but they would muddle through until he could move into one of the two-bedroom apartments on Crowfield Avenue. He still wasn't sure how he felt about having the Others as his landlords, but he knew he wouldn't find a safer place for Lizzy to live—or a more dangerous place if Lakeside exploded into a violent collision between the people who supported the Humans First and Last movement and those who believed that progress depended on maintaining peaceful relations with the *terra indigene*.

"So what's the deal with the bison?" Kowalski asked.

"Could be an isolated incident. Or it could be the first volley in Cel-Romano's war against the Others."

"But I thought Cel-Romano was preparing to wage war in their part of the world."

Monty looked out the side window. "Maybe that's what we're supposed to think."

Vlad set a small bowl on the sorting room table and smiled at Meg. "I brought you some strawberries."

She reached for a berry but didn't take it. "You're not giving up your share of the berries, are you?"

"No, I bought a quart of the berries that are for sale in the Market Square and decided to share them with you."

"Oh. Well, thank you."

He waited until she'd eaten a berry before broaching the real reason he was there. "Meg? What upset you this morning?"

He watched her throat work as she swallowed. Throats, with the blood in them so easily accessed by a kiss, always drew his attention. But with Meg, it was like looking at a delicate piece of art that could be admired but not touched because the *cassandra sangue* were Namid's creation, both wondrous and terrible, and their blood was not drunk by the Sanguinati.

"I had a bad dream. Then I woke up. I guess I was loud about waking up."

"You screamed and threw yourself on top of Simon." With windows open to cool the apartments, her scream woke everyone in the Green Complex. But Meg tended to scream when she saw a mouse, so they all wouldn't have come rushing into her apartment if Simon hadn't yelped like he was also in trouble. To the rest of them, that yelp meant physical trouble. In a way that had been true, since Meg had been clinging to Simon while he'd been trying to get out from under her without hurting her. At least, he'd put on a good show of trying to get out from under her when the rest of them came rushing into the room. "What did you dream about?"

Color blazed in her cheeks. "I don't remember."

Vlad studied her, wishing he could believe there had been some erotic element in the dream that she didn't want to reveal, but that wasn't the reason for the blush. Meg had just lied to him.

"Why is a bad dream so important?" she asked.

"It wouldn't be if someone else had the dream. But you're a *cassandra sangue.*"

"I didn't make a cut, and my skin didn't split because of weather or anything, so it wasn't prophecy; it was just a dream."

He nodded as if she'd convinced him, but he presented the one thought that troubled him, the thought that had brought him to the Liaison's Office. "It's just odd, don't you think, that three significant things happened at the same time of day? You had a bad dream, something compelled Hope to make a drawing that frightened her, and bison in Joe's territory were killed. All at daybreak."

"But daybreak in the Northeast Region is two hours ahead of daybreak where Hope lives."

"Two hours ahead of daybreak in Joe's territory as well. But you don't remember your dream, so we don't know if you had some kind of vision about the bison."

The sorting room filled with an awkward silence until a truck pulled into the delivery area.

"I have to get that," Meg said.

"And I have to get to work." He walked out the back door of the Liaison's Office, then stopped. He didn't want to go to Howling Good Reads yet, didn't want to talk to Simon.

Meg had lied to him about not remembering the dream. It wasn't that he'd thought she couldn't lie. She was human after all. But he'd never thought she would lie to any of the *terra indigene* who had befriended her.

Was their friendship less valued now that there were more humans around? Or was he making too much out of things that weren't important?

Too agitated to work, he headed for the Market Square to sit and think.

The moment the deliveryman walked out the front door, Meg rushed to the back room and peeked out the door to make sure no one was around. Then she opened the door all the way and leaned against the doorjamb.

She had lied to Vlad—and had lied to Simon and Henry and Tess earlier that morning when they asked her if she remembered the dream. She remembered enough. More than enough.

She'd dreamed about making a cut, had dreamed so vividly she could still feel the razor slicing her skin. Prior to the cut, she had run her hands down her arms, down her legs. But the buzz hadn't been in her arms or legs; it hadn't been on her back or her belly. In the end, she laid the razor along the right side of her jaw and pressed the blade against skin. Then her dreamself had endured the agony that came before a *cassandra sangue* began speaking prophecy, had continued to endure the agony by staying silent. And that dreamself had seen something so terrible that Meg had flung herself on Simon to protect him, to save him.

She had bled in a dream and seen prophecy. Something bad was going to happen to the Wolves. Unfortunately, *she* hadn't seen the prophecy, so she couldn't tell anyone what was coming, couldn't give a warning.

Were any of the other *cassandra sangue* who were living outside the compounds having similar experiences of seeing visions without making an actual cut? Hope was making drawings that, until that morning, had been a different way to reach the visions without cutting. What about Jean, who was living with a Simple Life family on Great Island? Was she sensing things now without cutting?

The visions the three of them saw seemed to intertwine, but were they seeing the same things? She and Jean and Hope had come from the same compound, had been taught the same images, so they had that much in common when they described their visions. But now their lives were so different. Jean lived on a farm. Hope lived in a *terra indigene* settlement in the Northwest. And she lived in the Lakeside Courtyard. Each of them was absorbing new images every day, but not the same images. That was true of all the girls who had been freed from benevolent ownership. Would the younger girls, growing up without that rigid training, be able to communicate at all when they saw the visions of prophecy? Would it matter?

Meg clenched her teeth as the skin over her entire head suddenly filled with that pins-and-needles feeling.

It would matter. Maybe not here, maybe not right now, but it would matter.

So how could girls living outside the compounds achieve the same kind of image consistency in order to communicate with one another?

She needed to find another, already available, source for images. Wasn't that part of her job as the Trailblazer, to help the other blood prophets find the tools they needed to survive?

The prickling beneath her skin faded. Going to the doorway between the back room and sorting room, she hollered, "Nathan? I'm going to the Three Ps. I'll be back in a few minutes."

"*Arroo?*"

Yes, it was unusual for her to leave the office during her work hours, but if another delivery arrived, Nathan—and Jake Crowgard, who was perched on the wall between Henry's yard and the delivery area—would let her know.

She hurried out the back door and across the access way. She'd been inside the Three Ps only once and had been overwhelmed by the amount of paper products Lorne Kates managed to carry in the small shop. She kept her eyes focused on the counter and rushed toward it as Lorne came out from behind the chest-high wall panels that separated the computers and printers from the retail part of the shop.

"Morning, Meg."

"Good morning." She braced her hands on the counter.

"You all right?"

Meg nodded. "I'd like some postcards."

"Do you want to take a look at what I have in the spin rack?" Lorne asked.

"No. I need sets of pictures, images. If I see Talulah Falls in a vision and need to convey that I'm seeing that particular waterfall, I want another *cassandra sangue* to pick up the same image so she knows exactly what I mean."

"Haven't you been creating a binder of images to help identify things in your visions?"

"The binders are too big." As soon as she said it, she knew it was true. Binders would be useful for collecting images that appealed to each girl, but the blood prophets needed something else for the consistent images, something about the size of a postcard.

Why was she so certain of that? Had she seen something during a cut, or heard about something that she couldn't recall?

They both turned toward the door when they heard the howl.

"Someone is looking for you," Lorne said. "I'll pull one of each postcard and drop them off at the Liaison's Office. After you look them over, you keep the ones you want and give back the rest. All right?"

"Yes. Thanks, Lorne." Huffing out an annoyed breath when Nathan howled again, Meg rushed across the access way but stuttered to a stop when she saw Blair Wolfgard leaning against the office's back door, waiting for her.

Blair was the dominant enforcer in the Courtyard and didn't have much use for humans. To be fair, she was pretty sure she'd caused him a considerable amount of trouble since she started working, and living, among the *terra indigene*. So there was always the possibility that Blair would forget—or ignore—the "don't bite Meg" rule.

"You caused a commotion at your place this morning," he said.

"I had a bad dream, and I sort of fell on top of Simon." How many times did she have to say it?

"What was the dream?"

"I don't remember."

Blair's amber Wolf eyes studied her. "You would tell me if I needed to keep watch for something, wouldn't you?"

"I would. And I will. But there's nothing to tell you now."

He opened the back door and stepped aside to let her enter.

"Meg!" Lorne hurried over to her, casting a nervous glance at Blair. "Take a look at these. And here's a catalog from the place that prints the postcards. Keep it awhile. You can make up a list of the images you want me to order for you."

Meg took the postcards and catalog. "Thanks."

With another glance at Blair, Lorne bolted across the access way and back to the safety of his own shop.

"I'm going back to work now," Meg said.

But the enforcer's eyes were focused on the second floor of Howling Good Reads and the Wolf standing at the window. Blair walked away without saying a word.

Shivering even though the day was turning warm, Meg went inside the office and laid out the postcards on the sorting room table.

Common images for blood prophets living in different parts of Thaisia. But these weren't the pictures she and Jean and Hope needed. These were scenic and pretty, and prophecy was rarely about things that were pretty. If that wasn't true, blood prophets wouldn't need the euphoria to veil what they saw and cloud their memories.

She had lied about the dream because Simon, Vlad, and the rest of her friends would be upset if she told them about the part she remembered.

There was no scar along the right side of her jaw. But there was going to be. Sometime soon she would make that cut to save Simon and the rest of the Wolves.

"Vladimir."

Looking up, Vlad forced a smile. "Grandfather. What brings you to the Market Square?"

In his human form, Erebus Sanguinati looked like an old man with a lined face. His hands had knobby joints and big veins, but the fingernails were not as yellowed or horny as they used to be—a slight adjustment in appearance that had been made after Meg began delivering packages to the Chambers, the Sanguinati's part of the Courtyard. His voice had a slight accent and belied the lethal nature of the vampire who commanded all the Sanguinati in Thaisia.

Erebus sat beside him on the bench. "Our Meg saw a couple of movies at the store here that she thought I might enjoy. So I have come to look. Then I saw you." He smiled gently. "You are troubled?"

Meg lied to me. Not something he would say to Erebus now or ever. Grandfather doted on Meg.

"Yes, I'm troubled," Vlad admitted. "I keep coming back to what happened this morning and how prophecy usually works."

"Prophecy is about the future, about something that is going to happen. Is that not so?"

"Yes. And sometimes that future possibility is just minutes away, leaving a person with very little time to act." Vlad blew out a breath. "Daybreak. That's what is bothering me. A *mound* of bison is bothering me. They must be connected with the dream Meg had and the drawing Hope made, but Joe Wolfgard said the bison fell where they died. They weren't mounded."

"You think the sweet blood saw something else, something that hasn't happened yet?"

Vlad nodded. "And whatever Meg and Hope saw, each in her own way, is connected to something that will happen around a place called Prairie Gold."

Erebus said nothing in a way that kept Vlad silent. A minute passed. Then two.

"We are more suited to hunting around larger human cities than other forms of *terra indigene*," Erebus finally said. "Not so well suited for small human places, like so many of the towns in the Midwest Region."

"I'm aware of that, Grandfather."

"But now the leader of the Lakeside Courtyard and our sweet blood are connected to two places that have no Sanguinati among the *terra indigene* who are keeping watch over the humans. You are concerned that the Wolves will not relay information?"

"No, it's not that. I trust Simon, and he trusts Jackson and Joe. But Wolves and Sanguinati have different strengths. I'm just wondering if our not being present in so much of the Midwest makes other kinds of *terra indigene* more vulnerable to an attack."

Erebus's laugh sounded like skittering dry leaves. "You would tell the Bear and the Panther that they are not capable of defending their land? You would say such a thing to the Wolves?"

"We've fought well together here. We can fight well together in other places."

Another silence. Then, "This place where the bison died. Could the Sanguinati shelter there?"

Vlad nodded. "There is a motel, so there are a few rooms that can be rented. I asked when I was speaking with Jesse Walker, the woman who runs the general store."

Erebus smiled. "Very well, Vladimir. Perhaps it is time to reassess our presence in the Midwest Region. I will ask two of our kin to visit this Prairie Gold."

"We could supply them with a legitimate reason to visit. The *terra indigene* collect the gold that is found in the streams that flow in the Elder Hills. Sanguinati could trade human money for the gold and bring the gold back here or take it on to Toland. Also, Jesse Walker didn't sound like she trusted the humans in Bennett, the railway town where the Intuits buy many of their supplies. We may be able to supply some merchandise directly."

"All right. But, Vladimir, you will inform the Wolf there that the Sanguinati will be arriving. As a courtesy."

"Of course, Grandfather."

Erebus stood. After giving Vlad's shoulder a pat, he walked over to Music and Movies to consider the movies Meg thought he would like.

Vlad sat for a moment longer before returning to Howling Good Reads. The Sanguinati who were heading for Prairie Gold could take the first order of books with them.

One window of Nadine's Bakery & Café was fitted with a piece of plywood, replacing the broken glass. Painted across the door and other window were the words *Wolf fukker.*

"I guess the vandals do need a dictionary if they can't spell *that* right," Kowalski said.

Guilt produced a queasy burn in Monty's stomach. He'd talked Nadine into providing baked goods and sandwiches for A Little Bite. The Others had come to her place early two or three times a week to pick up an order. They'd come quietly, in a minivan that looked no different from a thousand others in the city. But someone must have figured it out, must have said something.

Monty walked into the pretty café, with its handful of tables and the big glass display cases that were usually full of mouthwatering treats.

Not much in the display cases today.

Nadine walked out of the back room where she did the cooking and baking. "Lieutenant."

"Ms. Fallacaro, I am so sorry this happened."

"Could have been worse. Those little bastards could have—*would have*—done more if Chris hadn't run downstairs with a baseball bat and started swinging."

Chris's father was Nadine's cousin and the owner of Fallacaro Lock & Key—and a member of the Humans First and Last movement. Chris's refusal to join the HFL was the reason he was currently staying with Nadine. Monty wondered whether Fallacaro knew or cared that the HFL had targeted members of his family.

"He thinks one of them might have a broken arm," Nadine continued.

"He's lucky they didn't jump him," Kowalski said.

Nadine gave Kowalski a bitter smile. "They belong to the *right* kind of human. They didn't expect the likes of us to object to anything *they* chose to do, so they weren't prepared for someone to fight back."

Not this time, Monty thought. *But if there's a next time?* "I'll explain the situation to Tess. I think she, and Mr. Wolfgard, will understand why you can't provide—"

"You'll do no such thing." Nadine sniffed. "If I give in, then the next demand will be to join the HFL. You think I didn't notice how many stores are sporting that decal this morning? No, Lieutenant. I'm not closing my café, I'm not letting fools with an agenda tell me who can buy my baked goods and other foods, and by all the gods, I *am not* putting an HFL decal in my window." She sniffed again and squared her shoulders. "Besides, anyone who wants to defy the HFL in this neighborhood needs to buy food somewhere."

Monty extracted one of his business cards, turned it over, and wrote his mobile phone number on the back. "If you or Chris have any more trouble, you call me." He held out the card. "You call me."

"You going to the Courtyard?" Nadine asked.

"I am."

"Could you take a delivery?"

"I can." Monty turned to Kowalski. "Officer, why don't you drive the car around to the delivery door."

"Yes, sir." Kowalski walked out.

"Discretion, Lieutenant?"

"Practicality."

Nadine rubbed her hands over her arms, as if trying to warm herself. "You tell Tess that I'll have the extras she asked for next week."

"I'll tell her." A ringing sound startled him.

"Have to take those cookies out of the oven. Come around to the door over there."

She opened the Employees Only door for him, and he followed her as she hurried to the back of her shop to pull out the cookies.

Looking at the food she'd already made that morning, Monty figured she'd been up since the wee hours, cleaning up the glass and sealing up the broken window. And then cooking, baking, doing whatever she could with her hands, to ease the hurt in her heart.

"I wasn't the only one who was targeted last night," Nadine said as she boxed up the food. "Why do *those people* think anything will be better if we start fighting among ourselves?"

"I don't know," Monty said gently. Then he looked around. "Where is Chris?"

"He's been trying to find some glass to replace the window. If we can't get new glass, he's going to the hardware store to figure out a way to seal up that opening a little better than just using plywood."

After receiving Nadine's assurances that she and Chris had things under control, Monty and Kowalski loaded the food in the back of the patrol car and drove away.

"We're not a delivery service, and we shouldn't be doing this," Monty said since Karl wasn't saying anything quite loudly.

"I don't think she's expecting many customers today," Kowalski said. "She unloaded a lot of what she'd made."

"I know."

Kowalski glanced at him. "What's on your mind, Lieutenant?"

Monty sighed. "If things are starting to unravel like this in Lakeside, how bad is it in other parts of Thaisia?"

The computer finished downloading the first picture from Jackson. Simon put two sheets of the special glossy paper into the office printer and printed two copies. Then he went on to the next e-mail from Jackson and gave the commands to download the second picture.

He took a copy of the first picture out of the printer as Vlad, Blair, Henry, and Tess walked into the office. He held up the picture for all of them to see as the printer spit out the second copy.

"A mound of bison," Henry said grimly.

"Hope is good," Vlad said. "I've never seen a real bison, but part of me believes that if I touched the paper, I could feel the shaggy fur, the horns."

"Smell the blood," Simon said. "Well, Jackson certainly smells blood on the original drawing."

Tess stared at the picture. "Bloody footprints—*Wolf* prints—all over the bodies piled up. Why?"

"We wouldn't hunt that way," Simon said. "We *don't* hunt that way."

Vlad shook his head. "We're missing something—or misunderstanding something. Are you going to show this to Meg?"

A terrible picture. Wanton killing. Not for food or defense.

"Is that a huge paw print?" Vlad pointed at the bottom of the picture, at a shape that looked like it had been created in blood and absorbed until it was a faint impression in the grass near the bison mound.

"Could be a print in the foreground," Tess said.

Simon looked at Henry. "The Hope pup couldn't have seen any of them."

"Who?" Blair asked. "Are you saying there are *giant* Wolves in the Midwest or Northwest?" He looked at Simon, then at Henry. "Not Wolves."

"No," Henry said. "Not Wolves. The primal *terra indigene* in their true form. The Elders are very large—even when they take a form close enough to what shifters like us have taken."

"Even then, none of us are actually *seen* when we're in our true form." Simon looked at Henry, who was large in human form and massive as a Grizzly. But when Henry walked in his true form as spirit bear, he was even bigger.

Compared to the Elders, even Henry as spirit bear was small.

"Could they do that?" Tess asked, pointing at Hope's drawing.

Simon hesitated, then nodded. "Some of them are big enough, and strong enough, to drag a full-grown bison and haul it onto a pile of carcasses. But they don't hunt that way." But like the rest of the *terra indigene*, the Elders studied other predators—and learned from them.

"Simon, you have to show this to Meg," Vlad said.

The computer pinged, the signal that the second picture from Jackson had finished downloading. Simon put two more pieces of glossy paper into the printer and hit the Print key. "I'll talk to Meg, but not just . . ." He looked at the printer. Stared at the picture printing on the paper.

"Simon?" When he said nothing, Vlad pulled the sheet from the printer the moment the first copy was done. "What is this?"

An old woman wearing a straw hat, her bare arms browned by the sun so the thin scars showed white. She sat behind a little table, pointing to the cards that were spread out over the top. Her other hand held two cards. One was the image of a young Wolf—Simon recognized it as a picture of himself when he was a juvenile. The other card was a picture of Meg. But not Meg as *he* knew her. Younger. Lost. Eyes that held little hope. And yet just a touch of defiance in those eyes.

"Simon?" The sharpness in Vlad's voice made Simon focus on the other *terra indigene* in the room.

"Part of a memory," he replied. "And part something else." The old woman hadn't known about Meg specifically, so why would the Hope pup draw the picture like that? "Which females are working in the Courtyard today?"

"Merri Lee and Ruthie are downstairs, pulling stock to send to Jesse Walker in Prairie Gold," Vlad said.

Simon reached for the picture Vlad held. "I want to show them this picture. I'd like you to e-mail it to Jesse Walker and Steve Ferryman. Maybe the Intuits will have a feeling for what it means."

"Just this picture or both of them?"

"Would the Intuits on Great Island care about bison?" Henry asked.

Vlad shrugged.

"Send both," Simon said. Taking the picture of the old woman, he went downstairs and found both girls in the stock room, busily depleting the stock he wanted in the store for next week's visitors. "Look at this."

They stopped and stared at the picture.

"I'm not sure what we're supposed to see," Ruthie finally said.

He wasn't sure either. That's why he showed them the picture.

"What kind of cards is she pointing to?" Merri Lee asked.

Simon growled softly. Couldn't help it. "I don't know. She told fortunes. With the cards." Except she hadn't used the cards the day he stopped by her table. That day, the old woman had opened a silver razor and cut her skin.

They cocked their heads, such a Wolflike gesture it startled him.

"Tarot?" Merri Lee said, looking at Ruthie.

"Maybe," Ruthie replied. "But the woman is like Meg, a *cassandra sangue*. Would one of *them* use tarot cards? And how can you tell from the picture that she used the cards to tell fortunes?"

"I saw her once when I was a juvenile." Simon studied the females. He wasn't going to back away. Or run. But predators had that same focused look in their eyes just before they sprang at their prey.

They have little teeth and little claws that aren't very sharp. And I can run faster.

"You met her," Merri Lee said slowly. "So this is a . . ."

"Vision drawing," he finished. "That's what we're calling the pictures the Hope pup makes."

"A message." Ruthie pointed to the bottom right-hand corner. "For Meg."

That look again. "I'm going to show her," he said, sounding, and feeling, defensive.

"There are some stores around Lakeside University that might sell tarot cards," Merri Lee said.

"Better if you stay away from the university stores," Ruthie said. "Karl and I can go after he gets off work."

Simon nodded agreement. Not that they were considering his opinion at this point. But Merri Lee had been attacked by four students at the university because she worked in the Courtyard, and other students might recognize her if she went into a shop in that area of the city. The possibility of her being hurt by other humans was the reason she was staying in one of the efficiency apartments and hadn't returned to school. For her to go back would be like a bunny wandering into a field full of wild, hungry dogs.

"All right. I'll check the phone book and see if I can make a list of potential places," Merri Lee said.

They started pulling stock again, then stopped.

"Is there anything else, Mr. Wolfgard?"

"No." Since they were between him and the back door, Simon headed for the front of Howling Good Reads, then went through the archway that connected the bookstore with A Little Bite. Going out the coffee shop's back door, he headed for the Liaison's Office.

He wished he didn't have to stay in human form to talk to Meg about the picture. He wished he could shift to Wolf and give her hand a couple of licks. He always felt better after giving her hand a lick. Couldn't do that when he looked human. Could he? He hadn't observed Kowalski or Debany licking their mates' hands.

Just one more thing he didn't know about humans.

Then he walked into the sorting room and found Meg standing at the table with postcards spread over the top—and wondered if, in her own way, she already had the answer.

"Meg?" Simon waited until she looked up. "I have something to show you."

CHAPTER 9

Windsday, Juin 6

J esse Walker watched Shelley Bookman enter the general store in a way that made Jesse think of stories where the heroine snuck around searching for clues—and usually ended up in a lot of trouble. "Shouldn't you be at the library?"

"One of my helpers is watching the desk," Shelley replied, hurrying over to where Jesse was stamping prices on canned goods. "This came for you. You *did* tell me to monitor your e-mail, and this is from *him*, with a request that we pass along a copy to Joe Wolfgard."

"What is it?" Jesse took the envelope from Shelley and noted the tremble in the other woman's hands. She opened the envelope and pulled out two pieces of paper.

The first picture made her stomach roll, but she studied the dead bison and the bloody paw prints that dotted the carcasses like children's handprints painted on a large sheet of paper.

"I'll want to show this to Tobias." Jesse put that picture back in the envelope. "He was out there this morning with Joe Wolfgard. He can say if this picture is about us."

The picture of the scarred old woman disturbed her in a different way—and gave her the feeling that she'd seen this before.

The bell above the door jingled. Before Jesse could put away the second picture, Abigail Burch rushed over to them.

Abigail and Kelley Burch were newcomers to Prairie Gold, having arrived last summer. Kelley was a goldsmith who'd quickly realized most of the people in their small town couldn't afford the kind of jewelry he could make, so he made pieces out of silver and semiprecious stones and eked out a living.

Abigail was a few years younger than Kelley and had blue eyes and strawberry blond hair and a preference for long dresses of a style that Jesse's grandmother had worn in her younger years. No one would ask, but everyone wondered if Abigail was a bit simple or just a bit peculiar, because she was the only one among them who wasn't an Intuit. Either way, Kelley, who was an Intuit, loved her, and that was sufficient for the rest of them.

"Jesse?" Abigail always sounded a little unsure and a little breathless. "You've talked to the Wolf who's in charge of the . . ." She waved a hand in the general direction of the hills and the *terra indigene* settlement. "Could you ask him about the tallow?"

"Tallow?" Jesse looked at Shelley.

Abigail nodded. "I use tallow to make my candles and soaps. I make really nice candles and soaps."

"You do," Shelley agreed. "I've bought some of them."

"Tallow, Abigail?" Jesse prompted, hoping for more explanation.

"Kelley heard about the dead bison, and he's gone over to Floyd Tanner's to help out however he can. I usually have to buy some of the fat when sheep or cattle are butchered for meat, but I got to thinking about the bison. *They* would have fat too, wouldn't they? And I guess some of them are just going to go to waste? So I was wondering if I could harvest some of the fat? If bison have fat?"

Jesse's left wrist started to ache. She had feelings about everyone in Prairie Gold, and most of the time it was just an easy sense about the person. But when her wrist ached, it was a warning, and she didn't ignore such warnings. "I'll ask Mr. Wolfgard. But don't you go out to that field and try harvesting fat by yourself. There are plenty of predators of all shapes and sizes that are going to be out there feasting. Since Kelley is helping Floyd, he could ask about getting a bit for you to try out."

Abigail beamed a smile at both of them. Then she looked at the picture in Jesse's hand. "What's that?"

"Just a picture someone sent to me."

"Is the woman reading tarot cards? I read tarot cards. My grandmother read tarot cards. She gave her cards to me when she got feeble. And I bought a set for myself when I was . . . traveling." Abigail studied the picture. "Why does that woman have so many scars?"

"I think she's a *cassandra sangue*."

"Like those girls who . . ." Abigail blinked. "Why would she need tarot cards?"

"Not tarot," Jesse said softly. "Something close. Something I almost remember. Could I see your sets of cards?"

"Sure. I'll bring them right over." Abigail dashed out of the store, almost running into Tobias as he tried to enter.

"Need cold drinks. Whatever you've got," he said.

"Why don't I fill up a wire crate while you talk to Tobias," Shelley said.

"Talk to me about what?" Tobias wiped his face on his sleeve.

"About this." Jesse pulled the picture of the bison out of the envelope and watched her son pale. "Did it look like this?"

Tobias shook his head. "Mom, you can't show that picture around."

"I was asked to give it to Joe Wolfgard. You and Shelley are the only ones in town who have seen it. The only ones who *will* see it." She wanted to rub the ache in her wrist, but he knew her tell just like she knew why he sometimes pressed a hand against his right ribs when he was sensing something strong. "What spooks you about this?"

"Can't say."

"Can't or won't?"

Tobias gave her a hard look. "Won't. Truman and I saw something this morning, something humans don't usually see and live to tell about it."

Jesse looked at the one paw print that was different from the smaller Wolf prints painted on the bison. "All right, Tobias. I still have to give the picture to Joe Wolfgard." She hesitated. "Abigail Burch wondered if she could have some bison fat for making her candles and soap."

"Mom . . ." Tobias didn't continue, and Jesse heard the tick-tick-tick of her old clock. "I'll ask, but you make sure Abigail—and Kelley—knows she can't be wandering out there by herself."

Shelley put the wire crate on the counter, filled with bottles of juice and soda. "I figured Floyd has water."

"He does. Thanks Shelley." Tobias lifted the crate, gave Jesse a look that was both hard and pleading, then walked out of the store.

"Trouble?" Shelley asked.

"Could be." Jesse put both pictures in the envelope and stashed them under the counter as Abigail returned.

"I brought both sets of cards," Abigail said, setting silk-wrapped bundles on the counter.

Not tarot cards, Jesse thought as Abigail showed them her grandmother's deck, then did a reading for Shelley with her own deck. *Not tarot, but something similar. Something I've seen before.*

"I'm going to meet a stranger full of danger and darkness." Shelley watched Abigail dash across the street toward her own little shop. Then she snorted. "How likely is that here in Prairie Gold?"

"You didn't get a feeling?" Jesse wished she could put some ice on her now-throbbing wrist.

"Nothing." Shelley gave her a curious look. "Did you?"

"You need to get back before your helper gets bored and starts rearranging the books again." Since Shelley's helpers were usually the older children who liked books and wanted to earn pin money, they tended to be responsible—up to a point. "Do some research for me."

"You want your own set of tarot cards?" Shelley teased.

"I want to know who makes them. I especially want to know if any Intuit-run company makes them or something like them."

"You getting a feeling?"

Her vision grayed for a moment, a terrifying sensation. "Yes, I have a feeling."

CHAPTER 10

Windsday, Juin 6

J ean clenched her hands on either side of the bathroom sink. The Gardners, the Simple Life family who were allowing her to stay in their little guest cabin, never commented when they saw evidence of cutting, but she knew they reported it to someone.

Some days she could resist the need to cut by sitting outside the door of her cabin and watching the activity around the farm, listening to the sounds of children playing. Some days she could resist, but today an old scar itched so much it burned.

Dangerous to cut an old scar and have new images overlaying the previous vision. More dangerous to cut *across* old scars and jumble together the images of several prophecies. Such a cut was rarely useful. More often it drove a blood prophet insane or broke her mind in some other, smaller way. And this scar wasn't a true cut. This was damage that had been done to her while the Controller's men were beating her in order to get blood to make the drug called gone over wolf.

Had to cut. And, worse, had to remember what she saw.

Jean pulled out her razor. Then she rolled up a clean washcloth and bit down on it as a gag. Finally, she carefully cut the old scar and set the razor down moments before the agony filled her body and images filled her mind.

Two images, repeating over and over. Ones she had seen before while the Controller's men beat her.

She stood on a hilltop, looking down at a big map of Thaisia, its boundaries scratched into the earth. *Scattered throughout the continent were tiny candles. In the first image, some of the candles were clustered together, perhaps indicating human cities with a lot of people. In most places, there was a single candle. Probably a marker for a town. All those candles. Heavier concentrations along parts of both coasts. More human places than she would have guessed existed.*

The second image. The same map of Thaisia, seen from the same hilltop. So few candles still burning now. So few. But a candle still burned for Lakeside, and another burned for Great Island. Only two candles burned for Toland instead of many.

Some candles burned in the Midwest and Northwest, but their position didn't match the names of any of the towns she'd learned.

Jean spit out the washcloth, then pressed it against the cut. She was on the bathroom floor, and her body hurt too much to try to stand just yet.

Should she write down what she'd seen and share it with Meg? Should she burden the one blood prophet who, as the Trailblazer, was trying to help the rest of them stay alive?

"Meg's Wolf," Jean whispered. Yes. He was a leader of the Lakeside Courtyard. He'd rescued her because Meg had asked him to help her. Maybe knowing that Lakeside *could* survive what was coming would help him make the choices that would ensure that the city *did* survive.

Shaky, Jean got to her feet. She washed and bandaged the cut, then cleaned her razor and ate a small meal. Having properly cared for herself, she sat down and wrote a letter to Simon Wolfgard.

To: Simon Wolfgard and Vladimir Sanguinati

Intuits in the Midwest and Northwest have heard about bison being killed in dozens of places throughout those regions. No reports about the bison killings in the news; however, there were reports of cattle or sheep being killed, and outraged ranchers and residents of the neighboring towns were interviewed. Everyone ignored the simple fact that Wolves, Panthers, and Grizzlies don't shoot their prey, so the animals weren't killed by the *terra indigene*. Maybe a few of you should learn how to use a rifle. Less work catching your dinner and much less chance of being kicked or trampled.

Received a request from Jesse Walker, who runs a general store in Prairie Gold. She says Vlad gave his consent for her and a Shelley Bookman to be included in our e-mails about *cassandra sangue*. Please confirm.

Received the pictures. Wish I could thank you for them.

—Steve Ferryman

To: Steve Ferryman

Jesse Walker's request confirmed. We want to further the connections between Lakeside, Great Island, Prairie Gold, and Sweetwater.

You can thank Jackson Wolfgard for the pictures. Since a blood prophet drew them, consider them a warning. However, Simon would like any information your people might have about fortune-telling cards.

—Vlad Sanguinati

To: HFL, Lakeside Chapter

Stage one of the urban cleansing has revealed the problem areas. Proceed with stage two at the designated time.

—NS

CHAPTER 11

Joe Wolfgard helped Tobias Walker lift the fifth shipping container of bison meat into the dairy farm's small refrigerated truck, which Tobias had parked outside of Floyd Tanner's butcher shop. He didn't understand why the whole Prairie Gold community was proud to have such a truck, but he could appreciate its usefulness in moving food that would spoil during transport in the days when Summer ruled the land.

Besides, Vlad had already done some of the things he'd promised, and Jesse Walker and Shelley Bookman were now on Steve Ferryman's particular information list. Shelley had also set up an e-mail account for him at the library so that Simon and Jackson—and Vlad—could send him news if they didn't want to send a telegram, which would have to be brought out to the *terra indigene* settlement, or call him at Jesse Walker's store to have a message delivered that way.

In the *terra indigene* settlement where he'd lived before coming here, there had been a communications cabin that had a telephone and computer, and the settlement had been close enough to a human village that they could use mobile phones at least some of the time. But Prairie Gold was a simpler place, and communication was no longer as direct. The *terra indigene* settlement here didn't have a telephone or computer, didn't have the poles and wires that made such things work. The Others hadn't felt the need for such things. More important, the Elders didn't want those human things touching their hills.

But having a way to communicate with other *terra indigene* beyond howling range was important now that humans were causing trouble in so many places. He would need to chew on his problem for a while. Maybe the Eaglegard would be willing to act as couriers if he needed to send a message quickly to another part of Thaisia or receive a message from Simon or Jackson? If not, then the Crowgard or Ravengard would certainly enjoy being the first to have news.

Did humans who worked in telegraph offices choose that work because they had the same desire as Ravens and Crows to know the news first?

"What do you think?" Tobias asked.

Joe blinked, then remembered the question Tobias had asked as they loaded the meat into the truck. "Bison fat? Do humans eat it?"

"No, Abigail wants to try making candles and soap from it. She usually purchases tallow from Floyd Tanner when a steer or sheep is butchered for meat, but there are a lot of carcasses out there, and the fat on them is going to waste, so she wondered if she could have some."

There aren't that many carcasses left out there now, Joe thought. A Wolf could cover a hundred miles in a day. The Elders could cover even more ground. Many of them had come down from the hills to consume the available meat instead of hunting. And, he suspected, they had become sufficiently curious and wanted a closer look at the Intuits who had settled near the southern end of their hills—humans who were working hard to be friendly with the *terra indigene*.

"She would give you some of the candles and soap as a kind of payment for the tallow," Tobias added.

That was fair. Candles were sometimes useful. He would have to see about the soap. The Others had built places where they made the soap that they preferred to use when they were in human form. It wasn't stinky with added smells and it didn't foul the land. He would have to ask Jesse Walker if she carried that soap in her store. But if Abigail Burch could make an acceptable soap, they wouldn't have to buy it from another part of Thaisia.

"We can pick up some fat on our way back from the train," Joe said.

Tobias closed the truck. "Speaking of the train, we'd better get going. We need to stop for gas before we head out."

"Hey, Tobias!"

Tobias nodded at the man striding toward them from the direction of the general store. "Tom."

Tom Garcia wagged a thumb toward the store. "Jesse said you should stop at the store on your way out. She has a basket of food and drinks for the two of you to take with you."

"Appreciate that. We need to stop there anyway to pick up a couple of big containers that will hold tallow for Abigail."

Tom nodded at Joe and went inside the butcher shop, where every available adult human had been helping Floyd handle the glut of bison meat.

"Anything you need to do before we go?" Tobias asked.

"No." The rest of the *terra indigene* already knew he was going to the train station with Tobias, and plenty of Hawks, Eagles, and Ravens would be watching them from the sky.

They picked up the food and drinks from Jesse, filled the gas tank on the way out of town, and started the two-hour drive to Bennett.

"You sure you're not looking for tarot cards?"

Jesse hung on to patience. Shelley had found three Intuit companies that, among other things, printed tarot cards and fortune-telling cards, which, she'd been told, weren't quite the same thing. This was the third company. The other two either didn't know what she was talking about or weren't willing to admit anything to anyone—which made her wonder how they were staying in business. But she had a feeling that trust had become a commodity more precious than gold.

"I'm sure," she said to the woman on the phone. "I remember seeing decks of cards that were used by some women to get a sense of something coming, but that was four decades ago, and I'm trying to find out if cards like that are still being made."

Silence. Then, "What kind of women?"

"Blood prophets. I'm looking into this for one of the *cassandra sangue*." Not quite true, but close enough.

"You have one of those girls living in your community?"

"No, but we're looking into fostering one or two of the girls." Another gray truth since it had been a passing thought. When the other woman said nothing, Jesse continued. "The leader of the *terra indigene* settlement at Prairie Gold has connections to two of the girls. One of the girls had a vision about cards."

A crackling silence. "Gods," the other woman breathed. "You're looking for the Trailblazer deck?"

"I—" Jesse's left wrist throbbed. "Maybe I am." Now it was her turn to hesitate. "There's really a deck of cards called that?"

"Not officially. Not yet. Yesterday I pulled a few decks of fortune-telling cards from our stock. I had a feeling that a new deck was needed, but I didn't know *what* was needed."

"Maybe you're not the one who is supposed to decide. Maybe you're the one who is supposed to produce a special deck of cards that will be used by the Trailblazer." Jesse thought for a moment. "You could produce a deck of cards from new art?"

"Sure, but we don't have new art."

Not yet. "The decks you pulled yesterday. You must have been drawn to them for a reason. Can you send me two of each of those decks?"

"Yes, I could." The woman's voice softened. "Yes, I could."

Jesse gave the woman the mailing information for Prairie Gold, thanked her, and hung up. Then she threaded her fingers in her hair and pulled hard enough to relieve some of the tension in her scalp.

Need to stock up, she thought as she studied the shelves in her store and tried to ignore the increasing ache in her left wrist. *Canned goods, dried goods, anything in a jar that will last until . . .*

"Until what?" The sound of her own voice startled her, made her stop and consider why her thoughts had jumped from fortune-telling cards to the certainty that she needed to hoard supplies, and she needed to do it *now*.

As she looked around her store, her gaze rested on the shelves that held the books. Couldn't purchase books from the publishers anymore. Couldn't buy books from the bookstore in Bennett. Some might argue that books were a luxury, not a necessity. She didn't agree, but as a test for depriving an isolated community of merchandise? People would be unhappy about the loss of new books to read but not angry. At least, not at first. But what if things they considered more necessary suddenly couldn't be purchased? Things like food and clothes and, gods, even something as basic as toilet paper?

Two years ago, they'd had a rough winter, had been isolated for several weeks during a series of fierce storms. She'd had a feeling that year and had started stocking up on supplies in late autumn, ignoring the teasing from Tobias and Shelley about becoming a canned goods and paper pack rat. Then the storms hit a few weeks later. By the time they'd gotten the road cleared and could drive to Bennett for supplies, she'd had half a dozen cans of soup and two boxes of spaghetti on the shelves and had been breaking up the last packages of toilet paper and selling it by the roll so that every family would have some.

As she looked at the stock in her store, she had the same feeling, only this time it felt worse. Much worse.

Pulling out the notebook she used to keep track of items to order, she began reviewing the shelves and making a list. She'd completed the dried goods section when Shelley rushed into the store.

"Joe Wolfgard received an e-mail," Shelley said. "From Vlad Sanguinati!"

"Joe has gone to Bennett with Tobias," Jesse replied.

"Do you think we should read it?"

"No."

"I can access his e-mail and—"

"No."

"But it might be important!"

Jesse turned and eyed Shelley. "Even if it is important, there's nothing anyone can do about it until Joe and Tobias get back."

"But we could look—"

"Just because you set up the account for him doesn't mean you're entitled to read his mail or even check his account to see if he received any." Jesse's voice turned sharp. "The library and the post office are the only places in Prairie Gold that have computers. Anyone who wants to communicate through e-mail has to use those machines. Do you read the mail of everyone who uses the computers in the library? Do you violate the trust of your friends and neighbors?"

"Of course not! But this is different!"

"No, it's not. The fact that Joe Wolfgard is sharing anything with us is more communication than we've ever had with the *terra indigene*, and, Shelley, *we can't afford to lose that trust*. Not now." Jesse wrapped her right hand around her left wrist. "Not now."

"You're right," Shelley said, sounding chastened as she stared at Jesse's wrist. "You're right. But don't you wonder what they talk about?"

"I think it's better for all of us if we don't know."

"We filled out the paperwork, the containers are clearly labeled, and we paid the haulage for two hundred pounds that requires refrigeration," Tobias said hotly.

"Like we said." One of the handlers gave Tobias and Joe an oily smile. "Refrigeration car is full up this trip."

Stay in control, Joe thought. *Don't shift. And don't bite the baggage handlers. It won't help.*

Tobias pointed at the railroad car that was puffing clouds of cold air out the open door. "There's plenty of room in there for our five boxes."

The handler closed the door. "We're full up."

<Wolf? I am Air. Do you need help?>

The female voice—and the offer—surprised him. He'd never dealt with any of the Elementals directly until the night they'd all gathered to attack the Controller's compound. How many of them lived in Thaisia, let alone the rest of the world? Were there a thousand of them called Air? Ten thousand? More? Being a form of *terra indigene,* there were males as well as females. Was there someplace in the wild country where they gathered to mate and raise their young? Was there some lush valley where their steeds bore foals that played and grew until their natures were revealed? Was a wisp of a tornado a colt just learning what it was, while a lethal funnel was a stallion in its prime?

The Elementals called themselves by what they commanded and offered no other name—at least, not to anyone beyond their own kind. So while this female called herself Air, he didn't think she had been at the Controller's compound, and he was fairly certain she wasn't the Elemental who lived in Lakeside.

Joe considered her question. <We want to send some meat to Simon Wolfgard and Meg Corbyn at the Lakeside Courtyard, but the humans are saying the car with cold air doesn't have room for the boxes of meat.>

<We have heard of the Meg who lives near Etu. She likes this meat?>

<She has never tasted bison, so it will be a treat—if it doesn't spoil before it reaches Lakeside.>

A wind lightly whipped around the platform. The door of the next car opened. <Put the meat for the Meg in this box,> Air said.

<That baggage car isn't cold.>

<It will be.>

"We'll put our shipment in this baggage car," Joe told Tobias. "Come on, let's get these boxes inside."

"But that's not—"

"*Do it,*" Joe growled.

They hauled the five boxes of meat into the empty baggage car, setting them to one side of the door.

The baggage handlers smirked—until the female who looked like she was wearing a long dress made out of clouds walked across the platform with a barrel-bodied, chubby-legged white pony.

"Gods," Tobias whispered.

"Ssh," Joe warned. <Thank you for your help.>

She smiled at him. Then she looked at the baggage handlers, and her smile changed to something sharp and feral. She and the pony entered the baggage car. She closed the door.

"What the fuck was that?" one of the baggage handlers said.

Joe didn't answer. His sharp Wolf hearing picked up sounds in the baggage car that the humans didn't hear or were choosing to ignore—sounds of a storm in the making.

"All aboard!" the conductor called.

"Wait!" A man ran onto the platform with a cart full of boxes. "These need to be loaded."

"If you put them in that baggage car, they'll get wet," Joe said, making a token effort to be helpful.

"You and the Wolf lover can go fuck yourselves," a handler snapped.

"Why?" Joe asked, not seeing the connection between baggage and mating.

No one answered the question, because the handler pulled the baggage car door open—and wind-driven snow slapped him in the face so hard it knocked him back a step.

"Gods," Tobias said again.

"No, that's Air and Blizzard," Joe said. "They'll keep the meat cold. Come on. It's time to go." He walked away but had to wait for Tobias to stop staring at the baggage car and catch up.

On the way back to Prairie Gold, he wondered if he should call Simon and tell him the Elementals were going to be interested in knowing if Meg Corbyn liked bison meat.

Their footsteps filled the land around Bennett with a terrible silence.

For hours they circled the town, sniffed around the railway station, listened to the chatter of the little two-legged predators. They didn't understand much of the chatter. Unlike the sounds made by the ones who helped the shifters, this chatter was of little interest to Namid's teeth and claws. But they still listened. And they watched. And they learned.

To: Jesse Walker

A shipment of books will arrive at the Bennett station on Watersday, Juin 9. Please arrange for someone to pick up the shipment. Also, please arrange transportation and motel accommodations for two individuals who will be staying in Prairie Gold for a few days. Separate rooms are preferred.

—Vladimir Sanguinati

To: Simon Wolfgard

Five boxes of bison meat are on their way to you. I hope your Meg likes the meat since Air and Blizzard made a special effort to keep it cold. Also, a human female is making soap and candles out of bison fat. I will send you some.

—Joe

CHAPTER 12

Firesday, Juin 8

Simon held out a letter when Vlad walked into HGR's office. "Read this."

Vlad took the letter and looked at the signature. "This is from Jean."

"Yes. She sent it to me. Read it."

While Vlad read the letter, Simon read the e-mail from Joe. His mouth watered at the thought of tasting bison again, even if the meat wasn't fresh off the hoof. He really hoped Meg liked it.

He stared at the computer screen. He wasn't sure how much farming—or what kind of farming—was being considered at the River Road Community being developed by the Lakeside Courtyard and the Intuits at Ferryman's Landing. Sure, the land around Lake Etu wasn't like the grassland found in the Midwest, but there was grass. And he wasn't thinking of a *herd* of bison. Just a few at River Road, a few in the Courtyard. Substantial meat. Even with the deer that were already in the Courtyard, there would be enough grass to feed a handful of bison. Wouldn't there? Of course, it would be safer to ship little bison and let them grow up once they were here. So they would have to be fed for a few years before they were of sufficient size to be a meal for all the carnivores living here. But one bison *would* feed all of them for several days.

Something to think about.

Vlad sank into the chair on the other side of the desk. "When you were told to consider how much human the *terra indigene* would keep, we thought it meant the things humans make. But this prophecy sounds like something is going to happen that will cause a lot of the human cities in Thaisia to disappear."

"I know." Simon pushed aside the happy distraction of fresh bison. "But Lakeside and Great Island survive."

"Prophecy is not a guarantee of the future."

No, it wasn't a guarantee. Choices could change the outcome of the future.

Vlad set the letter on the desk. "I'd like to show the letter to Grandfather Erebus—and to Stavros. Blair is picking him up at the station. Tolya came with him from Toland and will travel with Nyx to Prairie Gold. They'll deliver the books to Jesse Walker and Shelley Bookman, and they'll talk to Joe Wolfgard."

"You didn't have to thin our stock quite that much," Simon grumbled.

"I've already sent in the reorder. We still have plenty of books available for the Addirondak Wolves to experience shopping in a bookstore. Besides, I sent Jesse Walker the rest of the kissy books we couldn't send to anyone else." Vlad gave him a long look. "The inventory didn't match the books we had left. You wouldn't know what happened to the rest, would you?"

"Oh. Well. I didn't want to get rid of all of them in case Meg wanted to read that kind of story. Not now, but sometime."

"I think it would be smart to ask a human male if that's the way human females typically respond to mating before assuming a *story* provides useful information."

Well, of course. Something scary had happened to Meg in the compound, so a naked human male was still a confusion for her. But that didn't mean she wouldn't come into season someday and *want* a mate. No reason not to gain some understanding of what would make one male more attractive than another when a female wanted to do more than take a one-night walk on the wild side.

"Why is Stavros coming here?" Simon asked, changing the subject.

Another long look from Vlad. "He has things to discuss with Grandfather—and the Business Association."

He'd been the leader of the Lakeside Courtyard for several years, but until tonight, Simon had never set a paw inside the Chambers, the part of the Courtyard where the Sanguinati resided. Plenty of game made use of the land and water—deer, ducks and geese, wild turkeys. The Hawks, Crows, and Owls might fly over that part of the Courtyard, but fly over was all they did.

Meg had been the first to receive permission to enter the Chambers, to walk up to the door of Erebus Sanguinati's home to leave a package. Because of Meg, Simon's nephew Sam had been inside the Chambers, protected by Erebus while Meg led the enemy away from the pup—an act of bravery that had almost killed her.

They drove up to one of the gates in the ornate black fences. Simon, Elliot, Tess, and Henry got out of the minivan and waited by the gate. The full moon was waning, but for a Wolf's eyes, it was enough light to see the smoke flowing toward them. Four of the Sanguinati moved to either side of the gate. Only Vlad shifted to human form. He opened the gate, a silent invitation.

Tess's green hair coiled tighter, a sign she felt uneasy.

I guess that means even a Harvester couldn't survive a fight with this many Sanguinati, Simon thought as he followed Vlad down a curving path and across a footbridge to a weathered pavilion sheltered from sight by the surrounding trees.

Stavros Sanguinati, the Toland Courtyard's problem solver, was already inside with Erebus Sanguinati.

"Welcome," Erebus said. "Sit. Be comfortable. We have some refreshments. Vladimir?"

<Can we decline refreshments?> Elliot asked Simon.

<No.> Being there at all was unprecedented. They would consume whatever was offered.

"None of us enjoy the soda beverages humans are fond of, so I've brought along bottles of apple juice and made a pitcher of lemonade," Vlad said.

"You know how to make lemonade?" Tess asked, eyeing the pitcher.

"After enduring a vigorous debate between Merri Lee and Ruthie about how many lemons and how much sugar make the best-tasting lemonade, I can't say I *know* how to make it, only that I followed the instructions I eventually received."

Tess laughed. "I'll try some."

"Sure," Simon said.

Vlad poured glasses for all of them. Erebus and Stavros took a polite sip and set their glasses aside. So did Henry. But Tess seemed to enjoy the lemonade, and while it would never replace the good taste of water, Simon decided it was tolerable—and something he would drink if Meg decided to make it.

"Stavros has things to tell us," Erebus said.

"About the Sanguinati?" Simon asked. He couldn't think of any other reason they would be meeting within the Chambers—unless Stavros wanted to be certain that no one would overhear what he had to say.

"About many things, but, yes, about the Sanguinati and the Toland Courtyard," Stavros replied.

"And the Toland police?" Scaffoldon, a police captain in Toland's Crime Investigation Unit, went missing shortly after the murder of Lizzy's mother, Elayne. Elayne's mother also disappeared around the same time.

Did Lieutenant Montgomery realize yet that Stavros was the reason the humans who had posed a threat to his daughter were no longer a threat?

"They are not our concern." Stavros made a dismissive gesture with one hand. "There have been no reports on the radio or television about bison being shot. This isn't surprising; such a thing is not of interest to humans, especially in a city on the East Coast. Some stores and shops in Toland, particularly ones who do business with our Courtyard, were targeted by vandals, just as some places were targeted here. Broken windows, writing on the walls and remaining glass. Stores that showed an HFL sign the next day had no difficulty finding replacement glass or getting repairs done. Store owners that refused to bend aren't doing as well."

"The impression I had from speaking with some of Lakeside's government officials is that this difficulty is the same everywhere," Elliot said.

Stavros nodded. "Tolya and I have been monitoring the television and radio news as well as reading the human newspaper. Nicholas Scratch has been oddly silent about the vandalism. He has not made any speeches about it or spoken to reporters. This is curious because he has voiced opinions about everything else that connects a group of humans with any of the *terra indigene*."

"Not so curious if he knows the Humans First and Last movement was behind the vandalism," Elliot said. "Maybe he left Toland?"

"No, he's still there, and he's still meeting with members of the HFL." Stavros took a sip of lemonade, then set the glass down again. "I've already discussed this with Grandfather, and it has been decided that we're going to abandon the Toland Courtyard."

Simon stiffened, while Elliot, Henry, and Tess made wordless protests.

"The humans are driving you out?" he asked, shocked.

"Not the humans," Erebus replied. "But Toland is a city filled with humans. Too many humans. They covet the land we hold in that city."

"They covet all of Thaisia," Henry rumbled.

The hair framing Tess's face turned red. "If they aren't held to the land they already infest, they'll swarm the continent and consume everything."

"No, they won't." Simon looked at Vlad. "Show them the letter."

"I'll read it." Vlad took the paper out of his back pocket, unfolded it, and read Jean's prophecy about the human cities in Thaisia.

"Fools," Henry said. He looked at Erebus and Stavros. "If the humans aren't driving the *terra indigene* out of Toland, who is?"

"While the *terra indigene* were distracted by the bison being killed, and while humans were distracted by the vandalism of stores not affiliated with the HFL, a dozen ships left three human-controlled cities on the East Coast. Five of those ships left from Toland; the other ships sailed from the other two cities. I don't know what cargo they carried, but we think it must have been some kind of contraband because each ship carried barrels of poison that they dumped into the water, killing all the fish that came in contact with the stuff."

"Sharkgard?" Simon asked.

Stavros nodded. "Oh, yes. The poison killed sharks and Sharks. It killed dolphins. It killed the schools of fish sought by fishing boats. Some of the Sharkgard survived long enough to send a warning. The ships were avoided to prevent further deaths, but they were followed until they reached the Mediterran Sea and Cel-Romano."

"What happens now?" Tess asked.

Stavros laughed, a bitter sound. "Ocean is going to vomit the dead fish onto the shores of those three human cities. She will vomit the poisoned water into the streets of the cities responsible for killing the *terra indigene* who live in her domain. And then she will give the humans a taste of her wrath."

"That is why the Sanguinati are leaving Toland—why all the *terra indigene* are leaving Toland," Erebus said.

"We're going quietly," Stavros said. "Most of the Wolves have already left. They're heading up the northern coast or toward the Addirondak Mountains. The Hawks, Owls, and Crows leave the Courtyard as usual, flying over Toland. But not as many return to the Courtyard as leave each morning or evening. Since the

Sanguinati were the dominant form there and the least vulnerable to the Elementals' wrath, we're packing up what possessions we can and using earth native trucks late at night to move items to other locations, or we're sending a trunk of smaller items with someone who is traveling."

"It sounds like we should order as many books as we can from the Toland publishers," Vlad said.

Stavros nodded. "I've made that suggestion to several Courtyards."

"How much time do we have?"

"Not much. Dead fish are starting to wash ashore."

"One last order, then," Simon said. "After that, there are Intuit and *terra indigene* companies that publish books and print books. We'll buy from them."

"We already buy from them," Vlad said. "They don't publish that many books."

"They can expand a little to publish more. Besides, if Ocean is going to strike out for killing some of the Sharkgard—and dumping poison in a part of her water—there may not be any books in Toland left to buy." He looked at Stavros. "What about you? Do you . . ." He stopped. Despite being the Courtyard's leader, he wasn't the one who should offer Stavros a place here at Lakeside. Not when Erebus was sitting right there.

Erebus smiled. "There will be many in the days ahead who would like a place in Lakeside, but too many predators in the same land causes strife. However, I would like Stavros to have a place here when he is not in Hubb NE, keeping watch over the human government. I think they will need careful watching in the days ahead."

Simon drank the rest of the lemonade in his glass. Was it his imagination, or had it gotten a little more sour while it sat? "You're not going to tell any of the humans, are you?"

"Why should we?" Stavros replied. "They brought this on themselves."

"Not all of them."

"There are no sweet blood in Toland now," Erebus said. "Stavros and the government agent, O'Sullivan, removed them."

"I wondered if Lieutenant Montgomery has family there."

Silence.

"Ah," Erebus finally said. "The helpful policeman. What could you tell him?"

Simon thought about that. No way to know when Ocean would strike. If too many humans tried to leave Toland, where would they go? Except for the human farms that supplied food for the city, there wasn't any human-controlled place between Toland and Hubb NE, which was an hour's train ride away. There was only wild country and the *terra indigene*, who, like Ocean, had less and less tolerance for the clever monkeys.

"I don't know what I could tell him," Simon said.

"Captain Burke's cousin is visiting all the way from Brittania," Henry said. "It would not be strange to ask if any of Lieutenant Montgomery's kin were planning to visit him and the Lizzy."

"Meg should ask. Otherwise Montgomery will wonder why we're suddenly so interested in his kin."

Everyone agreed that was a good idea. Meg asked questions. She talked to humans about all kinds of things. She might already know if Montgomery still had kin in Toland.

Nothing more to say. Not tonight. Simon wanted to shift to Wolf and run for a while in the moonlight. He wanted to curl up next to Meg while she watched TV or read a book. He wanted humans to go back to being annoying instead of a real threat.

Nothing more to say. Except . . .

"There's trouble here too, but we're not leaving Lakeside."

"No, we're not," Erebus agreed.

"Nothing else is at risk by leaving Toland," Henry said. "But if we're gone from Lakeside, Great Island will be vulnerable, especially since it hasn't been decided yet if all the remaining humans in Talulah Falls will be sent away and replaced by Intuits and Others who can work the machines. As it is, Steve Ferryman doesn't want his people going there because it's too dangerous. That means almost everything that comes from other parts of Thaisia—or the rest of the world—comes to them through Lakeside."

Erebus stood—and the meeting was over. Vlad led Simon, Elliot, Henry, and Tess back to where they'd parked the minivan. Four Sanguinati, still in smoke form, kept watch at the gate.

They drove back to the Green Complex in silence. Henry parked the minivan in one of the visitors' parking spaces across from the complex, and they all went to their apartments.

Simon stripped and tossed his clothes on the sofa before shifting to Wolf and going out again. He sniffed around the complex, watered a couple of trees, then returned to the summer room below Meg's apartment, shifting one paw just enough to open the door.

"Hi," she said.

He stopped just inside the door. He'd thought she'd be asleep since there was no light on.

"It's going to be a busy weekend, isn't it? The Addirondak Wolves will arrive in a few days for a week of people watching." Meg laughed softly. "I don't think it sunk in until Merri Lee, Ruth, and I were talking this evening that that's what this is about—people watching."

Interacting, actually. The Others *watched* humans all the time. Not that watching had stopped things from going wrong.

Nothing he could do about Toland. Nothing he could do about dead bison in Joe's territory. But he could help Joe by sending books for the Others and the Intuits. He could help Jackson deal with the Hope pup. And he and Meg and the human pack and the *terra indigene* here in Lakeside could show the Elders who were watching closely that *terra indigene* and humans *could* work together to keep Thaisia a good place for all of them.

He gave Meg's hand a couple of licks, then settled down next to her lounge chair and fell asleep.

Jerked out of a light sleep, Monty grabbed the phone on the second ring, scrubbing a hand over his face as if that would make his brain function—or convince his heart that Lizzy was still safe. "Hello?"

"Crispin?"

Monty's heart banged against his chest as he turned on a lamp and looked at his watch. "Mama? What's wrong?" Had to be something wrong for her to call him at midnight.

Twyla Montgomery sighed, a sad, tired sound. "I got handed my walking papers today. Security guard watched me clean out my locker, even checked my bag afterward to make sure I wasn't taking anything that wasn't mine before walking me out the door."

"Fired?" Monty couldn't get his mind around that bit of information. "You were fired?"

"Wasn't needed anymore. Have to provide jobs for those more deserving."

"They said that?" Then it clicked. "They wanted you to join the HFL in order to keep your job."

"As if I need to belong to some organization in order to clean the toilets those fools mess up every day."

"Gods." Monty rested his head against the back of the couch. "Mama, you did right not joining the HFL. They're doing nothing but stirring up trouble."

"You think I can't see that?"

The dry tone made him smile. His mama didn't tolerate fools—especially fools who wore suits that cost more than she made in a month. But his smile faded as he realized what losing the job meant for her. "When do you have to move out of your apartment?"

"Soon. I can stay with your sister for a few days, but she's got her troubles too."

How long since he'd talked to Sierra? His sister sent letters, breezy bits of news that, he realized now, didn't actually tell him much.

Monty looked around his apartment. Lizzy was spending the night with Sarah Denby, Eve and Pete's daughter. He'd intended to crash at the efficiency apartment in the Courtyard, but Captain Burke made a comment about possession being nine-tenths of the law—a pointed reminder that his landlady had a key and could decide he'd abandoned the place, which she could rent for twice as much as what he was currently paying. He wanted to keep this one-bedroom apartment until his lease ran out at the end of the year—or until the Courtyard took possession of the two buildings on Crowfield Avenue and he and Lizzy could move into one of the two-bedroom apartments.

"You often say that opportunities come out of bad moments as often as they come out of good."

"Where's the good in me being fired?" Twyla demanded.

"I need help taking care of Lizzy. Some friends are looking after her while I'm at work, but Eve has a job and her own two kids. I've been thinking about this ever since Lizzy arrived in Lakeside. She needs you, Mama. So do I."

A thoughtful silence. "Any chance of me finding work where you are now?"

Monty hesitated. "Maybe."

"I'm not living off my children, Crispin. Not you, not Sierra."

He noticed she didn't mention Jimmy, Monty's younger brother. Then again, Jimmy still came around looking for a handout, despite being a married man with two children of his own. And he always left feeling resentful when he didn't get that handout.

"There might be work available, but I'm not sure how you'd feel about the employers."

"Are they more of those HFL fools?"

"No, Mama. They are definitely not members of the HFL."

"Well, I'll think on it."

"You have enough money for a train ticket?"

"I've got enough put by. Might take the bus instead."

He bit back a protest. Plenty of people traveled by bus. "You let me know when you're coming and where to meet you. I'll be there."

A soft sigh. "Thank you, Crispin. Talking to you has eased my heart. I'll say good night now."

"Good night, Mama."

She hung up first. She always did since he just couldn't hang up on her.

Monty stood up and stretched. He was already entangled with the Others at the Lakeside Courtyard. He wasn't sure he wanted to ask Simon to give his mother a job.

CHAPTER 13

Watersday, Juin 9

"We don't usually come up to Bennett more than once a week to pick up supplies," Tobias Walker said as he pulled into a parking space at the train station.

Joe Wolfgard tried to identify the tone in the man's voice. "Are you complaining about this second trip because Bennett is a long way from Prairie Gold?"

"Nope. Just providing information that you might find useful." Tobias crossed his wrists over the top of the steering wheel. "We try to conserve fuel in the general way of things. It's especially important right now because the fuel truck that fills up the underground tanks at the gas station didn't show up yesterday when it was supposed to. We've got one emergency vehicle that's equipped to bring someone here to Bennett if the person is too sick or injured for the doctor to handle at our little clinic. That vehicle gets its tank filled before any others. The dairy farm's refrigerated truck also gets priority. Folks tend to fill up near the time when the next delivery is due so that we receive our full allotment of gasoline."

"Can we buy fuel for the pickup truck here?" Joe asked. Was finding out what happened to a fuel truck part of his responsibility now, or was it considered a problem between humans? Simon might know, although Blair might be the one he should ask because the Lakeside Courtyard's dominant enforcer spent more time driving vehicles and probably had more experience buying gasoline.

"We can—providing the gas station here received its scheduled supply of gasoline." Tobias hesitated. "The guests you're expecting. Do they know all we've got to offer is simple rooms at a motel?"

"Jesse Walker told Vlad what was available, so he knows."

"Is there a reason your guests don't want to stay at your settlement? Just asking."

"Vlad was specific about the living arrangements." But not specific about who was arriving with the books. That made him uneasy, but there was no point howling about it until there was a reason to howl.

They reached the platform just as the train pulled in. Half the station was a waiting area for humans. The other half was an area for merchandise and packages that came in by train. It made Joe think of Meg Corbyn's office with a person at the counter and a separate room to hold packages until someone came to collect them.

Humans hurried down the steps of the two passenger cars. Some looked pale, smelled weak. If he were hunting with a pack of Wolves, he would focus on the weak-smelling prey as the easiest to bring down.

"Must have some la-di-da folks on the train this time," Tobias said.

"La-di-da?" Joe had never heard of such a human.

Tobias lifted his chin to indicate the third passenger car. "Rich. Important. Don't always see a private car."

Rich. Important. *Or lethal,* Joe thought as he watched a male with a carryall descend, then turn and offer a hand to the female. The male was dressed in a black suit with a pale gray shirt. The female wore a long, old-fashioned black velvet gown with draping sleeves. They both had olive skin, black hair, and dark eyes. The male, by himself, could have passed for human and blended into a crowd— at least for a little while. The female made no effort to hide what she was.

"Gods above and below," Tobias breathed. "Are they . . . ?"

"Sanguinati," Joe finished. "Come on." He moved quickly, more to keep the humans from panicking if they realized who was now among them than because he was in a hurry to meet his guests.

The male saw them and smiled, while the female glided down the platform to watch the men who were unloading the baggage cars.

Joe smelled fear in Tobias's sweat. Not a good way to begin with predators like the Sanguinati.

"Joe Wolfgard?" the male said. "I am Tolya Sanguinati. We met a few months ago in Lakeside." He moved his hand in a slight gesture that indicated the other Sanguinati. "Vlad told you to expect us?"

"He did." Joe glanced toward the men who were carefully unloading boxes near the female, stacking them as if to build a wall between the humans and her.

The Sanguinati had been among the *terra indigene* who had destroyed the Controller and the compound where he had kept *cassandra sangue* like Meg Corbyn. Joe could appreciate them as predators, but he wasn't sure he could be friends with one the way Simon was friends with Vlad.

Now I know why Vlad wanted them staying near humans, although, when they're smoke, they could hunt anything at night.

"This is Tobias Walker, the foreman of Prairie Gold's ranch," Joe said.

"We brought many books for Jesse Walker and Shelley Bookman," Tolya said as the female joined them. "This is Nyx."

"Ma'am." Tobias brushed the brim of his hat with a finger before turning to Joe. "Mr. Wolfgard, we should get the boxes loaded and be on our way."

Hearing wariness, Joe looked around. There were too many humans paying attention to them. "Yes, we should."

Tobias wrangled a cart from the baggage handlers. Joe helped him stack the boxes on the cart and roll it out to the parking area while Tolya and Nyx trailed after them.

After they loaded the boxes into the pickup's bed, Joe remembered Tobias's comment about making trips up to Bennett. "Do we need to buy anything while we're in town?"

"Just gas for the truck." Tobias shifted his eyes in Nyx's direction but didn't look at her. He simply opened the passenger door. "Ma'am."

She shifted to smoke from the waist down and flowed into the pickup.

"There's room on the seat for you, too, Tolya," Joe said. "I can ride in the back."

Tobias shot him a panicked look before lowering his head enough for his hat to hide his face.

"I can ride in the back with you," Tolya said.

Joe shook his head and patted a hand against his leg. "This clothing fits in with riding in the back of a pickup. Your clothing does not—at least while we're in the human town." Once they left Bennett, it wouldn't matter, and he thought Tobias would feel less threatened if there was only one Sanguinati riding up front with him.

"You are more familiar with the customs in this part of Thaisia." Tolya got in and pulled the passenger door shut.

Joe jumped into the back and settled in the remaining space. Lots of books. More than he'd expected Simon and Vlad to send to the humans. Then he noticed his name on two of the boxes and happily realized they had sent books for the *terra indigene* settlement too.

Tobias came around and closed the tailgate. "Mr. Wolfgard . . ."

"They aren't going to feed on you," Joe said, then added silently, *At least not while you're driving.*

Tobias got behind the wheel and drove to the gas station. As he pulled in, Joe studied the human males who were gathered around watching a man in overalls tape a hand-printed sign above the pumps.

<Your human is angry,> Tolya said. <I don't understand all that he's saying— he speaks differently from the humans in Toland—but I understand some of the swearwords mixed in with the rest.>

As soon as Tobias pulled up to the pumps and shut off the truck, Joe vaulted over the tailgate and came around to stop Tobias from biting the man with overalls. Or punching him. Punching was more likely, since Tobias had strong hands from ranch work but small teeth.

"What kind of crap is this?" Tobias demanded. "You doubled the price of gas when you saw us coming?"

"Supply and demand," Overalls said, giving Tobias a nasty smile. The smile slipped away when Tolya opened the passenger door and stepped out of the pickup, but Overalls focused on Tobias. "You should know about supply and demand."

"We do," Tolya said so pleasantly it made Joe shiver. Then the Sanguinati gave Tobias a look that warned the human not to make trouble. "Since you had to make the trip on our behalf, I will pay for the gasoline." He took a wallet out of his suit coat, then held up two fifty-dollar bills as he focused on Overalls. "So that you know we can pay."

Wanting to get away from the town and this pack of humans who seemed ready to attack, Joe opened the gas cap and snapped, "Tobias." Then to Tolya, <Letting them change the price because we wanted some gas is no different from letting smaller predators run you off a kill before your own pack has fed. If you pay them this time, they'll keep making the Prairie Gold humans pay more.>

<Not for long.>

The ominous words made him uneasy, but the scent in the air—there and gone as the wind shifted—was more disturbing.

"What they're doing isn't right," Tobias said as he started to pump the gas.

Joe growled at him because this wasn't the time or place to discuss human meanness or greed—not when the Elders were so close to the town their scent was in the air.

Tobias filled the tank, Tolya paid for the gas, and they drove away as the pack of men made what Joe assumed were insulting comments.

<Do you need any food?> Joe asked Tolya.

<No, thank you. We ate on the train.>

As soon as they crossed the Bennett town line, Tobias pulled over and Nyx and Tolya got out. Joe, riding in the bed of the pickup, removed his shirt, then pulled off his shoes.

"I need to be Wolf." He stood up and unbuckled his belt.

"Wait a minute," Tobias protested.

Joe shook his head. "I need to be Wolf." He pushed the jeans down his legs and stepped out of them, kicking them aside before he shifted into a form that felt natural and had sharper senses. He gave his fur a good shake, then sat down and looked at Tobias, who had turned his back to the truck.

"We can continue now," Tolya said politely.

Tobias looked over his shoulder, then turned to face them. "I've got things to say."

When he didn't continue, Tolya said, "We are listening." Then to Joe, <He is angry, but I think he fears punishment.>

That was Joe's opinion too. <I want to hear why he's angry.>

Tolya relayed the message.

"They expected us," Tobias said. "Maybe they knew the fuel truck hadn't reached Prairie Gold yesterday, and anyone coming up to Bennett would be looking to buy gas. You could afford to pay that price today, and I do appreciate it. But tomorrow the price might double again, and what's the next person coming to town supposed to do? Gamble they'll have enough fuel to get home because they can't afford to pay those prices? Hope the fuel truck will have made the delivery to our gas station?"

"I can assist Joe in finding out why the fuel truck didn't arrive in your town,"

Tolya said. "Between us, we should be able to find a more reliable vendor—in other words, an oil refinery that belongs to the *terra indigene* and is run by Intuits."

Tobias blinked. "There are such places?"

"One or two. Enough to ensure that Intuit villages have what they need for essential transportation and machinery. Production is limited, but I think we can arrange for your town to be supplied that way from now on."

Joe tried not to growl. Had Tolya come to Prairie Gold to take his place as the leader of the *terra indigene* settlement? If that was the case, he should have been told, since he'd been selected as the new leader here less than a month ago. Although having a *terra indigene* around who knew about these human things like refineries would be useful. He had been among the *terra indigene* who could pass for human, and he'd had some human-centric education, so he could deal with humans on behalf of his own kind. But unlike Simon, he had never wanted to run a Courtyard or even live in one.

"We understand about supply and demand, Mr. Walker," Tolya said. "When there is a glut of prey, predators come in from other territories to hunt and feed. There is enough for all of us, and our young survive and grow strong and, in their turn, learn to hunt. When the prey becomes thin, predators travel back to their own territories, or else they end up fighting among themselves for a share of the kill. Not all of their young survive, nor do the weakest among them. Eventually Namid's balance is restored, and there is enough food for both predators and prey."

Tobias swallowed hard. "So you're saying there's a glut of prey in Bennett?"

"I'm saying Bennett isn't the concern of the *terra indigene* located in Prairie Gold," Tolya replied. "Shall we continue?"

Tobias slipped into the driver's seat and started the truck. Nyx slipped out and flowed over the side of the truck, settling in back next to Joe, while Tolya sat up front with Tobias.

<The humans in Bennett *are* the concern of the Prairie Gold pack,> Joe told Tolya. <We're supposed to keep watch and collect the payment for the land the humans leased around here. That includes the ranches as well as that town.>

<If they break the agreements, the Others can reclaim the land and force them to leave—isn't that so?> Tolya countered.

<Yes.> Joe didn't like the trail the Sanguinati was following.

<Perhaps you should allow them this kind of petty meanness, let the humans' own actions prove they should not be allowed to remain here.>

<But the Intuits have been promised protection from other kinds of humans in exchange for skills we do not wish to learn but know are needed,> Joe argued. <Letting those humans raise the price of gasoline until Intuits can't afford it isn't protecting them.>

Tolya said nothing for a minute. <I have always lived around larger human cities, so this part of Thaisia is very new to me. I felt something in Bennett that I recognized as *terra indigene* but had never encountered before.>

<Elders. The *terra indigene* who live in and watch over the wild country. They don't usually come that close to a human town.>

<If that is the case, perhaps you shouldn't depend on Bennett for the supplies needed in Prairie Gold.>

There was a warning in those words.

But Tolya had a point, Joe thought with a sigh. He'd learned enough about his new territory to know that the humans living in Bennett hated the Others for setting the boundaries of what humans could and couldn't have, and they resented the Intuits because Prairie Gold had something the human-owned ranches didn't have: water that flowed down from the hills and followed natural channels to watering holes that made it easier for the Intuits to run their dairy farm and produce farm and the ranch that raised cattle and horses. And a few men, over the years, had gone into the hills and come out again with gold. But what one man might be able to do, a dozen could not. Believing there was untold, and unclaimed, wealth in the streambeds that could make a man rich beyond his wildest dreams but couldn't be reached was becoming a different kind of sickness in some humans. They wanted what they couldn't have because something already claimed that land and that water, not for wealth but for life.

Joe didn't know exactly where Tolya and Nyx stood with their pack, but he wouldn't be surprised if their jobs were the equivalent of enforcers or guards. Why send them here to deliver some books? Or did their arrival have more to do with the drawings made by Jackson's prophet pup?

When Prairie Gold came into sight, Joe shifted back to human form and got dressed. Their first stop was the motel, so that Tolya and Nyx could check in and drop off their personal luggage. That's where they heard the news that a fuel truck had exploded on the highway the day before. The two men who drove the truck were killed. There was some argument about whether the explosion was an accident caused by driver error, or if the drivers were already injured or dead when the truck exploded.

"Supply and fucking demand," Tobias said when he heard the news. Then he looked at Nyx. "Pardon my language, ma'am."

Whether it was deliberate or not, Prairie Gold wasn't going to receive its expected—and needed—fuel until the Others arranged for a different supplier.

The worry over a gasoline shortage dimmed Jesse Walker's pleasure when they brought in the boxes of books for her store, but she was gracious in her thanks and polite to Tolya and Nyx. Shelley Bookman, on the other hand, took one look at the Sanguinati when they entered the library and seemed to have trouble catching her breath.

After receiving Tobias's promise to drop off the boxes of books at the place where the terra indigene received human goods, Joe watched the human drive away before giving the two Sanguinati a tour of the town. Humans watched them from doorways and windows.

"How long are you staying?" Joe asked. "Should I ask some of the terra indigene to stay close to town?"

"This is an Intuit settlement on terra indigene land," Tolya countered. "Is there a reason to fear these humans?"

"No. They remind me of the humans who make up Meg Corbyn's pack. They want to be members of a larger pack."

"That is wise," Nyx said. "I will be staying a few days before returning to Lakeside. Tolya will stay longer."

"If that's acceptable to you," Tolya said, looking at Joe. "Grandfather Erebus wants the Sanguinati to be more present in the Midwest. He wants us available to help the shifters. And my staying at the motel means I can keep an eye on the Intuits while you keep watch over everything else." He paused. "I think the terra indigene should visit Bennett as little as possible."

Joe agreed with that, but he hadn't liked being there to begin with. "We don't need to go anywhere in Bennett except the train station." As the implication of his own words struck him, fur sprang up on his chest and shoulders, and his canines lengthened to Wolf size. He stopped walking and took a moment to shift back to fully human.

"Our scent here becomes a sign of acceptance," he said. "It sends a message, an indication that these are humans who work with us." Would the Elders respect such a marker?

Tolya nodded. "That lack of scent also sends a message, does it not?"

Another warning under the words—especially after Tolya's suggestion that the Others avoid visiting Bennett and his earlier remark about reclaiming the land.

They walked back to the motel. Nyx wanted to explore beyond the town. Tolya wanted to make a couple of phone calls. And Joe wanted to shake off thoughts of troublesome humans, go home, and find out what books Simon had sent to the Wolves.

At Tolya's invitation, he stripped out of his clothes, folded them, and put them in the bottom drawer of the dresser.

"You may want to become a long-term renter of one of these rooms," Tolya said. "It would be a convenient place to store clothes and have water to wash in when you had to be in human form."

It was a good suggestion, and he would consider it. Instead of a Courtyard, the Others often had a house in a small human town, but there weren't any empty houses in Prairie Gold. They had built only what they needed. A room would be sufficient, and having it might encourage more shifters to experience limited contact with humans.

Tired but satisfied, Joe left the motel and headed home, slipping behind buildings instead of trotting down the road. But thinking about markers and who could be a more devastating enemy to the people here than the yappy humans living in Bennett, he stopped long enough to lift a leg and mark Jesse Walker's store.

CHAPTER 14

Earthday, Juin 10

Jackson Wolfgard knocked on Hope's bedroom door and waited to hear the words permitting him to enter. Not that he should need permission. He *was* the dominant Wolf, and she *was* living with his pack. But human females Hope's age were . . . peculiar. It wasn't *his* fault that, when he heard alarming sounds coming from her room the other day, he'd burst in, thinking she was hurt or under some kind of attack. And the jumping around and . . . caterwauling . . . turned into screams because he saw her without clothes. As if that made any difference to him. He had a mate. Besides, Hope was not only human; she was too fragile to be considering a mate, so he couldn't see why particular body parts made any difference.

Of course, her screams brought more Wolves running, so plenty of Wolves saw those body parts—and wanted to know more about the thatch of fur between her legs and under her arms. Were those things that should be present on the females when they shifted to human form?

They were still waiting for Meg Corbyn and her pack to answer that question.

But it wasn't fair to growl at him for responding the way he had. How was he supposed to know that sound had been *singing*? It hadn't sounded like any human singing that *he'd* heard. In fact, it sounded more like a young Lynx whose paw had gotten trapped in some rocks. Which was why he'd thought Hope was in trouble.

Jackson knocked again and heard a timid, "Come in." He stepped into the room, leaving the door open.

"Enough, pup," he said. "Grace and I don't mind if you draw every day, but not *all* day. The pack's nanny is taking the pups for a walk, and you're going with them. Get your shoes and your hat."

"I lost my hat," Hope mumbled.

Meaning the pups "accidentally" got hold of the hat and tore it to pieces. "Grace bought you another one." Several, in fact.

He studied her. She usually obeyed, but she'd been a bit odd since the vision drawing she'd done of the dead bison. Since she continued drawing instead of putting her things away, he came over and crouched beside her.

"I'm making sketches of cards Meg will need," Hope said.

Not finished drawings. Rough compared to her usual work. "Why does Meg need these?"

"I don't know."

"Are you going to make the final drawings?"

She shook her head.

When the pencil stopped moving on the paper, he knew she was done, drained of whatever she needed to reveal. "Go outside, pup. Breathe in the good air. Play with the other pups." He noticed the corner of another drawing that had slipped under her bed. "What's that?"

Silence. Then Hope sighed and pulled the drawing from under the bed and handed it to him. "Are you going to leave forever?"

"I wasn't planning to leave," he replied as he studied the overlapping images. He was the Wolf herding ten . . . no, eleven . . . young bison. Then, in the center of the page, a train, its engine heading east through the grasslands of the Midwest. Then Talulah Falls, distinctive and unmistakable, and those houses she had drawn once before. The last piece of the picture was of him and Simon herding the bison.

"You wouldn't leave Grace, would you?"

"I wouldn't leave either of you. But I might have to make a trip to Lakeside." He took the drawing and pulled her to her feet as he rose. "Outside. Walk, play, study the creek."

She blinked. "Study the creek?"

"Yes. It's clear water, not that deep. Look at what lives there. Then you can draw a picture of it when you get back."

She gave him the same brilliant smile that she'd given him when she'd told him her name was Hope.

She put on socks and sneakers before bounding out of the room ahead of him. Grace, in Wolf form, held a straw hat between her teeth and blocked the outside door until Hope took the hat and obediently tied the ribbons under her chin.

They watched the girl leap off the porch and run to catch up with the pups, who raced back to meet her.

Jackson showed the drawing to Grace. "I need to go down to the communications cabin and call Simon."

<It's Earthday. He won't be at the bookstore.>

"I have the number for his mobile phone. Even if he doesn't answer, he'll call back as soon as he gets the message." He ran his human hand over her white head, enjoying the feel of her fur against the naked skin. "As soon as I get back, we'll go for a run, just the two of us."

Laughter filled her amber eyes. <You'll have to find me first.> She ran out of the cabin.

He wanted to forget about drawings and visions and pesky humans. He wanted to run with his mate and have fun. But he would go down and make the phone call because he wondered what Meg Corbyn might have told Simon about the images in Hope's drawing.

Simon trotted to the back door of Howling Good Reads and shifted a paw just enough to turn the knob. He'd had an enjoyable morning, even if it was spent with humans, and the Wolves who had accompanied Kowalski, Debany, and the gaggle of girls had learned the Squeaky Dance game, which was great fun even if it didn't last very long.

The Wolves from the Addirondak Mountains were arriving tomorrow, and Vlad had been a bit sharp about not getting help restocking the shelves. John Wolfgard had made the mistake of pointing out that Vlad was the one who had decimated their stock before this visit, which was why Simon was spending a couple of hours at the store helping Vlad instead of John coming in to work. Verbally nipping at Erebus Sanguinati's most trusted weapon here in Lakeside was beyond foolish.

And even though no one *said* anything, Simon figured Vlad was concerned about Tolya and Nyx being so far from any Sanguinati stronghold.

Simon shifted to human form and reached for the pair of jeans he'd left on the chair next to the door. He growled at the empty chair, then did a quick search.

Damn females! There was a reason he left clothes on that chair! They had to stop *taking* things and "putting them away."

Not finding anything, he strode to the front of the store, hoping to meet one of the human pack who would squeak about his being naked. But he hadn't gotten that far when Vlad called out, "Simon? Is that you?"

He bounded up the stairs and into the office. "The next time I find *anything* any of those females have left around the store, I'll—" He stopped when he saw Vlad's face. "Your kin?"

"They're fine. Joe met them at the train station yesterday. Tolya called me last night to give me the phone number of the motel as well as his room number in case I needed to reach him." Vlad held out the receiver. "It's Jackson."

Simon leaped toward the desk and grabbed the receiver. "Jackson? What did Hope do now?"

Hesitation. "What do you know about bison?"

What an odd question. "They're tasty. Hard to hunt unless you're with a strong pack or bring down a young one." Things Jackson already knew. "Joe sent us packages of bison meat. They arrived yesterday. The female pack is cooking a roast to give all the humans a taste."

"What about live bison?"

"What about them?" Then he remembered Meg's prophecy about the River Road Community. "Meg saw some bison grazing at a mixed community we're building—Others and Intuits." *And she saw you there.*

"Hope's newest vision drawing shows me bringing young bison to you at a place around Talulah Falls." A waiting silence. "Is this how it works with blood prophets in the wild?"

"I don't know," Simon replied. "Maybe it's because Hope, Meg, and Jean—because she's part of this too—grew up in the same compound. Or maybe it's because those three have a connection to *terra indigene* who have bonds to each other. This is new for the girls as well as for us."

Jackson sighed. "Hope sees me traveling to bring bison to you, and she's asking me if I'm going to leave her and Grace forever. Your Meg sees me there. I don't know what to do. Traveling alone . . . Things feel strange around here. Close to Endurance, the human-controlled town, the water tastes sour and the air feels hot. The Intuits who have gone there for supplies felt it too."

"You need books?"

Vlad looked at Simon and showed his fangs. Simon revealed his own fangs.

"We're taking care of a human pup. Physically a juvenile, but you know what I mean."

He did. "It would be good for her to have books. We'll see what we can send." He'd have the female pack make a list of what a juvenile would like to read.

"Nyx," Vlad said quietly. "If Jackson is coming here, could he go to Prairie Gold first? Then he and Nyx could travel together."

Simon relayed the request.

"I'll do that. We didn't have any trouble with bison being killed around here, but if trouble is heading west, I'd like to know about it."

"Let me know when you're coming. We'll meet the train and arrange transportation." He'd make a call to Jerry Sledgeman on Great Island and see if Sledgeman's Freight could haul livestock.

"Our Hope and your Meg," Jackson said. "They could be wrong."

"One of them, maybe, but not both." Not when Jean was seeing a Thaisia cleansed of so many human cities. "Vlad has a number for the motel where Nyx and Tolya are staying. He'll call her so that she knows you're coming."

"All right. Simon? Tell Meg we're doing our best to keep Hope well."

"I'll tell her." As he ended the call, Simon thought about Jean's prophecy and what it meant to the Others. He looked at Vlad. "We can't trust humans anymore."

"Did we ever trust them?"

"No. But we counted on their desire to survive being stronger than their greed. I don't think we can count on that anymore."

Dear Jean,

Earthday in the Courtyard is a day when the stores are closed and the Others stay feathered or furry for the entire day because they don't have to interact with humans. But it was hot and humid today, and Henry said he and the Wolves usually spend time around the swimming hole on a day like this. It's not a hole full of water; it's actually the small lake in the Crowgard's part of the Courtyard. Anyway, Simon invited some of my human friends to come with us. It was a test, I think, to see how they would behave in a part of the Courtyard that was usually off-limits to humans besides me.

Theral MacDonald rode in the BOW with me and Simon. Merri Lee, Michael, Ruth, and Karl rode bicycles. I'm not sure if the Others had never seen bicycles before or if they had never considered them as a useful form of transportation, but something about the bicycles made the Wolves quite excited. There was a lot of sniffing once we reached the lake, but everyone was polite and didn't pee on the tires.

The lake is one of three that, along with the creek, supply a lot of the fresh water in the Courtyard. The Others drink it, swim in it, and catch fish to eat. Michael and Karl wanted to know what kind of fish, but no one was interested in shifting to human form to tell them, and I didn't know, so that's something they can discuss tomorrow.

Because the lake is waist-deep at one end and well over my head at the other end, it was fine for Wolves but not much fun for the Crows. So when Simon took over leadership of the Courtyard, he, Henry, and Blair created a connected wading pool where the water is only a few inches deep so that the Crowgard can splash around and play.

When it was time to go into the water, no one knew what to do. At least I didn't. After staring at us for a moment, Simon, Blair, and Nathan jumped into the water, then climbed out and shook water all over us.

It was <u>cold</u>! Merri Lee, Ruth, Theral, and I hopped around, making noises and saying, "It's cold, it's cold, it's cold."

The Wolves jumped in, climbed out, and shook water all over us again! The third time the Wolves shook water on us girls, we were sufficiently wet that it didn't feel that cold anymore—and the Squeaky Dance game was done. Unfortunately, I think this is a game the Wolves really enjoyed, so I suspect we're going to be on the receiving end of surprise soakings for the rest of the summer.

But once we got in the water, it felt so good! At one point, Nathan bumped into me and I went under and came up sputtering. That's when Ruth asked me if I could swim, and I said no.

Simon shifted to human form and just stared at me, shocked. How could I not know how to swim? All the puppies knew how to swim.

I pretended that Simon was wearing swimming trunks like Michael and Karl, and even though the water was pretty clear, the shade of the nearby trees kept the obvious from being obvious.

Michael offered to teach me how to dog paddle. He got snarled at from three directions, because no one was going to teach me to paddle like a dog! The Wolves don't mind dogs; they just don't want to be mistaken for a dog, and I guess they don't want me to be mistaken for one either.

I think Michael deliberately exaggerated the movements because Simon huffed, shifted back to Wolf, and began paddling around us to show me how to do it. Michael held me up while I tried kicking with my legs and paddling with my arms. Then I tried on my own with Simon and Nathan swimming on either side of me. When I got tired, we all climbed out and sat on blankets under the trees.

I must have fallen asleep for a little while, because I woke up feeling so content.

But contentment isn't going to last, is it? Dead fish are washing up on the shores of three East Coast cities. I heard Vlad tell Tess the fish were the storm's herald. I didn't feel any pins and needles under my skin because of that comment. I don't know if I should be relieved or worried.

I hope you're doing well at the Gardners' farm. Steve Ferryman is supposed to come by this week to show Simon—and me—plans for the new campus for the cassandra sangue. Steve says the girls are doing well, and the caretaker he hired for them is very intuitive about when to introduce something new and when to stay with the familiar.

I'm trying not to use the razor. Some days that's easy to do. Other days it's so hard. Maybe the younger girls will be able to escape the addiction. And if they can't escape altogether, maybe cassandra sangue like you and me and Hope can find other ways to reveal some prophecies. I'm just not sure those other ways will veil our minds *sufficiently, or if the euphoria that comes from cutting—and the likelihood of an early death because of it—is the cost of staying sane.*

You always believed we could survive in the outside world. I'm doing everything I can to give at least some of us a chance of not only surviving but truly living.

Your friend,
Meg

It is not enough to say we should have food and water and timber and oil. It is time to say we will have the food and water and timber and oil to feed our children and build our cities and heat our homes and run the machines that make us greater than the creatures hiding in the so-called wild country. It is only wild because it has not felt the bite of the ax or the plow. It is only wild because we still cower from the phantasms that were the stuff of stories we heard as children. Abolish the phantasms and see the creatures for what they are—animals that have not yet been conquered. It is time to banish the stories of childhood. It is time to claim our true place in the world.

—Speech written by Nicholas Scratch,
delivered at chapter meetings by HFL leaders throughout Thaisia

CHAPTER 15

Moonsday, Juin 11

A few minutes after Meg opened the Liaison's Office for morning deliveries, Steve Ferryman and Jerry Sledgeman drove into the Courtyard and up the access way, pulling into the employee parking lot. Alerted by Nathan's howl and the Crowgard cawing a warning, Simon left Vlad to finish restocking HGR's shelves so that they looked full when the Addirondak Wolves arrived that afternoon.

He met the two men at the access way. "We'll talk in the Liaison's Office so that Meg can see the plans too." He smiled, showing longer-than-human canines as a friendly reminder that trying to poach Meg wouldn't be tolerated. Not that he thought either Intuit would, but it never hurt to reestablish territory.

Not that Meg was *his* territory, but he did have a responsibility to the whole Courtyard, and Meg was a vital connection to the nonedible human element that was now underfoot every time he turned around.

Simon led them through the back room and into the sorting room.

"Hi, Steve. Hi, Jerry," Meg said, giving Simon a puzzled look.

"Morning, Meg," Steve said. "Can I use the table?"

Meg moved a couple of stacks of catalogs. Steve unrolled the plans for the *cassandra sangue* campus on Great Island.

"We have thirty acres to work with, but we're thinking to put most of the buildings together," Steve said. "That will make it easier to run the water and sewer lines, as well as the electricity. And we wanted to keep plenty of grass and trees for the girls as well as the wildlife that's already there. Eventually, we'll build for a hundred residents. Older girls and adults will have studio apartments and some common areas for socializing. The younger girls will have rooms and common areas in their building. Pam Ireland, who's working with the girls now and will be the administrator of the campus once it's built, will have her own residence on the grounds. We'll have a stable with a handful of horses—a couple of them to pull carts and the rest for riding. The Liveryman family is donating the horses and training them. They'll also have someone looking after the horses as part of their contribution to the campus. Since the idea is for the girls to learn to do things and be independent, there will also be a small farm with a dairy cow or two, and some chickens. We thought about pigs, but figured cows, chickens, and horses will be enough for girls between the ages of eight and eleven to take in. Plus, we'll have a kitchen garden, but that will probably happen next year. Our first priority is the living quarters." He looked at Meg. "What do you think?"

Meg studied the plans. "You should have a place to swim."

Steve winced. Simon didn't think Meg noticed.

"We have a swimming pool at our community center," Steve said, giving Simon a "help me" look. "We didn't put a pool into the budget for building this place."

"Not an official kind of swimming pool." Meg looked at Simon. "Something like the one in the Crowgard part of the Courtyard."

"She means a swimming hole," Simon said. "I'll show you the one we have here." He felt reluctant to take more humans to a part of the Courtyard that was usually off-limits. In fact, they had recently put up a larger Trespassers Will Be Eaten sign to remind the human pack that they were allowed to go *only* up to the Green Complex but no farther, and unchaperoned humans driving down the road that led to the Pony Barn were just asking to be hit by Tornado or struck by Lightning.

"Library?" Meg asked.

"With only the five girls, we figured some bookshelves in the common room would be enough," Steve said.

They studied the plans for a few more minutes. Not a compound, Simon thought. Not a prison with cells. A steady place where *cassandra sangue* could count on the routine of daily chores to balance the things that would keep changing.

He wondered if Jean had said anything to Steve about the prophecy she had seen where so few human cities remained.

When familiar trails disappeared, you had to find new ones—or make new ones—to take care of your pack.

"You need the building supplies for the young girls' den, the Pam's den, the stable, and the barn and other buildings for the animals and other food," he said.

"Yes, but we can start with—," Steve began.

"You need to buy all the building supplies you can."

"Sure, but we have a budget and—"

"Now."

Silence. Finally, Meg said, "Simon?"

He kept his eyes on Steve. "You need to buy supplies for your village. You need to buy the human supplies used by the Simple Life folk and the *terra indigene*. You need to prepare now for a hard winter."

Meg looked at the three men. "But . . . it's Juin. Summer is just starting."

Steve stared at Simon. "How long and how hard a winter?"

"Long. And very hard," Simon replied. "If you buy a product from another city, make sure you buy enough of it to see you through to spring." That would give them all a few months to figure out new ways to get what they needed.

"My wife starts buying extra toilet paper in September to make sure we're not trying to grab the last roll in the grocery store when the ferry can't make a supply run," Jerry said. Not looking at any of them, he added, "And the female supplies."

But that was as far as Jerry ventured into that dangerous territory. Simon hoped it was enough for Meg to take the hint.

"Do we know when winter will arrive this year?" Steve asked.

Simon shook his head, relieved that Steve understood they weren't actually talking about the season. This talking about one thing and meaning something else felt strange, but there were things he didn't want to share with humans, even ones he trusted. "When it comes, it will come hard and fast." He and Vlad had heard a news report about a speech being given by all the HFL leaders in Thaisia. Did Captain Burke and Lieutenant Montgomery think it odd that all these leaders were howling to reporters but Nicholas Scratch was so conspicuously absent from the news?

The *terra indigene* knew that a storm was coming. The only questions were when it would hit and what would still be standing when it was done.

"Wait by your car," Simon said. "I'll show you the lake."

Steve rolled up the plans. He and Jerry said good-bye to Meg and went out the back way.

Simon watched Meg rub the crosshatch of scars on her left upper arm.

"You know something," she said.

"I know we should buy human supplies while humans will still sell them to us."

"They have to sell them to us."

"They've gotten bold. They don't believe we'll do anything if they break the rules. Why should they? The HFL is telling them what they want to hear—they can take without consequences." Simon gently pulled Meg's hand away from the scars. "You and the female pack need to start buying the things that are essential for you. I don't know how much longer those things will be around. Some companies might go out of business."

Meg stared at him in disbelief. "How can companies that make things like toilet paper go out of business?"

Should he show her the letter from Jean? Was it wrong to want to protect her from that information when she already had so many things to think about?

Before he could take the letter out of his pocket, Meg got that look in her eyes—the look that told him she was reviewing training images and memories.

"A while ago, Ruth told us—the female pack—about a list she had found in an old book," Meg said with a care that made Simon think of a Wolf testing the ground with each step. "It was a list of human towns and cities that didn't exist anymore. I suppose you could say that the companies in those towns went out of business."

"You could say that," he agreed. "Maybe another company in another town would start making some of the same products, but it would take time."

"I understand."

Did she? He hoped that was true. "However much you decide to tell them, you need to keep this just within the female pack, Meg. Make the other girls understand that they have to keep this within the pack."

Meg nodded. She didn't look happy, which made him unhappy, but sometimes you couldn't share a carcass—or information—if you wanted your own pack to have enough to eat.

"Steve and Jerry are waiting for you," she said.

He wanted to press his lips to her skin, but he didn't think she would let him right now, so he walked out to join the other males.

"She's going to want to buy toilet paper for every person she's met, isn't she?"

Steve asked as he opened the back door and got in, leaving the front passenger seat for Simon.

"She can't." What was this obsession with toilet paper?

After a moment, Jerry said, "Where to?"

Simon directed him to the road and the turn toward the Crowgard's part of the Courtyard—which meant passing the new sign. He smelled fear, but neither man said anything.

"The information you received that makes you think a big storm is coming," Steve said. "You didn't get that from Meg, did you?"

Simon shook his head. "From Jean."

"Gods above and below."

He could hear Steve trying to steady his breath. "Simon, Jean is . . ."

Simon hesitated, thinking of what he'd just said to Meg about keeping information within the pack. But he'd already told Steve and Jerry that a storm was coming. He didn't feel easy about telling them more, but he removed the letter from his pocket and handed it to Steve. "Her brain is sick. That's not why she sees what she sees, but maybe it's the reason she chooses to remember what she sees."

"Gods," Steve said again after he read the letter. "All right, we'll purchase what we can afford."

"Buy what you can get. The Courtyard has money. We'll pay for it. You'd better buy what you can for the River Road Community too."

"Yeah, all right." Steve handed back the letter. "One thing the 'Meg, the Trail-blazer' e-mails have done for us is provided us with an expanded network of Intuit settlements. We've started a second list of what each settlement makes and what it wants to buy. The village council already decided to purchase as much as we could from our own."

"Send that list to Meg and Vlad, since Meg doesn't remember to check e-mail." He pointed. "Pull up at the bridge. That's the lake Meg wants you to see."

"The campus doesn't have a lake, but there is a creek that runs through that land. I think we could find a spot that could be opened up to make a natural swimming hole," Steve said. "We'll take another look when we get back to the island."

They drove back to the Market Square, letting Simon out when they reached the access way.

"By the way," he said as he opened the door. "Can Sledgeman's Freight haul livestock?"

"Sure," Jerry replied. "We have a big trailer for livestock. Mostly use it for horses, but it will work for other kinds of animals. You need something relocated?"

"Yes. They will be coming soon." Simon got out of the car, then waited until Steve moved to the front passenger seat before adding, "And you need to find someone who can ride a horse and look after some young bison."

They stared at him. "Bison?" Steve said.

"Eleven of them. We can split the herd between the River Road Community and the Courtyard."

Their expressions reminded him of Skippy when the juvenile's brain wasn't working quite right. Hoping Jerry had enough sense not to drive before he could think, Simon went into Howling Good Reads to get ready for their guests.

Meg called the female pack, including Eve Denby, assuring everyone it would be a quick meeting but it needed to be *now*.

"Girl stuff," she said and started to close the Private door. As she expected, Nathan scrambled off the Wolf bed and let out a protesting *arroo* at being shut out. But when he saw the rest of the girls, he turned around and went back to the bed. Guarding against feral deliverymen was one thing; dealing with the human females, whom he couldn't bite, was something else.

Meg glossed over the meeting with Steve Ferryman. While the campus on Great Island was interesting, it didn't have anything to do with them. But the part about supplies . . .

"I don't usually slip into squirrel mentality until autumn, but with more and more companies being owned by HFL members, Simon has a point about buying what you can while you can," Merri Lee said.

Meg frowned. "Squirrel . . . ?"

"Buying cans of soup, jars of spaghetti sauce, and boxes of spaghetti. Stocking up on toilet paper, paper towels, and tissues. And the things we girls need because no one wants to run out of those supplies in the middle of a blizzard."

She looked at them, surprised that no one felt the alarm that she had. "So this is normal?"

"In Lakeside? Sure."

She blinked.

"Meg, you weren't thinking about these kinds of supplies last winter, but when the radio announcers warn of a big winter storm, we pay attention," Merri Lee said. "And believe me, we don't take TP for granted."

Ruth nodded. "You expect every last roll in the store to be bought when that happens." Then she frowned. "Why do you think Mr. Wolfgard is so concerned about stocking up?"

Because more human cities are going to disappear. "Because of the sanctions that were imposed recently, there are delays on any merchandise being shipped from one region to another," Meg said, offering a less frightening explanation. "Maybe the delays will get longer and there is more chance of running out of some supplies?"

"If there are restrictions about the amount of paper supplies one family can purchase at a regular grocery store, the humans who work in the Courtyard will be looking to make up the difference by buying items in the Market Square stores," Eve said. "And speaking as the property manager, once the sale of those two apartment buildings goes through, there will be the potential for ten human families, with human needs, living there. Maybe the Business Association heard a rumor about shortages."

Or heard more than a rumor. Meg felt her heart thumping against her chest. Pins and needles filled her arms, and she suddenly craved the relief and release of a cut.

Not now, she thought. *Not now.* "Simon said we need to keep this between us, that we shouldn't tell anyone else about storing supplies." She rubbed one arm and then the other, ignoring the way the other women tensed.

"Maybe we shouldn't worry about the why and focus on getting the supplies while we can," Eve said.

The others agreed.

"I think we should buy some canning jars," Ruth said. "We'll need them to preserve some of the fruit. Maybe buy some jelly jars too. Meg? Is there any way we could ask some of the Simple Life women for help in learning how to preserve food or make jelly?"

"I can ask," Meg said.

"Gauze, bandages, and splints." Theral pointed to Merri Lee's splinted finger, which had been broken a couple of weeks ago during the fight at the stall market. "Over-the-counter medicines. Other medical supplies."

Eve nodded. "Speaking as a mother, having some prescription drugs available would be a good idea."

"Simon said we're not supposed to, but should we tell . . ." Meg faltered when she saw the resignation and bitterness in her friends' eyes.

"Tell who?" Merri Lee asked. "The friends who won't speak to us anymore?" She tipped her head toward Ruth. "The family who won't acknowledge us?"

Meg looked at Ruth. "But I thought they were coming over on Windsday to help you and Karl move into your new place."

Tears filled Ruth's eyes. "My mom told me all the stuff I'd stored at her house was going out on trash day unless I picked it up before then. It was already at the curb when Karl and I got to the house. My mom stood in the doorway and watched us. Didn't come out to talk to us. And you know what she yelled to my father when Karl and I finished putting my things in the car? 'The trash picked up the boxes.'" A sob escaped Ruth before she regained control.

"Problem?" Tess stood in the doorway leading to the back room, her hair completely red and coiling.

"No," Meg said. "No problem." How much had Tess heard?

They made room for her when she walked up to the sorting room table and set down the carry sack. "Fresh muffins," Tess said. "Have a snack. Then it's time you all got to work." She walked out.

Everyone let out a sigh of relief.

Ruth wiped her eyes. "Muffin. Work."

"Where did you put your stuff?" Meg asked Ruth.

"My aunt and uncle are holding on to it until Ruth is ready for it," Theral said. "They want to help. They haven't forgotten that Mr. Wolfgard is letting them have Lawrence's share of the produce from the Green Complex's garden. He didn't have to do that."

"Muffin. Work," Merri Lee said, opening the sack and taking a muffin. "The Courtyard's guests are arriving this afternoon, and we all need to set a good example." She eyed Meg. "You okay?"

"I'm sad for all of you, but I'm okay." The pins-and-needles feeling was gone, leaving no indication that a cut would reveal anything of use to her friends or the Courtyard.

Without a question that needed an answer, without some kind of justification, she couldn't make a cut without upsetting her friends, not to mention Simon.

They ate the muffins and went to their jobs. Meg opened the Private door and ignored the stare she received from Nathan. "You can sulk about being left out, or you can have one of the fresh Wolf cookies Jerry Sledgeman brought from Eamer's Bakery."

Sulking as a sport could not compete with fresh, beef-flavored cookies. Since Meg had a feeling Simon was going to be a little sulky too, she set aside two of the beef-flavored cookies for him.

Walking back to A Little Bite, Tess stopped when she saw Henry looking at her over the wooden gate that opened onto his yard. She glanced at the Liaison's Office and the sorting room's open window. <You heard?>

<I heard,> he growled. <Nothing to be done about that sow.>

<Nothing to be done,> she agreed, then silently added, *Yet.*

<Kowalski asked to borrow a van or the pickup from the Utilities Complex tomorrow to move the possessions he stored at his family's den. I will go with him and discourage any more talk of trash.>

The coils in her hair relaxed. The Grizzly's presence would discourage many things, but it wouldn't hurt to suggest to Simon that the Hawks keep an aerial watch while one of their own was in enemy territory.

CHAPTER 16

Windsday, Juin 13

" **P**ull into the customer parking lot," Monty told Officer Debany. Kowalski was taking a couple of personal days to move into the two-family house across from the Courtyard, so Debany was standing in as Monty's driver and partner.

Many police officers in the Chestnut Street station supported the idea of cooperating with the Others, of keeping things peaceful with the beings who controlled most of the world and had the final say in what happened to humans living in Lakeside. But being supportive wasn't the same as being willing to stand on the front line and interact with the *terra indigene* on a daily basis—especially when family members could be ostracized by their friends and neighbors because of the officer's decision. That was a real possibility—as Louis Gresh and his family well knew. So far no one had stepped forward to be Michael Debany's new partner and the fourth member of the team assigned to deal with the Lakeside Courtyard.

Monty didn't know what to do about that. Apparently, neither did Captain Burke. Or maybe Burke, understanding that the assignment wasn't just about another officer in the patrol car, didn't want another personality added to the mix right now because in the back of the minds of the officers who were already closely involved with the Others was a single word: extinction.

The other concern about assigning a new officer left a bad taste in Monty's mouth, but he had to acknowledge the truth: they couldn't afford to have an officer who belonged to the Humans First and Last movement infiltrating the Courtyard and spying on the Others so that the HFL leaders could plan effective attacks.

As he and Debany walked to Howling Good Reads, Monty paused and studied the two-family house. "How is the move going? Wasn't Karl picking up his furniture and possessions yesterday?" He'd heard what happened with Ruth; he wondered if things had been that bad for Karl.

Debany hesitated. "Karl's parents aren't bad people. Lawrence and I and a few other officers were at a cookout at their house last summer, and it was great. But now they're blaming Karl's assignment for everything from the butcher selling the last pot roast before Mrs. K. got to the shop to the price of gasoline. His brother, Tim, was halfway drunk when Karl got to the house yesterday morning, and abusive because of it. Karl wasn't getting any help loading the furniture—and some of that stuff you really couldn't lift alone. Then Henry and Blair drove up in the pickup. Didn't say anything; just loaded furniture in the back of the pickup while Karl packed the van with boxes. Then they drove off."

"Did Karl's parents say anything about the *terra indigene* helping out?"

Another hesitation. "Probably, but he won't talk about it."

Monty kept his eyes focused on the building across the street. Gods, his men were taking an emotional beating for doing what they *knew* would help everyone in the city. "What about you and your family?"

"My folks are worried, especially after Lawrence was killed at the stall market, but they're supportive. They've taken some flak about me being a Wolf lover, which ticked them off." Debany gave Monty a sheepish smile. "My sister wants a job where she can ride a horse and work with animals, so she keeps asking about the River Road Community—what sort of job skills are they looking for, when are they taking applications."

"Why don't you talk to Roger Czerneda? As a fellow officer, he might have more information and be willing to tell you something." Monty sighed. "Well, let's hope that Karl's and Ruth's families come around."

"Karl's not holding his breath." Another hesitation. "They postponed the wedding."

He had wondered why nothing had been said lately but thought Karl and Ruthie had just decided to keep the ceremony private and have a party to celebrate once they moved to their new place.

"I don't think their families were going to show up anyway," Debany added.

It made his heart heavy to hear that—and it made him wonder if his mother and sister coming to Lakeside was such a good idea.

As he started to turn toward Howling Good Reads, Monty realized the For Sale signs were gone from the front yards of the two stone apartment buildings on either side of the two-family—confirmation that the Courtyard's purchase of the buildings was going through. So far there had been no protests about the Others owning property outside of the Courtyard, but sooner or later someone would make that bit of information available to the TV and radio news. Monty suspected that the current owner of the apartment buildings wanted his money before he started stirring things up.

"Why don't you pick up something at A Little Bite, get a feel for anything that might become a problem," Monty said.

"Yes, sir. Are we talking about human problems?"

"Anything and everything." He wanted to talk to Kowalski about things that weren't being said. But first he needed a word with Simon Wolfgard.

Debany went into A Little Bite. Monty went into Howling Good Reads. The Residents Only sign was on the door, but he was, for the time being, a temporary resident, so he went in. Kowalski, dressed in sweat-darkened T-shirt and cutoff denim shorts, stood at the display table in the front of the store, reading the cover copy of a book. He looked up when Monty walked in.

"Aren't you supposed to be arranging furniture?" Monty asked. Karl looked a little strained, but Monty couldn't tell if that was because of family pressures or from moving into a new place.

"Oh, please," Kowalski groaned. "How many times can you move one piece of furniture?"

Monty smiled. "That's a trick question."

"Yes, it is, especially since Ruthie is working today, interacting with the guest Wolves. Pete Denby and I are the muscle, and Eve Denby is supervising the placement of the big pieces based on notes Ruthie left with her, but Eve is a bit distracted because Jester Coyotegard is in the downstairs apartment watching the three kids. The third time she told us to move the couch because we'd put it in the wrong place—which meant putting it back where we'd had it the first time—Pete and I rebelled. That's why we have a thirty-minute break. Plus, Eve has to negotiate with Jester on his choice of babysitting activities. He's been teaching the kids to howl."

Monty sighed. One of those children was Lizzy.

"Kowalski." Nathan walked up to them, trailed by a teenage boy who was dressed in a short-sleeve pullover shirt, jeans, and sneakers. The boy clutched some paper in one hand and looked ready to bolt.

One of the guests, Monty decided. Nothing obvious about the boy's looks, except the amber eyes, but he couldn't quite pass for human.

"Nathan," Kowalski replied, smiling at the enforcer and then at the boy.

"Kowalski is a police officer." Nathan turned his head enough to make it clear he was addressing the young Wolf, but he kept his eyes on Kowalski and Monty. "He is not in uniform today."

"Officer Debany is in A Little Bite if you want to see an officer in uniform," Monty said.

Nathan nodded, then focused on Kowalski as he pointed at the paper. "We have a question."

Kowalski held out a hand. After a moment's hesitation the boy gave him the paper, which had been folded to make a four-page document.

Monty moved closer when he saw the banner for the Courtyard's newsletter. The majority of the newsletter that Lorne Kates printed each week held lists of new books and movies that were available, as well as what movies were being shown in the social room located in each gard's complex.

"It's on the inside," Nathan said.

Kowalski opened the newsletter. "The 'Others Etiquette' column?"

Nathan nodded, then tipped his head toward the juvenile Wolf. "He wants to know if that's true."

Monty read over Kowalski's shoulder.

Dear Ms. Know-It-All:

Last night a human female invited me for dinner and some four-play. (It turned out to be two-play since no one else showed up.) After dinner she wanted to sit in the back of her car to play. Since this was my first social interaction with a human, I was trying to be polite, so I didn't point out that the nearby field provided a lot more room to run around. I also didn't point out that she didn't have any toys. Anyway, she started patting me with her hands and licking at my mouth. When she put her tongue in my mouth, I thought she was hungry despite having just eaten a large dinner. So I obliged and gave her a mouthful of pre-chewed food.

After she got done spitting and screaming, she told me to get out of the car. Then she drove off, and I had to walk home.

Why did she do that?

Signed,
Baffled Wolf

Dear Baffled,

One of the challenges of interspecies relationships is that a particular gesture or signal can mean two very different things. As a Wolf, you responded as you would to a puppy who licked your mouth: you provided food, and your confusion about her reaction is quite natural. However, humans do the licking and tongue maneuvers as play to stimulate the urge to mate. So your companion wasn't asking for food; she was sending out an invitation to experiment with the first stages of sex. That is what she meant by foreplay. (This is not the same as four who are playing, although Ms. Know-It-All's research indicates that humans sometimes do that too.)

The Dimwit's Guide to the Female Mind might assist your efforts in under-standing human females. But it must be pointed out that this subject can be a dan-gerous adventure and should be undertaken with extreme caution. After all, human males have been trying to understand their females for generations, and most of the time they come away from these encounters looking like someone stuck their tails into an electric socket.

Kowalski kept making sounds like something was stuck in his throat. Finally, he managed, "Yeah." He handed the newsletter back to the boy. "Yeah, that's true."

The boy looked at the newsletter, said "Huh," and walked over to the archway that led into A Little Bite.

Nathan gave the men a nod, then followed the boy.

"*The Dimwit's Guide to the Female Mind?*" Monty asked. "Is that a real book?"

"They have one for sale here, and there's one in the Market Square Library. That one's been chewed on, so I think someone tried to read it."

"Have you read it?"

Kowalski choked on a laugh. "Gods, Lieutenant."

Monty took that to mean *no*. "You're getting moved in across the street?" He knew the answer, but the question was an invitation for Karl to tell him some of the things that were going unsaid.

The momentary light mood vanished as if it had never been. Kowalski gave him a look, then focused on the display table, his back to the checkout counter.

Nobody in sight, but that didn't always mean much with the Others.

"We went to MacDonald's house this morning to pick up Ruthie's things," Kowalski said quietly. "Eve Denby busted ass to get the apartment cleaned and painted for us, and we'll help her and Pete do the same in the downstairs apartment. Simon Wolfgard came through with his promise to fetch their personal possessions from their old place in the Midwest. The *terra indigene* in that area packed everything they could, starting with the things that the Denbys had indicated were most important."

"Personal things," Monty said just as quietly.

Kowalski nodded. "A lot was left behind. Big stuff like the appliances. Couch. Mattresses."

Monty understood the outlay of cash that would be required to start over. He was looking at the same. His ex-lover, Elayne, had kept all the furnishings they had bought for the apartment they had shared in Toland. Elayne's brother had been found dead, and her mother was still listed as missing, so he wasn't sure who would have to deal with the liquidation of Elayne's estate.

He supposed Lizzy was now Elayne's next of kin. He should have a chat with Pete Denby soon to make sure Lizzy's interests were protected.

"Has Eve or Pete Denby talked to you about registering Lizzy for school in the fall?"

"No." Monty studied his partner. "Is there something I should know?"

"Eve went to talk to the principal of the school that Sarah and Robert should be attending next fall."

Monty felt a chill. "Should be?"

"She was told that *her* offspring had no right to use up resources needed for *proper* humans."

"How did they know she wasn't a proper human?"

"She gave them her new address. I think the school administrators were waiting for the opportunity to reject Eve's children and use them as a test case for refusing any children whose parents were Wolf lovers."

"They can't do that," Monty protested. "It's not a private school. We're talking about a public school run by the city."

"Ruthie saw a small article in the *Lakeside News* about a vote that's about to be taken to privatize *all* schools. If that happens, they will be able to choose who is admitted."

"Gods above and below." Another twist of an emotional knife. How many parents would become members of the HFL if that was the only way their children could be educated?

"Thought you should know," Kowalski said.

"I appreciate the heads-up."

"I'd better pay for this book and get back to work before Eve comes looking for me."

"I'll see you at the station tomorrow," Monty said.

"I'm so ready to come back."

Monty smiled. His smile widened when he heard Simon Wolfgard's voice coming closer.

"The library is a place where you can borrow books your Courtyard or pack has purchased for everyone to read," Simon said as he entered the front part of the store, followed by five Wolves. "But a bookstore like Howling Good Reads is where you buy books you want to keep for yourself instead of giving them back." He walked behind the checkout counter and looked at Kowalski.

"Just this one today." Kowalski set the book on the counter, then pulled his wallet out of the back pocket of his cutoffs.

"What book did the human buy?" one of the Wolves asked, looking at Simon. Kowalski held up the book so the Wolves could see the cover.

"Alan Wolfgard wrote that book."

"Yes. I enjoy his stories."

The Wolves stared at Kowalski before venturing another comment. "There are bad humans in his stories."

"Sometimes there are bad humans in stories written by humans," Kowalski countered.

Another long stare before the Wolves looked at Simon.

"I can show you some of the authors who write those kinds of stories," Simon said. "Lieutenant Montgomery?"

"A minute of your time, if you can spare it," Monty said.

Simon nodded before leading the pack of guests to the shelves that had the thrillers. Kowalski waved and left.

"Looks like you're busy," Monty said when Simon returned to the counter.

"I am. We are." Simon paused. "No one had considered that the gaggle of girls would have as many questions as the Addirondak Wolves."

"Gaggle?"

"It doesn't sound as dangerous as 'female pack,'" Simon grumbled. "And Charlie Crowgard arrived last night to visit for a couple of days. We got to hear his song about Teakettle Woman and Broomstick Girl. Charlie told the Wolves that the song was based on Meg and Merri Lee thwarting an attack here in the Courtyard, and that Merri Lee *was* Teakettle Woman. After that, none of the Wolves wanted to get near her while she was holding a coffeepot."

Monty laughed. Dealing with the Others was dangerous work, no mistake about that, but the absurd moments like a column in a newsletter or the reaction to a song gave him hope that humans and the *terra indigene* could still find a way to work together. Then he sobered. "I'm here to ask a favor on Captain Burke's behalf."

"What kind of favor?"

"His cousin is visiting for a few days. Shady Burke assisted in bringing some special girls safely to land." The Others had diverted a ship bound for Cel-Romano that had *cassandra sangue* as part of its cargo, bringing the "lost" ship to Brittania. Shady had participated in the girls' rescue.

"I remember."

"Shady would appreciate an opportunity to interact with some of the *terra indigene* to better his own ability to work with them when he returns home."

No response. Then, "Different forms live in different parts of Namid. The Shady Burke may not meet the same forms here. Although the Crowgard may live in Brittania. They live in many places."

"He understands that. But Shady has never seen a Courtyard."

A thoughtful silence. "Charlie Crowgard is going to play some music tonight in the Market Square. Theral is going to play some songs on her fiddle. This would be a good time for Captain Burke and his kin to come to the Courtyard. They could have food at Meat-n-Greens."

And be another kind of entertainment? Monty thought. "I'll let them know."

"Simon?" a Wolf called out.

Monty didn't move aside to let Simon vault over the counter to talk to his guests about books.

"Something else?" Simon asked.

Did he really want to ask? Was there a choice? "My mother is going to spend some time here with me, helping me look after Lizzy. And my sister and her two children may join her for a visit."

Those amber Wolf eyes studied him. "Is that your whole pack?"

"I have a brother, but we haven't heard from him in a while."

"Simon?" the Wolf called again.

"I'll be there in a minute."

Monty couldn't even guess what Simon was thinking. A Wolf pack might be quite comfortable in a one-bedroom apartment, but it wouldn't work for three human adults and three children.

"Where is your mother now?" Simon asked.

"She lives in Toland. So does my sister."

A long silence. Monty could hear someone talking behind the shelves. Someone else must be helping the Wolves.

"Humans have important papers," Simon said, not looking at him. "Things they need to keep."

"Yes."

"Your mother and sister. They should come soon, and they should bring the important papers with them."

"They don't need to bring such things for a visit," Monty said, smiling. But that was a good thought if his mother was going to relocate to Lakeside.

Simon looked at him. "They should come soon, Lieutenant, and they should bring whatever is most important to them."

Another chill went through Monty. This wasn't a misunderstanding about what humans brought when they visited someone. This was a veiled warning.

Simon walked away from the checkout counter and disappeared among the shelves.

Monty went into A Little Bite and bought a cup of coffee. Instead of taking it with him as he usually did, he sat at a table near the window, ignoring Debany's puzzled looks.

Typical of Simon to give him a veiled warning. But the message was clear enough: get your family out of Toland because something is going to happen soon.

If it hasn't already started, Monty thought, remembering the news report about dead fish washing ashore around Toland and two other East Coast cities.

He finished his coffee, brought his cup over to the counter, then signaled for Debany to join him as he left A Little Bite.

"Where to, Lieutenant?" Debany started the patrol car.

"Back to the station. No." Monty got out of the car. "Wait here. I have to make a phone call. I'll be back in a few minutes."

Monty went up to the efficiency apartment, where he would have privacy. Pulling out his mobile phone, he called his sister's residence and wasn't surprised when his mother answered.

"Mama? It's Crispin."

"Crispin? Are you all right? Why are you calling at this time of day?"

"I'm fine, Mama." Monty took a deep breath and let it out slowly. "I'm fine. But I need you to listen very carefully."

CHAPTER 17

Windsday, Juin 13

A breeze danced over the Courtyard, softening the heat of the day as Simon and Sam trotted down the road. Meg and Tess had driven to the Market Square, so they had brought clothes for the two Wolves. Sam might remain in Wolf form, but Simon felt he should look human tonight as a courtesy to the humans who would be joining them.

<Remember, pup, we don't howl during every song,> Simon said. <Charlie Crowgard will tell us when to participate.>

<I *know*,> Sam replied. <I know how to behave.>

Which meant someone else didn't know. Did human pups tend to misbehave during public events? Should he warn Lieutenant Montgomery and Pete Denby that anyone disrupting music would get nipped? He thought the humans were attending the concert out of politeness, but he could be wrong. Theral was going to play her fiddle, and those songs would be familiar to the other humans. The female pack was excited about the concert, both to hear Theral play but also to hear Charlie Crowgard. And Kowalski and Debany had asked him twice if Charlie was going to sing the song about Meg and Merri Lee defeating the bad human, Phineas Jones.

When he and Sam arrived at the Market Square, Kowalski and Debany already had three short rows of chairs set up in the open area that made up the center of the square.

"Vlad told us to do it this way," Kowalski said when Simon approached. "And Henry said to put some perches behind the chairs and around both sides."

Not all the *terra indigene* would attend this concert. Some still needed to stand guard. But tonight was as much about mingling with humans as it was a chance to hear music. Charlie would give a private performance for those who couldn't attend tonight—or didn't want to mingle.

Tess came out of Meat-n-Greens, followed by Meg, Merri Lee, Ruthie, and Eve.

"We're all set," Tess said. "We have pizza from Hot Crust that we can warm up, fresh-picked berries, sandwiches and sweets, and ground bison already shaped into patties for those who need, or want, their burgers cooked."

Charlie sat in a chair, tuning his guitar. He had a few more feathers than usual in his black hair—a sign that he was feeling anxious about performing in front of humans.

Henry walked in with a big drum. Nathan followed him, carrying a wooden flute, which he set on a stool near Charlie before taking his place in the audience.

<If you're playing your flute, who is going to play the drum?> Simon asked Henry.

<We'll have to see,> the Grizzly replied. He stood next to Charlie as Theral came out of the medical office, where she must have done her grooming before the performance.

The air carried the smell of her nerves and sweat, but the smile she gave Charlie seemed genuine, and Simon noticed the nervous scent faded as she showed her fiddle to the enthusiastic Crow.

The Wolves entered the Market Square: Blair, Elliot, Jane, and John, along with the six Addirondak Wolves. Thirteen Wolves, including him, Sam, and Nathan. Enough to balance out the humans who would be there—especially when Simon saw the smoke flowing toward the other side of the chairs. Erebus and two other Sanguinati took human form, while the other two columns of smoke settled into the shadows to keep watch.

Owls glided in and settled on the perches on one side of the square. Hawks flew in and took the perches behind Erebus and his kin. That left the perches directly behind the chairs for the Crows—and gave them the best view of Charlie.

He was glad to see Jake fly in, followed by Jenni and Starr. Crystal's death had hit all the Crowgard very hard, and the Courtyard's Business Association wondered if Jenni and Starr would remain in Lakeside, and if they did, if they would continue to run Sparkles and Junk.

Not a question to ask tonight. They were here among humans, a species who were, for the most part, becoming true enemies of the *terra indigene*. Simon hoped their presence was a good sign that the Crows could make the distinction between friends and enemies.

Now the humans arrived. The Denbys came with their two pups, and Lieutenant Montgomery was with them. So was the Lizzy.

Sam bounced over to greet them but returned a minute later.

<Sam? Do you want to shift? Meg brought clothes for you if you want to play with the human pups.>

<They are being silly,> Sam replied. <I want to stay with you and Meg. And I want to hear the music.> Sam bounced back to Meg and wedged himself between her feet. If her bare legs got too warm from brushing against fur, she would move him. But that was between Meg and Sam. The humans, on the other paw . . .

The human pups seemed to be willfully disobedient, deliberately acting up to be disruptive. Wolves knew the difference between high spirits and troublemaking, and they were eyeing the two-legged pups a little too sharply. So was Ruthie. *She* had a look in her eyes that reminded Simon of a pack's nanny just before she put a stop to some nonsense.

Discussion among the Denbys and Montgomery. Then Pete, giving Simon an apologetic look, herded the youngsters away while Eve went into Meat-n-Greens and came out with containers of food. She said something to Tess before following her mate.

<They don't think the pups will behave tonight,> Tess said in response to his and Vlad's inquiring looks. <They don't want to spoil things for the rest of us, so they're taking the young home to watch a movie. But I suspect Pete and Eve will take turns going outside to listen as best they can.>

<A nip would encourage good behavior,> Simon replied.

<Every adult Wolf here is probably thinking the same thing, which is why Pete and Eve are taking the children home.>

Simon wondered how the three adults had decided who would stay to hear the music and who would tend the pups. Then he saw Captain Burke and another male enter the Market Square and understood that there was no decision. Montgomery had stayed because the police were another kind of pack that brushed the edges of the Courtyard, and he needed to be here with Burke, the police pack's leader.

"Simon?" Meg didn't raise her voice; she didn't need to in order to catch his attention. But hearing it reminded him that it was time to shift to human form so that he could meet the stranger Burke had brought among them.

He returned to Meg and looked at her expectantly.

"I put your clothes just inside Meat-n-Greens," she said.

He trotted off to put on clothes and fulfill his duties as host for the evening. And, as his reward for being human tonight, he would hold Meg's hand during the concert.

Meg had seen images of orchestras and music halls and theaters. But those images didn't fit this experience. The center of the Market Square had three broad steps down to an area that sometimes had benches and tables where the Others could sit and eat or read or simply be around the shops as a social interaction when they were in human form.

She identified the guitar and drum as musical instruments, and Henry had shown her his wooden flute during one of her visits to his studio.

Leaning over, she placed a hand on Sam's shoulder so the pup wouldn't bounce up and whack his head on her chin.

"This is exciting," she whispered, idly petting him. "Have you been to a concert before?"

"*Arroo.*" Sam tipped his head back and licked her chin.

She wasn't sure if that meant yes or no but decided it didn't matter.

Captain Burke, Lieutenant Montgomery, and the stranger approached her. Her fingers tightened on Sam, and he let out a little *whuff* of concern.

No reason to be afraid. She was in the Courtyard, and she trusted Captain Burke and Lieutenant Montgomery. They wouldn't bring someone here who posed a danger to any of them.

"Ms. Corbyn?" Burke smiled at her. "This is my cousin, Shamus Burke. He came all the way from Brittania to visit me and see a bit of Lakeside."

"Hello, Mr. Burke," Meg said.

"It's a pleasure to meet you," Shamus replied with a smile. "Call me Shady. Everyone else does."

Relaxing her hold on Sam, and feeling better about Shady when the man crouched and held out a hand for Sam to sniff, Meg returned his smile.

She didn't need to see them to know all the Wolves had edged closer, watching the unknown human who was too close to a pup. She just watched the way Shady quickly rose and stepped back. Then Simon, now in human form, stepped between the humans and Wolves and was introduced to Shady.

Charlie Crowgard strummed a chord, and everyone hurriedly found their seats. Merri Lee and Michael Debany sat on Meg's right, leaving a seat on her left open for Simon. Karl and Ruthie were in the row behind them, along with Lieutenant Montgomery and Tess. Looking over her shoulder, Meg saw Burke and Shady in the third row, along with Vlad and Erebus. When everyone else was seated, Simon sat down next to Meg.

The perches, as well as the rooftops, were full of Crows, Hawks, and Owls. Sanguinati, slipping into the Market Square so quietly Meg wondered if anyone else realized they were there, now sat on the broad steps on one side of the square, while Wolves filled the other side.

Oil lamps, grouped at the corners of the steps nearest the performers, provided lights for the musicians, and several shops around the square were dimly lit as well.

Seeing Henry strike a match and light another oil lamp, Meg leaned down and rubbed the skin above her right ankle.

"Meg?" Merri Lee whispered when she sat up. "You okay?"

Simon leaned so close she could feel his heat—and that skin above her ankle prickled a little.

"Just an itch," she whispered back, wanting to believe that.

"I brought some bug lotion." Merri Lee looked at Simon and made a face. "It probably smells really stinky to you, but we don't know yet how Meg will react to a bug bite, so I brought some with me."

Charlie began singing. The prickle faded.

"I'm fine," Meg whispered.

She held Simon's hand and listened to music, marveling as Henry played some *terra indigene* music on his flute—music she'd heard on CDs he listened to when he worked on his sculptures and totems. She and Merri Lee cringed when Charlie sang "Teakettle Woman and Broomstick Girl." And cringed even more when the Crows cawed, the Wolves howled, the Sanguinati clapped, and Karl and Michael laughed and whooped their approval.

Theral played a song on her fiddle. Then Shady went up and joined the musicians in a folk song originally from Brittania, singing the words in a fine tenor voice.

Everyone applauded. Meg rubbed her skin above the ankle and gently nudged Sam away from her legs. The pup obeyed, whining a soft protest as he moved to a spot right in front of her chair.

"Meg?" Simon said. Concern, warning, and demand all wrapped in one quiet word.

"Not pins and needles," she whispered. "Just a little too warm." She gave Sam an apologetic smile.

Just a little too warm. Merri Lee had described sunburn as a prickling heat that caused skin to peel. Which sounded disgusting—and possibly dangerous for a *cassandra sangue*, even though the skin wasn't actually cut. Could she have been in the sun too long today? Did that little bit of skin really feel hotter than the rest of her leg, or was it warm because of Sam, or even from her own rubbing?

"We need a drummer," Charlie said. "Anyone willing to try?"

No one moved. Then Captain Burke rose and made his way to the drum. "Let's see if I remember anything from my misspent youth."

He spent a minute tapping the drum and learning the different sounds it made. Then he nodded to Charlie.

"Give us a rhythm," Henry said. "We'll find something to fit it." Then the Grizzly nodded to Simon, who looked at the Wolves.

Catching his uncle's look, Sam sat up in anticipation.

A simple rhythm that filled the square. Henry and Charlie joined in, their instruments reminding Meg of the sound of leaves stirring in the wind. Then Theral joined in, and her fiddle became the sound of a shallow stream. And then the Wolves sang—and the Courtyard, with its human shops and human instruments, embraced the sound of the wild country.

When Simon tipped his head back and howled, Meg joined him, and Merri Lee and Ruth joined her. Then Karl and Michael added their voices while the Crows cawed and the Owls hooted. Only the Hawks and Sanguinati were silent.

Meg looked to her right, where the Sanguinati sat on the steps or hovered as columns of black smoke.

Smoke, she thought as the skin above her ankle prickled. *Grilled cheese sandwich. Merri Lee saying, "Don't worry about it, Meg. It was your first try. So the crust burned a little. We'll trim off the burned bits, and the sandwich will be fine."*

Meg looked at the oil lamps providing light, how the flames, even protected within the glass globes, flickered and danced.

Smoke . . . and fire.

The annoying discomfort she'd felt on and off during the concert suddenly turned into a buzzing under her skin that felt so painful it burned.

She cried out and clutched her ankle. In the silence that followed her cry, she thought she heard a distant siren, but she wasn't sure if the sound was real.

"I have to cut," she gasped. "I have to—"

No time to explain or argue. No time.

Meg rushed out of the Market Square. Had to reach the Liaison's Office. Privacy. Bandages.

"Meg!" Simon howled as he ran after her.

She fell against the back door of the office, and almost fell again when she turned the knob and the door swung open.

Simon rushed in behind her, grabbing her to keep her from falling. She felt his claws pricking through her T-shirt.

"What can we do?" Charlie asked, piling into the back room with some of the Wolves.

"Let me through. *Move.*" Merri Lee shoved her way through the Wolves, who, surprised, lifted their lips in a silent snarl.

"Everyone, get out."

Meg couldn't see her, but Tess's voice sounded oddly harsh.

The Wolves and Charlie took one look at Tess, coming in behind them, and bolted for the sorting room.

"I have to cut," Meg gasped, pulling the silver folding razor out of her pocket. "I have to." Too desperate now to walk the few steps to the bathroom, she sat on the floor and opened the razor with shaking hands.

"Okay, you have to cut, but we're going to do this the right way," Merri Lee said, her voice stern yet shaking. She grabbed the pen and pad of paper Meg kept on the table in the back room.

Yes. Had to do it right.

Smoke. Fire. Sirens.

Meg looked at Simon, who stared at her with amber eyes that held flickers of red—a sign of anger. Not fully human now. Too upset to hold the form.

"Can't . . . wait," she gasped.

"Focus on us," Tess commanded, kneeling in front of her. "You know what you need to tell us. Speak, prophet, and we will listen."

Command and promise. Meg's hand steadied as she set the razor where the skin above her ankle burned—and made the cut.

Monty pushed into the back room, following Tess. Burke and Shady came in behind him. Feeling a change in the air, he guessed someone had opened the delivery doors in the sorting room to let more of the Others crowd into the office without antagonizing Tess—or Simon.

"You know what you need to tell us," Tess said. "Speak, prophet, and we will listen."

He saw the change in Meg as Tess said the words. He was sure that Burke and, especially, Shady, who hadn't seen this before, were watching everything, from the way Merri Lee knelt beside Meg, pen poised over paper to record everything that was said, to the agony stamped on Meg's face when she made the cut and how her expression changed to a blank wantonness as she began to speak.

"Woman," Meg said dreamily. "Dark hair. A loaf of bread. Blackened crust. Blackened arms. Smoke. Fire. Screaming. Bread is burning. Woman is screaming. Burning."

Sighing, Meg stretched out on the floor.

"Oh, gods," Merri Lee said, staring at the pad of paper.

Tess twisted around in Monty's direction, but she kept her eyes focused on the floor as the coils of black and red hair moved around her head.

"Nadine's Bakery and Café," Monty said, sick with the certainty. Then he turned to Burke, horrified. "Her apartment is above her shop. She lives above her shop."

Pushing his way clear of the bodies crowding around the back door, Monty pulled out his mobile phone. He didn't know Nadine's home number, but he knew the business phone number. He checked his watch, surprised at how late it was. If Nadine was asleep, would a ringing phone in the shop be enough to wake her?

Burke walked out of the office, already punching numbers into his own mobile phone, his big strides and furious expression scattering the girls and his own men, who were waiting for their orders.

Vlad hurried around the corner of the office with an open phone book. "Is this the number?" He pointed to a listing.

"That's it." Monty disconnected and dialed the home number.

Nadine answered on the second ring. "Chris? Where are you?"

"Nadine, it's Lieutenant Montgomery. Your building is on fire. Get out *now.*" Was it already on fire, or was the warning just ahead of what was going to happen?

"I— Chris."

"We'll find him. Get out, Nadine."

She hung up.

"Do what you can," he heard Burke say before his captain ended the call and swore viciously. Burke looked at all of them—his police officers, the girls, Simon, Vlad, and Tess, who was still not meeting anyone's eyes. "A handful of businesses have been torched on Market Street, and there are more fires around the city. Too many. Lieutenant, you're with me."

"Hold up a minute, Lieutenant," Kowalski said. "I'll fetch your service weapon."

None of them, with the possible exception of Burke, were carrying a gun this evening. "Kitchen cupboard. Top shelf." He pulled out his keys and handed them to Kowalski, pointing out two in particular. "Apartment key. Lock-box key."

Kowalski took the keys and ran to the steps leading up to the efficiency apartments.

"I'll wait for you here and do what I can to help," Shady told Burke.

"Debany, you and Kowalski call the hospitals and other precincts," Monty said. "We need to locate Chris Fallacaro."

"You think he's been harmed?" Vlad asked.

Monty glanced at Simon and wondered if the Wolf was capable of human speech. "I hope not, but we need to locate him." Chris, who was a locksmith, also did work at the Courtyard and could be a target.

"Lieutenant!" Kowalski returned and handed Monty his weapon and holster. "It's loaded. And here are extra rounds if you need them."

Monty slipped the speed loader into his jacket pocket.

"Lieutenant!" Burke shouted.

Monty ran to catch up with Burke, who had already reached the employee parking lot where he'd left his car, had the blue light on the roof, and was ready to go. He'd barely closed his door before Burke backed out of the space. But the captain eased the car out of the lot and down the access way, aware of Wolves and humans milling about. He turned right, then right again, flipping on the sirens and light as he raced along Crowfield Avenue to Parkside, where he headed north at what would be a reckless speed if anyone else had been driving.

"We can't fight a fire," Monty said quietly. Prophecy could be changed. Burned bread? Yes, the shop would be lost. But . . .

"No, we can't fight a fire, but we can make sure Ms. Fallacaro survives if she gets out of the building," Burke replied.

"Survives?" He felt sick. "You think someone would be waiting for her?"

"Don't you?"

Sirens. A harsh—and human—kind of howling.

Simon listened to all the voices around him, struggling to contain his rage. The Nadine hadn't hurt anyone by selling bread and pastries to Tess for A Little Bite. In fact, by honoring the agreement the city had made with the Courtyard, her bakery was the reason the rest of the bakeries in the city had been allowed to continue.

Too many *terra indigene* from the wild country were close enough to the city to notice this fighting among humans. This wasn't an understandable dispute— two bakers battling to show who was dominant and would control the bakery, forcing the loser to find a new place to work. No, this destruction was a deliberate attack against the Others as well as the humans whose dens and businesses were burning.

<Tess?> he called.

<Leave me alone, Wolf. I need some time alone.>

He wasn't sure where she was, but he guessed she'd gone into A Little Bite to avoid being seen until she wanted to be seen.

"Simon, I'm going to let Kowalski and Debany use the phones in Howling Good Reads to make their calls," Vlad said. "I'll stay in the store with them."

<Meg.> He wanted to stay with Meg, wanted to sniff the cut and assure himself that it smelled clean. But by now, Merri Lee would have put the stinky healing ointment on the cut and wrapped it in bandages to discourage licking.

"She's fine." Vlad nodded toward the back door.

Simon turned. She stood behind Ruthie and Merri Lee. The girls looked pale, smelled afraid.

"Meg should eat," Vlad said. "The female pack should stay with her. They're going to Meat-n-Greens. Grandfather Erebus will look after them. So will the Shady Burke."

<The monkeys. They're turning rabid.>

"Yes. But this disease has a name: Humans First and Last."

Simon watched Jester Coyotegard navigate around Wolves and human males, his tail tucked between his legs. When he reached Simon, the Coyote rose up on his hind legs, probably intending to shift to human form. Then he caught sight of Meg and the other girls and dropped to all four paws.

Jester looked at Simon. <I'm delivering a question.>

<Ask.>

<Do you want them to act?>

Simon considered the question—and who was asking the question. *Did he want the Elementals to respond to this attack on humans who honored the agreements that had been made between humans and terra indigene?* If the Courtyard did nothing, would humans see that as a weakness, encouraging them to continue testing and attacking? But the *terra indigene* in the wild country, the *terra indigene* who were Namid's teeth and claws, were already considering the elimination of this troublesome species, already wanted to purge humans from Thaisia.

That purge was coming. The Sanguinati and the rest of the *terra indigene* were abandoning the Courtyard in Toland. No doubt humans would think it was because the Others were acknowledging human superiority. But the Others weren't leaving Toland because of the humans; they were leaving to get out of the way of the fury that was coming.

That was Toland. Jester and the girls at the lake were waiting for his decision about Lakeside.

Too many fires burning in the city tonight. More than the firemen and firetrucks could handle on their own.

Too many fires. And not enough fires.

<Simon?> Jester said. <Do you want them to act?>

Simon looked at Jester. <Yes.>

The fire at Nadine's Bakery and Café was fully engaged by the time Monty and Burke pulled up halfway down the block.

"Where are the fucking firetrucks?" Burke snarled. He slammed out of the car, its bubble light still flashing, and opened the trunk.

Monty got out of the car and decided the answer to Burke's question was obvious. All he had to do was look at all the flashing lights from the trucks as firemen tried to control the other fires farther up the street.

Monty scanned the street but didn't see Nadine or Chris Fallacaro.

Burke slammed the trunk. He had removed his sports jacket, and his shoulder holster and weapon were visible over his casual shirt. He carried a length of pipe.

Monty had expected the gun. He didn't want to think about why Burke carried a length of pipe in his official vehicle. "Captain?"

"You see her?"

"No. But there are a couple of parking spaces behind her building."

Burke strode in that direction. Monty followed, keeping an eye on the building. Gods, what kind of accelerant had been used for it to go up this fast? Had Nadine . . .

They heard a scream. Recklessly ignoring the heat and flames, they ran to the back of the building. Nadine had reached her car. She'd had enough warning that she hadn't been trapped inside the building, but not enough time to get clear of the pack of men who had come to burn her out. They'd smashed the car windows and were dragging her out of the car when Burke arrived, swinging the pipe with a fury that put two men on the ground and scattered the rest of Nadine's attackers.

"Police!" Monty shouted, pointing his weapon at the attackers. "Down on the ground!"

A piece of burning debris fell between him and the attackers, and he didn't expect them to obey.

"Lieutenant! Get her out of here!" Burke yelled.

Monty holstered his weapon and ran to the car. Nudging Nadine into the passenger seat, he started the car and barreled out of the narrow driveway, almost hitting a couple of people who were either coming to help or just there to gawk.

He drove past Burke's vehicle and parked behind it, blocking in the cars that were already parked on the street. "Stay here." He bolted out of the car, intending to back up his captain, when he saw Burke walking toward him. Watching Burke, he leaned down enough to talk to Nadine.

"Are you hurt? Do you need medical attention?"

When she didn't respond, Monty wondered if she was in shock. Did Burke have a blanket in his trunk?

"After you called," Nadine said suddenly, "I got dressed and grabbed my purse, my keys, and the two file boxes where I keep all my important papers. I put the file boxes in the trunk and heard shouts, heard . . ."

"We'll get a statement later. Right now—"

"They were going to throw me into the building, into the fire." Her voice held a note of bewilderment. "They *said* that. They were going to throw me into the fire."

Monty joined his captain as Burke opened the trunk of his own vehicle, tossed the pipe inside, and took the sports jacket out.

"You have a blanket in there?" Monty asked.

Burke pulled one out and handed it to him. Monty hurried back to Nadine and tucked the blanket around her before rejoining Burke. "Captain . . ."

"Lots of debris falling," Burke said idly, putting on the jacket. "A couple assailants tripped on some debris during a criminal act."

"Gods, Captain. What if they accuse you?"

The smile Burke gave him was beyond his usual fierce-friendly smile; it was terrifying. "You think any of those men are going to want the *terra indigene* to know who set fire to Ms. Fallacaro's business and tried to kill her? I hurt a couple of them, but I wasn't trying to inflict real damage, so I doubt the blows were serious enough that those men will see a doctor, let alone end up in the emergency room. But if they want to come forward so that a whole lot of beings can recognize their faces, I'll take whatever penalties come from it."

"What happened to those men?"

"Went over the fence into the next property. Or so I'm assuming."

He hadn't heard gunshots. At least Burke hadn't shot any of them.

Monty's mobile phone rang. "Montgomery."

"Lieutenant, it's Kowalski. We found Chris Fallacaro. He was at the university precinct, brought in with a handful of other young men who were fighting. I talked to Captain Wheatley. He's of the opinion that Fallacaro was the victim of an attack and wasn't doing much fighting to defend himself after someone broke his left hand with a hammer."

"What stopped the fight?"

"The kid with the hammer raised it above his head for another swing . . . and was struck by lightning. He's heading for the morgue."

Gods above and below, Monty thought.

"Fallacaro has made a statement and is on his way to Lakeside Hospital. Do you want me and Debany to meet him there and stay with him?"

"Wait a moment." Monty relayed the information to Burke.

"That's a plan," Burke said. "They can head out now. Shady will keep an eye on things. I'll call Captain Wheatley with an update as soon as we get back to the Courtyard."

They heard the explosion and watched a fireball rise from a building two blocks away.

"Let's go," Burke said quietly as a second building exploded. Then a third. And a fourth.

Lightning struck nearby, and the boom of thunder, sounding more like giant hooves striking the ground, made Monty's skin crawl.

"Let's go," Burke said again.

Monty returned to Nadine's car and followed Burke's flashing blue light back to the Courtyard as a punishing rain struck the northern part of the city, putting out the fires and flooding the streets.

"What do you think?" Eve Denby asked.

Henry looked around the room above the Liaison's Office—a room that had occasionally been used for sex with a human—and wondered what he was supposed to think. More, he wondered why he'd been chosen to provide the answer. Then he looked at Ruthie, Theral, and Eve. They must have considered the members of the Business Association and had decided he was the most approachable right now.

Tess had slipped away from the Courtyard. No one was sure where she was, but he was certain a few members of the Humans First and Last movement were going to die of a mysterious plague that had already struck humans in the city a couple of times over the past few months. Simon had gone off to consider a simple yet difficult question: was Lakeside worth saving, and if it was, how much could their Courtyard save? Vlad and Blair were coordinating the defense of the Courtyard and its property. Wolves were patrolling the boundaries of the Courtyard and guarding the three gates that provided the easiest access. The Sanguinati were guarding the Market Square and the buildings on Crowfield Avenue, making sure no one attacked the Denbys' apartment or threatened the children. The Crows and Hawks were maintaining a lookout around the buildings, while the Owls glided along the fence line, looking for intruders. Nathan, Erebus, and the Shady Burke were in Meat-n-Greens with Meg and Merri Lee.

And that left him to provide an answer to a question he didn't understand.

"This isn't much different from a hotel room," Ruthie explained. "It has its own bathroom. We gave the room a quick dust and vacuum and put clean sheets on the bed—not that we thought the ones on it had been used, but . . ." She stopped, then plowed through the thorny words. "Ms. Fallacaro is going to need a place to stay, at least for tonight. She would be alone at a regular hotel."

"And no one who has been targeted is going to want to be alone," Eve added.

Now he understood. "You want permission for her to stay here?"

They nodded.

"And we wondered if someone could check on Lorne," Ruthie said. "He said he would be here for the concert, but he didn't show up, and he's not answering his home phone or mobile phone. He doesn't live far from here."

"We will try to find him," Henry promised. He would talk to Vlad about finding Elizabeth Bennefeld and Dominic Lorenzo, the other two humans who provided services to Courtyard residents. "Anything else?"

"Do you have any storage space we humans could use?" Eve asked. "We need to stock up on what we don't want to do without."

"I'll talk to Simon." Human settlements in the wild country were often cut off from supply towns during the winter months and stocked up on many things. He was pleased to hear these females preparing for the same kind of isolation.

He walked out of the room. Catching the sound of cars driving up the access way, he hurried down the stairs behind the Liaison's Office, his hands shifting to the more useful paws and claws of a Grizzly. But these weren't intruders. He didn't recognize the car that had most of its windows smashed, but Lieutenant Montgomery was driving it, and Captain Burke was driving the black car.

Henry followed the cars. Burke pulled into the employee parking lot, but

Montgomery drove to the spaces where delivery trucks parked for the Market Square. As soon as he parked the car, Montgomery hurried around to the other side and helped a woman out of the car. Wolves approached the Market Square, then turned away when Simon and Vlad stepped out of the library, along with Elliot.

"Is there anyone in the medical office who could take a look at Ms. Fallacaro?" Montgomery asked when Simon walked up to him.

"We'll call our bodywalker," Simon said.

"I'm fine," Nadine said. "Just a little cold is all."

Simon took a step toward her and sniffed the air. "You are not fine. I can smell blood." He paused. "Not a lot of blood, but you are not fine."

Montgomery escorted Nadine to the medical office. Moments later, Merri Lee looked out the door of Meat-n-Greens and came running.

Made sense, Henry decided. She was the human who most often helped Meg after the cutting. Even if someone else had to do the tending because Merri Lee still had sticks around one finger, she would know about human bandages and medicines.

Burke joined them, and the males, except Montgomery, returned to where Vlad and Elliot had waited.

"The mayor has called twice, wanting to know if we have any information about the fires," Elliot said.

"Strange that His Honor is working so late," Burke commented.

Elliot gave Burke a sharp smile. "I thought so too."

"What did you tell him?" Simon asked.

"I told him he should ask the police commissioner about the fires since the man is a member of the Humans First and Last movement and would be better informed about these escalated attacks on innocent humans. He hung up."

Burke barked out a laugh.

"Tess called," Vlad said. "She's bringing Lorne here, but she thinks he should be taken to a human bodywalker. She says it isn't wise for her to go to such a place right now."

No, it wouldn't be smart for a Harvester to go to such a place.

"I can drive him to the hospital," Burke said. "Chris Fallacaro should be there by now. I'll find out when he'll be released and then figure out where he can stay."

"Bring him here," Simon said. "I left a message on Dr. Lorenzo's phone, warning him about the fires, and Vlad called Elizabeth Bennefeld. She received threatening phone calls tonight because she works in our medical office a couple of days a week. Vlad told her to come here because we can't assume the monkeys won't try to burn out anyone who works for us." He gave Burke a challenging look.

"No, you can't assume that," Burke agreed. "Gods, the world has gone crazy tonight."

"Not the world," Henry rumbled. "Just your species."

They went their separate ways, guarding and protecting—and preparing for the storms that were coming.

"Arsonists and mobs are being blamed for dozens of fires that burned down buildings in several of the city's neighborhood business districts. The first wave of fires struck businesses that had been vandalized last week. Some accusations have been made that the Humans First and Last movement was behind the vandalism and the first wave of fires. The second wave of fires that swept through the city targeted bakeries, especially the bakeries displaying HFL signs, but investigators are refusing to comment about the cause of these fires. Police Commissioner Kurt Wallace has pledged that these fires will be thoroughly investigated and wrongdoers will be punished, regardless of their political affiliation or species.

"The bakeries that survived last night's torching are closed until further notice. The owners of the businesses refused to comment about this decision, but other people in the neighborhoods speculated that the owners feared a run on their stores.

"Adding to last night's troubles, a sudden storm blew in off Lake Etu. The driving rains put out the fires that firemen had battled all over the city, but the flash floods stranded many motorists and tore debris from the damaged buildings, damming up roadways and trapping people who tried to escape from the fires. At least twelve people have been reported drowned in the floodwaters and more are still missing. Market Street is currently closed to all traffic while police, firefighters, and volunteers search the debris of the buildings that were burned or flooded. We'll be back at the half hour with a full list of road closings. This is Ann Hergott at WZAS."

To: Joe Wolfgard

I have a ride to the nearest train station. Leaving Sweetwater now.
Should arrive in Bennett on Thaisday. I will call you with the arrival time as
soon as I know.

—Jackson

CHAPTER 18

Thaisday, Juin 14

Tess poured a mug of coffee for herself, then sat at the table where Nadine stared at the plate of food. The woman had dark circles under her eyes, as well as cuts and bruises caused by the men trying to pull her out of the car.

"Humans First and Last," Nadine said, her voice barely audible. "I thought they were strutting blowhards who enjoyed the sound of their own voices. I expected some trouble from them, but not this." She looked up. "They were going to throw me in the fire. How can someone call himself a human and do that?"

Since she thought that savagery was completely in keeping with human behavior, Tess said nothing.

"I need to do something."

"What?"

"I don't know. Work. Something to occupy my hands while I . . . I'll talk to my insurance company. Not that it will do much good if they're sporting an HFL decal on their door, but I'll file the paperwork."

"Then what?"

Nadine shrugged, then winced. "I appreciate you letting me stay here last night, but I'm not comfortable living on charity."

Tess stood. "Come with me." She led Nadine to the work area in her shop. "Does this have everything you would need?"

"Appliances? Yes. But you'd need to get your hands on some loaf pans if I was going to bake bread here." Nadine pointed to the cookie sheets and muffin pans. "Someone already does some baking?"

"I do when I'm in the mood," Tess said. "I don't do enough of it to supply A Little Bite with food." She hesitated. She should discuss this with the rest of the Business Association first. Then again, Simon had been making a lot of decisions on his own, and this *was* her shop. "You're welcome to use the room above the Liaison's Office until you get yourself sorted out. You can make the food for A Little Bite as your rent. We can sell loaves of bread so that people like the Denbys can make their own sandwiches. Or I can take you over to Meat-n-Greens to have a look at the kitchen there if you want to cook other things."

Nadine studied the workspace. "How do we get supplies?"

"Make a list of everything you usually ordered for your bakery, and give me a list of tools you would like to have here. I'll see what I can do about getting them. We may not be able to purchase everything we request, but I think we'll have enough." Supplies shouldn't be a problem. The *terra indigene* who grew food on humanlike farms between Lake Etu and the Feather Lakes had sent a message that they would sell their crops only to other *terra indigene* or to Intuit settlements that belonged to the *terra indigene*. If all the Others throughout Thaisia were making that choice, Tess figured the Lakeside Courtyard could trade fruits and vegetables for Midwest wheat to make flour.

"What about Chris?" Nadine asked.

"Last I heard, the doctors needed more time to work on his broken hand, and he was still at the hospital," Tess said. "Police officers from the Chestnut Street station are there standing guard. No one will hurt him. One of the girls can drive you over there to visit."

Nadine nodded. "He should have family there. Chris's father joined the HFL, so I don't know if either of his parents will be at the hospital to help him—or will let him come home to heal."

Simon was right, Tess thought. *We keep getting tangled up with more and more of these humans.* "We'll figure out something when he's ready to leave."

Nadine sniffed once, then squared her shoulders. "Well, I'm going to warm up that breakfast you kindly made for me and get started on those lists."

Tess stayed at the counter and let Nadine bustle around in the back.

What would the Humans First and Last movement say when they realized the Courtyard had the only bakery left in the city of Lakeside?

CHAPTER 19

Thaisday, Juin 14

Jackson stepped off the train at Bennett station and wanted to run. A sourness filled the air. Had a sickness spread among the humans here?

<Joe?> Noticing three rough-looking men heading toward him, Jackson stepped closer to the station—and away from the tracks and the wheels of the train. <Joe? Are you there?>

He had called the general store in Prairie Gold and told the Jesse female what time the train was expected to arrive. Had Joe received the message?

Jackson watched the three men and struggled not to shift to a between form that would surely cause panic and, perhaps, provoke other humans into an attack.

"Mr. Wolfgard!"

A human voice. Not Joe's. Not the voice of anyone Jackson knew.

One of the three men looked back at the sound of the voice. Then he stopped abruptly and slapped the arm of his nearest comrade.

Barely controlled fear rolled off the disembarking humans who had to walk past a column of smoke in order to go into the station.

Sanguinati.

Jackson walked toward a man dressed in a checked shirt and jeans who was standing beside the smoke. The three rough-looking men stepped out of his way, but one of them said in a low, harsh voice, "Gonna nail your fucking hide to a barn wall, Wolf."

The smoke took human form when Jackson reached that spot. The Sanguinati smiled, showing a hint of fang. "I'm Tolya. We met at the Lakeside Courtyard."

Jackson nodded. "I remember you."

"This is Tobias Walker, the foreman of the Prairie Gold ranch."

Walker. Same name as the Jesse female.

"Jesse is expecting a package. I'll check and see if it's come in." Tobias looked at Jackson. "Anything in the baggage car that I can pick up for you?"

Jackson held up the carryall. "No. This is all I brought with me."

"Will you be all right fetching the package on your own?" Tolya eyed the three men who still lingered on the platform.

"I should be fine. Why don't you wait for me by the truck?" Tobias went inside the station.

"This way." Tolya led Jackson to the pickup truck.

"Where is Joe?" Jackson asked, dumping his carryall in the pickup bed.

"He is escorting the earth native fuel truck to Prairie Gold," Tolya replied. "The last fuel shipment didn't arrive—at least, the allotment of fuel designated for Prairie Gold didn't arrive—so we made other arrangements."

We? Jackson wondered, lowering the tailgate when he saw Tobias hurry out of the station carrying a box big enough to fill his arms. Trailing behind were the three rough-looking men who had been on the platform.

After helping Tobias load the box, Jackson said, "I can ride in the back."

"There is room for the three of us in the cab," Tolya said with a pleasantness that made it hard for Jackson not to shift to Wolf. "And Tobias feels more comfortable when there is someone between him and me."

He noticed Tobias Walker didn't deny that observation, so he took the middle position on the seat.

"Please drive around the town square," Tolya said.

"Not a good idea," Tobias protested. "There's a bad feeling in the air today."

"I feel it too," Jackson murmured.

"Please drive around the town square," Tolya repeated. "I've been instructed to look at the businesses."

Clearly unhappy, Tobias put the truck in gear and obeyed.

"What would you say are essential businesses?" Tolya asked. "The railway station, of course, for transportation and to send and receive food and merchandise.

The gas station because vehicles would need fuel and servicing. The bank. What else?"

Jackson wasn't sure if the question was for him or the human.

"People need a place to buy supplies," Tobias said. "Hardware store is useful. And someplace that sells feed as well as ranch and farm supplies and equipment."

"A place to eat and a place to sleep," Jackson said. He thought of Hope. "Someplace you can buy books and music and pencils and paper for drawing."

"A clothes store, unless the general store is going to carry basics along with shoes and books," Tobias said.

Jackson thought, *If the Tobias was a Wolf, he'd be panting and whining.* <Why are you asking, Tolya?>

<I was asked to consider how many humans would need to be replaced to maintain the buildings and essential businesses.>

<Are the humans in Bennett going to be replaced?>

<I don't know, but I don't think this is an idle consideration.>

<Could the Intuits here take over those businesses?>

<Not easily. They have only the people they need for their own settlement. Besides, Intuits or not, they're still human, so I don't think it would be wise to ask it of them. Not at first.>

That sounded ominous. What had he walked into?

They circled the town square a second time, but no one had further suggestions beyond a barbershop or similar place.

Tobias breathed a sigh of relief when they drove away from the town. So did Jackson. Tolya didn't seem concerned, but he could turn into smoke and out-maneuver almost any adversary.

They didn't speak. If Simon wasn't expecting him, if he didn't want to talk to Meg Corbyn in person about the Hope pup, Jackson would have shifted to Wolf and headed home on his own four feet, despite the distance.

Daniel Black swore fiercely as the wind slammed against the pickup. The dust that covered the road and filled the air was as thick as a mean bitch of a blizzard.

"Mr. Black?" His foreman braced a hand against the dash. "We have to stop. We're not going to make it to the crossroads in time."

"We damn well *will* make it," Black snarled, fighting to keep the truck on the road. Fighting to *see* any part of the road. "The longer that *community* receives supplies, the longer they'll hang on, and until they're gone, we won't have a way into those hills and the riches they hold."

The men riding in the pickup's bed pounded on the back of the cab.

"They can't breathe in this dust," the foreman said. "We have to stop."

"We're not—" A wall of fence posts and barbed wire suddenly appeared in front of him. Black slammed on the breaks and yelled, "Fuck!" as the truck became tangled in the posts and wire.

He threw the truck into park, then slammed his fist against the dash, over and over.

The wind died. The dust settled. Black listened to the men in the back struggling to sit up, struggling to breathe.

Should have been as easy as the last time, he thought as he saw the dust of at least one vehicle driving down the road to Prairie Gold.

He tried to open his door and swore when he realized he was trapped by the barbed wire. So was his foreman. They would have to wait for the men in the back to pull away the wire.

While he waited, he watched the pickup that belonged to the Prairie Gold ranch hesitate at the crossroads, as if whoever was driving was thinking of stopping to help. Then it drove on when four of his men climbed down from the truck bed.

"I'll get the men started on restringing that wire," the foreman said.

Black didn't reply.

"Any word yet about the attack?"

"We're supposed to wait until the special equipment from Cel-Romano arrives. Once the designated HFL chapters have that equipment, we'll be ready to make a coordinated attack." Black didn't like taking orders from anyone, especially some slick prissy-boy from Cel-Romano. Scratch's plans had worked just fine at first, but they'd started to unravel when the scandal broke about that farming association selling grains and feed to Cel-Romano that ranches and towns here needed. Without the feed to help the cattle through the coming winter, would he be expected to sell his beef at a loss because he wouldn't be able to feed the whole herd? No, this next strike would drive the fucking *terra indigene* so deep into the wild country no one would need to kowtow to them again.

"We'll wait for the order to attack." Black opened the door that his men had freed from the barbed wire and posts. "Let's get to work on those fences."

Joe Wolfgard stood at the doorway of Tolya's motel room and watched Prairie Gold's residents drive up and form a line of vehicles, waiting for the fuel truck to fill the storage tanks at the gas station across the street.

Nyx drifted toward him. "I heard some of the humans talking. The fuel truck driver will stop now so that the humans can fill their vehicles. Then he'll continue filling the storage tanks."

That made sense. After a hunt, Wolves would allow all the members of the pack to eat before caching some of the meat.

A Hawk glided in and landed on the roof of the motel. <Air and Earth played with some humans, making lots of dust and stopping the humans from meeting the big truck.>

He had seen the dust storm when he'd escorted the fuel truck to Prairie Gold. He'd wondered if the Elementals had been involved in preventing humans from stealing the fuel again or harming the driver. He'd never heard of them being involved in shifter concerns until the Elementals in the Lakeside Courtyard became interested in Meg Corbyn.

He was about to ask if the Hawk had seen Tobias and Tolya when the ranch pickup drove past and stopped in front of the general store.

<Jackson?> Joe called.

<Joe.> Jackson sounded relieved. Too relieved?

Joe hurried to Jesse Walker's store, aware that Nyx had turned to smoke but stayed behind him instead of racing ahead to meet up with Tolya.

He glanced at the pickup. It looked dusty, but no more than usual. "You missed the storm?" he asked when Tobias stepped out of the truck.

"I think at least one vehicle got caught in it, but that dust storm didn't reach the crossroads," Tobias replied. "At least, not when we drove by."

"That's good." He studied the human, whose voice sounded odd. "That's not good?"

Tobias glanced toward Tolya and Jackson, who had gotten out on the other side, then leaned toward Joe. "Is that the way it usually works? I always thought . . . Storms. Lightning strikes and starts a fire. Blizzard sweeps in and you have to wait it out and hope your stock survives. But that's the land; that's weather. At least, we always thought it was."

"Most of the time, it is," Joe said. "But there are *terra indigene* who can guide weather, even shape it." *Or turn it into a weapon against an enemy.* "When we sent the bison meat to Lakeside, Air and Blizzard made sure it arrived without spoiling. That was a good thing."

"If we started doing something wrong, you'd tell us, wouldn't you? Give us a chance to fix things before . . . Well, before weather became something more than weather?"

He smelled fear. "I would tell you." He looked at Tolya and Jackson, who had joined them, and wondered where Nyx had gone. "Was the train late?"

"No, I wanted to take a look at the town," Tolya said. "Get an idea of what sort of businesses are there."

<More like getting an idea of what needed to be maintained if the humans went away,> Jackson told Joe.

<Are they going away?>

<Tolya doesn't know. Maybe that's a question for Simon . . . and Meg Corbyn.>

Not a comforting answer. If it wasn't for the train station, he would steer clear of the town of Bennett—except collecting the payments for the land lease and water rights for the town were the responsibility of the Others living in the Prairie Gold settlement.

He thought about the rancher, that Daniel Black, who also owed the *terra indigene* for the land and water he used. Somehow he didn't think that Daniel Black was going to turn over the payment when it came due next month.

"I rented a room at the motel for Jackson," Tolya said. "Actually, Jesse Walker reserved the room. She had a feeling you would need it."

Jackson frowned. "I'm here to pick up eleven bison."

"We're going to have to herd them," Tobias said. "Well, first we have to find the ones you want."

"Yearling calves," Joe said. "We can ask the Hawkgard and Ravengard to help us look."

"Nyx and I can help you keep the animals complacent to some extent," Tolya said, smiling.

Joe thought about the weak-smelling humans who had disembarked at Bennett when Tolya and Nyx arrived. Sanguinati looked like smoke but didn't *smell* like smoke in their other form. Would bison see them in the dark? Would they sense any danger when that smoke curled around them and drew blood through the skin?

"You boys going to stand out there all day, or are you going to let our guest come in and have something to drink?" Jesse Walker stepped out of her store. "Tobias, you should fill up that truck while you have a chance."

"Fuel truck's not going anywhere for a while," Tobias said.

<Dominant female?> Jackson asked.

<Yes,> Joe replied. <Tobias is her pup.>

<Ah.>

"Did that package arrive for me?" Jesse asked.

"I've got it," Tobias answered.

"Then bring it in here, since half the items are going on to the Lakeside Court-yard with Mr. Wolfgard and Nyx."

"They are?" Jackson looked at Joe.

"I'm just helping you with the bison. The rest?" Joe shrugged.

Tobias unloaded the box and brought it into the store. The four *terra indigene* followed. Joe barely got out of the way before the door opened again and two females entered. He recognized Shelley Bookman but didn't know the other female.

"Did they come?" Shelley Bookman asked. "We saw Tobias's truck and wanted to see."

"The box is exciting?" Nyx asked, eyeing the two women.

"Introductions first," Jesse said. "This is Shelley Bookman, our town's librar-ian. And Abigail Burch is the person experimenting with bison tallow for making soaps and candles."

That explained why she smelled a bit like bison. Should he mention that?

"Do I need to know what's in the box?" Tobias asked.

"Doubt it would interest you," Jesse replied, using a box cutter to slice the packing tape.

"Then I'll get in line for gas." Tobias looked at Joe. "I'll stop by on my way to the ranch, in case you want a ride back to the settlement."

"Okay." Somehow he'd been pushed to the back of the crowd watching Jesse open the box. Didn't need to look now. If Jackson was taking things to Lakeside, he could look when they hauled the box to the motel room.

"Cards?" Tolya sounded puzzled. "I think stores in Lakeside sell cards for games."

"These are fortune-telling cards," Jesse said, holding up two sealed boxes that had different drawings. "There are several different decks of cards. I'm keeping a set of the decks here." She looked at Jackson. "The other set goes to Lakeside with you for Meg Corbyn's use. I have a feeling these may help her find a way for at least some of the blood prophets to see visions of the future without cutting their skin."

"Why didn't you arrange for the cards to go directly to Lakeside?" Joe asked.

Something about the look Jesse gave the Others made Jackson growl and caused Joe's fangs to lengthen to Wolf size.

Jesse said, "I had them shipped here because, even though I trust the woman I spoke to when I placed the order, I had a strong feeling that it was better for everyone if the cards weren't sent directly to anyplace where a blood prophet lives."

CHAPTER 20

Firesday, Juin 15

The Wolves, along with ranch hands on horseback, cut eleven yearling bison from the Prairie Gold herd. Then smoke wrapped around the animals' necks, and Tolya and Nyx fed on each animal just enough to make it easy for Wolves and men to pen the bison in a makeshift corral that held tubs of water and feed.

After giving the bison time to drink and eat, they headed for Bennett, a pickup filled with supplies leading the way while the men and Wolves kept the bison moving.

Tolya had called the train station to let them know a livestock car would be required for the train going east to Lakeside. Joe hadn't heard what the human at the station said, but he'd heard Tolya's reply: if the *terra indigene* couldn't reserve a car for livestock, *no* livestock would be permitted to travel by rail from this part of Thaisia. That meant the ranchers who sent cattle to the slaughterhouses located in cities beyond the Midwest Region would be stuck with animals they couldn't sell and couldn't move overland without losing half their herds to the predators who would gather for the feast.

Could he have stopped Tolya from making such a threat? Did it matter? The Sanguinati was far more skilled at dealing with the humans in Bennett than he could be. Besides, Tolya deferred to him whenever decisions involved the Intuits, who were the humans the *terra indigene* settlement needed to interact with on a regular basis.

They kept the herd moving at a steady pace.

Joe wanted to push on while they still had light, but Tobias argued that there would be nowhere to set up camp for the night once they passed the crossroads. There was nothing but human-controlled ranchland between the crossroads and Bennett, and once they arrived in town, they would have to hold the bison in the stockyard until the train was scheduled to depart. The less time they spent in town, the less time for people to stir up trouble.

Since Tolya agreed with that assessment and Tobias was confident they could reach Bennett in plenty of time to catch the train if they headed out at first light, Joe went along with them. They set up camp within sight of the crossroads—and not that far from the spot where bison had been shot the previous week. No one mentioned the incident, or said anything about the number of carcasses that had been stripped down to bone already, but the Wolves sniffed the area for any sign of intruders, and Tobias and the ranch hands put on their gun belts and checked their revolvers before setting up the watch for the night.

The next day, they started out right after breakfast.

As Joe snapped at a yearling to encourage it to keep up with the other bison, he noticed the trucks parked on the side of the road and the men who stopped working and watched their little herd trotting toward Bennett.

<What are the humans doing?> he called to one of the Ravens.

<Fixing the fence that Air and Earth pulled up the other day.>

That was sensible. Cattle that strayed off the land used by humans were considered edible, and the Elders who had come down from the hills last week to feed on the dead bison were still prowling the edges of human land. It was their lingering scent, as much as the herding skill of humans and Wolves, that kept the bison from trying to break free. There was also the sound and smell of water as it sloshed in the two barrels loaded in the back of the pickup—and Nyx hand-feeding the bison when the humans stopped to rest, teaching the animals that she was not something they needed to fear.

Joe wondered if the Sanguinati did something similar with humans, lulling them into a trust that allowed vampires to feed without their prey being aware.

And that made him wonder how long Tolya planned to stay around Prairie Gold.

When they finally reached the train station, there were two livestock cars being loaded with cattle. After being told they could load the bison into the third stock car once the cattle were settled, Joe and Jackson took advantage of the wait to shift to human form and pull on clothes.

A human noticed them and the bison, then said something to a couple of men on horseback before walking over to them.

"I'm Stewart Dixon." He tipped his head to indicate the bison. "You boys need a hand getting them loaded?"

Tobias glanced at Joe, and Joe understood it was his decision. He also understood that Tobias didn't feel wary of this man the way the Intuit did around that Daniel Black.

"Thank you," Joe said.

A wave of a hand had the men on horseback approaching slowly, nodding to the men from Prairie Gold.

Tobias eyed the cattle that had been loaded into the two stock cars. "Pardon me for saying, but your cattle look a bit young and underweight to be sent to market."

The Stewart smiled. "Shows you've got a good eye, and you'd be right if they were going to market. But I wanted to reduce my stock, and there were two settlements east of here that were looking to buy some cattle to start their own herds. From what they said, they already have a small herd of dairy cows—enough animals to provide their communities with milk and such—and would like to be able to eat something besides elk when roads and weather make it impossible to drive to a bigger town for supplies."

"Don't humans like eating elk?" Joe asked.

"Sure. One of the freezers at my ranch is filled with elk meat every hunting season, but it's a delicacy for most folks, same as milk and cheese might be for you."

Joe, Jackson, Tobias, and the Stewart moved out of the way as the men on horseback herded the bison into the empty livestock car.

"If you don't mind *me* saying, those bison look a little young if you're sending them to market," the Stewart said.

"They aren't food yet," Joe replied. "They're going east to a city on the shores of Lake Etu. Sending smaller bison was sensible." Besides, Simon wanted everyone in the Lakeside Courtyard to have time to get used to bison living there before they were old enough to breed.

"I'll help Nyx and Tolya load the box going to Lakeside," Jackson said. Then he added, <See you on the platform before I go?>

<Yes.> Joe looked at Tobias. "Give him a hand?"

"Sure."

That left him alone with the Stewart Dixon. "Thank you for your help."

"Happy to lend a hand."

"You aren't connected to the Prairie Gold settlement."

The Stewart shook his head. "My ranch is several hours north of here, but Bennett is the closest rail line, as well as the largest town when we need supplies or want a night out. It's a day's drive in any direction to find another town with a music hall and a movie theater. A different group of *terra indigene* watch over the land north of Bennett. At least, I'm assuming it's a different group, because I haven't seen you around before."

"It's a different group," Joe agreed. Had the Wolves north of the hills felt the presence of the Elders?

The Stewart hesitated. "Look, I don't want to step on anyone's toes, or cause trouble between you and the Wolves I usually deal with, but . . ." He took a small pad of paper out of his pocket and a short pencil, wrote on the paper, and handed it to Joe. "That's the phone number of the ranch house. Like I said, we're north of Bennett, so I'm not sure what we could do, but if you need help, you call and ask for me."

Joe studied the number. "Why would you do this?"

"Anyone but a fool can see trouble is on the horizon. My family has never had any problems with your kind, and I don't want problems now. Your people have been good neighbors. I try to be the same." The Stewart looked over when someone shouted his name. "I'm needed."

He held out a hand. After a moment's consideration, Joe shook hands.

"See you around." The Stewart walked away.

Joe headed to the platform to say good-bye to Jackson and Nyx.

"Safe travels," Tobias said as Jackson and Nyx boarded the train.

"They'll be fine," Tolya said, joining them. "The train will be watched all the way to Lakeside."

Joe found that comforting. Jackson was away from his pack, but he wasn't alone. He glanced at Tobias and wondered if a human felt the same kind of comfort, knowing the residents of the wild country were keeping a closer watch on everything and everyone who traveled through their land.

When the train pulled out of the station, Tolya turned to Tobias. "Mr. Walker, do you and the others want to remain in town for the night? You worked hard bringing the bison here."

"I was told this town has a music hall and a movie theater," Joe added. "Having entertainment seemed important to the Stewart Dixon."

"I had overlooked those two businesses when we drove around the town square the other day," Tolya said, then added privately to Joe, <I will amend my list.>

Tobias looked at both of them. "I talked it over with the men. None of us have a good feeling about staying here. If it's all the same to you, I'll check the baggage room at the station to see if there are any packages for us to bring back. Then we'd like to put some distance between us and this town."

"All right," Joe said. "Won't the humans returning on horseback need food and water? Should we purchase some here?" They'd carried food and water in the pickup, but most of it was gone now. He wanted to get away from this place as soon as possible, and he knew the other Wolves felt the same way, but humans were part of his pack for this trip and they weren't as hardy as the *terra indigene*, who could do without food and water until they reached Prairie Gold.

"I'll call Jesse, tell her we're on our way back. She can send up another truck with supplies to meet us," Tobias said. "We can make camp in the same place we did last night—on *terra indigene* land."

<He wants to be away from here,> Tolya said.

<Let's help him check for deliveries and get out,> Joe replied.

They carried out two boxes of books from Howling Good Reads, and eight boxes of goods from different parts of Thaisia, all addressed to Walker's General Store. And all around them, humans who should have left the station by now stood around and stared, their hatred pulsing in the air.

Why so much anger, so much hate? Joe wondered. He looked at Tobias, whose hands were tight on the steering wheel as the pickup followed the Wolves and ranch hands on horseback out of town. "Has it always been like this between you and the other humans?"

"Not like this," Tobias replied.

"Is it because of us? Because some of the *terra indigene* came into town with you?" Trains couldn't go from one place to another without the tracks that ran through the wild country, and that right-of-way was predicated on the *terra indigene*'s being able to travel by train. So the Others had to come to town once in a while to pick up guests or packages. But they didn't need to go beyond the train station. Even when Tolya asked to see the town during the last visit, Tolya and Jackson—and Tobias, for that matter—never got out of the pickup.

"There have been stories lately that the creek beds in those hills are filled with gold nuggets," Tobias said. "That you can scoop them up by the handful."

Wasn't *that* easy, but he'd been told by the Wolves who had been living in the *terra indigene* settlement for a while that there were some places where the yellow pebbles were fairly easy to collect—a gift from the Elders that allowed the Others to trade with the Intuits.

But if humans invaded those hills . . .

Joe shuddered.

"You okay?" Tobias asked.

"Yes. I will be glad to get back to our own territory."

"You and me both."

Tolya said nothing, but when they stopped to rest the horses, he shifted to smoke and headed down the road as a scout. Joe stripped and shifted to Wolf, letting another Wolf ride in the cab for a while, along with one of the ranch hands.

Aware, aware, aware. They moved on, alert for anything and everything.

The Stewart was right; there was trouble on the horizon. As he trotted along, Joe thought about the Intuits. They had a few pups in their settlement, and no good places to hide if other humans turned rabid.

Joe didn't like bringing himself to the Elders' notice—he was a small shifter in comparison—but he would go up to meet them and ask them to allow the Intuits to hide in the hills if Prairie Gold was attacked.

CHAPTER 21

Moonsday, Juin 18

A vigorous debate between members of the Courtyard's Business Association ended minutes before Jerry Sledgeman drove in from the train station, his livestock truck filled with bison. None of the Others had been happy about allowing Jerry so far into the Courtyard, but everyone agreed that unloading animals in the Market Square wasn't a good idea, particularly if the bison stampeded down the access way and thundered into the traffic on Main Street.

That was the reason five yearlings were unloaded at the Pony Barn, and the female pack and Kowalski were on hand to witness the arrival of a future item on the menu.

Simon itched to shift out of his human skin and help herd the bison to the part of the Courtyard where they would be settled—once everyone decided exactly where that would be. Henry had just laughed, saying deer roamed throughout the Courtyard's three hundred acres and the bison would do the same. Since Simon agreed with him, he didn't offer any opinions. A full-grown bison would go where it chose, but most of the Others in the Courtyard hadn't lived in the Northwest and had no experience with prairie thunder.

Meg looked at the bison and then at him. "You said we were getting little bison."

"They are little bison," Simon replied.

She waved a hand to indicate the female pack. "We thought you meant *baby* bison."

"Yearlings are close to babies."

"Don't go there," Kowalski muttered.

"Besides," Simon continued, ignoring the man, "if we'd brought calves, we'd also have to bring the mothers, and they're *big*."

"Oh," Meg said. She and the female pack stared at the bison.

"Even if they're bigger than we'd expected, they are kind of cute," Ruthie said. "And so docile."

Jerry Sledgeman scratched his head and looked at the trees. Vlad pressed a fist against his mouth and stared hard at the ground. And Nyx gave everyone the complacent smile of a well-fed vampire.

Jackson was currently in Meat-n-Greens quieting a sharp appetite, but Nyx hadn't gone hungry during the journey. Docile bison were testimony to that.

"What are you going to call them?" Meg asked.

"Lunch?" Simon offered.

The female pack gave him a look that made him think running away would be a good idea, if he wasn't the leader and couldn't back down.

"Simon? Shouldn't you and Jackson be heading to the River Road Community to settle the other bison?" Vlad gave the female pack a pointed look. "And shouldn't the rest of us be getting to work? I know some of you have to review the items Jackson brought from Prairie Gold."

Ruthie and Theral rode off on bicycles. Meg and Merri Lee drove off in the BOW.

Simon looked at Kowalski, who was usually at work by now.

"Where *are* you going to put them?" Kowalski asked, nodding at the bison.

"Why?"

"Out of sight, out of mind. If they're around where the girls see them every day, they'll end up with names, and I don't think the girls will forgive you if you put a platter of Fred or Henrietta on the table."

Jerry nodded. "Oh, yeah. What he said."

Simon thought this over. The Wolves wouldn't be serving up *their* bison on any platters, but *some* of the meat would be sold at the butcher shop in the Market Square for the humans to buy. How would they know which bison had become a roast? Would it matter?

Humans were no end of trouble even before they did anything.

"Right," he said. "Don't name the food."

"Jackson said males and females remain separate most of the time," Nyx said. "We can keep the females in the Chambers. It's fenced."

It was also off-limits to everyone but the Sanguinati—not the best choice to establish the bison where they couldn't be hunted. Then again, deer were plentiful, so there was no reason to hunt bison for another year or two, and the land inside the Chambers offered plenty of grazing and fresh water.

"Will Erebus agree to this?" Simon asked. "Bison aren't dainty when they poop."

Vlad shrugged. "Deer roam inside the Chambers. I don't see . . ." One of the bison lifted its tail and demonstrated not being dainty. "Ah."

"It will be fine," Nyx said.

"I'd best be getting back," Jerry said. "Anything you want me to deliver to Ferryman's Landing?"

Simon shook his head. "Not today."

The bison wandered across the road and began to graze.

"Anyone want a lift to the exit?" Jerry asked.

"Sure," Kowalski replied. "It's time for me to head out to work."

"I'll walk," Simon said.

Nyx shifted to smoke and flowed in the direction of the Chambers.

Vlad set out with Simon, heading for the Market Square, where Blair and Jackson would meet them with the van, since two of the juvenile Wolves from the Addirondak packs were coming with them to the River Road Community.

"Wouldn't a few cattle be easier to manage if you'd wanted something . . . exotic?" Vlad asked.

"We have access to beef and to dairy foods from *terra indigene* farms," Simon replied. "Don't need cows here. Besides, bison don't need tending as long as they have food and water. And in another year, one of them can feed the whole Courtyard for days."

"You think humans in Lakeside are going to continue to let earth native trucks reach the Courtyard to supply us with beef, eggs, and milk?"

"You think this city will survive if they don't allow those trucks to reach us?" Simon countered.

"No. Fortunately, there are those in the Lakeside police who understand that too."

They didn't speak for a minute. Then Simon said, "You'll keep an eye on Meg?"

Vlad nodded. "Henry is working in his studio—or, more precisely, he says he's sanding a piece and is working in his yard. With the sorting room window open, he'll hear enough of what Meg and the other girls are saying about the decks of cards Jackson brought—and what they think of the sketches Hope made for Meg."

Blair passed them but didn't stop, giving Simon a few more minutes before he reached the Market Square and had to deal with the next task.

Meg opened one deck and laid the cards on the sorting room table in rows.

"Lovely artwork on these fortune-telling cards," Ruth said. "It's almost like the illustrations make up an entire fantasy world."

"Lovely, yes, but not realistic," Meg replied.

"The art is supposed to be symbolic of what the cards represent, not realistic."

"That's the problem, isn't it?" Merri Lee said, watching Meg. "You're not going to see visions about people or events in that fantasy world, so you need a picture of fire, not a picture of a dragon that represents fire."

"Yes," Meg said. "And we need to call the cards by a different name because saying we're telling fortunes sounds like a kind of entertainment, and we're trying to use the cards as a tool for prophecy."

"Then that's what we'll call them—prophecy cards." Merri Lee swept the rows of cards into stacks, her movements hampered by the splint on the left index finger.

"How much longer?" Ruth asked, pointing at Merri Lee's hand.

"Hopefully the splint comes off tomorrow after Dr. Lorenzo checks the finger. Gods, I'll be glad to have both hands to wash my hair."

"At least it was a simple break. It looked . . ."

"Like the bone was sticking through the skin. Lucky for me it was a shard of bone china from all the dishes that had broken during the fight at the stall market. Sure looked like bone, especially since my finger hurt." Merri Lee blew out a breath. "Most of us were lucky."

Meg didn't say anything. Girls had come and gone in the compound where she'd been raised and used, but she hadn't known any of them well enough to feel the loss—not the way she felt the loss of Lawrence MacDonald and Crystal Crowgard. They had been friends.

I don't want to lose any more friends, she thought as Ruth put the deck into its box and opened the next deck.

The next deck didn't appeal to any of them, but the third . . .

Meg's hands tingled lightly as she touched the cards. Realistic illustrations. She pulled out all the pictures of water—lakes, streams, waterfalls, surf.

"Here's an illustration of the Great Lakes," Merri Lee said, setting the card with the ones Meg had already culled.

"Specific and general." Meg went to a drawer and took out the postcards she had gotten from Lorne. She pointed to one of the prophecy cards. "A waterfall would be a general image that could be anywhere." She laid a postcard of Talulah Falls under it. "But this would mean a specific place."

"How many specific places did you learn?" Ruth asked. "We had the impression that you were taught one image to represent a particular thing, like one image to stand for small dogs and one for large dogs, but no particular breed of dog."

"But Talulah Falls is a distinctive landmark," Merri Lee said. "Maybe different combinations of cards could mean different things. Meg, what does seeing these two cards together mean to you?" Merri Lee set the postcard of Talulah Falls on top of the card illustrating the Great Lakes.

"Lake Etu," Meg said as soon as she placed her fingers on the cards, surprised that she didn't have to think about it at all.

"It could also mean Lake Tahki," Ruth said. "A third card might be needed to narrow down the location."

"That's a good point." Merri Lee handed Meg a card that showed the sun setting behind a mountain range. "What about this?"

"West."

"And together with this?"

She took the second card. "Sunset."

Ruth eyed her. "How do you feel?"

"My hands tingle a little, but they've been tingling since we opened this deck of cards."

"That doesn't prove anything." Ruth sounded disappointed.

"We haven't asked a question," Merri Lee said. "Let's arrange these cards in categories, the way Meg did with the water, and then do a test. We'll include the postcards too."

"What about the other decks of cards?"

"Let's start with what we have and see what happens. Ready?"

Meg nodded.

"Where did the Courtyard's bison come from?"

"I already know the answer to that."

"Yes, but if you had to give us the answer using cards, which ones would you choose?"

Meg looked over the cards and chose the card she'd said meant West, then a card that showed tall grass and little else. Then she frowned and rubbed her right hand. "It's not here. The yellow pebble isn't here."

"Wait a moment." Ruth opened another deck of cards and quickly went through them. Then she held up a picture of several bars of gold stacked in a vault.

"Yes," Meg said, taking the card and setting it beneath the other two.

"West as a direction or region, a picture of what I'm guessing is prairie—Mr. Wolfgard could confirm that when he returns—and bars of gold." Merri Lee sounded pleased. "The answer to the question is Prairie Gold, which is west of us."

The tingling faded.

Meg stared at the cards. Could this work? Could she really answer questions this way?

"We would need cards that have pictures of bad things," she said.

"Yes," Merri Lee agreed. "But a picture of a bad thing doesn't have to be graphic."

"Okay," Ruth said. "Is there anything in this landscape deck that doesn't feel right to you, Meg?"

After looking at all the cards, Meg shook her head. "None of them feel wrong."

Ruth reclaimed the card with the bars of gold before they collected the rest of the cards and put them back in their box. "That was the landscape deck. This deck is called cityscapes."

Meg hugged herself while Merri Lee and Ruth sorted the cards into categories.

"Meg?" Merri Lee said.

The calves and thighs of both legs burned, burned, burned—the prelude to prophecy. Meg clenched her teeth and held one hand above the cards, moving slowly from one category to the next. Her hand buzzed painfully when it brushed against the last category. She pushed those cards to one side, then backed away from the table until her hand stopped buzzing and her legs stopped burning.

Merri Lee and Ruth looked at the cards and then at her.

"Meg?" Ruth said softly. "Why did you set these aside? They're all cards that show skylines of different cities."

Burned, burned, burned. She'd had the same sensation above her ankle when she'd seen the prophecy of Nadine's shop burning. If she made a cut, if she saw . . .

No. She didn't want to see what was going to happen in those places. And she didn't want her friends to carry that much of a burden of knowing.

"Meg?" Merri Lee said. "Why did you set these cards aside?"

She shuddered and swallowed hard. "I don't think we'll need them." Her stomach rolled. "I can't look at anymore today."

She ran to the bathroom, but once she was out of the sorting room, her stomach settled. When she returned, the cards were put away, the decks set out in their boxes on the counter.

"We didn't want to put them away," Ruth said.

"But we can," Merri Lee added.

"I made a note on the deck that was too fantastical for you, and on the deck that wasn't of interest, as well the two decks we've looked at. And there's one other deck that might be too fanciful to be useful."

Meg nodded. "We can look at more tomorrow."

Her friends exchanged a look.

"I don't need to cut," she assured them. That was true in a way. She didn't need a cut, but she craved the euphoria that came from cutting. "I just need some routine now."

"Anything we can do?" Ruth asked.

"No. Thanks."

"Should we tell someone about what you said about not needing those cards?"

"We don't know anything for certain." When the Controller had cut her for his clients, she hadn't known what she'd seen and certainly hadn't had any say in who was told about the prophecy. "If you tell someone . . . make sure you tell them we don't know anything for certain."

They nodded. Promising to return during the midday break and have lunch together, Merri Lee and Ruth went out the back door of the Liaison's Office.

Meg opened the Private door and studied Nathan, who looked too casually sprawled on his Wolf bed under one of the front windows. She'd bet a week's pay that he'd been leaning on the counter, listening to everything they'd said so that he could report to Simon.

She watched the mail truck pull into the delivery area and felt relieved that she would have something routine to do for a little while. Before the mailman stepped out of the truck, she said to Nathan, "Make sure you tell Simon we don't know anything for certain."

CHAPTER 22

Moonsday, Juin 18

The six remaining bison weren't as docile by the time Simon, Jackson, two juvenile Wolves, and Jerry Sledgeman reached the River Road Community. As soon as Simon and Jackson lowered the ramp on the livestock truck, the bison trotted away from the houses and the creatures who stood on two legs but smelled like Wolves.

"Do you want us to watch them?" a voice asked.

Simon looked at two Sanguinati males who had drifted close to them in their smoke form before taking human shape.

"Yes," he replied. "It will be helpful to keep track of them."

The two males shifted back to smoke and flowed in the direction the bison had taken.

Simon watched them as the other four juvenile Sanguinati joined them. At least bison watching would give them something to do.

Jackson studied the land. "Back home, the land stretches out and you can see a long way. Here it won't be as easy to keep track of a herd."

"You may want to purchase a couple of all-terrain vehicles that the farmers and livestock wranglers can use," Jerry said. "Steve wants a couple of them for the *cassandra sangue* campus along with a couple of small carts that can be attached to haul gear or feed."

"Or the humans could use horses," Simon said.

"If you want horses, you should talk to Liveryman. But you'd need to build some kind of shelter and a place for feed. The ATVs could be stored in the old industrial building."

"Some of these houses will belong to *terra indigene*. Most will not have a car and the garage will be empty. Wouldn't a garage be big enough for a horse?"

Jerry scratched the back of his neck. "I'm not saying it wouldn't be useful to have a couple of horses here, but you'll do better to build a structure meant for a horse than to try to refit a garage into a safe stall. You could store feed in a garage if you put wooden pallets on the floor to keep the hay dry, but that will attract mice that will get into the house through the attached garage. I suppose you could get a couple of cats."

"The Panthergard don't usually eat mice because it takes a lot of little rodents to make a meal," Simon said. "But there are other *terra indigene* who would eat mice." If the Others promised to consider them nonedible, maybe having a few domestic cats living in the community would reassure the humans. With the way humans hoarded possessions where mice could nest, cats that lived with humans would find hunting in a house easier than an Owl would. Maybe there were spare cats on Great Island?

Horses, cats, and all-terrain vehicles. More things for the list the next time he talked to Steve Ferryman.

"Anything else you need?" Jerry asked.

Simon shook his head.

"Almost forgot." Jerry opened the passenger door of his truck and pulled out a carry sack, which he handed to Simon. "We have tennis courts at our community centers, both on the island and the mainland part of Ferryman's Landing. Don't know if any of your folks play the game, but Ming Beargard saw Pam Ireland throwing a tennis ball for her dog, and he thought you might like a few of the balls for the youngsters."

"Thank you." The Wolves already knew about this kind of ball. Bouncy—and soft enough that it didn't hurt a pup if he missed the catch and got conked on the head. But he didn't tell Jerry that this wasn't a new thing for the Lakeside Courtyard. Besides, these balls could stay here for the Wolves who would settle in the River Road Community.

Jerry drove away, turning north on River Road to head back to Ferryman's Landing.

Jackson reached for the carry sack. "Can I see one of those?" He studied a yellow ball, squeezed it, then threw it.

The juvenile Wolves watched the yellow ball disappear in the long grass.

"You're supposed to run after it and bring it back. That's the throw game," Simon said.

Jackson threw another ball in the same direction, and this time the Wolves raced after it. After finding both balls, they trotted back to Jackson, who threw the balls again.

Simon watched his friend and felt excitement bubble inside him. Jackson throwing a ball was part of the prophecy Meg saw for this community. "Roy Panthergard is going to resettle here. A female might be coming with him."

Jackson aborted the next throw and looked at Simon in surprise. "A mate? The Panthergard aren't as solitary as regular panthers, but would two of them— could two of them—live so close together?"

"Don't know. Don't know if the female is planning to stay or just wants to look at this part of Thaisia before deciding. Either way, Roy is going to settle here." Simon hesitated. "What about you?"

"Me?" Jackson's next throw was so short the Wolves barely had to move to catch it. "You thought I would be staying? Why?"

"Because Meg saw you here." Simon shrugged. It was still too easy to believe that everything a blood prophet saw would happen in the future, especially when Meg had been right so often. But you couldn't make assumptions about the visions.

When Jackson looked uneasy, Simon continued. "This is what Meg described— you throwing a ball for juvenile Wolves. I thought it meant you would live here."

The Wolves dropped the balls at Jackson's feet, then trotted off to explore the land around the houses, having had enough of the game.

"I like living at Sweetwater," Jackson said. "And Grace is from the High North and would miss the snow."

"We have snow."

Jackson laughed. "You don't have what Grace calls snow."

He hoped no one relayed that comment to the Elementals in Lakeside. He didn't want Winter to feel the need to prove she could provide as much snow as some of the Elementals in the Northwest or High North.

"Besides," Jackson continued, "the Hope pup is settling in, learning the land

and how to take care of herself. And it's different now, isn't it? The Intuits are more interested in talking to us, exchanging information about the prophet pups, asking what would be helpful for the ones they're looking after. It's not just a weekly visit to the trading post anymore."

"And you're the leader they talk to." Simon nodded. "Like Joe is talking to the Intuits in Prairie Gold."

"You and your Meg showed Others and Intuits that it's possible to really work together."

"Not all humans feel that way," Simon warned.

"Not all the *terra indigene* feel that way either." Jackson picked up one of the tennis balls and frowned. "Don't think you want to put this in with the clean ones."

"We'll take those two with us and put the carry sack with the clean balls in the garage attached to the Sanguinati's house." When they were ready to leave, Simon called the juvenile Wolves. <Time to go back to Lakeside.>

<We're not done sniffing!> <We could stay here and help guard the bison.>

Help chase the bison was more like it. Trouble was, the bison knew about wolves; these young Wolves knew just enough about bison to get themselves into serious trouble. And two packs of juveniles with no adults of any kind around? Not going to happen.

<Get in the van,> he growled.

They returned, looking sufficiently chastened. Simon suspected that had less to do with actual obedience and more to do with not being banned from the next outing.

<You're disappointed that I'm not going to stay,> Jackson said when Simon drove away from the community.

<Yes. But I wouldn't want to relocate and leave Meg, so I understand why you don't want to leave the Hope pup on her own.>

<I had an aptitude for holding the human form and for understanding many of the things they use, but I didn't want to run a Courtyard or even live in one. Not like you did. Now I deal with more humans and human things in a week than I used to face in a whole season.>

<Humans do have a way of sticking to you. Like burrs.>

Jackson laughed quietly. <But a few humans are worth the prickles.>

Simon thought of the way Sam looked when he was with Meg, how much the pup had grown since that first night he'd caught her scent and curiosity had quieted fear. And he thought of how he felt about having Meg as a friend. <Yes, some of them are worth the prickles.>

Meg crumpled that day's issue of the *Lakeside News* and threw it into a corner of the sorting room. Then she retrieved it and smoothed it out before placing it in the wire bin she used for the recycled newspapers.

How had Merri Lee put it? Same news, different day: Governor Patrick Hannigan still urging city governments to show common sense instead of giving in to the sensationalism being thrown about by the Humans First and Last movement, and Agent Greg O'Sullivan saying the Investigative Task Force was still investigating the cause of the dead fish that continued to wash up around Toland.

Those articles made her hands tingle while she read them, but the article that quoted Nicholas Scratch . . .

Humans were powerful. Humans were right. Humans deserved all the riches the world could offer. People shouldn't have to be grateful for handouts that were doled out according to the whims of *animals*.

Her skin burned so much as she read the article she couldn't touch the newspaper anymore.

Too soon to cut, she thought as she went into the bathroom to wash her hands. *And no point cutting now that the burning has gone away.*

Returning to the sorting room, Meg set the decks of prophecy cards on the table and opened each box. She hesitated a moment, then retrieved the discarded cards from the cityscape box—the cards that identified Thaisia's larger human cities. She even included the two sets of the more fantastical images. Last, she spread out the sheets of paper that held Hope's sketches of the cards that should be included in this new Trailblazer deck everyone expected her to create somehow.

Hope's sketches showed a mix of cards. Some were scenes that might be taken as a whole or be relevant because of one image, and some were images of things. Was that mix already in the decks? She hadn't really given the cards a proper look the last time she'd touched them.

Meg wasn't sure how long she'd been staring at the decks, feeling overwhelmed even before she began looking at images, when she realized she wasn't alone. She looked up at the big man standing on the other side of the table.

"Henry?"

"You sighed. I wondered what was wrong."

"You heard me sigh?" She looked toward the open window. She and her friends hadn't considered that anyone might overhear them when they talked in this room, especially since they usually spoke quietly to avoid Nathan eavesdropping from the front room.

"I was working outside and heard you. Jake heard you from his perch on the wall. And Nathan heard you. It was a loud sigh."

She hadn't thought her sigh had been *that* loud, but all the Others had excellent hearing, so it could have sounded loud to them.

"Reading the newspaper bothers me," she admitted.

"This is recent?"

She nodded. "Every time I read about the HFL movement or something Nicholas Scratch said, my skin prickles or burns. I'm trying not to cut. I really am."

"That Nicholas Scratch and the HFL humans are trouble. You don't need to cut to tell us what we already know." Henry gestured to the decks of cards. "And those?"

"I don't know what I'm doing with these cards. I don't know how to combine images from these decks to make one that will be useful to *cassandra sangue*. What if I leave out something that another girl needs but isn't significant to me?"

Henry pursed his lips. The scar on the right side of his face still looked raw and painful, a daily reminder of the HFL's agenda where the Others were concerned.

"Why do you need to know right away?" he finally asked.

"So that other girls can use the cards instead of cutting." Other girls. Was she that addicted to cutting that she didn't want an alternative? No. Cutting would kill her in the end. She could—*would*—learn how to use the cards for her own sake as well as that of other blood prophets.

"First you learn the nature of a thing," Henry said. "We have a teaching story among the Beargard. A young bear is hungry. He goes to the river looking for fish. He waits by the river for days and days until he is weak with hunger, but there are no fish. Why?" Henry looked at her expectantly.

"I don't know this story. I don't know why there are no fish."

"He arrived too soon. If he had learned the nature of the fish that spawned in that river, he would have looked for other things to eat and come to the river at the proper time." Henry gave her a careful smile. "Look. Learn. Then you will find what you need."

Meg sighed.

"*Arroo?*" Nathan queried from the front room.

"She is fine, Wolf," Henry said. Then he gave her a long look. "Are you fine, Meg?"

She touched one of the decks. "The cards might reveal an answer to a question, but using them doesn't produce the euphoria. Using them doesn't feel as good as cutting."

"Until you learn their nature, how do you really know that is true?"

She didn't have an answer, but she did have a question. "Henry? Are the bison going to roam around the Courtyard?"

"The two males have been taken to the Chambers. The fences should keep them from roaming beyond the Sanguinati's part of the Courtyard. The females are grazing where they will. Why?"

"They're going to get bigger."

"Much bigger."

"Do they chase things?"

At first she thought he was amused. Then he said, "Ah. The BOW."

"Sometimes a deer is in the road when I'm making deliveries, but it moves out of the way. I don't think a grown-up bison needs to move out of the way of much." Merri Lee had promised to check Howling Good Reads and Ruth said she would check the Market Square Library for information about bison. Mostly they were concerned that the new residents would devour the kitchen gardens. Meg wondered how bison felt about a Box on Wheels that chugged along on the Courtyard's roads.

"I will give you an answer when I have one," Henry said.

When he left, Meg moved over to the window but kept out of sight. She heard the wooden gate open and close, heard footsteps on the path. But they stopped before Henry reached his studio because Jake cawed, announcing that a truck had pulled into the delivery area.

On impulse, Meg opened a random deck of cards. Unsure how to shuffle cards, she fanned them out in one hand with the images facedown. Picking a card, she turned it over.

Basket of ripe apples, looking so . . .

Rotten. Wormy.

Meg blinked. No. The *card* showed a basket of ripe, unblemished apples—a delicious harvest.

The office door opened. She heard Nathan scramble off the Wolf bed to meet the deliveryman at the counter.

Meg dropped the cards and hurried into the front room.

"Hi, Harry."

"Miz Meg."

Harry's voice. Worn. Drawn. "Is something wrong?"

"Got a package here for Miz MacDonald. Says to keep it cool."

"Harry?"

Nathan stood on his hind legs, resting one front paw on the counter.

"Might not be making deliveries much longer." Harry lowered his voice and leaned toward Meg. "There's been talk about Everywhere Delivery becoming Everywhere Human Delivery."

"*Arroo?*" Nathan asked at the same time Meg said, "What are you going to do?"

"Hand in my notice; that's what I'll do," Harry replied hotly. Then he looked over his shoulder, as if afraid of being overheard. "Course, I don't know what the wife and I will do without my paycheck, but I've also heard talk that if you're fired for being a Wolf lover, you forfeit your pension, what there is of it. So I would rather resign and get what money I can. But that means you might have some trouble getting deliveries. And something like this"—Harry tapped the box—"might not arrive before it spoils."

Meg thought about the prophecy card and shivered.

"*Arroo?*"

"I'll tell Mr. Wolfgard what you said." Meg stepped back from the counter. "Thanks, Harry."

"You take care." Harry looked at Nathan. "Both of you."

Meg pressed both hands against the Private door's frame and waited until Harry drove away. Then she focused on Nathan, clenching her teeth to keep from biting her tongue to relieve the buzz and burn. "Get Henry."

Nathan cocked his head.

"Something is wrong with that box." She didn't dare unclench her teeth to speak clearly. "Get Henry. Get Tess."

Nathan howled.

Running through the sorting room and back room, Meg clawed at the back door until she finally got it open and bolted outside.

"Meg?" Pete Denby ran down the stairs from his office and caught her as her legs gave out. He half carried her to the stairs, sat her down, and gently pushed her head between her knees.

"Meg?" Tess's voice, as sharp as a razor.

"Package. Something bad," Meg mumbled. "Tongue burning."

"What does that mean?" Pete asked.

"That means you don't let her out of your sight." Tess went into the Liaison's Office.

"Are you cut?" Pete patted Meg's shoulder. "Did you see something?"

"Heard a truck. Picked one of those prophecy cards from a deck. Saw rotten apples, but the picture was of a basket of ripe apples."

"Gods. Okay. How's your tongue now?"

Meg raised her head. "Better."

"Because you spoke the warning. Isn't that how it works?"

"I don't think someone sent a basket of apples to Theral. The box isn't big enough."

Pete pulled his mobile phone from his pocket.

"I'll be all right." Who would he be calling anyway?

"Doug? You or Lieutenant Montgomery need to come to the Courtyard ASAP. Suspicious package." Pete paused, looking at Meg as he listened. "Don't have the impression we're dealing with anything explosive."

Meg shook her head.

"Human law doesn't apply in the Courtyard," she said once Pete finished the call.

"Theral is human. The threat is coming from another human. That's police business." Pete stood and held out a hand. "You feel well enough to go back inside?"

"I'd rather sit out here for a bit longer, but I would like a glass of water."

He made a face. "I'm not going to try to explain to Tess that I left you on your own."

She sighed. She really wanted some water.

Jake flew over the back wall of Henry's yard, landed near the stairs, and shifted to human. "I will get water for our Meg."

Pete made a choked sound, and Meg averted her eyes. She was becoming accustomed to these quick shifts from fur or feathers to naked human and back again—as long as it wasn't Simon. It was *different* when it was Simon.

"Don't eat my lunch while you're looking for the water," Meg shouted.

Jake didn't reply, which made her think that half of his reason for helping was being able to poke around the back room for anything a Crow would find interesting. But he returned quickly and handed her the glass of water before shifting back to his Crow form and flying to his favorite spot on the wall.

She heard sirens at the same time she heard a vehicle drive up the access way and suddenly stop. Before she could twist around to see who had arrived, Simon was crouching beside her.

"Meg?"

"I'm fine." That's as far as she got before Jackson crouched beside Simon, being less subtle about sniffing the air for the scent of blood.

Then Merri Lee ran out of Howling Good Reads' back door. "Michael says the police were called. There's trouble? Meg, are you all right?"

"Suspicious package," Pete said. "Something the police should investigate. Meg had a bit of a reaction to the package and needed some air. No need for alarm."

"You, Ruth, and I need to talk later," Meg told Merri Lee.

"A lot of us have something to talk about," Simon growled.

Meg drank some water. Learn the nature of a thing. Until she knew what was in the package, she wouldn't be able to understand the connection between it and a basket of apples—or why she'd seen something that wasn't there.

Monty walked into Captain Burke's office, followed by Kowalski and Louis Gresh, who closed the door.

Burke eyed the door, then folded his hands on the desk blotter and gave the men his fierce-friendly smile. "I'm usually the one who decides if it's a closed meeting."

"This needs to be a closed meeting," Monty replied.

"There was a ruckus in the Courtyard?" Louis asked.

"Of sorts. Theral MacDonald is all right. She didn't know anything had happened, or that it concerned her, until I went to the medical office to talk to her. Meg wasn't available, but Nathan Wolfgard was forthright about what had occurred."

"So was Pete Denby," Burke said. "He called me again while you were taking a formal statement from Nathan. The package was inspected?"

Monty nodded. "A box of expensive chocolates, with a card that read, 'Sweets for a sweet girl.' No signature on the card, and the only thing the clerk at Everywhere Delivery could tell us was the package was brought to their receiving window just before closing yesterday and the man paid the extra fee for perishable merchandise that needed to be delivered the next morning. The clerk didn't remember much about the man; just that he looked like he'd been working outdoors—had grass stains on his clothes and dirt on his work boots. There is nothing to indicate the package was sent by Jack Fillmore, Theral's abusive ex."

"But?" Burke prompted.

"There are signs that the chocolates had been tampered with. There were no foreign objects inside the chocolates that were examined, so the lab will have to run tests to figure out what was inserted." Monty swallowed anger. If Meg Corbyn hadn't reacted badly to the package, Theral could have given the chocolates to the children as a treat. What might have happened to Lizzy, or Sarah and Robert Denby, if anything in the chocolates was intended to incapacitate an adult?

"On our own time, Officer Debany and I have called hotels and rooming houses, particularly those that offer suites that are rented by the week, and haven't found anyone registered under the name Jack Fillmore," Kowalski said.

"Which means he's coming into town for each of these emotional hit-and-run attacks, or he's staying here under an alias," Burke said.

"Most likely using an alias, even if he is living and working in another town," Louis said.

"That might explain the gap in time between when he sent the flowers to Theral to confirm she was working in the Courtyard and this delivery of tampered sweets," Monty said. "There are a limited number of human-controlled towns and cities within a reasonable drive of Lakeside, and even staying overnight to check on the MacDonald house or watch Theral to try to establish a routine would mean using the scheduled days off work. If Fillmore took any other time off from a job, that would be recorded and form a pattern."

"We have no proof that Fillmore sent the flowers or these chocolates," Burke pointed out. "We've made assumptions based on Theral's history with this man, and we were more inclined to take her word because Lawrence MacDonald was her cousin and one of us."

"So far he—or someone—has tried twice and hasn't gotten past the front counter in the Liaison's Office. Actually, it's the Liaison's Office that I wanted to talk about." Monty relayed the information Nathan had given him about Everywhere Delivery becoming Everywhere Human Delivery.

Burke blew out an angry sigh. "Damn fools. If people keep pulling this crap, humans *will* be evicted from Lakeside. I'm going to ask Pete to check on the land leases, see how much of the city could be lost and how soon. Only the gods know what we'll do if trains coming and going from Lakeside completely lose the right-of-way through the wild country and the city is no longer a viable destination."

"The roads between cities are also a leased right-of-way," Louis said. "And ships moving cargo on the Great Lakes are already in a precarious position. We could be isolated."

"Every human-controlled city on the continent can be cut off. People have been forgetting that lately." Burke looked at the three men. "Anything else? No? Then let's do what we can to keep things smooth."

Monty, Kowalski, and Louis left Burke's office.

Thinking about the loss of the right-of-way between cities, Monty went to his desk and called his mother to urge her, again, to pack up and come to Lakeside as soon as she could.

Simon, Jackson, Blair, Henry, and Vlad stood in a circle around one of the BOWs.

"Your Meg drives around the Courtyard in that?" Jackson asked.

"Can't drive it around on the city streets, but she does just fine here," Simon replied, feeling defensive. Meg's driving *had* improved over the past few months, so "just fine" was an accurate assessment of her skill. But as he looked over the top of the BOW at Jackson, he understood the real question. "When the bison grow up, they're going to be bigger than the BOW."

"Bigger and heavier." Jackson set both hands on the BOW's frame and pushed. The little vehicle rocked. "This will buckle if a bison hits it."

A shiver of fear went through Simon. The BOWs could chug on the roads in the Courtyard; they could keep someone dry during rainy or snowy weather. They could, with the right driver, chug along on wet or snowy roads without mishap. Could a BOW—and its driver—survive a collision with something as big as a bison? "They would have no reason to chase the BOW or charge at a BOW." That didn't mean one of the bison *wouldn't* confuse the BOW with something that should be chased or challenged.

"Are they going to be a problem for the deer?" Blair asked. "The Courtyard's land can feed the herd that lives within its boundaries, and that herd is large enough to feed the pack and provide meat for the rest of the Courtyard's residents. How much of the deer's food will the bison consume?"

Vlad frowned. "Tell me again why we have bison in the Courtyard?"

He had room to move, but Simon still felt cornered. "Because Meg saw bison at the River Road Community, and the Hope pup did a vision drawing of Jackson bringing eleven bison to us." Then it occurred to him that, perhaps, they had misinterpreted the *cassandra sangue*'s visions. After all, what was seen didn't always happen.

Maybe having bison right in the Courtyard wasn't a good idea after all.

"Well," Henry said, "if the bison are a problem, we'll just eat them sooner."

Unhappy about making a bad decision, Simon scrubbed a hand through his hair and wanted to forget about the bison for a little while. It wasn't too hot today. Maybe he could convince Meg to play a game of chase before they ate dinner. Or he could chase her to and from the Green Complex's garden if she was going to pull weeds. "If we ate everything that was a problem—"

"—we'd all be fat," Blair finished.

Henry snorted a laugh. "Until we decide what to do with them, we'll make sure someone keeps watch on the bison when Meg is out in the BOW."

That much decided, they pushed the BOW into one of the garages behind the Green Complex and attached the power cord to charge the vehicle.

"You're taking the early train tomorrow morning?" Simon asked Jackson as they all walked through the archway that provided access between the garages and the apartments.

"I want to get home. With so many humans acting aggressive and strange, I don't feel easy being so far away from Grace and Hope." Jackson looked around. "Can we take one more run?"

Vlad stopped suddenly, a peculiar look on his face.

"What?" Simon asked.

"Tess says one of us needs to talk to Meg about her prophecy skills," Vlad replied. "You and Jackson have your run. I'll deal with this."

"Do you know what 'this' is?"

"No." Vlad shifted to smoke and headed for the Market Square and the Liaison's Office at a speed that could outpace any prey on foot.

"Go," Henry said. "Run. You'll feel better for it."

He couldn't argue with that, so Simon, Jackson, and Blair walked over to Simon's apartment to shed clothes and human form—and remember who they really were.

Vlad stopped in the shadows of the access way and shifted to human before walking to the front of the Liaison's Office and entering through that door.

Meg is suddenly doubting her ability to see visions accurately, Tess had said. *She says she isn't performing well. She's upsetting me, so you or Simon needs to talk to her.*

Not a problem. He had plenty to say to Meg Corbyn.

<I need to talk to Meg,> he told Nathan.

Nathan eyed the Private door. <She's unhappy. I don't know why. No one bothered her.>

Vlad wagged a finger at the other Wolf bed. <Where is Skippy?>

<Playing with Sam. They were playing with the human pups for a while, but the humans kept whining about being bored. What is bored?>

A human trait we don't want to acquire, Vlad thought. <Sam and Skippy aren't with Meg?>

<No, Sam left his clothes at Howling Good Reads, and he and Skippy headed back to the Wolfgard Complex by way of the swimming hole.>

That much settled—and feeling assured that this conversation wouldn't be interrupted—Vlad opened the go-through that gave him access to the Private door. As he closed that door, Meg turned away from the sorting table, clearly surprised to see him.

"Vlad?"

He closed the door to the back room before walking over to the table. "I understand that you're looking for a performance review. Isn't that what humans call it?" He heard the sharpness in his voice.

"Why are you angry with me?"

He had eleven reasons, but the bison really weren't her fault. "Not you. But I am angry. More than I realized." To give himself time to gather his thoughts, he looked at the decks of cards on the table. "How do these work?"

"I'm not sure."

"What does *that* mean?"

"It means I'm not sure!"

The shrillness in her voice made him look at her, really look at her. Was the anxiety in her eyes, the strain he saw in her face, because the Others had asked too much of her, expected too much from someone who was just a fledgling regardless of her physical age?

"You seem to think there is something wrong with your abilities as a prophet. Why? And don't tell me 'I'm not sure.'" He pitched his voice to sound like a girl's and made the tone so insulting Meg was either going to burst into tears or come up swinging.

"Even a little child can tell the difference between a box of chocolates and a basket of apples!" she shouted.

Anger. Good. He preferred that to crying.

"If you showed a child a picture of both those things, I assume they would know which was which—if they were old enough to know such things," Vlad said mildly. At random, he cut one of the decks of cards and turned over the top card. It showed a table laden with food: mashed potatoes, a salad, a basket of bread, cooked vegetables, and in the center, a huge roast.

My answer to what should be done with the bison, he thought as he restored the card to the deck.

"So all this emotional fuss is about you selecting a card that didn't match the specific danger?" He didn't wait for her to answer. "Did anyone ask you a question? Did anyone, including you, ask, 'What is in that package?'"

Meg's brow wrinkled in concentration. "I selected the card with the apples when the delivery truck drove up. Before the package was in the office. But, for a moment, the picture . . ."

When she trailed off, he finished the thought. "It was like one of your training images had been superimposed over the card, showing you a truth beyond what the eye could see."

"Yes. And when I went to the front counter to talk to Harry, my tongue began burning, like that was where I needed to cut to reveal the prophecy."

He'd seen the amount of blood that flowed when a tongue was bitten or cut. He didn't want to think about Meg putting that silver razor in her mouth.

"But you didn't need to do that because you already sensed that there was something wrong with whatever was in the package." Vlad touched one of the other decks, an idle movement. "Meg, you made a connection between two things and gave warning. How is that inadequate?"

"Because I have to figure out how to make this work for everyone!" She waved a hand to indicate all the decks of cards.

"No, you don't," he snapped. "You were asked to consider if using these cards is a possible alternative to girls cutting themselves to release the visions, not to figure out everything in a couple of days. And we're not talking about the other girls right now. We're talking about you. Just you. So what is this really about?"

"My prophecies used to be accurate," Meg cried. "It cost a lot to buy a cut on my skin because my prophecies were accurate."

"They still are."

She shook her head so fiercely he feared she'd hurt her neck. "I'm not accurate anymore. Not like I was in . . ." She swallowed hard. "In the compound."

"When you speak prophecy, you don't remember what you see; you don't remember what you say. How do you know you were more accurate?"

"The Controller's clients wouldn't have paid so much if I wasn't," Meg whispered. She avoided his eyes. "Where is Simon?"

"He's having a run with Jackson and Blair while he tries to figure out what to do with eleven large, smelly mistakes." Vlad sighed. "Maybe it isn't your prophecies that are suddenly inaccurate; maybe it's the skills of your interpreters. After all, this is a new experience for everyone in the Courtyard. But you've never had anyone show you what you said or draw little pictures like Merri Lee has done to figure out the images. You've never seen your own prophecies come to pass, so you've never seen if they were true."

"Until now." Meg looked around the sorting room.

"I haven't been keeping score, but I think at least half of the time since you've been living in the Courtyard, what you've seen hasn't happened *because* you saw it. Think about it, Meg. The ponies didn't die of poison, because you saw them dying and identified where we'd find the poison. Nadine Fallacaro didn't die when her shop was set on fire, because you saw images that warned enough of us about who and where. So many of the blood prophets were rescued because you saw the danger." Anger burned in him again. "In fact, Ms. Corbyn, your prophecies have been so accurate, it *is* your fault that we ended up with those stupid bison!"

She took a step back, despite the table being between them. "But I saw them! When Simon wanted to know about the River Road Community, *I saw the bison*. And . . . and Hope drew a picture of them!"

"You saw them. Hope drew a picture of them. And everyone just followed all the steps that would make that happen without stopping to think if it was something that *should* happen!"

Meg blinked.

Vlad paced the width of the room a couple of times, the only thing he could think to do with his agitation.

"The Sanguinati are urban hunters for the most part. What do we know about bison?" Nothing at all until he did a little research, but the bison were already on the train by the time he received a message from Tolya expressing some concern about the scheme. "Henry, who grew up in the Northwest, didn't oppose the idea. Neither did Elliot. And Simon . . . All right. I understand his thinking to some degree. Fresh meat on the hoof. *Lots* of meat. Enough to feed the *terra indigene* and the human pack. But it takes a pack experienced in hunting an animal that big to succeed without getting hurt."

"Hurt? The Wolves could get hurt? No one said they could get hurt." She sounded bristly, and the fierceness that filled her eyes made him wary.

Vlad stopped pacing. He could picture her, a human who could be felled by a paper cut, waving her broom at a bison, ready to smack it senseless to protect a Wolf pup. The idea that she might try to do exactly that was funny and frightening in equal measure.

Time to steer Meg away from thoughts of critters with hooves. A Wolf could be hurt by a deer's well-placed kick, or be injured by antlers. Since the Wolves weren't going to stop hunting deer, he wasn't going to volunteer information that might cause friction in the Green Complex every time someone trotted home with a hunk of meat.

"You could get hurt too, which is something we hadn't understood," he said. "These bison are still young, still growing. But there's no way to tell how they'll react to the sight of a BOW, especially once they mature." And the thought of Meg injured and bleeding in the BOW was beyond anything he wanted to imagine. Not that she wouldn't be found quickly; even when she drove around alone, there were plenty of *terra indigene* keeping her in sight.

But it wasn't a thought he wanted Grandfather Erebus to entertain. Once that happened, the bison would be bled out before Simon had a chance to make a decision as the Courtyard's leader—and that might create tension between the Sanguinati and Wolfgard that neither form could afford when there was all this turmoil with the humans.

"The point is, two blood prophets saw bison coming to this area," Vlad said. "But we should have asked if that was the future we wanted—and what the consequences might be when we brought an animal into an area that wasn't part of its natural territory."

Meg took a deep breath and blew it out. "Pick a deck."

"What?"

"You wanted to know how this worked. Pick a deck."

He picked the same deck he'd looked at previously, then watched Meg's fumbling effort to shuffle the cards before setting the deck on the table with her hand resting on the top card. "Ask your question."

"What should we do with the bison?" Then he added silently, *Speak, prophet, and I will listen.*

Meg closed her eyes, breathed in and out a couple of times, then cut the deck and turned her hand to reveal the card.

It was the same card he'd drawn—the table full of food and the big roast in the center.

Vlad laughed. "Show that to Simon."

Meg looked at the card and made a face. "Simon was so excited about the meat Joe sent, and he and Sam liked it so much I didn't want to spoil their pleasure, but . . ."

He laughed again. "You didn't like the bison burgers."

"No."

If she'd told Simon, that would have settled the question of bison in the Courtyard before the damn things were put on the train, Vlad thought.

<Delivery truck is pulling in,> Nathan said.

"Time for both of us to get back to work." He walked around the table and smiled at her as he opened the Private door. He followed her to the counter and leaned against it, noticing that Nathan was on his feet and watching the human who got out of the truck. Not a regular, then.

Meg frowned at her clipboard as she wrote down the name of the company on the side of the truck.

"Delivery." The man set a package on the counter.

It was the way Meg shrank away from the man and package that warned Vlad and Nathan that something was very wrong. Vlad stepped up to the counter, gently nudging Meg toward the Private door while Nathan silently moved to block the front door.

"Wait," Vlad said when the man backed away. "I haven't agreed to accept this package."

"You have to accept it."

"No, I don't." The package was addressed to Ms. Wolflover MacDonald. The "company" address said "Dead Cops Club."

Smiling enough to show a fang, Vlad picked up the phone on the counter and called Burke's direct line at the Chestnut Street station. "Captain? We've just received a package from something called the Dead Cops Club. What would you like us to do with the man who delivered it? Yes, he's still here. Well, you can arrest him, or we can eat him."

The man gasped. Meg dropped her clipboard on the sorting room table and made an odd sound. Since she was safe from the stranger, Vlad ignored her, more interested in Burke's moment of silence before saying he would send a car.

Vlad hung up.

A long minute later, Officer Debany, in uniform, entered the office at a run, almost tripping over Nathan, who still blocked the front door.

Must have been getting ready for work when Burke called.

"You're under arrest," Debany said.

"I just delivered a freaking package!" the man protested.

Hesitating, Debany looked at Vlad. "Do you believe that?"

Vlad looked over his shoulder to check on Meg and saw her slice the underside of one finger on her right hand.

"Arrest him or we'll kill him," Vlad snapped. "Either way, I want him out of here!" <Nathan, go outside with Debany.>

<Why?> Nathan snarled.

<Go.> Vlad rushed into the sorting room, cursing Meg and himself. After calling Burke, he should have let Nathan guard the stranger while he kept watch on Meg.

He pulled the razor out of her hand and set it on the table. No obvious blood on the razor; nothing to run onto the cards. And no time to grab anything to soak up the blood dripping off her finger, so he cupped his hand under hers, struggling not to shift to smoke and consume the drops of blood as they hit his skin.

"Speak, prophet, and I will listen." How much time had passed as she'd tried to swallow the words along with the agony that preceded the spoken words of prophecy? <Tess! Liaison's Office, now!> Not his first choice since she was already upset with Meg, but she had experience dealing with the girl during these prophecies.

"Rotten eggs," Meg whispered. "Hands. Feet. Bones. Maggots." A hesitation before she breathed out one final word. "Bullet."

She sank to the floor. Vlad went down with her, still cradling her hand to keep her blood off the floor.

He felt Tess sweep into the room and out again. When she returned, she crouched beside Meg, lifted the bloody hand, and wrapped a towel around it, dropping a second towel under Vlad's hand. He quickly wiped Meg's blood off his skin.

"Put the towel in the sink. Run cold water over it while you rinse off your hands. The female pack says that works for removing blood from cloth so we don't waste what we might need later," Tess said.

<Can you take care of her?> Vlad asked as he hurried into the bathroom. <I need to talk to Lieutenant Montgomery and Captain Burke.>

<I hear sirens. I don't think you'll have to go looking for either of them.> Tess studied him when he returned. <Bad?>

<Let's hope our Meg is wrong this time.>

<She hasn't been wrong yet. Not really.>

At another time, the truth of that might have made Meg's self-doubt amusing. But not now.

Monty retrieved the mail from his letter box and climbed the stairs to his apartment. He wasn't sure he would spend the night there. He wasn't sure a man alone, even a police officer, who was known to work with the *terra indigene* would be safe in this part of the city. Between the fires that burned down so many businesses on Market Street and the flash floods caused by the localized storm the same night of the fires, this part of Lakeside was in turmoil, and the police were breaking up several fights a day between members of the HFL, who blamed the *terra indigene* for all of the city's troubles, and people who now blamed the HFL for the city's troubles.

And then, today, the package that was delivered to the Courtyard. He believed the deliveryman when the fool claimed he didn't know what was in the package. The hysteria after they had shown him what he'd delivered hadn't been feigned.

Two hands with some of the bones showing through where the flesh had been eaten away. Two feet covered in maggots. And a bullet. Not a spent round. Nothing they could test.

After impounding the delivery truck, and ignoring the shrieks of the company's owner about customers waiting for the items in the truck, Louis Gresh and his team checked every package, making a record of each item. They found three other packages from the Dead Cops Club—three other packages with the same items. Those were handed over to the forensics team after the bomb squad confirmed the packages weren't booby-trapped.

They were searching for four bodies, or, at least, the identities of the deceased. Burke didn't think they would be found since cremation was standard except for the wealthy, who could afford a family crypt and literally be buried with their ancestors. None of the hands and feet were fresh enough that the body would still be in the morgue or at a funeral home for the final viewing.

But the police would search for the bodies, and they would search for the people who were responsible for directing such ill will toward a member of Lawrence MacDonald's family.

According to Burke's grapevine, the delivery company's owner and all its employees belonged to the Humans First and Last movement, and the workers at the crematorium, who were also HFL members, swore they hadn't left any body unattended for "more than a minute" and hadn't noticed any hands or feet missing on their return. And it seemed like, when fingerprints confirmed that the hands that had been sent to the Courtyard had belonged to Lawrence MacDonald, every police officer in Lakeside knew about it within an hour. And after hearing that news, every officer who had secretly, or openly, belonged to the movement removed his HFL pin and threw it away.

No matter what they thought about people who worked with the *terra indigene*, no police officer saw the Dead Cops Club as a harmless prank. This time, the HFL had crossed too many lines.

Because he was tired, Monty read the note from his mother twice before he understood what she was saying. Because he was tired, his temper, usually so slow to rise, ignited.

Tossing the letter aside, he picked up the phone and called his sister's apartment.

"Sissy?" Monty said, struggling for control. "It's CJ. I want to talk to Mama."

"Mama wrote to you? When she heard about the phone call, she got a mad on and said she would write. It's just that, Jimmy called to see how we were doing . . ."

"He called to squeeze some money out of you." Monty sincerely hoped she hadn't had a penny left to give.

He'd been twelve when his parents adopted Sierra. The toddler had needed a home; his parents could give her one. For him, there was nothing to discuss.

But for nine-year-old Cyrus James, known in the family as Jimmy, Sierra's arrival meant a smaller piece of the pie. Money for clothes, for toys, for anything he coveted—and he coveted almost everything—had to be split among three children now instead of two. Jimmy never let Sissy forget that he never had enough because of her. If they each got a cookie, Jimmy ate his and half of hers because, he said, he would have gotten both if she hadn't been there. Every time she saved up her spending money for something she wanted, he'd find something *he* wanted that cost more money than he had and she would make up the difference, and have to wait and save some more to buy something for herself.

Monty had stood as a buffer for as long as he'd lived at home—and he'd breathed a sigh of relief when Jimmy left home too, to make his own way.

In many ways, Sierra was a strong young woman, and she was smart. But Jimmy could twist her up so much she never stood a chance when she had to deal with him.

"No, he didn't," Sissy began. "Not really. He asked what we were doing, and I said Mama and I and the girls were going to Lakeside to visit with you for a bit. And he said a visit sounded like a fine idea, but if I didn't have any money, how were we going to get there."

Monty did not want to hear this. "Let me talk to Mama."

"And he said how maybe he should come and visit you too, seeing as it's been a while."

More than a while. Jimmy liked booze and drugs, and he preferred having money without working for it. Having a cop for a brother didn't make his friends feel easy.

"Did he suggest that he and his wife should come to Lakeside with you and leave Mama in Toland looking after four children?" When she didn't answer, he felt the blood pounding in his head. "Either I talk to Mama *now,* or *no one* is coming to visit."

A moment later, Twyla Montgomery was on the phone.

"Mama."

"Don't you use that tone with me, Crispin."

She had taught him the value of courtesy. Her voice turned sharp only when she'd been pushed too hard. "I'm sorry, Mama. Some bad things happened today." He took a moment to gather himself. "Mama . . ."

"You don't need to be telling me," Twyla said. "I already told Sierra that I'm coming to Lakeside to help you look after Lizzy. You were kind enough to provide the means for her and her children to come with me. And since she just lost her job too, there's no reason to stay in Toland, but suddenly she's dragging her feet and saying she can't decide. So I said if she wants to stay that's her choice, but I'm not giving her train fare to Cyrus to spend as he pleases. If he wants to come to Lakeside, he can do it on his own and make his own arrangements for a place to stay, since I got the impression that some folks wouldn't be comfortable with the arrangements you made for us."

"You're going to be surrounded by cops and Wolves."

"Huh."

Monty had to smile. Twyla Montgomery wouldn't be intimidated by either kind of enforcer.

"You're set, then?"

"I'm packed. Have the important papers you said I should bring. I think that's what spooked your sister. She felt obliged to tell your brother there's trouble coming. Not that anyone but a fool can't see that." Twyla paused. "Maybe he'll have sense enough to get his family out of the city."

"Maybe." If Jimmy's wife didn't grab onto his coat, he'd leave her and his children behind without a second thought. "Did Jimmy leave a number where you or Sierra could reach him?"

"The number changes every time he calls. Since Sierra couldn't give him what he wanted, he didn't leave even that much this time." A pause. "Crispin? The trouble that's coming. It will be bad?"

Need to know. "I can't say."

"Does it have anything to do with the news report today that the folks cleaning up all the dead fish found some pieces of arms and legs?"

Probably. "Come soon, Mama."

"I heard the words the last time you called, Crispin, and I understand what you're saying. But I want to give Sierra a little more time to see what's best for herself and her girls. If she can't see it, I'll be coming alone."

Monty waited until she hung up. Then he called his captain to find out if Burke had heard that news report—and if there was any possibility that some of the hands and feet found in the packages had been in salt water and had been shipped from Toland.

To: Simon Wolfgard

Four of the six bison released at the River Road Community have been killed. We found two carcasses well away from the houses. Scavengers were feasting when we arrived, but whatever attacked the bison must have been very big and very hungry to have consumed so much of the animals in such a short time.

The other two carcasses were left at the Talulah Falls' town line. I know this because one of the *terra indigene* leaders called me to say the meat was appreciated. While talking to him, I had the feeling that the *terra indigene* who were sent to take control of the Falls are tired of dealing with humans and want to return home—or at least go to some other place that has minimal contact with humans. Another feeling from that conversation: if the humans who have the training necessary to run things like the hydro-electric plant and any other businesses that can't be left unattended choose to stay, the *terra indigene* would allow the rest of the humans to leave town.

Like I said, this is just a feeling, but it's the first time the Others have initiated contact with anyone in Ferryman's Landing since the Falls was locked down a few months ago.

The Hawks and Crows are looking for the other two bison. We'll let you know when we find them.

I'm pretty sure Ming Beargard knows what killed the bison, but I think he's afraid to say. Is it safe for my people to be working at the River Road Community?

—Steve Ferryman

To: Steve Ferryman

Your people should be safe, but, for now, Ming or some other *terra indigene* should be with the Intuits if they need to go beyond the houses to look at the land we want to set aside for pasture and crops. The Others who live in the wild country are curious about what we're doing at the River Road Community. They are observers.

We have decided that bison are too dangerous to live in a Courtyard, and it seems like providing wild meat to the *terra indigene* in Talulah Falls will help all of us. We have enough room to store the meat from one bison. Ask Jerry Sledgeman to bring his livestock truck and take the other four bison to Talulah Falls. That will be plenty of meat for everyone.

—Simon Wolfgard

To: Stavros Sanguinati

Have tried to contact you several times. I'm concerned about the rumors that the *terra indigene* have been driven out of the Toland Courtyard. Please contact me at your earliest convenience.

—Greg O'Sullivan, Investigative Task Force

CHAPTER 23

Cel-Romano

The men and women in the small villages that dotted the border separating Cel-Romano from the wild country led simple lives. They farmed, raising the crops that suited the land. They raised some animals for food and others for fleece. They stopped in certain shops in the village proper to listen to the radio or use a telephone because such things weren't found in most houses. They laughed; they sang; they married and made love and raised children.

And every village had one or two families who had the special duty of following a path into the wild country to a designated place and leaving a gift at the full moon. Sometimes it was special food; sometimes a length of cloth or a rug. Sometimes it was a book purchased by the whole village just for this.

Members of the families would go to that designated place and say, "For our friends," as they held their offering. Sometimes a wolfman or a foxman would come out of the woods and accept their offering. Sometimes it was a Crow or a Hawk that would land nearby and indicate the gift was acceptable.

Generation after generation, each side carried out the ritual. A gift in exchange for the men in the village venturing into the wild country to cut wood to warm their houses, for the women to pick fruit. And when the Important Men from the Big Cities came to the villages to take most of a harvest, or the horses that were needed for the farms, or the animals that would have been sold to the butcher for the coins that would provide the income the family needed for the next year, sometimes there was a basket, woven from vines and filled with fruit, left on a doorstep. Sometimes there was a rabbit for the pot or a small deer that kept many families in the village from going hungry.

"For our friends." The people knew the wolfman, the foxman, the Crow, and the Hawk were messengers. They knew there were things in the wild country— and in the sea—that were too ferocious and should not be seen. They lived at the border of the wild country; they lived in fishing villages at the edge of the sea. They had always known what the Important Men from the Big Cities refused to know—that being friends was the only way to survive.

Since the New Year, the Important Men had come to the villages and taken more than food and animals; they had taken the strong, healthy sons because "we need workers in our factories; we need soldiers for the great battle."

There would be no battle. The people in the villages had passed down the old stories and they knew this, but the Important Men wouldn't listen. They claimed that they needed more food, more animals, more fish for the cause. They needed more wood, more glass, more metal, more cloth, more leather.

More men.

"Do not forget," fathers whispered to sons. "You will come home to us if you do not forget."

Day after day, the people tended their flocks and their fields. They baked bread and wove cloth. And they traveled the paths to the special places, bringing not only gifts but also precious photographs of their sons.

"He is a good boy. Let him come home."

There was no answer. But as the villagers returned to homes all along the border of Cel-Romano, the land was filled with a terrible silence.

CHAPTER 24

Fingerbone Islands

Rising out of the surf that caressed the Fingerbone Islands, she waited a moment, allowing most of the crabs and small fish to spill out of her gown before she made her way to the treasure rooms. There were chests filled with gold coins and tables heaped with necklaces so encrusted with gems she thought of them as rocks covered with colored barnacles.

Coins and necklaces had no particular interest for her, but maps were her delight. To see what she knew in a different way, to see where her kin lived. When she rose to walk on land, maps of any kind provided knowledge and entertainment.

But today she wandered from room to room, looking at what had been salvaged over centuries, and felt no curiosity, no pleasure. The creatures who made these things had been an enemy in the past and were an enemy again. They had killed her Sharkgard. They had killed fish of all kinds with their poison. And for what? To fill their little ships with gold or some other kind of treasure and scurry from one shore to another?

Let them fight among themselves. That was no more significant to her than male crabs maintaining a territory in order to entice a mate. But they had touched *her* domain, had spilled poison into *her* waters.

Because the Sanguinati were land predators the Sharkgard respected, she had sent her warning to give them time to withdraw inland. Soon she would strike. But not quite yet. Air said strange noisy things had been flying lately. Ancient

Tethys was stirring, roused out of her benign watchfulness of the Mediterran Sea. Even Indeus slapped at the shores that bordered his domain, disturbed by a change of temper in Earth and Air.

Two shores—Thaisia and Cel-Romano. Where was she needed?

Leaving her treasure rooms, she returned to the water and flowed toward the west. The poison had come from Thaisia. She would deal with the enemy there first.

As she followed currents, she listened to the news the Sharkgard and Orcasgard passed along to her. And she waited for the right moment.

Other forms of *terra indigene* referred to her Elemental form as Ocean. Among her kin, she was known as Alantea.

And humans, those two-legged upstarts, called her domain the Atlantik.

CHAPTER 25

Windsday, Juin 20

The Lakeside Wolfgard knew how to hunt deer together, and they knew how to fight together to defend the Courtyard, but they didn't know much about hunting bison until they tried to round them up. After chasing one of the yearlings, the pack made it clear that this wasn't an animal they wanted to hunt unless they were very hungry and had no other choice. In fact, the only Wolf who really wanted to chase bison was Skippy. The juvenile's suicidal enthusiasm was one reason that Simon decided to send four of the bison to Talulah Falls as a gesture of friendship to the *terra indigene* currently living there.

Unlike the Wolves, who didn't know how to hunt bison, the bison already knew how to defend themselves against Wolves. But they weren't prepared for a Grizzly dressed in a T-shirt and jeans to jump toward them and roar, and when faced with a small tornado that trotted after them, they stopped fighting the Wolves' efforts to herd them into the truck.

Tired and thirsty, Simon watched Jerry Sledgeman drive away with the bison. <Well, it's done,> he said when Blair joined him.

Blair shook out his fur. <Boone Hawkgard says there is enough room in various freezers to store half of the meat from the yearling the Sanguinati brought down. The other half of the meat will be available now to all of us, including the human pack.>

Simon sighed. <Meg didn't like the bison burgers. I don't think Ruthie or Merri Lee did either.>

<Their mates ate what they left on their plates. We can sell bison burgers and hunks of roasted meat at Meat-n-Greens. Kowalski and Debany will eat them. So will Captain Burke and the Shady Burke if we allow them to visit again.>

<The humans are another pack who want to eat from the land inside the Courtyard.> Simon headed for the Pony Barn, where Meg had watched the "roundup" from a safe place.

<They eat like Wolves and gather in numbers that rival the Crowgard in any Courtyard.> Blair said nothing for a moment. <How many humans can live in that pack? How many will want the supplies that come into the Market Square? We can't bring down more deer to feed another pack. The herd wouldn't produce enough offspring to make up for that.>

He could accept for himself being hungry some days. But not Sam. Not Meg. Not the other *terra indigene* young who lived in the Courtyard.

<Our human pack has been sensible so far.> Of course, hunger could drive out sense. But that was a maybe problem. Food of all kinds was growing in the Courtyard, and there was plenty of meat, even if things like pork and beef were in short supply until they received the next delivery from a *terra indigene* settlement that raised a few of those animals. And how the human pups drank milk! He'd run out of milk for Sam, and Meg didn't have any either until the earth native truck made the next delivery. They couldn't ask for more from their current sources, so they would all have to make do with a little less.

Except Sam and Meg.

<I'm going to the swimming hole,> Blair said.

He'd like to do that too, but he headed for Meg when she stepped out of the Pony Barn, and Blair went on without him.

"You must be hot," Meg said, tunneling her fingers through his fur.

Yes, he was.

"Where is Blair going?"

This was one of Meg's tricks: asking questions when he couldn't answer because he was in Wolf form.

Jester Coyotegard stepped out of the barn, grinning. "He's going for a swim."

Meg looked at Simon. "Don't you want to go for a swim?"

Of course he did. He was hot and his fur was dusty. He gave her a hopeful look.

"No. I'm not hot, and I don't want to do the Squeaky Dance."

Simon sighed. This day was full of disappointments.

"I'll wait for you here," Meg said.

"Which is convenient," Jester added, "since your clothes are in the back of Meg's BOW."

Grumbling to himself, Simon trotted to the swimming hole. The cool water tasted good and felt even better. And since there weren't any human females nearby to get all squeaky about it, when he'd paddled around enough as a Wolf, he shifted to his human form and enjoyed floating on his back while cool water played over sun-warmed skin.

Meg returned to the folding chair that Jester had set out for her. She picked up another deck of prophecy cards that she'd brought to show the Coyote. Then she sighed. "Simon really wanted to have bison."

"Your seeing and his wanting made it happen." Jester repositioned the other chair and sat beside her. "That brought the bison here, where they've done a lot of good. The *terra indigene* in Talulah Falls are talking to Ming Beargard and the Steve Ferryman because the bison meat is the first thing that has made them happy since they came to the Falls to control the humans. Henry, Elliot, Vlad, and Nyx have gone to Talulah Falls with Jerry Sledgeman to deliver the Courtyard's bison, and the Steve Ferryman and Ming are going to join them there for a meeting with the *terra indigene* leaders and some humans."

"How do you know who is going to be at that meeting?"

"I have my sources." Jester winked at her. "I think Talulah Falls will be under new management soon. Isn't that the phrase humans use? So you showed me the city deck, which isn't so interesting, and the nature deck, which I liked. What's that one?"

Stuck on the image of a sign saying UNDER NEW MANAGEMENT hanging over the road leading to Talulah Falls, it took Meg a moment to catch up to Jester's change of subject. "This is a deck of fantastic drawings—imaginary creatures."

Jester's smile faltered. "Can I see the cards?"

She handed him the deck. "They're just make-believe. I don't know how the Intuits would read them, but I don't think they'll be useful to the *cassandra sangue*. Why would we speak prophecy about something that doesn't exist?"

She thought about the cards of city skylines that she had put aside because she didn't think they would be needed. And she watched Jester's ears shift to Coyote, watched fur spring up on his neck and hands as he looked at the drawings. He let most of the cards fall into his lap, but a few he handed to her.

"Jester?"

"Who else knows about these cards?"

"I don't know. I think Jesse Walker has the same decks that she sent to me." Jester slanted a look at the cards in her hand. "Don't tell *anyone* about those cards. You should keep them. Learn them. But don't talk about them with anyone else."

Meg studied the cards that upset Jester. The creatures walked upright, but that was all they had in common with humans. The cards weren't intended to convey a blended form of *terra indigene*. Or if they were, she didn't recognize the animals these creatures had absorbed.

Separated from the rest of the cards, the drawings frightened her—and made the backs of her legs prickle.

"Promise you won't tell anyone about these," Jester whispered. "Put them in with the nature cards and hope you never see any of them again."

"But these are just something someone imagined."

The prickle became a burn when Jester said, "Or remembered."

She realized the Coyote was shaking. Her fingers tightened on the cards in her hands. "They're make-believe."

"No. They're not."

To: Erebus and Vladimir Sanguinati

The remaining *terra indigene* have left the Toland Courtyard. Some of the Crowgard and Sanguinati will remain near the train station to keep watch and report any suspicious activity or any sign that an unusual number of humans are leaving the city.

I and a few of our kin will watch the ships leaving Toland for a while longer. The Elementals promised to help keep watch—and to warn us when the taste of the storm touches the beaches and fills the air so that we, and other *terra indigene* along the East Coast of Thaisia, have time to move inland.

—Stavros Sanguinati

Recognizing the superior might of the human race, the Others have abandoned the Toland Courtyard, giving us much-needed acres to grow crops and provide pastures for some domestic animals. Some people think a few acres is not a significant victory. I say it's the first step in acquiring all the land and resources we deserve.

—Nicholas Scratch, speaking at Toland's city hall

To: Greg O'Sullivan

Humans were indirectly responsible for our decision to close the Toland Courtyard, but it is not accurate to say humans forced us to leave the city, as Nicholas Scratch would like you to believe. We left because human behavior has made it prudent for us to get out of harm's way.

—Stavros Sanguinati

To: Simon and Jackson Wolfgard

Wolfgard throughout the northern Midwest and Northwest are howling about bison being killed and left to rot for a second time. We have lost
more bison from the Prairie Gold herd, and Tobias Walker reported that
some cattle have disappeared from the ranch. He says this is called rustling.
Since we didn't find horns or hooves to indicate the Elders ate the cattle,
I think Tobias Walker is right but don't know how to find the thieves. The
Prairie Gold Wolves are keeping watch, looking for scents beyond the town
that don't belong to the humans we know. Tolya Sanguinati continues to
watch Prairie Gold as well as Bennett. He says there is a bad feel in
Bennett—poisonous smiles—and he thinks something will happen soon.

Jesse Walker says nothing but continues to buy extra supplies for her
general store. Tolya is lending her money to do this. She rubs her left wrist
when she thinks no one is watching. Tobias says that is a sign of trouble.

Has Meg or the Hope pup been itchy?

—Joe Wolfgard

CHAPTER 26

Windsday, Juin 20

Vlad sat back and let Steve Ferryman and Elliot Wolfgard do the talking. Or, more truthfully, let them be the focus of the humans and the *terra indigene* from Talulah Falls who were attending this meeting.

Maybe he'd never been so close to a source to see how much influence small things could have on the fate of so many. Simon had hired Meg, who was a *cassandra sangue*. Her combination of childlike sweetness, the prophecies she'd seen, and her desire to learn and live shifted enough of the *terra indigene's* perception of humans that the humans working in the Lakeside Courtyard reacted by becoming a little more friendly to the Others. Lieutenant Montgomery's efforts to forge a connection between the Courtyard and the police also gave both sides more opportunities to interact without hostility.

He saw the results of those actions. The Talulah Falls humans hadn't brought government officials—if there were any who had survived. They brought a supervisor from the hydroelectric plant and a police captain. Vlad could hear Captain Burke's influence in the way the Falls captain expressed his concerns about how to keep the peace for the humans who would remain in Talulah Falls, and how to release the humans who wanted to leave. The captain, at least, understood the danger that faced anyone who wanted to flee from the Falls: with the friction building between humans and the Others in so many regions, the towns and cities still under human control provided only the illusion of safety.

But the surviving Talulah Falls residents *had* worked with the *terra indigene*, explaining the value of clearing at least one lane of the cars that had been abandoned during the first effort to flee the Falls a few months ago. There were parking lots full of cars that hadn't been reclaimed—some because the owners had been tourists who had been allowed to leave or had run away in the first chaotic days and weren't seen again. And some vehicles belonged to people who had been killed outright during the *terra indigene*'s initial furious response to the explosion that had killed several of the Crowgard.

No one talked about how many humans had died. No one talked about the Harvester who had been brought to the Falls to act as the enforcer and consumed the life energy of anyone suspected of wrongdoing. Instead, the humans presented a list of what they considered vital businesses and industries. The power plant provided electricity for the whole area, including Talulah Falls, Great Island, and Lakeside. It would provide most of the power for the River Road Community. If they could have some reassurance for their safety and that of their families, the men and women who worked at the power plant would remain in the Falls, doing their work to the best of their ability, even making entry-level jobs available to the folks from Ferryman's Landing to train more workers in all areas of the business.

As far as Vlad could tell, this seemed to be the message the humans wanted to convey: this was their home; they wanted to stay; but they didn't want to die if they stayed. And they understood that any sign of the HFL movement would mean the end of the citizens and town of Talulah Falls.

From the *terra indigene*, he heard a different message: they were tired of dealing with humans; they didn't like feeling enclosed by so many human things; they wanted to go home, go back to limited contact with the clever monkeys. But they also wanted an opportunity to observe humans without the responsibility for so many things they didn't understand.

In other words, they wanted to play tourist for a day or two in a place like Ferryman's Landing or the Lakeside Courtyard and then retreat to the land they knew and loved.

<What do you think?> Vlad asked Henry and Ming.

<They see Lakeside surviving and Ferryman's Landing surviving,> Henry said. <They want to survive too.>

<Yes,> Ming agreed. <I smell no lie-sweat. And Steve Ferryman did not say the words that were the signal that he felt something wrong here.>

An Intuit who was the mayor of his village would have a feeling about any deceit that might threaten his own people.

"The Sanguinati have adapted to living in and around human places," Vlad said, finally ready to say what Erebus had commanded him to say. "We are willing to take over the rule of Talulah Falls, with the help of other forms of *terra indigene*."

He saw fear in the humans' eyes, but not as much as there would have been a few months ago. After having a Harvester walking among them, the idea of vampires running the town was a relief.

"The Sanguinati who would be the leader is known to many in the Lakeside Courtyard. He also has contact with Governor Hannigan's Investigative Task Force, so he is in a position to consider the needs of the human citizens as well as the *terra indigene*." Vlad looked at the *terra indigene* leaders. <With others willing to take over for you, you can go home if that is what you want to do.>

<When?> they asked.

<Soon. The problem solver has one more task to complete if it can be done. Then he'll be on his way to Lakeside and then here.>

Done. Since Talulah Falls was now a town controlled by the Others, there would no longer be a Courtyard as such. Vlad and Nyx, along with a couple of human residents, would take a look around the Falls and recommend places where the Sanguinati might live. The rest of the *terra indigene* who would settle in the Falls would select their new homes according to their nature.

People were in desperate need of some supplies. Could something be done?

Yes, something could be done. Checkpoints would remain, but an effort would be made immediately to bring in supplies—and find drivers who would be willing to bring a truck into the Falls.

Vlad gave the police captain his e-mail address. Steve Ferryman did the same. Between them, they would do what they could while the transition of leadership took place.

As a last gesture, they all followed Jerry Sledgeman's livestock truck to the fenced acres that used to be the Falls Courtyard and released the four bison. Maybe the humans would value the meat; maybe not. But the gesture of help was building links among Talulah Falls, Ferryman's Landing, and Lakeside.

How much human do the terra indigene *want to keep?* Vlad thought as Henry drove the minivan back to Lakeside. *Are the Sanguinati, who can adapt to urban environments better than most forms, going to become separated from the rest of the Others? Or are we going to be the stronghold that maintains the bits of human the terra indigene want while the other forms take care of the land? There's a storm coming. We all know it, even if humans don't want to see it. No point worrying about what might be until we see what is left.*

Simon ran through the Courtyard. Ran and ran and ran. Talulah Falls wasn't his responsibility. If the *terra indigene* there wanted to yield to the Sanguinati and go home, that was their business, not his. In Lakeside, the Sanguinati and Wolves were complementary predators, and they were strong predators. They made an effort not to quarrel with one another. Okay, they had snarled at each other a bit about Meg, but they were both being protective because she was not only a friend; she was Namid's creation, both wondrous and terrible.

He stopped suddenly and spun around. In smoke form, the Sanguinati had no scent. They made no sound. But he'd sensed something in the dark.

<Are you running from something?> Vlad asked.

<Maybe I'm just running for the fun of it.>

<You move differently when you're having fun.>

Did he? Why hadn't he known that?

He settled into a trot until he came to one of the creeks. He swam to the other side, shook the water out of his fur, then shifted to human and sat on the bank. A moment later, Vlad flowed across the water, shifted, and joined him.

"Why didn't you tell me the Sanguinati were going to take over Talulah Falls?" Simon said.

"Until I felt confident that the *terra indigene* who were already there wanted to leave, I wasn't supposed to say anything." Vlad stared at the creek. "Sanguinati have ruled the Toland Courtyard since the first humans built houses on the land that became the city. We've seen Toland bloat around us, fill itself to bursting with humans. To abandon that Courtyard . . . It feels wrong. Like you would feel if all the Wolves were driven out of the Northwest and High North."

"But you didn't leave because of humans."

"No, but we won't be going back there."

Simon studied his friend. "It makes you sad."

"Yes. But I like it here, so the loss of Toland doesn't feel as sharp for me."

"Why Talulah Falls? Wouldn't Stavros prefer settling in Hubbney, where the region's government is located?"

"We're already strongly established in Hubbney. Many of the Toland Sanguinati will resettle there, but Stavros . . ."

"His being there would mean a fight for dominance."

"Not something we need at any time, but especially right now." Vlad smiled. "Besides, I think Grandfather is doing a little of what humans call matchmaking."

Simon blinked. Blinked again. "He's bringing Stavros here to find a mate? Who?" The second he asked, he knew. "Nyx. What does she think about that?"

Vlad shrugged. "Grandfather is providing an opportunity since Nyx has shown no interest in the males here."

"Maybe she doesn't want to mate yet."

Vlad laughed softly. "But it's good to be available when a female changes her mind."

Simon growled. "Are we talking about Nyx?"

"Of course."

"Meg has been very quiet since her visit to the Pony Barn this afternoon."

"Did Jester say why?"

"He was very quiet too."

"That's not good. The Coyote is rarely quiet when he knows something the rest of us don't."

"Henry picked up the Elders' scent on the outskirts of Talulah Falls and on the way home. He thinks they're just curious, just poking around."

"He would know better than I would," Vlad said.

"He thinks we'll be okay, and humans will be okay. He doesn't think the Elders are considering extinction anymore."

"You think he's wrong?"

"I think I'd like to know why Meg is so quiet." *And why she kept rubbing the right side of her jaw when she thought I wasn't looking.*

CHAPTER 27

Thaisday, Juin 21

J esse stocked the store shelves with canned soups, tomato sauce and tomato paste, and a variety of canned fruits and vegetables. In the back room, she had big plastic bins that were airtight and mouse-proof. One held five-pound bags of flour; another held bags of sugar, both white and brown; and the third held boxes of pasta that she couldn't fit on the shelves out front. The fourth she had filled with bags of rice and packages of egg noodles.

Hopefully the supplies would still be good when the people in Prairie Gold needed them.

Enough supplies to last until next spring, Tolya had told her after she'd mentioned her feeling that Prairie Gold might be denied access to other supplies, the same way the bookstore in Bennett had stopped her from buying new books for her store. *Food. Medicines. What females need when they come into season and become snappish.*

Somehow, having a vampire mention PMS and menses as part of the preparation checklist was more unnerving than having him push her to order food that could be cached for the coming months.

And not just food. Clothes too—everything from underwear and socks to jeans and T-shirts and sweaters and coats. Shoes. Boots. Anything that could be outgrown or worn out.

Something was coming. Everyone in Prairie Gold felt it. The *terra indigene* knew what they were preparing for, but they weren't sharing specifics.

More bison had been shot—someone's idea of malicious fun. The adult Wolves, especially those who were the hunters and guards, were away from their settlement, roaming to find the human culprits and put an end to this waste of food.

Food wasn't the only thing being wasted. Someone had poured gasoline down prairie dog holes and set them alight. The fire spread over acres of grassland, coming within yards of the settlement's food crops. Then the wind changed direction, blowing the fire back on itself, saving Prairie Gold's fresh food for the coming year.

She and Phil Mailer, the postmaster and editor of the *Prairie Gold Reporter,* had driven to Bennett to report the incident, but no one had seen anything. What was the law enforcement in Bennett supposed to do? The fire didn't happen in town or on any *human* land.

She had hoped she was wrong about preparing for isolation, but that isolation had already begun with frightening speed. The Intuits couldn't make purchases in any of the Bennett shops. You had to show your residence card in order to buy anything. When Truman Skye and Billy Rider, two men from Prairie Gold's ranch, had asked if that rule applied to people stopping overnight or visiting for a day or two, they were roughed up by a gang of men. After returning home, Truman had told Jesse and Phil—and Joe Wolfgard and Tolya Sanguinati—that the sheriff had been writing out a parking ticket within sight of the fight and didn't notice two men being attacked by eight. As it was, Truman and Billy escaped with a few scrapes, some bruised ribs, and a couple of black eyes because a tree in the town square uprooted suddenly and crushed the cab of a pickup parked on the street.

The rumor was that something had hooked its claws into the tree and ripped it out of the ground.

Warnings issued from both sides. At least that's how Jesse read that encounter—and Joe hadn't disagreed with her assessment even if he wouldn't confirm there was something besides Wolves and Wyatt Beargard watching the land between Bennett and Prairie Gold.

So, no merchandise available from the nearest town. Everything they needed had to come by train or truck now. Trouble was, they were buying far more than the town residents or businesses could afford, and they wouldn't have been buying much of anything if Tolya, as spokesman for his kin, wasn't loaning them the money.

No one had a *feeling* about borrowing money from the Sanguinati, but no one felt easy about it either. Still, it was either that or ignore the warnings that they needed to tuck in supplies.

Diapers and baby powder. Blankets and bed linens. Towels. Toothbrushes and toothpaste. Toilet paper. Gods! How was a shopkeeper supposed to make an estimate about something like that?

And where was she supposed to put all these supplies?

The bell on the door jingled. Jesse turned away from the shelves, glad to be distracted by a customer.

The girl looked to be about sixteen or seventeen. A stranger wearing one of the dresses Jesse knew had been in the window of the used-clothing store just last week. Sandals on her feet. Her hair was a light ash color and hung halfway down her back. Her eyes were amber, and the ears that suddenly poked out from beneath the hair were furry and not human-shaped.

A *Wolf*, Jesse thought, smiling as she moved slowly toward the girl. "Hello. I'm Jesse, the owner of this store. Can I help you find something?" She spotted Joe Wolfgard and a stranger—another Wolf?—standing outside talking to Tobias.

Chaperoned independence.

"What's your name?" Jesse asked.

"Rachel. I'd like a book?"

A statement phrased as a question. The girl wasn't really sure she was allowed to ask for such a thing.

"The books are over here." Jesse led Rachel to the shelves. "These two shelves are new books. New books usually cost more. These two shelves have used books." Jesse chose a paperback at random and handed it to Rachel.

Rachel studied the cover. Then she sniffed the book, made a face, and handed it back.

Interesting. She wanted to ask what the girl smelled on the book, but that would have to wait for the next visit.

"You can also borrow books from the library."

"Borrow means we can't keep it?"

"That's right. You read it and give it back to the library."

"We want a book to keep."

Jesse nodded. "A book for you?"

Rachel hesitated. "A book of stories for puppies? To read to the puppies? I can read pretty well."

This girl threw out lures to snag the curious.

Another time, Jesse promised herself as she studied the selection of children's books that she had available. "Well, I have a book of animal stories." When Rachel squatted beside her, she wanted to ask if the girl was wearing underpants beneath that summer dress, but that was a question that could cause embarrassment, especially if this was a first attempt at interacting with a human.

"We like animals," Rachel said.

"I don't know if the animals in these stories behave like the animals you know."

Rachel nodded. "Make-believe." She held the book. Sniffed the book. And didn't hand it back.

"Would you like to pick out a book for yourself?"

"I—" Rachel looked at the price sticker on the book of stories. "I don't have enough money to buy another book."

"I'll give you a book for yourself."

Rachel shook her head. "Supposed to buy it."

"Usually that is true. But today I would like to give you a book as a gift. As a way to say welcome."

"Oh." The girl looked at the shelves of books, her amber eyes filled with delight and confusion.

Bit by bit, Rachel told Jesse about the books she had read and which ones she liked the best. Finally, Jesse nudged Rachel toward an Intuit mystery writer who wrote a series of stories about a human who had a couple of *terra indigene* acquaintances who helped solve the mysteries. She wasn't sure if the portrayal of the Others was sufficiently accurate. She hadn't thought twice about that when she'd read some of the books.

Well, it will be interesting to read one again with what I know about the Others now—and see what Rachel thinks of the characters. Would any of the terra indigene *be interested in attending our monthly book club? Something to ask Joe Wolfgard.*

Jesse rang up the one book and watched through the window when Rachel left the store. The girl almost glowed with the triumph of a successful encounter. And turned shy when introduced to Tobias, who tipped his hat and did everything proper for an introduction.

As Tobias came into the store, Joe looked at Jesse through the window—and smiled.

We're going to be all right, Jesse thought as the Wolves headed in the direction of the *terra indigene* settlement. *If the Others accept us as friends, we'll be all right.*

To: NS

Troops are in position and are drawing unwanted attention. We must strike now or lose the element of surprise. Create the final distraction.

—Pater

To: NS

The special deliveries from Cel-Romano have arrived. Awaiting your instructions.

—HFL Leaders, Midwest and Northwest chapters

To: HFL Leaders, Midwest and Northwest chapters

Proceed with third stage of the land reclamation project.

—NS

CHAPTER 28

Firesday, Juin 22

H ope stared at the sheet full of drawings and felt her stomach roll.

No. No, no, no! She'd had a happy day yesterday sketching the Wolf pups and juveniles. She'd drawn her *friends* as they napped and played and chased one another. Why, today, had she drawn them looking like *this*?

She tore the page in half, then in half again, before shoving the pieces under her bed. This wasn't a vision drawing. It *wasn't*! Her friends were whole and healthy! They weren't missing limbs. They weren't trying to crawl away from danger with their heads bashed to pulp. They weren't lying in a field burned beyond recognition.

"It's a *bad* drawing." Hope sprang to her feet, intending to leave the cabin, to get away from the pencils and pastels and paper that told *lies*. "Won't be real. Can't be real."

She reached for the door but didn't touch the knob.

She hadn't seen the reason for these drawings. If it *was* a vision drawing, she still didn't know why the young Wolves might look like that. Would the next drawing give her the answers? Would it give Jackson and Grace what they needed to know in order to save the pack?

Turning away from the door, Hope settled on the floor with her large sketchpad and closed her eyes.

What is going to happen to the Wolves?

She opened her eyes and stared at the drawer in the desk, craving the euphoria that came from using the razor. Instead, she picked up a pencil and let the vision sweep her away as her hands drew the answer to her question.

CHAPTER 29

Firesday, Juin 22

Annoyed and oddly out of sorts, Meg gathered the prophecy cards that were scattered all over the sorting room floor. "Darn it, Sam," she muttered. "I *told* you these cards weren't playthings."

He'd been curious about them. Of course he was. Wolf pups were curious about everything. But she'd told him these cards were special. And she knew that Simon *and* Henry had talked to the pup, explaining that these special cards were tools for visions. Like the razor. Something potentially dangerous. Not something for pups to play with.

And now the cards felt odd, off, filmed in a way she couldn't explain.

She spread the cards over the surface of the big table, backs facing up. Each deck had a distinctive design on the back, so it would be easy enough to sort the cards into their proper decks. But she didn't try to restore order. Instead, she touched the cards, and as she shuffled them around the table, a suspicion rose in her.

Sam wouldn't play with something that belonged to her. But what about Lizzy, Sarah, and Robert? The back door of the Liaison's Office wasn't locked when she was working. Pete Denby had an office on the second floor, and Sarah and Robert sometimes played up there when Eve Denby needed some child-free time. And Lizzy spent a lot of time around the Market Square playing with Sarah and Robert.

Unlike the *terra indigene* young, who alternated between being interested in everything around them and napping to rest their little brains, human children quickly became bored with what they could have and whined to have the next thing they saw. At least, it sounded like they were always pestering their parents for "this," and if they couldn't have "this," then they wanted "that." If they'd been told they weren't supposed to do something, it seemed that was the very thing they just *had* to do.

And they had been told they couldn't play with the prophecy cards.

Maybe those things were normal for a human child. Having been raised in a compound where she had lived a very regimented life, she didn't have any experience with "normal" when it came to children. She couldn't tell the difference between youthful exuberance and misbehavior that would make the Others angry and cause trouble for all the humans. She'd made a mistake when Lizzy first came to the Courtyard, and the consequences of that had left her feeling anxious about everything the children did.

When she wasn't feeling so out of sorts, she would talk to Ruth, who had taught school, or Eve Denby, who was a mother, and get some guidelines so she would know when the anxiety justified a cut and when it should be dismissed as normal. She'd like to feel as easy around the children as she did around the Wolf pups, whose games were a lot more rough-and-tumble but didn't make her afraid.

Which brought her back to the prophecy cards someone had dropped on the floor.

Meg braced her hands on the table. Had she locked the door when she'd left for her midday break? Had Jenni, who had a key to the back door of the Liaison's Office, come in to pick up the mail for Sparkles and Junk and forgotten to lock the door on her way out? Had the children, bored with themselves and their available toys, tried the door and, finding it open, come inside to poke around? And finding the cards, had they decided to play a game, and then dropped the cards when they lost interest—or heard something that reminded them they weren't supposed to be in the Liaison's Office in the first place? Nathan would know. If she asked, he could sniff around the room and tell her exactly who had been there. But that would get the children in trouble.

Meg stared at the cards and realized two designs were missing. She rushed to the drawer where she'd kept the decks. The nature deck was still there in the back of the drawer. She pulled it out, removed the cards from their box, and shuffled them in with all the others scattered over the table.

Shuffled all of them in, including the cards with the drawings Jester had warned her to keep a secret.

After making a space at the top of the table, Meg closed her eyes and ran her hands lightly over the backs of the cards. Dozens of cards. Hundreds, maybe thousands, of combinations. Wasn't that always true with prophecy? Thousands of learned images and sounds and smells still came down to the particular images and sounds and smells that answered the question the blood prophet was expected to answer.

She didn't have a question, didn't know why she was fiddling with the cards instead of sorting them back into their decks and getting on with her work. She just felt odd today and made a decision to see what she might see.

Three sets of three, she thought as she selected cards based on the severity of the pins-and-needles feeling that stabbed her hands, her legs, her chest. *Three sets of three. Subject, action, result.*

She opened her eyes and flipped over the first set of three—and realized the prickling along the right side of her jaw increased as each card was revealed.

Bison. Rifle. Tombstone—a thing that still existed in some parts of Thaisia from a time when cremation wasn't required to conserve space in city burial grounds.

She flipped the next set of cards.

Wolf. Knife. Hooded figure with a scythe.

"No," she whispered as she turned over the last set.

City skyline. A montage of Elemental forces—tornado, tidal wave, fire. And the last card . . .

Put them in with the nature cards and hope you never see any of them again. That's what Jester had said. But there was one of those cards representing the result of something that was going to happen.

The prickling along her jaw became a buzz.

"Where?" Meg cried in frustration. "When? How will I know?"

"Arroo?" An idle, conversational query from Nathan, who was snoozing in the front room.

Her right hand buzzed. The index finger burned. Meg turned over the card beneath that finger.

A communication card—drawings of a telephone and a telegraph key.

Breathing hard, Meg looked at the phone on the counter.

"I'll get a call."

"*Arroo?*" No longer an idle query.

"It's nothing." Meg raised her voice enough to carry to Nathan. "I'm just talking to myself."

That would stall him for a minute, maybe two. Then the watch Wolf would come into the sorting room to have a look around.

The prickling faded in her hands, in her jaw.

Meg retrieved a notepad and pen and wrote down the three sets of cards in their proper order, and then added the communication card. She left the pad on the counter, facedown. Then she scooped up all the cards and dumped them in the drawer. She would ask Henry to make her a special box big enough to hold all the decks. A box with a lock. A lock with two keys. She would keep one. Who should hold the other? Simon? No, too easy to find a key if left at Howling Good Reads or his apartment. Henry or Tess?

Grandfather Erebus. Yes, the Sanguinati should hold the other key to the box.

There was no evidence of what anyone had been doing in the sorting room by the time Nathan leaped over the counter and came in to sniff around. A Wolf didn't need evidence. His growls made it clear that he knew exactly who shouldn't have been in the sorting room.

He trotted into the back room and returned a minute later in human form, wearing a T-shirt, denim shorts, and sandals—clothes he'd left in a bin in the storage area.

"I need to talk to Simon." Nathan gave her a hard stare. "Are you expecting any deliveries?"

"No." A message, yes, but not a delivery.

"Jake will keep watch and give warning if anyone comes in."

"Okay."

She waited. Winced when she heard HGR's back door slam. Then she braced her hands on the counter beneath the sorting room's open window and shouted, "Henry? Henry, I need to see you."

Not telling Nathan about the cards was one thing. But someone needed to know. And it had to be someone who could know about the *terra indigene* prophecy cards that were mixed in with make-believe images.

When Henry walked in, Meg picked up the notepad and hugged it to her chest. "I don't know what it means, but there's something you need to see."

_____

Gathered in HGR's office with Henry and Vlad, Simon stared at the paper with Meg's list of images. "We don't have any bison in the Courtyard—at least, not on the hoof." They'd killed the one yearling they kept and had packed every available freezer with bison meat, but there was no reason for Meg to see a vision about that. "And the *terra indigene* in Talulah Falls wouldn't use revolvers or rifles to kill the bison we gave them."

"Rifles," Henry said. "The bison are killed with rifles."

"There's a revolver on the card too."

"I don't think Meg saw the revolver. She wrote down 'rifle' because that's what she saw."

Vlad rubbed his chin. "Selective seeing when there is more than one object on a card? That's an interesting thought."

"But not one for immediate concern." Simon studied the list. "Wolves being attacked with knives? Not a smart thing for a human to do, especially if there is more than one Wolf."

"Rifle card was already used," Henry said. "Maybe Meg needed another human weapon. Rifle or knife, the result is the same. She saw death."

Simon looked at the last set of words and shivered. *How much human will the* terra indigene *keep?* He remembered the words the Elders had spoken, but it was Vlad who pointed to the list and said, "It looks like we've run out of time."

"We were out of time when the humans disregarded the significance of the Elders declaring a breach of trust and decided to cause more trouble," Henry rumbled.

"How did Meg know that card was supposed to be a *terra indigene* form?" Simon asked.

"Jester knew," Henry replied.

Which meant at some point in his life, the Coyote had actually seen one or more of the *terra indigene* who were Namid's teeth and claws.

"He separated the forms from the make-believe creatures and told Meg she shouldn't send that deck to other blood prophets," Henry continued. "The Jesse Walker already has that deck, but only Meg knows that not all the images are make-believe."

Simon handed the sheet of paper to Henry. "We don't know when it will happen."

Henry folded the paper until it fit in the back pocket of his jeans. "Meg will receive a phone call, and that will be the battle cry. At least for us."

Simon felt grief already clogging his throat. "Some of us are going to die. If the Elders have made their decision, why are they going to hold back until some of us die?"

"I don't think shifters like us are that important to the Elders," Henry replied. "But even if we do matter to them, maybe they have to wait for something to be set in motion before they act, even if waiting means watching some of us die."

CHAPTER 30

Firesday, Juin 22

Hope dropped the gray crayon, horrified by the drawing. She leaped up then half fell on the bed when her feet, asleep from being tucked under her for so long, couldn't hold her. She felt warm liquid run down her legs, barely understanding that she'd wet herself.

Shaking, sobbing, too scared to call for help—too scared that no one would answer—she forced herself to look at the drawing again.

More than death. A horror that would never be forgotten.

She looked closer. She didn't know that face. He didn't live in Sweetwater. Had she drawn that face before? She couldn't remember.

Fear grew inside her, its sharp edges slicing through her ability to think.

Had to find Jackson and Grace. Had to run, escape, hide. Had to tell . . .

A face in the corner of the paper, apart from the rest of the drawing.

. . . the Trailblazer.

Hope pushed to her feet. She could run fast now. She could run to the communications cabin and call the Trailblazer. She remembered the number. She would call because the danger would strike somewhere else before it came to Sweetwater. So she would call, and then she would find her friends and they would run and hide.

She stumbled out of the Wolfgard cabin, almost fell down the steps.

Caw!

One of the Ravengard, watching her.

No time to explain. Not until she had sent the warning.

Hope dashed between the cabins that made up the *terra indigene* settlement until she reached the dirt road. Then she ran as fast as she could to the communications cabin, chased by the image of a drawing full of death.

Joe Wolfgard scratched on Tolya's motel room door, then turned away and listened to the howl of Wolves in the distance.

The Song of Battle.

<What's wrong?> he demanded.

<Humans!> came the answer. <They're shooting our bison again! They're killing our meat!>

<Wait! They can shoot you too!>

But the pack's hunters and guards, enraged by more wanton slaughter, didn't listen.

Tolya opened the door. "Joe?"

<Humans are killing bison again.>

"In daylight? When we can recognize them?" Suspicion in Tolya's voice.

The humans had been careful so far. They had stayed inside vehicles so the Wolves couldn't pick up their scents. But Tolya was right—humans wouldn't reveal themselves unless they were doing something else that was sneaky.

<I have to stop the pack.>

"Go. I'll keep an eye on the humans here."

Joe raced in the direction of the pack and wondered if he had missed some new sign that humans were turning rabid.

CHAPTER 31

Firesday, Juin 22

Hearing Nathan's growl and Jake's scolding *caws*, Meg rushed to the front counter to find out what was wrong. Then her mouth fell open as she stared at Robert, Sarah, and Lizzy playing with a large ball *in the delivery area*—a place where a large delivery truck, pulling in fast, could hit them. A place that was not a playground. They *knew* that.

"Robert!" Lizzy shouted. "Grr Bear says we're not supposed to play out here! We're supposed to play out back!"

Meg gasped and grabbed the counter as a painful buzz filled her abdomen and lower back. When she heard the creak of someone moving around upstairs, the buzz faded as quickly as it began, leaving an echo of pain.

"Grr Bear is a poophead!" Robert threw the ball at Lizzy, who swung Grr Bear like a bat and managed to connect with the ball, sending it in a high arc.

"Robert!" Pete Denby shouted from an upstairs window.

Robert froze for a moment at the sound of his father's voice. Then, seeing the ball arcing over his head, he turned to run after it.

Pain. Abdomen, back, legs. Remembering training images of people injured in car accidents, Meg's vision grayed, and she screamed, "Nathan, stop him! *Stop him!*"

Footsteps pounded overhead as Nathan hurled himself out the door and caught Robert when the boy was just two steps away from the street—and brought him down in a way that guaranteed skinned elbows and knees. Then Pete Denby was there too, and the girls were crying because Pete was angry and Nathan was snarling . . . and the phone kept ringing and ringing.

The pain in Meg's body faded again, leaving her feeling weak, but the skin along the right side of her jaw began to burn.

Focused on Pete and Nathan squaring off, she grabbed the receiver and said, "What?"

"Meg?"

The voice shook so much she wasn't sure she recognized it. "Hope?"

"Meg . . . run . . . hide. Death."

"Hope, what . . . ?"

"*Run!*"

"Hope? Hope!"

The girl wasn't there anymore. Meg listened to the dial tone, then dropped the receiver back into the cradle. She rushed into the sorting room and locked the Private door.

Whatever vision she might have seen about Robert . . . That was done. She still felt weak and sick, but there was no prickle or buzz in her lower body. The pain was along her jaw now—the spot where she had dreamed of making a cut.

Run. Hope's screamed command burned under her skin. But run from what? The cards hadn't supplied the answer.

Meg opened her silver razor, laid the blade against the right side of her jaw, and made a long cut. Setting aside the razor, she braced her hands on the table and swallowed the agony as well as the words in order to see this prophecy.

Images piled up like a stack of photographs being seen so fast she could barely understand. Wolves. Blood. Death. That was common in all the images. But the land . . . Similar places but not the *same* places. A sea of grass. Cabins built near mountains. More places that became a backdrop for death. So many more.

For a heartbeat, she saw Simon at the Wolfgard Complex, one side of his face covered in blood. Then she saw . . . she saw . . .

Turning away from the table, Meg bent over and vomited on the floor.

Run. Hide the pack.

"Sam," she whispered.

Turning away from the mess, she spotted the phone on the counter. She had seen . . . She knew that face.

The address book, recently purchased at the Three Ps, sat beside the phone. Meg flipped to the W section and called the number.

"Walker's General Store. Jesse speaking."

She forced the words out. "This is Meg Corbyn."

"Meg?"

If she didn't get out of there soon, something inside her would break. Still she struggled to lay out the images in a way that Jesse Walker would understand. "Bison. Rifle. Death. Wolves. Trap. Death. Bodies. Bodies. Joe's face. Fire, fire, fire."

"Meg?" Alarmed now.

The images swam in front of her eyes, too horrible to bear. "Run. Hide the puppies. Hide the children. Run. *Run!*"

Fear spurred her, and Meg followed her own warning. She snatched the BOW's key out of her purse and ran out the back door, colliding with Vlad but unable to stop, unable to speak. She flung open the garage door, leaped into her BOW, and barely missed running over Simon as she backed out.

"Meg!" Simon yelled.

She looked at him, trying to find words, and could find only one. "Run!"

She stomped on the power pedal, careened around the corner, and headed for the Wolfgard Complex as fast as the little vehicle could go.

CHAPTER 32

Firesday, Juin 22

Jesse Walker ran into the middle of Prairie Gold's main street and screamed, a sound that was part fear, part battle cry. People working in nearby stores ran out, but it wasn't humans who could help her now.

Hearing *caws*, she looked up and spotted several Ravens circling above her. And when she looked toward the other end of town, she saw smoke rushing toward her.

"Meg Corbyn says the Wolves are heading into a trap! Sound the alarm! Stop them!"

The Ravens flew away. The smoke continued to rush toward her. Just before it reached her, it rose into a column and shifted into human form.

"Did Meg say anything else?" Tolya asked.

"She saw Joe's face. She said . . ." Jesse swallowed hard. "She said 'bodies' twice and 'fire' three times. She said to hide the puppies and children."

"Joe made a special arrangement with . . . Well, that doesn't matter. What matters is there is a hiding place in the hills above the *terra indigene* village. Did he tell you?"

"Yes."

"Then grab only what you need and take the females and all the young to that place."

"But—"

"Do it, Jesse Walker. Neither of us has time for words now." Tolya shifted to smoke and raced toward the open land beyond the town.

Neither of us has time. Gods above and below.

"Jesse?" Phil Mailer started walking toward her.

She shook her head. "Ring the alarm bell. We have to get out of here." She ran back into her store and stared at the two wire crates on the counter that were already filled with jars of peanut butter, boxes of cereal, chocolate bars, cans of fruit. For the past hour, she'd been feeling uneasy without knowing why, had started packing emergency supplies for something to do.

"What's going on?" Shelley Bookman asked, running into the store.

Jesse shoved an empty crate into Shelley's hands. "Bottles of juice. Anything else that might quickly feed children. Get moving!" She dropped a box of flatware into one of her crates and two loaves of bread into the other. Rushing to the display of kitchen utensils, she grabbed a can opener and tossed that in the crate.

"Should I put in some cans of soup?" Shelley asked.

"Nothing we need to cook or heat in order to eat," Jesse snapped in reply. She set her full crates by the door, then went into the back room and returned with a daypack, her rifle, and two boxes of ammunition.

Shelley's eyes widened. "Jesse?"

"You got that crate filled? Then go grab your purse and be back here in five minutes. I mean it, Shelley. Five minutes. Then we head out."

"Head out where?"

"Clock's ticking." *Hide the puppies. Hide the children.* The words were a whip that wouldn't relent until she obeyed.

The alarm bell stopped ringing. Jesse walked to the middle of the street and looked at the people who were waiting for an explanation. "We have to evacuate. A *cassandra sangue* called me to give warning." *And I don't know what it cost Meg Corbyn to give that warning.*

"What's the warning, Jesse?" Phil Mailer asked.

"Death. Traps. Fire. It's coming for us." *Maybe already found some of us.*

Couldn't think about that.

Billy Rider had taken a wagon and team of horses from the livery stable and drove up to the general store. "Tried to get hold of Tobias," he told Jesse. "Tom Garcia said some kind of miniature twister tore up a bit of fence and spooked the horses, so the men are out rounding them up. I told him about the alarm. He said he's staying at the ranch, but he'll be on the lookout for trouble and will ring the bell there if he sees anything. Ellen Garcia is driving in to meet up with you. She'll bring her kids and any *terra indigene* youngsters she spots on the way."

Wasn't likely that Ellen would find many *terra indigene* youngsters that far from their settlement without any adults nearby, but every warning was better than none.

Prairie Gold's small bus and the minivan that served as a taxi pulled up.

"Stop dawdling and get on the damn bus," Jesse snapped at Shelley and Abigail Burch. "We have got to *move*." She pointed at the taxi. "Swing around that end of town and pick up whoever you can. The bus will head toward the hills and pick up the folks at that end."

Phil Mailer stepped in front of her. "Who else can I contact? I'll send out messages until the wires go down. You've had the most experience with the *terra indigene*, so you need to go. But some of us are going to stay. This is our town, our home. These buildings are packed to the rafters with supplies that we need to see us through the next year. I'm not letting some yahoos burn us out."

Murmurs of agreement from other men.

"Go on now, Jesse. Go and do what you can for all of us."

Nothing to say to that, so she climbed onto the wagon seat beside Billy Rider and led the women and children into the hills—and wondered if there would be anything left when they returned.

Joe howled, then waited for a response. He howled again. <Answer me! I am leader of this pack!>

He heard the Song of Battle and ran in that direction.

<Joe! Stop!>

Joe slowed to a trot. <Tolya?>

<It's a trap! Meg Corbyn saw and called Jesse Walker. It's a trap for the pack.>

His ribs tightened and he struggled to breathe. <Why would Meg see prophecy about us?>

<Does it matter why? She sent the warning. Joe, come back. Jesse Walker is going to take all the young to the hiding place you arranged in the hills. The town is in danger too. You need to come back.>

<I have to stop the pack before the bad happens. You take care of the town. Send on the warning to whoever you can.>

Having made his choice, Joe ran hard and fast to find the pack before the humans sprang the trap.

CHAPTER 33

Firesday, Juin 22

Vlad rushed into the sorting room, then stopped when he caught the stink of vomit that almost overwhelmed the scent of Meg's blood.

"What . . . ?" Simon stopped beside him. "Nathan heard a phone ringing just after he stopped the Robert from running into the street. Jake heard it too."

Vlad stared at the razor on the table. "Go after Meg. I'll try to find out who called."

"She didn't speak." Simon wrinkled his nose and took a step away from the vomit. "She saw the visions."

"She's scared sick. You have to find her before she gets hurt."

Simon pulled off his clothes and tossed them aside. Then he shifted to Wolf and ran out of the Liaison's Office.

Vlad pulled a section of newspaper out of the recycling crate and dropped it over the vomit. He would clean up the mess later. Right now, they needed answers.

As he reached for the telephone, Pete Denby stormed into the room.

"Gods above and below! I know they were playing where they weren't supposed to, but they're just kids, and I was coming down to deal with it. Did Nathan have to throw Robert to the ground like that? The kids are terrified."

"The next time we won't stop your pup from running into the street," Vlad snapped. "Don't leave your young by themselves until they've learned to avoid the things that will kill them."

Pete drew in a breath, then made a face. In that moment, Vlad saw the man replace the father.

"What happened?"

"Don't know yet, but Meg is running scared. Is there a way to find out who called her, or is that something only the police can do?"

"There's a way unless she placed a call afterward. Then you would need the police to get records from the telephone company." Pete joined Vlad at the counter and pointed to a small button beneath the others on the phone. "I would try 'redial' first and see what you get."

He pushed the button and listened to the phone ring and ring and ring.

"Walker's General Store."

A beat of silence before Vlad said, "Tolya?"

"Did Meg Corbyn say anything else?"

A chill went through Vlad. "She's not saying anything at the moment."

"The Wolves are running into a trap. Joe Wolfgard is trying to stop them. The town is preparing for attack. Jesse Walker is taking all the youngsters to a hiding place in the Elder Hills."

"Who is with you?"

"The men in the town. Vlad, are the humans going after all the Wolves? Or are they after all of us?"

"I don't know. Do what you can, Tolya, and I'll do the same." He hung up.

"Bad?" Pete asked.

"Very." He opened Meg's address book, found the number for Sweetwater, and dialed.

"What?" A male voice, already stirred up and angry.

"This is Vlad Sanguinati at the Lakeside Courtyard. Can you get a message to Jackson Wolfgard? It's urgent."

"Lakeside? Has your prophet pup gone crazy too? Jackson's pup ran in here all pee-stinky, called someone, and then ran away yelling that they had to hide. Some of the Ravengard are following her to make sure she gets back to the Wolfgard den."

"Tell Jackson that the *terra indigene* and the Intuits are in danger. The other kind of humans have turned on us."

"I— I'll tell him."

Vlad hung up and looked at Pete, who was sickly pale. "Where are your off-spring?"

"Lorne from the Three Ps came out to help. He took them to the medical office."

"The Lizzy too?"

Pete nodded.

"Keep them there until I say otherwise."

Vlad left the Liaison's Office, turned to smoke, and raced off in the direction of the Wolfgard Complex.

Skidding to a stop in front of the Wolfgard Complex, Meg flung herself out of the BOW and screamed, "Sam! *Sam!*"

He ran to greet her, followed by the other puppies and Skippy.

Meg opened the back of the BOW. "Get inside, Sam. Get inside. We have to run. We have to hide."

He jumped into the BOW and immediately went to the passenger seat. The other pups hesitated, sensing something wrong in her behavior.

"Skippy. Come on," Meg panted. As soon as he jumped in the back, she grabbed a pup and tossed her into the BOW. Then another and another and the last one.

"Meg?" Jane, the Wolfgard bodywalker, hurried toward her in human form while the pack's nanny rushed toward her, snarling. "Meg, what are you doing?"

"We have to run!" Meg screamed. She closed the BOW's back door.

"You're bleeding."

"*We have to hide.*" She fell into the driver's seat, started the BOW, and shot away from the Wolfgard Complex. Sam whined and Skippy *arrooed*, which started the rest of the pups howling.

"Quiet! We have to be quiet!" Where to go? Where could they hide from an enemy who could do . . .

Meg swallowed hard and drove blindly and recklessly along the dirt trails that were barely wide enough for even a vehicle as small as the BOW. She glanced in the side mirror once and saw Wolves chasing the BOW. But not the Wolf she needed to see.

"Simon," she whispered.

Then the trail ended at a dip in the land. She drove the BOW into the dip, bouncing on the way down. Flinging the driver's side door open, she tumbled out of the BOW and ran to the back to open that door. As the rest of the pups and Skippy leaped out of the back, she grabbed Sam, who was more than a double armful now, and staggered a few steps away from the BOW.

Shaking, she sank to the ground and held on to him. Had to hide because she'd seen . . .

Her stomach rose, and she threw up over both of them.

Simon sniffed around the Wolfgard Complex. Where was Meg? Where were the other Wolves?

<The pack went this way,> Nathan said. <And Meg. Simon . . . she's still bleeding. There are drops of blood on the road.>

<Uncle Simon! *Uncle Simon!*>

<Sam!>

<Help! Meg is sick!>

Simon lifted his muzzle, intending to howl. If the other Wolves had followed Meg, their reply would help him pinpoint where she was in the Courtyard. But he stopped before the sound rose. Why were the other Wolves silent? Why wasn't Sam howling?

He and Nathan followed the road, running toward the Hawkgard part of the Courtyard. They had to find Meg. There weren't *that* many roads in the Courtyard that could accommodate a vehicle, even one as small as a BOW.

<Over here!> Jenni Crowgard flew toward him. <Our Meg is over here!>

<There's no road over there, just a wide trail the ponies and deer use,> Nathan said.

Jenni flew over their heads, back the way she'd come.

When he reached the spot, he raced down the incline. How had Meg gotten the BOW down there? And how were they going to get it out?

<Meg!> He slowed down to avoid stepping on the pups who were sufficiently scared now that they wouldn't move far enough away from Meg to receive protection from Jane or the nanny. The rest of the adult Wolves remained on the incline in a protective circle, with Blair and Nathan at the top keeping watch.

Sam gave him a pathetic look. <Meg *puked* on me!>

<She's sick, pup. She's really sick.>

The cut along her jaw was starting to clot, but her neck was streaked with blood and her shirt reeked of vomit, erasing the usual lure of her blood's scent.

Pretty sure that she was too sick to be confused about him being naked, Simon shifted to human and crouched beside her. "Meg? What did you see?"

"We have to hide. Have to hide from . . ." She retched. Sam whined. The other pups backed away, finally seeking protection from the adult Wolves.

"Who has to hide?" Simon asked.

"We do. The Wolves." She focused on him. Her eyes looked weird—too big, too black instead of gray. "Joe's face looks like that."

Like what? Simon wondered. Before he could ask Vlad was beside him, reaching past him to wrap a hand around Meg's arm.

<You're between forms,> Vlad said. Then to Meg, "Did you see anything about the rest of us? Meg? Do the rest of us need to hide or just the Wolves?"

She stared at Vlad with eyes so blank Simon wondered if something had broken inside her brain.

"Just . . . Wolves," she finally said. "And people living in little wood houses." A pause. "Cabins. Fire. Burning."

"Okay." Vlad gave her arm a gentle squeeze before releasing it. "The Wolves will hide with you until it's safe. The rest of us will send the warning to as many packs as we can."

Simon looked at Vlad. <Jackson?>

<His prophet pup is scared sick and running, just like Meg,> Vlad replied grimly. <Both of them, in different parts of the continent. This is not good, Simon.>

Joe's face looks like that. <Joe?>

<The warning was sent. I don't know if it will be in time.> Vlad rose, his legs already shifted to smoke. <Stay here. The rest of us will do what we can. It's not just the Wolves. The attack is also aimed at the Intuits.>

Everything he and the rest of the *terra indigene* in Lakeside had tried to do by working with humans was breaking apart. How far was it going to break?

He shifted back to Wolf form, instinctively understanding that it would calm Meg.

<Simon,> Vlad said.

<Go. Do what you can. Warn Steve Ferryman.>

<I'll do that first. He'll get the warning out to other Intuit settlements within

reach of the bad humans.> The Sanguinati shifted all the way to smoke and raced over the ground.

<More Sanguinati going with Vlad,> Blair reported.

<We will help you keep watch over our Meg,> Jenni said as she, Starr, and Jake perched in the nearby trees.

<Uncle Simon?> Sam whimpered. <I don't wanna lick my fur clean.>

He didn't want to lick the pup either. <As soon as it's safe, we'll get you and Meg cleaned up.> And they would need to wash any of the other pups who were splattered with puke. For now, there was nothing any of the Wolves could do.

Resisting the temptation to lick her neck clean of dried blood and ignoring the bad scent of vomit, Simon rested his head on Meg's shoulder, offering silent comfort—and trying not to think too much about what was happening to the Wolfgard in other parts of Thaisia.

CHAPTER 34

Firesday, Juin 22

Jackson trotted back to the Wolfgard cabin. While troubling, the meeting with the Panthergard had gone well. Only one of the Cats now living in the Sweetwater area had gone through the first level of a human-centric education—enough to read, write, and do sums, as well as speak with humans and make a purchase at a trading post.

Enough education to distinguish between normal human activity like farming and tending animals and activity that felt . . . wrong.

Nothing suspicious around Sweetwater's Intuit village, but that wasn't true about Endurance, the closest human village. Something wasn't right there. Something had changed. But it was like trying to hook your claws into air, hoping to catch hold of the problem and deal with it.

<Jackson! Jackson!> one of the Ravens called. <Your pup is strange sick.>

He ran toward the cabin, momentarily relieved when he spotted Grace. Then Hope burst into view looking as terrified as a fawn being run down by a Grizzly.

"We have to hide!" Hope screamed. She ran past Grace, grabbing at the pups who had run to greet her. "We have to hide!"

"Hope?" Grace said, her white hair gleaming in the sun.

Jolting to a stop, Hope looked at Grace. "Fire. Death. *We have to hide!*" She ran toward the creek and the pups ran after her.

<Go with her,> Jackson told Grace. <I'll check the cabin.>

Grace pulled off her clothes, shifted to Wolf, and ran after the girl with the pack's nanny and the juvenile Wolves following.

Jackson rushed into Hope's room in the Wolfgard cabin. Where had the girl been? She wasn't supposed to go out of sight of the cabin without telling an adult Wolf.

He stopped at the smell. Wasn't Hope a little old to be piddling on the floor?

Spotting the scatter of pencils and crayons, he moved cautiously around the bed—and smelled a hint of blood that was almost overwhelmed by the scent of urine.

He came farther into the room, moving his feet with care to avoid stepping on Hope's drawing supplies. When he lowered his head to sniff the floor for the blood smell, he spotted the drawings under her bed. He pulled out the intact drawing and then the pieces—and snarled.

All the pups and juvenile Wolves in the Sweetwater pack. Dead. Mutilated. No wonder Hope wanted them to hide!

Then he looked at the intact drawing. Meg Corbyn's face in one corner. A hilltop view of the Intuit village at Sweetwater, all the buildings on fire. And filling the center of the paper . . .

He wasn't sure what he was seeing. It was like the drawing she did of the mound of bison except . . .

Joe.

Jackson tore out of the cabin and ran as if everything in his world depended on his speed . . . because, at that moment, it did.

<Help!> he called.

<Wolf? Wolf?> Replies from the Ravengard, Hawkgard, Eaglegard.

<The Intuits are going to be attacked. *We're* going to be attacked. Watch the road. Give warning if any humans head our way.>

<Jackson?> That was Grace.

<Hide the pups! Warn the Wolves. Get away from the settlement!>

<Where are you?>

<Have to warn . . . > Who? How many?

Reaching the communications cabin, he flung himself inside, shifting to human as he walked to the table that held the telephone and the computer.

"Jackson?" The Hawk minding the cabin stared at him.

Jackson stared back, then picked up the phone and called the number he had for Prairie Gold. Getting a busy signal, he hung up and called Howling Good Reads. No answer.

As he stood there, he smelled Hope and urine.

"The Hope pup was here?"

The Hawk nodded. "She used the telephone. She said 'Meg, run, hide, death,' and then she ran away."

Jackson wrote a phone number on the pad of paper next to the phone. "Call this number. Keep trying until someone answers. Tell whoever answers, even if it's a human, that the Wolves have to hide. They have to hide or they're going to die."

"Where are you going?"

"To warn the Intuits. Hope saw their village burning."

Shifting back to Wolf, Jackson raced down the road. It wasn't just Intuits who needed help in that village. There were the four surviving prophet pups living there too.

CHAPTER 35

Firesday, Juin 22

Joe pushed for all the speed he had. <Wolves! Wait!>

<They're killing our meat!>

Too angry. Not listening. He'd been chosen as leader of the *terra indigene* settlement because of his contact with Simon and the Lakeside Courtyard, because they needed someone now to actively deal with the Prairie Gold humans. But being the leader of the settlement wasn't the same as being the dominant Wolf. The pack had just proved that by ignoring his command. <The sweet blood says it's a trap!>

That slowed the other Wolves who had been racing toward men so focused on shooting bison that they didn't seem to notice the angry Wolves bearing down on them.

<Sweet blood?> The pack's dominant enforcer slowed to a trot.

<Simon's prophet, Meg, called Jesse Walker to warn us that this is a trap.>

More Wolves slowed down. The hunters among them were more reluctant to let the humans continue killing the meat the pack would need, but the enforcers, who had the job of protecting the pack, turned away from the humans standing in the beds of the pickup trucks and headed toward Joe.

Then they stopped, took a step back. Like them, Joe felt the thunder that meant only one thing: bison stampede.

Gunshots and shouts behind him. Behind the bison. Humans were driving the bison toward the pickup trucks, and the Wolves were caught in between.

<Run!> Joe shouted. The Wolves turned and ran toward the trucks and the bison that were already dead. Big bodies. Pressed against the belly, a Wolf might escape being shot—might escape being trampled. They had no chance in the open.

They ran toward the trucks and the men. Had to reach the dead bison before . . .

The men stopped shooting. Moving swiftly, a man lowered the tailgate of one of the pickup trucks while another man pulled a tarp off something that looked like a heavy rifle mounted on three legs. What . . . ?

The hunters, who were at the head of the pack, were the first to fall as the heavy rifle spit bullets that thudded into bodies too fast for the Wolves to change direction. And behind them, the bison thundered closer and closer, driven by other humans.

Now some of the men raised their rifles toward the sky, aiming for the Ravens and Hawks.

<Get away!> Joe yelled at the Ravens and Hawks. <Warn—> He felt the thud, thud, thud. His front legs slipped and he tumbled. Had to get away from the stampeding bison. Had to . . .

He got his hind legs under him and tried to leap, gain some distance between him and those hooves.

More thud, thud, thud that hit a hind leg and his side.

He tumbled again, one of his hind legs now useless. Still struggling to move, he managed to crawl until he was partially hidden by one of the dead bison.

So hard to breathe. So hard to . . .

He didn't really feel the hooves as bison trampled his back legs. He barely heard the triumphant shouts of the humans or the gunfire that turned the bison away from the trucks.

He didn't notice the silence.

How had Meg, so far away in Lakeside, known this was a trap? What would she have seen?

Could barely hear. Could barely breathe.

"This one's still alive."

"Not for long. Throw the carcass in with the rest."

Being dragged by his forelegs. Then lifted and tossed.

What had Meg seen? How had she known one Wolf from another?

She had seen me in Lakeside. She would remember my face.

Couldn't shift all the way to human. He didn't have the strength for that. But if Simon and Jackson saw him somehow, if *Meg* saw him now, they would know, would be . . . warned, could . . . escape other traps.

He made strange sounds as he tried to breathe, tried to change from Wolf to human form. He saw his hand, mostly human now at the end of a furry foreleg. He felt his face changing.

He felt a blow to the back of his head.

"Do you want us to pull this one off the pile, boss?" a man asked. "His face is halfway humanlooking."

Daniel Black glanced at the body of the last Wolf thrown on the heap of carcasses. "Leave him. That's proof we eliminated the enemy and not just a few dumb animals." He stepped away from the pile of dead Wolves and held out a hand. "Give me that camera. I'll take a couple of pictures of you boys standing up for humans everywhere."

They gathered on either side of the mound, rifles raised in triumph while Black took the pictures. He wouldn't be the only man making a record of this historic day. Men from dozens of HFL chapters throughout the Midwest and Northwest had participated in the third stage of the land reclamation project.

He wouldn't be the only man who sent one or two photos to the newspaper. But, by the gods, he and his men would be among those best rewarded for this day's work.

"Now," Black said, looking in the direction of the hills and the town called Prairie Gold. "Let's finish this and claim what should have been ours all along."

As he and his men headed back to their trucks, he didn't notice the absence of all birds—and he didn't notice the silence.

Nothing he could have done against a bison stampede, Tolya thought bitterly as he raced above the grass. He could have slowed one animal, or caught and killed one of the riders driving the animals. But that wouldn't have saved the Wolves. All he could do now was return to Prairie Gold and do whatever he could to help the Intuits save the town.

Wind stirred the grass. A shimmer of heat appeared just ahead of him. He rose to a column of smoke before shifting to human.

Two of the Elementals who watched over this piece of Thaisia took form in front of him. Air and Fire sat astride two of their steeds—one white, one brown.

Was there something the Elementals could have done to stop this? Pointless to ask. Dangerous even for a Sanguinati to say anything that might sound like an accusation.

And maybe the Elementals were never meant to *stop* this fight between Others and humans any more than they were meant to interfere with any two predators who were fighting over the same territory. But the Elementals at Lakeside had helped Simon. Elementals in another part of the Midwest had helped destroy the Controller and the terrible place where he had caged some of the sweet blood. Maybe the Elementals here *would* work with him now. After all, Air had helped Joe when he shipped the bison meat to Simon.

"The humans," Tolya said. "They're going to burn down the Intuits' town. They're going to try to kill all the young Jesse Walker is taking into the hills for protection."

"How do you know this?" Fire finally asked.

"Meg Corbyn spoke prophecy and warned Jesse Walker."

"Broomstick Girl?"

So Charlie Crowgard's song about Meg defending a Wolf had reached this far west. "Yes. Meg, the Trailblazer. Friend to the *terra indigene* in Lakeside."

"Our eastern kin know her," Air said. "She saved the ponies who live in the Lakeside Courtyard."

Tolya nodded. Then he waited.

Air looked up as some of the Ravengard flew by. "The humans who killed the Wolves. The Ravens say some are from the town and some . . ." She looked at Fire and smiled. "How many bison died?"

Fire just returned her smile.

Something about those smiles gave Tolya a sudden understanding of why the Elementals shouldn't be encouraged to become too involved in the lives of beings who were more anchored to flesh than their form of *terra indigene*.

Air and Fire said nothing as they turned their steeds toward the ranches that lay between the Intuit town of Prairie Gold and the human town of Bennett.

Shifting back to smoke, Tolya continued on to Prairie Gold. As he reached the truck stop at the edge of town, he saw a bolt of lightning strike the ground in the north and judged that it had hit something near the crossroads.

He kept going until he reached Walker's General Store. Men hurried over to meet him as soon as he shifted to human form.

"They're dead," he said. "The Wolves are dead."

"Ah, damn," Floyd Tanner said softly, sorrowfully. "Even Joe?"

Tolya nodded. He wouldn't tell these men how the Wolves died. Not yet.

"We're sorry for your loss," Kelley Burch said after a moment's silence. "We all liked Joe."

"He was a good leader," Tolya said. *And maybe, in the same way that Simon Wolfgard is with Vlad, he could have been a good friend.*

He didn't appreciate how much the loss saddened these humans until he saw the change in their faces and bodies and realized that they were, for now, setting aside grief.

Phil Mailer cleared his throat. "I guess we'd better prepare for the rest of the prophecy. I've warned every Intuit village or settlement I could. Got a response from Steve Ferryman at Ferryman's Landing. He's sending out the alarm too. He didn't have the feeling that all Intuit places would be in danger. A lot of our settlements are too deep in the wild country to be reached easily by other humans. But he also felt that the farther the warning could be spread, the less likely one of our villages would be caught unawares."

Tolya nodded. Then he looked north and pointed. "I don't think we're the ones who will have to worry about fire."

The fire funnel raced over the land, and everything burned in its wake. Wind whipped the flames that consumed fence posts and grass—and cattle—as the funnel headed for the ranch buildings still in the distance.

As they neared the crossroads, Daniel Black saw lightning strike the lead pickup's cab with a marksman's accuracy as a sudden gust of wind hit the pickup with enough force to shove it off the road.

The other trucks pulled over and men ran to help their comrades.

Black stepped out of his pickup. "They hurt?" he called to the men.

They backed away from the lead pickup.

"They're dead." One of the men, who had looked so triumphant a short while ago, looked frightened now.

Shouldn't be dead. Rubber tires. Grounding. That was supposed to protect a person in a lightning storm, wasn't it? How could his men be dead?

Then Black saw the funnel that appeared out of nowhere, and felt the first shiver of fear.

"By all the dark gods," he whispered.

"Boss?"

He looked at his foreman. Then he reached into his truck, pulled out the camera, and handed it to the man. "Tell the sheriff about this. Get someone out here to deal with . . . the men. Then get those pictures to the newspaper. You got that?" He waited until the foreman pulled away with reckless speed before turning to the rest of his men. "Come with me. We have to get to the ranch ahead of that thing and save what we can."

The men looked at the funnel, then at him.

"Move!" Black scrambled into the pickup. The men piled into the cab and into the bed, their only choice if they didn't want to be left behind.

He put the truck in gear. Then he hesitated. They couldn't outrun that twister. He wouldn't get to the ranch house in time. He should go the other way and finish his assignment, burn out that town of freaks.

"What the fuck . . . ?" one of his men shouted moments before hail the size of his fist struck the pickup, hammering metal and glass. The windshield cracked. His men riding in the pickup's bed cried out in pain as they tried to shield themselves.

A warm day in summer. No storm clouds. No clouds of any kind. And yet there was that damn funnel heading toward everything he'd built, and now *this* storm.

He looked at his side mirror and thought he saw a horse and rider racing toward him, taking no notice of the punishing hail. As they passed his truck, he saw a shape so shrouded by the storm he wasn't sure if he'd just imagined seeing figures. And yet the storm turned with no rational explanation and headed for the freaks' town, filling the road with hail. Then it slowed, stopped moving.

Waited.

If he headed for Prairie Gold, his men might be exposed to that storm the whole way and would be injured and useless by the time they reached the town. Of course, if they got caught by the twister or the fire, they wouldn't be much good either. But at least they'd be trying to save something.

Black headed for his ranch.

Jesse followed a wide game trail. By the time her people had reached the *terra indigene* settlement, the Ravens and Hawks had already spread the news about the humans killing the Wolves. Surprisingly, the adults in the settlement had no objection to her taking the Wolfgard young with her to the hiding place Joe Wolfgard had arranged. In fact, *all* the young from the settlement were with her. Fledglings from the Owl, Raven, Hawk, and Eagle gards were riding on human shoulders or on the backs of juvenile Wolves—or were balanced on the packs they'd loaded onto two burros.

When she had time—if she lived—she'd ponder the oddity of Wolves keeping a handful of burros as pack animals, and what it said about the Others that the burros knew they didn't need to fear *these* predators.

"Jesse?" Shelley gasped behind her. "Jesse? We need to stop. We need a rest break."

"We'll rest when we get there." Couldn't be much farther. Joe had said a couple of miles beyond the *terra indigene* settlement. Water. Shelter. A spot that could be defended.

Which could mean it was also a spot that, if overrun by an enemy, wouldn't give them any way out. The humans, anyway.

"*Arroo*," Rachel said softly, suddenly trotting ahead of Jesse.

The youngster had stayed close to her throughout the journey. Jesse wasn't sure if Rachel was helping to act as a scout or if the Wolf wanted to be near any adult she recognized.

The only adult Wolf who had been left at the settlement was the pack's nanny. The rest of the adults had gone out to deal with the humans and had died.

The pups are orphans now, all of them, Jesse thought.

"Jesse?" Abigail Burch this time. "Can't we stop a minute? The children are tired."

Tired was better than dead.

Jesse hesitated when Rachel rushed back to her. But the Wolf seemed excited, relieved. A couple of minutes later, Jesse shared that relief. Water flowed into a pool before the creek continued down the hills to the settlement. There were rocks that provided shelter, and trees that would provide shade. Couldn't make a fire here because they were in the wild country. Joe had warned her about that. But they could huddle up in blankets to keep warm if they had to stay up here overnight.

Once they had set up camp, she would figure out where they could set up the latrine—and where to picket the burros.

"We're here," she said, moving aside. "Step lively, now. Everybody in."

Not all the Prairie Gold women had come with them. A few had sent messages that they'd had a feeling they needed to stay at the farms and help look after the animals. But they had sent their children. In truth, they had a point. Meg Corbyn hadn't said to hide the women, just the children. Just the Wolves.

Feeling Rachel pressed against her leg, trembling, Jesse felt a pang of grief as she remembered Joe standing outside the general store, ready to step in if needed but allowing Rachel to make her first foray into a human store on her own. Jesse hadn't had time to get to know him well, and she regretted that. Working together, they could have bridged the differences between *terra indigene* and Intuits, could have built a partnership the same way other places were trying to do.

Rachel whined.

"Hush up," Jesse snapped at the women and children whose voices had been steadily rising. Stepping into the gap between rocks, she raised her rifle, prepared to fire.

The women fell silent or frantically tried to hush the children.

Nothing. Nothing. Except the pack's nanny had led the puppies to a hiding place behind a fallen tree. Except Rachel stood at her side, panting and trembling.

Nothing but an odd silence.

Then something shimmered on the game trail. Something her eyes couldn't quite see.

Something big.

"That's far enough," she warned.

A wet snarl—more a feel in the air than an actual sound.

"We have permission to be here, and we're staying until I'm told it's safe to bring the youngsters back to their homes."

Rachel suddenly shifted, now a human teenage girl crouching beside her. "Jesse Walker is our friend. She . . . was Joe Wolfgard's friend."

Where do you aim when you can't see? That dark glint. Was that an eye? Gods, how big *was* that thing?

It took a step closer. She couldn't see it, but she *knew* it had moved closer.

"If you're one of the *terra indigene* who lives in these hills, then you should know why we came up here, should know what happened to the Wolves." Jesse took a slow breath. "We've lost enough friends today. In that, I think, you and I are the same. So I'm telling you now that the only way *anyone* is taking any of these youngsters away from here is if I'm dead and can't fight for them anymore."

Hesitation. Then it was gone.

Jesse didn't know how anything that big could move that quickly or that silently, but she could feel it was gone.

"The Elders will watch the trail," Rachel whispered. "We'll be safe here tonight and can go . . . home . . . in the morning."

Jesse lowered the rifle. "That was an Elder?"

"Yes. They are old forms of *terra indigene*. They are Namid's teeth and claws."

Namid's teeth and claws. I believe that. I surely do. Gods above and below. "They live in the hills?"

"Yes. They allow us to take some wood and yellow stones to trade with humans. And our . . ." Rachel's breath caught on a sob. "Our pack could hunt up here." She looked at the other juvenile Wolves who had come with them. "We've been learning how to hunt, but we aren't strong enough yet . . . We can't . . . How are we going to feed the puppies?"

"We'll figure something out," Jesse said quietly. "You should shift back to Wolf now. You'll be warmer wearing fur."

The girl nodded. After shifting, she joined the other Wolves, who were huddled in one area. All the *terra indigene* young had chosen a particular spot, each gard keeping to itself. In the center were the Intuits, setting out blankets, pulling out cups for drinking and packages of food.

Ellen Garcia came up to Jesse, who leaned against a rock and divided her attention between the game trail and the camp.

"I've got about thirty pounds of raw meat packed on one of those burros," Ellen said.

"Told you not to bring anything we needed to cook." Thirty pounds? No wonder they'd had to leave a few things behind, even with women wearing packs of things babies and small children would need.

"Didn't bring it for us."

Jesse looked at the other woman. Tobias was the foreman of the Prairie Gold ranch, but Ellen and Tom looked after the buildings and vehicles, and Ellen cooked for the men. She also had some training as an accountant, so she kept the books for the ranch as well as the dairy and produce farms. While Jesse liked Shelley Bookman and considered her a friend, she recognized Ellen as a kindred spirit—a woman who got on with what needed to be done.

She huffed out a breath as she glanced at the *terra indigene* young. Meat eaters, every one of them. "Didn't think of that."

"No reason why you would. We have a couple of cattle dogs, so packing some raw meat in the provisions is second nature for me. I'll take care of that part of the camp."

"Thanks."

They enjoyed a comfortable minute of silence, just listening to the other women settling the children. Then Ellen said, "You trying as hard as I am to not think about what's happening on the ranch and in town?"

Jesse nodded. "I keep thinking we'd see the smoke if the worst happened, but I'm not sure that's true."

"Guess we'll find out in the morning."

"Guess we will."

"Well. I'd best get to chopping up some of that meat before all the youngsters realize they're hungry."

Jesse worked up a smile. "Feeding that crew should be interesting."

While Ellen went to work preparing meat for the furred and feathered, Jesse continued to keep watch. Had Rachel seen clearly what human eyes and brain refused to understand? What might have happened if a Wolf hadn't spoken up for them?

What would happen to any of them if there was no one like Joe Wolfgard left to speak for them when the Elders came down from the hills?

Jesse rubbed the ache in her left wrist.

They were coming. She knew that as surely as she knew her own name.

Ignoring the dead bison, they gathered around the Wolves who had been heaped into a mound. They sniffed, circled, considered.

<This killing,> one of them finally said. <This is what it means to be human. This is what humans do.>

The anger grew slowly, filled muscle and bone and blood. And in a few of them, it ... changed. They rose on their hind legs and shifted the shapes of legs and hips in order to stand upright. Front paws changed to hands, but the fingers still retained the claws of a predator. The body reshaped to a powerful torso and shoulders, a strong neck, and a head that retained the teeth and jaws that could bite through bone.

They would tower over their prey, but this shape would be able to enter dwellings, dig out what tried to hide.

One of them turned and took a few hesitant steps on its newly shaped legs. It grasped the horns of a bison with its new hands and, with all the strength of its true form, gave a savage twist and tore off the bison's head. Dropping the head, it raked its claws over the belly and watched the entrails slide out.

<This is what it means to be human,> it said. <This is what humans do.>

<This is what humans do,> the rest agreed.

Those who had taken this necessary but unwelcome shape shifted back to their true form.

Then they all headed for the human town called Bennett, and their footsteps filled the land with a terrible silence.

CHAPTER 36

Firesday, Juin 22

Jackson in Wolf form and five Intuits on horseback watched the pickup trucks burn. They had stopped—or exploded—yards away from the simple barricade that the *terra indigene* and Intuits had set up across the road that led to the Sweetwater settlement and village.

The fire sweeping over the land had begun at the two pickups, which must have carried many containers of gasoline as well as the men who had intended to burn down the Intuit village. Now it rushed toward Endurance, the human-controlled town in the distance.

"Gods above and below," one man said quietly. "If the wind turns again . . ."

The fire should have raged toward Sweetwater. Instead it had turned with a deliberation that couldn't be explained as anything but conscious choice and headed for the few human ranches that had been established on the land around Endurance, setting the pastures ablaze before turning toward the houses and stores.

"Supply trucks will charge more if they have to come all the way to Sweetwater," another man said.

"Assuming there's still a right-of-way and any trucks can reach us," the third man said.

Jackson noticed how careful they all were not to look at him as they spoke.

They were right. Supply trucks didn't want to waste the gasoline to drive to Sweetwater when they could leave most merchandise at a rented storage area in the human town. They were also correct that the right-of-way through the wild country would no longer exist, and there was no certainty that *anything* would be able to reach them, whether the town burned or not.

Trading post, Jackson thought as his eyes followed the dirt road that ribboned through the burning land. *We could build a trading post near the place where our road connects to the paved road that leads to the human town. There is already a gas station and little store at that spot. Even a depot where things could be dropped off for the Intuits and Others would be enough. Earth native trucks would still be allowed to use the roads, even if the Elders completely turned against humans. We could still bring in what we need—if those things still exist.*

"Nothing we can do about that fire except let it burn," the first man said.

A clump of wetness fell on Jackson's nose. He licked it, then looked up, surprised by the sudden cold.

Snow? *Snow?* Now? He'd already shed his winter coat. Why was there snow now?

"Shit," one man muttered. "Didn't come prepared for this."

Jackson licked another snowflake off his nose.

One flake. Two. Ten. A thousand.

"We need to get back to the village while we can still find the road," the second man said. "Jackson?"

One moment he watched the snow follow the path of the fire and lay a blanket over the land. The next moment, he could barely see the men and horses he'd accompanied.

The Hope pup was dressed for summer, and she'd been running toward the stream. If the Wolves got wet, they got wet. Their fur—even a summer coat—would protect them well enough from cold. But Hope . . .

Jackson headed back to Sweetwater, reminding himself to stay on the road since the Intuits would follow him and would end up lost and sick if he had to curl up and wait out the storm.

Then he trotted into bright sunlight and stopped so fast one of the horses almost stepped on him.

"By the gods," one of the men breathed.

Sunlight. Warmth.

Jackson moved out of the way and shook out his fur before looking back at the wall of snow that was quickly turning into a few fluffy, lazy snowflakes. Then even those stopped falling.

"Maybe we should . . ."

Seeing the men look back, Jackson shifted to human form and wished he had some clothes, not for modesty but for warmth. "Do you have any reason to believe the humans in those trucks are still alive?"

They hesitated, not quite looking at him after the first glance. Then they shook their heads.

"Then stay on this side of the barricade. Stay on the land the Intuits are permitted to use. At least for now."

"Going to have to deal with those trucks sometime. The remains will have to be returned to their families."

Jackson caught a scent in the air that made him shiver. He looked at the men who weren't quite looking at him. How to tell them what his instincts howled? "The wild country begins at the barricade now. It . . . surrounds . . . us. It surrounds that human town."

"It always did."

"Not like this." He watched them pale.

Silence. Then, "No way out?"

"Not for a few days." Didn't want to be in this skin, didn't want to look human.

Jackson shifted back to Wolf. Nothing more he could tell the Intuits anyway. Not yet.

He ran home to find Grace and the Hope pup near the stream with the rest of the pack. The sweet blood seemed dazed until he licked her cheek. Then she threw her arms around him and started crying.

<It's okay, pup. It's okay.> Hope couldn't hear him, but he said the words anyway. Then he looked at Grace. <Is it okay?>

<The Eagles and Ravens said there was fire, but it didn't come here,> she replied. <The Intuit village?>

<Safe.> He licked the Hope pup's ear since that was all he could reach. <Would have burned without her warning.>

When the Hope pup finally stopped crying, she washed her face in the stream while Jackson rolled in the grass to clean his fur. Then he and Grace led their prophet pup back to the Wolfgard cabin. He went in first and removed the terrible drawings, hiding them in the kitchen area until he could decide what to do with them.

Grace came in next. Together they opened the windows in the bedroom and bathroom and washed the pee smell off the floor as best they could.

Leaving the Hope pup dozing on the porch with the rest of the pack guarding her, Jackson and Grace trotted to the communications cabin at the edge of the settlement. The Hawk who had been answering the phone looked at them with sad eyes as he handed a message to Jackson after the two Wolves shifted to human form.

"Who is it from?" Grace asked.

"Vlad Sanguinati," Jackson replied. "Simon and the Lakeside pack are all right."

"Vlad asked about you," the Hawk said. "I told him the Sweetwater pack was all right too. I've been calling the number like you asked me to, but there's no answer."

"I already know part of the answer. The Hope pup drew a picture of it." But he'd been hoping Joe had received the warning in time.

Grace sucked in a breath.

"Phone is working, then not working," the Hawk said.

"It might be like that for a while." Nothing he could do right now. Nothing any of them could do right now except wait. "We'll be at the Wolfgard cabin if any more messages come in."

Grace waited until they were trotting back to the cabin. <Do you expect any more messages?>

<No.> How many packs had received a warning to run, to hide, to flee from the evil humans? How many of the Wolfgard were still out there?

They were safe. For tonight, all the *terra indigene* in the settlement were safe.

CHAPTER 37

Firesday, Juin 22

S imon felt the exact moment when Meg relaxed.

It's over, he thought. *At least for us.*

He'd lost track of time, had no sense of how long they'd been hiding in that dip of land. Since he didn't have to worry about Meg now, he considered the other problem.

<How are we going to get the BOW out of here?> he asked Blair.

<We can attach a rope. Then some of us will pull and some will push. We'll get it out.>

He considered the next, and more immediate, problem. <How are we going to wash Meg? She really stinks.>

<The BOW is my problem. Meg is yours.>

Simon sighed, then moved his head, resting it against Meg's back. It was the only part of her that smelled more like Meg and less like vomit.

Monty gave Kowalski full marks for his driving skills, but he still wished cars had brake pedals on the passenger side. As it was, Kowalski whiskered by the patrol car assigned to block the intersection of Parkside and Crowfield avenues.

They would have been heading for the Courtyard earlier if Captain Burke hadn't called everyone in for emergency assignments. No one, including Burke, was sure of what was going on. But after Burke received a call from Pete Denby, he had placed an urgent call to Agent Greg O'Sullivan, who, in turn, must have called Governor Hannigan. Despite the slim amount of information available, the governor had issued emergency orders that amounted to an ultimatum for the entire Northeast Region: block access to every Courtyard; block every street that led to a settlement controlled by the *terra indigene*; arrest anyone who tried to get around the barriers. Trains were detained at whatever station they were in. No travel of any kind between towns until further notice. The severest measures allowed by law would be taken against anyone who attacked, or attempted to attack, any of the *terra indigene* or any human who worked with the *terra indigene*.

Hannigan's orders were a declaration of war on the Humans First and Last movement, and he expected the police departments in every city to uphold that declaration. And any officer who couldn't, or wouldn't, obey those orders was expected to resign immediately.

Plenty of speculation but no explanations. And no one on Monty's team had told anyone outside the "police pack" about the frightened phone calls that had come in from Merri Lee and Ruth. There had been some kind of dustup between Robert Denby and Nathan at about the same time that something had happened to Meg, and now the Wolves were gone. All of them. Didn't close up the stores, didn't even close doors. They just ran off.

The girls couldn't find Tess, couldn't find Vlad or Henry, couldn't find a single Crow to tell them what was going on, but they believed there was a serious problem.

Pete Denby said much the same thing to Burke. Something very bad was happening, and not just around Lakeside. The children were in the Market Square medical office. The *terra indigene* were . . . gone.

Armed with that information, Burke had informed O'Sullivan and then circumvented the Lakeside police's chain of command by calling patrol captains Zajac and Wheatley for help. Before Police Commissioner Kurt Wallace, who was a member of the HFL, even knew there was a potentially lethal problem, the police were locking down the city—and bracing for whatever was coming.

"Gods, this feels creepy," Kowalski muttered as he pulled into the Courtyard's Main Street entrance and then eased the patrol car down the access way.

"Like a ghost town you read about in stories." Once the car was parked in a space usually reserved for the earth native delivery trucks, Monty hurried toward the medical office. "Did Ruth and Merri Lee say where they would be?"

"With the kids and Theral and Pete Denby. Safety in numbers."

He hoped that was true.

Vlad hung up the phone with exaggerated gentleness just as Eve Denby strode up to Howling Good Reads' checkout counter. He'd managed to avoid dealing with the female pack since the Wolves went into hiding. Now . . .

"Did my son cause whatever this is?" Eve asked.

Vlad shook his head.

"Then I'll hand out a suitable punishment."

He said nothing. Tolya's voice on the phone. So flat, so . . . empty.

"I'll clean up Meg's office. Being a mother, I've dealt with my share of puke."

He said nothing.

"Hey." Eve reached out. Almost touched his hand. "Is Meg really hurt?"

He looked at her. Honest concern. Would that make any difference now? "Joe Wolfgard is dead."

"Oh." Immediate sympathy. "Some kind of accident?"

"No. We called to warn him, and he tried to stop the pack from running into the trap, but . . ." Vlad sighed. "Except for the nanny who went with the pups, all the adult Wolves in the Prairie Gold pack are dead. Slaughtered. By humans."

Eve looked out the store's windows. She'd been working across the street. She would have heard the sirens, seen the police cars. Probably had a call from Pete since she knew about Nathan dealing with Robert.

Eve rammed her fingers through her short hair. "Does Simon . . . Does anyone else here know?"

"Not yet." He felt so strange. The Wolfgard and the Sanguinati were different forms of *terra indigene*, but he felt so strange. One death was sorrow, but a whole pack . . . Maybe it was because Tolya had sounded so empty when he called.

Or maybe it was because Vlad thought he would sound the same way if it had been Simon.

"Can I do anything for you?"

He focused on Eve. "No. Thank you."

She nodded. "I'll get Ruth and Merri Lee. We'll give Meg's office a good clean and airing. Put the Closed sign on the door."

"Yes. All right." Had to tell Grandfather Erebus.

Eve hesitated. "I heard on the radio . . . I don't know if it makes a difference, but it sounds like Governor Hannigan is doing what he can to support the *terra indigene.*" She walked out of the store.

I don't know if it will make a difference either, Vlad thought.

He checked the front door and made sure it was locked, then went through the archway to A Little Bite and turned the lock on that door. Maybe the coffee shop should stay open to give the police drinks and food, but he saw no sign of Tess—and no sign of Nadine Fallacaro, for that matter. Well, if Nadine showed up and wanted to serve food, she could.

Returning to HGR, Vlad went upstairs to check the e-mails, but after reading a couple, he shut off the computer.

Not just the Prairie Gold Wolfgard had been lost today. Tomorrow was soon enough for a reckoning.

In his official capacity as a lieutenant in the Lakeside Police Department, Monty placed Robert, Sarah, Lizzy, and Grr Bear under house arrest. The girls insisted that Grr Bear was innocent and that he'd *tried* to tell them they were playing where they weren't supposed to, but *Robert* wouldn't listen.

Because of the difference in their ages, he'd never had this kind of sibling squabble with his sister, Sierra, but if they'd been closer in age, he thought there would have been times when Sissy would have thrown him under the bus—or thrown him to the Wolves.

When Eve Denby stormed in and demanded he arrest the children and take them to jail for reckless endangerment and being a pain in her ass, he'd thought she was playacting and went along, especially when Pete, as the children's attorney, threw himself on the mercy of Mother Court and tried to plea-bargain.

It wasn't until Eve agreed to a week's house arrest with no TV, no movies, and no treats that Monty realized her mood wasn't driven by the children misbehaving. It wasn't until she took him outside and told him about Prairie Gold that he understood some of the reason Hannigan had locked down the Northeast Region. The HFL movement had stopped talking, stopped their petty attacks.

While Eve marched off with Ruth and Merri Lee, Monty called Burke to let him know the HFL had declared war on the Wolves, if not all the *terra indigene.*

Jester rushed outside as the BOW pulled up. Hadn't the human pups caused enough trouble? Why did the adults have to be stupid too?

"You're not supposed to be here," he snapped.

Eve Denby reached across Merri Lee, who was driving, and said, "Give that to Simon or the Wolfgard bodywalker."

Jester took the folded sheet of paper. "What is it?"

"I heard . . ."

Caw!

Jester looked at Jenni Crowgard and growled.

". . . that Simon has a girl and a puppy covered in puke. I wrote down instructions—what I would do if I had to deal with it. You can give it to him or not, but if I was in his shoes, I wouldn't want to go very far with them in that condition."

"Oh." Jester looked at the paper. "Good point."

"I told Vlad we would clean up Meg's office and air it out, so that's what we're doing now."

Merri Lee put the BOW in gear, did a five-point version of a three-point turn, and headed back to the Liaison's Office.

Jester put the instructions in a small cloth bag that had wooden handles suitable to be held by teeth, stripped off his clothes, and shifted. Then he ran to the place where the Wolves were still pondering how to get Meg and Sam clean without anyone having to touch them.

Rage became a scent in the wind, a taste in the water, a heat that rose from the earth. It rushed across Thaisia as fast as the news reports spilled out of radios and televisions.

Beneath the rage, these words shivered through the wild country: *This is what it means to be human. This is what humans do.*

To: Pater

All eyes are focused on the central part of Thaisia. Strike now and the human race will triumph on both sides of the Atlantik.

—NS

To: Erebus Sanguinati

It is not prudent to kill Nicholas Scratch at this time. He is too well protected, and striking at him now would make the humans in Toland vigilant to other kinds of attacks. However, I don't believe he will stay in Thaisia once Namid's teeth and claws respond to the deaths of hundreds of Wolfgard in the Midwest and Northwest regions. Ocean is rising in preparation for striking the East Coast of Thaisia, especially the cities that sent out the ships responsible for poisoning fish and killing some of the Sharkgard. The Sharkgard have guaranteed my safety from Ocean's wrath if I remain near the Toland docks and tell them when Scratch sets sail for Cel-Romano.

—Stavros

CHAPTER 38

Watersday, Juin 23

All the weapons and machines that had been built and tested in secret, and all the men who had been conscripted from all the nations that made up the Cel-Romano Alliance, headed for the borders that separated human land from the wild country.

When the airplanes flew overhead, carrying the weapons that would make this a swift war, the men who came from the big cities cheered at the metal promise of more land, more food, more space. But the men who had been conscripted from the villages that touched the wild country looked at the airplanes and whispered to their comrades, "You don't know. You don't know."

Bombs dropped from the airplanes destroyed the *terra indigene* settlements, those simple dwellings that provided a gathering place for the Others who watched the borders. The men and machines flowing up the roads in the wake of the bombs' destruction killed the wounded and the weak and the young. And they killed the *terra indigene* who turned and tried to fight to protect their wounded and weak and young.

It quickly became clear that the humans now had weapons that the shifters couldn't fight. So the gards fled in advance of this enemy.

For a full day, men and machines moved up the roads, killing and conquering. Then they stopped because there were no roads, and the machines could not move forward on the narrow game trails.

The leaders looked at the conquered land and declared the human race victorious.

That night, no one but the men who came from small villages on the border noticed the odd, and terrible, silence.

In all the Cel-Romano nations, old men and women slipped away from their villages and followed trails into the wild country that had been made by generations of humans. Or they slipped away to isolated places where the land met the Mediterran Sea. There they set out traditional foods that were given to families during a time of mourning.

"They were our friends," voices whispered to the night. "We share your grief. They were our friends."

Nothing answered them. Nothing stepped out from among the trees, or rose from the sea, to accept their mourning gifts. So they returned to their villages, and their neighbors asked the question: "Do you think it will make a difference?"

And they answered: "We will know soon enough."

They watched the two-legged predators. And they listened, not to the upstart species but to the world itself.

The humans had broken the boundary between the land Namid had given to them and the wild country that belonged to the *terra indigene*.

No boundary now. Not in this part of the world. And when there was no boundary, Namid's teeth and claws knew what they had to do.

Anger sharpened the wind as Elementals called Air raged through Cel-Romano, uprooting trees to form barriers across the roads. Anger quietly rumbled along the skin of Elementals called Earth, who tested the ground beneath the places that had built the flying weapons. Anger rained along the coastline and fell into the Mediterran Sea, drawing the attention of ancient Tethys, the Elemental who watched over the sea.

Then the wind and rumbling and rain were gone as if they had never been— and the humans in Cel-Romano began to believe this was all the *terra indigene* could do, began to believe they had conquered the Others and would hold all of this new land.

Began to relax.

Flowing around her home in the Fingerbone Islands, Alantea listened to the stories in the surf—stories that came through the seaway from the Five Sisters, who knew much about Thaisia. She listened to the cries of anger coming from Cel-Romano's western shores and the strait that connected her domain to Tethys's home.

There was a malignant current running between Cel-Romano and Thaisia, a current that didn't touch the other parts of the world. At least, not yet.

A question had come from Thaisia not long ago, and she and the gards living in her domain had helped find the answer. Might she not ask a question in return?

And when she had the answer, she would decide what to do.

To: Tolya Sanguinati

Grandfather wants you to stay in Prairie Gold and keep him informed about what is going on in that area. He is especially interested in hearing about things the human news *isn't* reporting.

—Vlad

To: Crispin James Montgomery

No trains running. Will leave with Sierra and her girls as soon as we can. Cyrus called several times, wanting to be included in this visit. Didn't say anything about bringing his wife or children. Once I told him we were staying with your boss, he lost interest. Doesn't mean he won't get interested again. Thought you should know.

—Mother

CHAPTER 39

Watersday, Juin 23

With the exception of Meg Corbyn, all the humans currently residing in the Courtyard had spent the night elsewhere, even if elsewhere was just across the street. Merri Lee had stayed with Ruth and Kowalski; Nadine Fallacaro had slept on the Denbys' couch, while Chris Fallacaro had bedded down in a borrowed sleeping bag; and he and Lizzy had stayed in the half of Captain Burke's duplex that had been previously occupied by the Denbys.

Burke had told him he was welcome to use that half of the duplex as a temporary residence or even rent it if he wanted to stay instead of squeezing into the efficiency apartment in the Courtyard or hanging on to the one-bedroom apartment he'd rented when he'd first come to Lakeside. While the offer was generous—and Monty had no doubt Burke would respect his privacy—he couldn't count on regular work hours, especially now, and he would end up leaving Lizzy with Eve Denby or Ruth Stuart anyway. Easier for everyone to have Lizzy staying across the street from her caretakers and playmates.

And despite yesterday's upset, the Courtyard was still the most protected place in the city.

So many things he'd like to discuss with Burke—and nothing either of them could say with his seven-year-old daughter and Grr Bear sitting in the backseat.

"Daddy?"

Monty looked over his shoulder. "Yes, Lizzy girl?"

"We really can't watch TV or movies today?"

"Mother Court passed sentence. No movies or TV for a whole week."

"But Grr Bear and I didn't *do* anything bad."

"You were accomplices." He saw Burke's lips twitch.

Lizzy conferred with Grr Bear. Boo Bear, Lizzy's previous stuffed toy, had been her constant companion. Grr Bear, whose wooden head and paws had been carved by Henry Beargard, seemed more like a conscience that was less inclined to go along with "cute naughtiness," let alone outright wrongdoing.

But Grr Bear couldn't discourage all misbehavior, especially when it was started by someone else.

Monty suspected that, from now on, Nathan Wolfgard's teeth would prove to be a more effective deterrent in that regard.

Lizzy tried again. "Grr Bear thinks maybe not a whole week if we behave?"

"Does Mother Court show leniency?" Burke asked so quietly the question wouldn't carry to the backseat.

"Not in my experience," Monty muttered. Until yesterday when he saw her in angry-mom mode, he'd thought of Eve Denby as a practical, energetic, amiable woman. Last night he considered what would happen to any appeal for mercy once Eve teamed up with his mother, Twyla.

Gods. If he were still a child, he'd give Pete Denby half his allowance each month to be the attorney on retainer.

Monty turned his face away to hide his smile.

"Daddy?"

"Don't know, Lizzy. I've never stood before that particular judge before."

"Oh."

The discussion lightened the mood in the car until Monty dropped Lizzy at the Denbys' apartment, and he and Burke drove to the Chestnut Street station.

"Didn't think about it last night," Burke said. "Was there anything in the kitchen for breakfast?"

"Not really, but Eve had said Lizzy could have breakfast with Sarah and Robert." And he would welcome a large cup of coffee—even what was served in the station's cafeteria. "Have you heard anything through your grapevine?"

Burke didn't speak for a long minute. "Some trouble around Market Street— again. Trouble around what is left of Lakeside University as well as the technical college. Nothing that wasn't expected here. Governor Hannigan locking down the region as fast as he did stalled any attempts to burn Intuit villages or any other settlements within the wild country. Or course, his actions might have saved the Northeast from at least some of what's coming, but it pretty much destroyed his chance for being reelected if the residents of Toland have anything to say about it. And when it comes to elections, they usually have quite a bit to say."

"What about other regions?"

"News bulletins on the radio this morning talked about human triumphs over the *terra indigene*."

"What does that mean?"

"I guess we'll find out."

Vlad stared at the images on the TV screen.

There hadn't been enough time to warn all the Wolfgard, and not all the Wolfgard keeping watch over human places had human allies.

When had the clever monkeys stopped being clever? Did they think only humans were seeing these pictures of them dancing around piles of dead Wolves? Did they think only humans noticed the bodies of the puppies that had been killed along with the adults? Of course, humans thought nothing of killing their own young, so why should they hesitate to kill other species?

So many places. So much slaughter. Hundreds, maybe thousands, of Wolves had been killed throughout the Northwest and Midwest regions. How many Wolfgard were left in those parts of Thaisia?

Then he saw it, the picture that was different from the rest.

Joe's face looks like that.

"Meg." Vlad shut off the TV, rushed out of his apartment, and raced up the stairs to Meg's place, just two doors away from his home in the Green Complex. Knocking softly, he tried her front door, hoping it was open, hoping . . .

He pushed the door open just enough to lean in. "Meg?"

"Vlad?"

He opened the door all the way and went in. "Where is Simon?"

"Peeing on trees." She bent her head and sniffed herself. "I don't know how many times Sam and I were washed yesterday, but I think I still smell like puke." She held out her arm.

He considered it an act of unrivaled gallantry when he walked up to her and sniffed her arm.

"Still?" she asked.

She sounded dismayed, so he said, "Not really." He didn't point out that Simon might have a different opinion.

Taking both her hands, Vlad stepped closer. "Meg? Don't watch the news today. Don't read the newspaper. Please. As a favor to me, to Simon, to all of us, just don't."

"Why?"

"Because you saw Joe's face." *And if you saw his face, you saw the rest.*

"It really happened?"

"Yes."

"Does Simon know?"

"He knows Joe is dead, but he didn't see . . ." Couldn't finish.

"All right. I'm going to the office. There will be mail, maybe some deliveries. But I won't look at the *Lakeside News* or turn on the radio."

"Okay." The female pack was bound to see something. He couldn't stop all of them from seeing what had been done, but Meg didn't need to see it again. "I'm not sure if e-mail is getting through. The phone lines have been jammed since yesterday. But I'll try to get through to Jackson and find out how Hope is doing." And he'd check with Steve Ferryman and find out how the five young *cassandra sangue* were doing—and Jean.

Simon hadn't intended to go to Howling Good Reads today. He hadn't wanted to do anything *human* except spend time with Meg. Outside.

But he ended up at the back door of the bookstore before he realized he didn't have his keys. Or clothes. He found the back door of A Little Bite open and crept inside, wary of running into Tess if she was in a deadly mood.

Instead of Tess, he found Nadine in the back room where Tess sometimes baked cookies.

"Couldn't sleep, so I've been here a while," Nadine said. She tapped a container that sat on the edge of her worktable. "Special delivery from Eamer's Bakery. Wolf cookies. I guess they were up early too, working. A lot of us are going to be up early. I heard you lost a friend yesterday. I'm sorry for that."

He whined to let her know he'd heard her. Then he went to the lattice door, let himself in to Howling Good Reads, and went up to the office. Not to deal with paperwork or read e-mail. He had added a simple wooden trunk—simple if you didn't count the carving Henry had done on the lid—to the office furniture as a place to store a set of clean clothes and a pair of shoes. He dressed and went back downstairs. He'd check the stock, shelve a few books. Wouldn't stay long since he hadn't told Meg he was coming to the store and she'd be expecting him at the apartment.

As he turned toward the stock room, he heard the familiar slap of paper on pavement. Copies of the *Lakeside News*.

Fetching the spare keys from the office desk, he opened the front door, grabbed the newspapers, and dumped them on the checkout counter. The headline said, "Humans Triumph!" Beneath the words was a photo that filled half the front page.

Simon stared at the photo. Stared and stared. Then he whispered, "Joe."

Pouring himself a large mug of coffee, Monty half listened to the television news report and ignored the looks from some of the other police officers packed into the station's break room to hear the news and see the "graphic proof" of the Humans First and Last movement's triumph.

"Humans have taken possession of thousands of acres of prime land through the HFL's audacious strike against the terra indigene, *creatures who have held a chokehold on Thaisia for decades. But not everyone is applauding the HFL's actions toward land reclamation. One rancher near the Midwest town of Bennett had this to say.*

"'They're damn fools, the whole lot of them. My family has been raising horses and cattle here for four generations, and we have never had trouble with the terra indigene.'

"When asked about the loss of livestock to Wolves, Stewart Dixon told the reporter, 'It's called rent.'

"And now here's a recap of the photographs that were sent to news stations all around the continent."

Monty watched the photos appear on the TV one by one. No one spoke, not even the officers who had supported the HFL. Then the last photo appeared and remained on the screen.

"Oh, gods," Monty whispered. The mug slipped from his hand. Had Meg Corbyn seen . . . ? Of course she had.

He looked toward the door where Burke stood. Yes, his captain recognized the Wolf on top of the mound of bodies. Burke gave him a nod.

"Lieutenant?" Kowalski said, suddenly beside him. "I'll get the car."

Monty walked out of the break room, his mind racing. The other photos had been terrible, but it was the half-shifted, recognizable face of Joe Wolfgard that made the loss of the Wolfgard in another part of Thaisia personal.

He doubted Simon Wolfgard would want to see a human today. He doubted Simon would want to see a police officer or be asked what ramifications these actions might have for Lakeside. But today he wasn't going to the Courtyard as a human or a police officer. Today he was going as a friend.

Burke moved aside when Montgomery and Kowalski hurried out of the break room. Then he filled the doorway, preventing anyone else from leaving.

"Gentlemen, there is a war coming. Despite what the HFL may want you to believe, it won't be against the *terra indigene*. It's going to be humans against humans. It's going to be between those who recognize that working with the Others is the only way to survive on this continent and those who mistakenly believe that killing the shifters will win us anything. It's going to be between the so-called Wolf lovers and the HFL supporters."

Burke scanned the room, noting who met his eyes and who looked away. "So I'm telling you now. If any of you, after looking at those pictures, are thinking of putting on an HFL pin again, I want the paperwork for your transfer or resignation on my desk first." He gave them all a fierce smile. "I know. I'm not the station chief. I'm just the patrol captain and I don't have any say about the personnel under other captains' commands. But I'm telling you here and now, if you can't—or won't—fight alongside the Others in order to save this city, I don't want you in this station, because being divided within the ranks will kill us all. I can't do anything for the rest of the continent, but I'm going to do everything I can to save Lakeside, and, if the gods are merciful, saving Lakeside might help Governor Hannigan keep at least part of the Northeast Region open to human habitation."

He turned away, then turned back. "Don't try to call my bluff about this. I am standing with the Lakeside Courtyard because I think it's the only way to save the people of this city. If you can't stand with me, you need to be gone by the end of the day."

He walked to his office and wasn't surprised when Louis Gresh came in right behind him.

"That was quite a speech," Louis said.

"You think so?"

"You usually get what you want when it comes to having men transferred out of this station, but . . . a humans-against-humans war when there's another potential enemy?"

"They didn't think it through." Burke settled in his chair. "You kill off one kind of predator, you leave a void. Sooner or later, something will fill that void, and in this case, I think it will be sooner rather than later. The HFL wants to talk about land reclamation? They have no idea what they started—and I have no idea who among us will still be here to see where it ends."

Deciding on visible police presence, Monty asked Kowalski to park in the Courtyard's customer parking lot.

"Check on the Denbys, warn them about the news reports," Monty said.

"Sure not something the children should see." Kowalski seemed about to say something more but changed his mind.

Monty smiled. "I'll check on them after I talk to Simon."

"Not sure what all they're doing, but the girls are working with Meg at the Liaison's Office this morning, and Theral is at the medical office."

"Then check on them too."

The lights weren't on in Howling Good Reads, but the front door was open. That door wasn't usually open anymore, so Monty went in cautiously, his hand brushing against his police issue revolver.

"Simon?"

A sound. Something moving on the other side of the main display table.

Careful, careful. He could draw his weapon against a human intruder but not against a Wolf. Not today.

Then Simon stood up, grabbing the table for balance.

"Simon."

"You did this." The voice sounded rough, not quite human. "You did this."

"I saw the picture. Simon, I am so sorry about Joe." What was he dealing with here? Shock? Rage? Overwhelming grief?

"How much human will the *terra indigene* keep? Well, you showed them the answer, didn't you? You showed them *this* as an example of what it means to be human."

Monty didn't have time to brace for the attack before Simon grabbed him and slammed him against the bookshelves.

"We tried to work with . . ." Simon snarled. "We . . . tried. *But you did this!*"

More than grief. More than rage and shock.

"What are you afraid of?" Monty asked. "Us? Humans?"

Simon released him and stepped back, shaking his head. "Fear you? You're going to be as good as extinct soon. Why should we fear you?"

Monty swallowed hard. "Did Meg tell you that?"

"No. Jean did."

Gods above and below.

Vlad stepped out of the back of the store. "Simon, Meg was looking for you." He glanced at the counter. "She's at the Liaison's Office now. You need to convince her to go home, let someone else take care of the mail and packages today. The humans will be talking. She doesn't need to hear more than she already knows."

Simon looked around, as if wondering why he was in the bookstore. "I didn't mean to be gone long. I . . ." He headed for the back of the store, but he stopped and wouldn't meet Monty's eyes. "We learn from other predators. Remember that, Lieutenant."

Then he was gone, and Monty was left alone with Vlad. "Is there anything any of us can do to help?"

Vlad walked over to the checkout counter. He took one copy of the *Lakeside News* off the stack, folded it, and placed it under the counter. "You could get rid of the rest of these. I'd rather not put them in our recycling bin. Too much chance of someone seeing what they shouldn't."

"Of course." He'd take them to the station. He didn't think Eve Denby would want the front-page photo in her recycling bin either. "Anything else?"

"What else do you think the police can do?"

"I wasn't asking as a police officer."

Silence. Then Vlad said softly, "Ask again in a couple of days."

Monty left the bookstore, dumped the newspapers in the backseat of the patrol car, then walked across the street to the Denbys' apartment.

Mother Court was in full swing at the breakfast table as the young wrong-doers tried to get their sentence reduced.

Wrong day to ask about watching TV, Monty thought.

"No means no," Eve said.

"But I got *hurt,*" Robert protested, displaying his scabbed elbows and knees before pointing out the bruises caused by Nathan's teeth.

"If there are any further outbursts over your sentence, you will be held in contempt of court, and 'no dessert' will be added to your sentence."

The girls, Monty noticed, were keeping very quiet. And judging by the look in Lizzy's eyes, he needed to have a talk with her about the injury she might cause if she whacked someone—like Robert—with Grr Bear since her new buddy had a wooden head and paws.

Then again, the boy was being a bit woodenheaded too.

"As your father, and your attorney, I advise you to accept the sentence you already have and not give the court any reason to add to it," Pete said.

That ended all discussion. Monty accepted a cup of coffee and a piece of toast—and wondered how much longer those things would be an ordinary part of a meal.

After the children went to their rooms to make their beds and do a general tidying for inspection, Eve poured more coffee for the three adults.

"We heard," Pete said quietly. "Saw just enough of the morning news to . . . Gods."

"Anything we can do?" Eve asked.

"A question to ask in a couple of days." Monty rose and put his cup and plate in the kitchen sink. A moment later, Eve stood beside him.

"What happens in a couple of days?"

He looked out the window at a pleasant summer day. Then he sighed. "I wish I knew."

CHAPTER 40

Moonsday, Juin 25

Computers in select newsrooms in each region of Thaisia chugged away as they downloaded a digital photo sent from the newspaper in Bennett. When the download was complete and a copy printed out for editors to review, most laughed harshly or swore or looked at coworkers and said, "What the . . . ?"

The photo was of a sign made from old boards nailed to a post. Painted in red were the words WE LERNED FROM YU.

Intuit editors had a very bad feeling when they saw the photo, and they sounded an alarm to all Intuit communities within reach. Most of the editors in charge of the newspapers in human cities decided it was some kind of prank to waste front-page space, but some sent a reporter to check out the potential story.

And a few television stations, after receiving the photo, sent reporters and cameras to Bennett to find out about the sign as a follow-up story to the Humans First and Last movement's triumphant land reclamation.

CHAPTER 41

Windsday, Juin 27

A young television reporter watched the land rush by as the train sped toward the town of Bennett.

"Think that's the same sign?" another reporter asked, pointing out the window.

WE LERNED FROM YU.

"Didn't learn much," someone else in the car said with a sneer.

The young reporter looked around the car and frowned. Reporters and their cameramen from various newspapers and television stations were the only passengers. Sure, there had been a travel lockdown in the Northeast by the loony governor, but that was over and done—just some kind of political maneuver. And there *had* been other people boarding the train in Shikago. Maybe the railroad had reserved a car for reporters?

WE LERNED FROM YU.

The reporter checked his watch. Another of those signs and the Bennett railway station just minutes away now.

Funny how the Bennett newspaper editor who had sent that first photo hadn't responded to e-mails or phone calls from any of the TV stations or newspapers that sent out reporters for the follow-up story. It was almost like the man couldn't be bothered with them after sending out that lure.

The train pulled into the station.

No passengers waiting to board. No station personnel in sight.

The young reporter disembarked with the rest of the newsmen. An odd silence filled the station, a silence that seemed to seep into his skin and awaken a primal understanding.

The newsmen left the station in a group, looking for a taxi or bus so they wouldn't have to haul their equipment. What they found were cars in and around the streets, many parked haphazardly, as if the drivers had left the vehicles in a hurry.

No people walking. No music coming from radios or television programs drifting out of open windows.

Some stores were closed. Others had lights on and doors open.

A cameraman suddenly stopped and gasped, "Gods above and below." He ran down an alley toward whatever he'd spotted, and the rest of the newsmen followed him to open land beyond the buildings.

The young reporter caught up to the others and stared at the mound of bodies. Young. Old. Some wearing the uniforms of their profession. Others wearing casual clothes. In front of the mound was another of those signs: WE LERNED FROM YU.

It's the whole town, the reporter thought, feeling his gorge rise in response to hearing someone else throwing up. *Something killed the whole town and piled the bodies to imitate the Wolf packs that were wiped out by the HFL, down to the last pup.*

He shuddered. "They're still here," he whispered as he backed away, trying to look everywhere at once—and wondering if any of the humans in the town had seen what had killed them. "We have to get back to the train, have to get away. They're still here."

Cameramen shot a bit of footage. Newspaper reporters snapped digital photos. But the fear of the train pulling out of the station and leaving them behind snuffed out any desire to do a live report in a dead town.

As they hurried back to the train station, the young reporter heard a sound that might have been the wind in the nearby trees—or the sound of something laughing.

To: Tolya Sanguinati

Grandfather Erebus has decided that you will take control of the town
of Bennett. Sanguinati from the Toland Courtyard are on their way to you
now, along with a few of the Wolfgard who worked with you. Some of the
terra indigene from Toland will join Stavros when he takes over the rule of
Talulah Falls. The rest will head to the Midwest and Northwest regions to
manage a few of the reclaimed towns that have railway depots. Those places
are still of value to us.

Give this warning to the humans who helped save the Wolf pups at
Prairie Gold: there is no safety in the dark.

—Vlad

To: Vladimir Sanguinati

Your message received and understood. I have considered what businesses are immediately necessary and will ask Jesse Walker for her recom-
mendations. While having some Wolfgard in Bennett as one kind of enforcer
would be beneficial, ask some of the Toland Wolves to come to the *terra
indigene* settlement at Prairie Gold. The pack's nanny is the only surviving
adult Wolf there, and someone needs to teach the juveniles how to hunt.
Much bison meat has already been cached, so the youngsters can be fed
for some time, but the Intuits, no matter how well intentioned, cannot
teach young Wolves all they need to know.

Also, all the humans who ran the ranches between Prairie Gold and
Bennett were killed. Most of the fences that divided the land were torn up
and are now fearsome balls of barbed wire and posts. Tobias Walker tells
me the beef cattle can manage on their own for the summer, but there are
other animals that require tending, including the ones in town that humans

kept as pets and the working animals on the ranches. We are doing what we can, but there are not enough of us to care for that many animals as well as handle so many other tasks. Would the Elders allow some humans—Intuits or Simple Life folk, preferably—to come to Bennett under the Sanguinati's supervision to deal with such things?

—Tolya

CHAPTER 42

Thaisday, Juin 28

M eg tried not to hover while Henry measured the drawer where she wanted to keep the prophecy card box.

"You'll want handles to lift the box out of the drawer without catching your fingers," Henry said.

"Okay." She hadn't considered the mechanics of lifting the box. "I would like a lock. With a key. Two keys."

The Grizzly gave her a long look. "We can get a lock and keys."

"It doesn't have to be a fancy box."

Another long look. "You'll take what I make."

"I just meant . . ." Something, not a prickle or a buzz, whispered across her skin. This wasn't a prophecy or vision. This was a flash of understanding. Despite—or perhaps because of—the turmoil going on throughout Thaisia, Henry wasn't working on his sculptures, but he needed something to occupy his time when he had to stay in human form to help Simon. "Thank you. Umm . . . Ruth and Merri Lee said there should be a fabric lining. They're going to look at information on tarot and fortune-telling cards to see if the box is supposed to have a certain kind of fabric, and then they'll check with the seamstress and tailor to find out what might be available."

"Tell them to talk to me about the size I'll need." Henry thought for a moment. "No, I'll talk to Ruth. The Business Association has other things to discuss with her."

"She's not in trouble, is she?" Meg couldn't think of anything Ruth—or Merri Lee or Theral, for that matter—could have done that might upset the Business Association.

"No one in the female pack is in trouble. At least, not with us." Henry closed the drawer and came over to stand beside her. "No more packages arrived that we should know about? You would tell us if there were?"

She blinked at his fierce tone. "Why wouldn't I tell you? We aren't receiving many packages for individuals. I don't think anyone in the Courtyard is ordering anything from catalogs right now, so that's not unusual."

"Nothing from that Jack Fillmore who is hunting Theral?"

Oh. *That* kind of package. "No. Nothing since those chocolates. Maybe he's left Lakeside."

"He has the scent of his prey, Meg." Henry's voice was a soft rumble. "He'll keep hunting until he catches her—or we catch him."

"Then I'll keep watching."

"*Arroo!*"

Meg looked through the doorway into the front room. "So will Nathan."

Henry folded the paper with the measurements for the box and tucked it into his pocket.

"Henry?" Meg considered the wisdom of asking the question. "Never mind."

Henry left the Liaison's Office. Meg listened but didn't hear the gate to his yard open. Must be going directly to his meeting with Ruth.

She took the supply notebook from the drawer that now held several notebooks covering a number of subjects—including *The Blood Prophets Guide*. No, there weren't many packages coming in for individuals, but they had been receiving some of the supplies she had ordered in quantity. She'd have to talk to Simon and the rest of the Business Association about how those supplies would be distributed among the Courtyard's residents, but that would have to wait.

She'd done as Vlad asked. She hadn't turned on the TV news or the radio or tried to peek at the newspaper. It hadn't been said, but it was understood between them that when the repercussions caused by the death of the Wolfgard in the Midwest and Northwest were concluded, Vlad would bring her the office copy of the *Lakeside News*.

She wondered if she would ever read a newspaper again—and as she wondered, she opened the drawer that held the prophecy cards and brushed her hand over the backs of the cards.

Don't know enough about working with them, she argued with herself. *No one knows if choosing some cards is really the same as prophecy. Blood prophets might be no better at seeing the future than Intuits are when they use these things.*

But she felt a pins-and-needles prickle in the hand brushing the cards—a feeling that quickly turned into a buzz.

All right, then. Ask a question. "What are the repercussions from the humans killing the *terra indigene*?"

She kept brushing her fingers over the cards, picking up a card when touching it turned a prickle into a painful buzz. Keeping her eyes closed, she set the prophecy cards facedown on the counter. One card. Two. Three.

Meg opened her eyes, turned the cards over, and stared at the answer to her question.

The first card was one she thought of as an Elemental card: tornado, hurricane, avalanche, earthquake. The second card was one of the creatures Jester insisted wasn't make-believe. The third card was the hooded figure holding a scythe.

Meg returned the cards to the drawer, then brushed her hand over all the cards again. "What will happen to Lakeside?"

No prickles of any kind. That couldn't be right. *Something* was bound to happen in Lakeside.

She closed her eyes and brushed her hand over the cards again, repeating the question over and over.

Nothing. Then the faintest prickle.

She moved the cards around, using both hands now to locate the source of that prickle.

Found it!

She opened her eyes, looked at the card, and frowned. The only thing on the card was a large question mark. How was that an answer?

Future undecided.

She returned the card and closed the drawer.

She wasn't going to discuss this with Simon or Vlad or any of her human friends. After all, turning over a few cards wasn't *prophecy.*

But what if she cut herself and saw the same image? She would waste skin on a question that had been answered, which would upset Simon and the rest of her friends. And since anyone she asked to listen to the prophecy would argue about the need to make this cut, she would have to swallow the words and endure the agony of not speaking so that the cut wouldn't be completely wasted.

Future undecided.

For one uncomfortable moment, she wondered if the answer was more about her than about the city. If she couldn't avoid the lure of the razor, how much of a future would she, or any other *cassandra sangue*, have?

She picked up her supply notebook and went into the front room, where she would have Nathan's snoozing company while she checked the list of things the humans—and the Others when they were in human form—would need over the next few months.

Undecided or not, Lakeside *would* have a future, and so would she. She wasn't going to believe otherwise.

<Ruthie smells nervous,> Henry observed.

<Might have something to do with the four of us standing between her and the door,> Tess replied.

<And it's a small room,> Vlad added. <But the rooms above our social center didn't need to be large for the way they had been used.>

Simon, Henry noticed, said nothing.

"The human pups need schooling," Henry began.

"Yes," Ruthie said. "I know Eve Denby and Lieutenant Montgomery are concerned about getting the children enrolled in a school this fall."

"They need schooling now."

She blinked. "Now? But . . . it's summer."

"Yes. So they should begin learning the things they must for this season, as our young do."

"The adults need to work, and the children need activities that will help them survive," Tess said. "Since they are old enough, and independent enough, to cause trouble, they are old enough to do some work, to learn some skills."

Ruthie looked alarmed. "What kind of skills? I mean, humans have laws about child labor."

"Human law doesn't apply in the Courtyard," Simon growled.

"The point is," Vlad interrupted, "the human children can receive supervised learning from a human teacher, which is you, or they can be banned from the Courtyard unless they are with a human adult."

"Or we can let someone like Nathan or Blair teach them about the value of obeying adults." Henry nodded when Ruthie paled. "You begin to understand. We tolerate much from all the young because they *are* young. But our young learn as well as play throughout the year. And our young now include any human young who spend time here."

"But I don't have any of the books or supplies or—"

"Order a dozen sets of books for all the grades of human schooling," Simon said. "Order the supplies—the chalkboards and other things a schoolroom needs."

"Where are they going to school?" Ruthie asked.

Vlad indicated the room. "Here?"

All right, even with the bed removed, it might be a cramped space since there would have to be desks for the children and the teacher.

"Maybe we could make one of the efficiency apartments into the human school," Henry said. "Lorne does not often stay overnight, and the police pack will soon have their own dens across the street. These rooms could be like . . . a dormitory? There is a sink and toilet up here. We could put a wave-cooker and small fridge in the social room and move things around."

"But I'm supposed to help the *terra indigene* learn human things, and help Meg with *The Blood Prophets Guide*," Ruthie protested.

"And you'll still do those things," Vlad said. "Perhaps you can teach the children in the morning and work on other tasks later."

"Lieutenant Montgomery asked me if there was work here for his mother," Simon said. "Maybe doing things with the children is something she can do since she is going to help look after the Lizzy."

Ruthie tugged on her hair. Henry wondered why humans did that. He'd tried it once after observing a human do it and didn't see the point.

"All right." Ruthie blew out a breath. "I can see the need to structure the children's time. I certainly see the value of their continuing to learn, especially since their school time was interrupted. But Lizzy and Sarah are seven and Robert is nine. Why do I need to order books for the earlier or later grades of school?"

"You need to order them now because they may not be available later," Vlad said. "Or they may not be easy to obtain."

Ruthie stared at them. "You're making this sound like the one-room class-rooms in frontier towns that I read about in history books."

"Yes," Henry said. "You should think of it that way."

Watching her, he wondered if they should have brought a chair in the room so that she could sit down. They hadn't thought they were asking for such a strange thing.

Finally Ruthie nodded. "I would prefer an efficiency apartment to one of these rooms. I'll need to think about what kind of desk will work best if it has to accom-modate younger children and teenagers later. And I'll see what we can come up with right now with the furniture we have."

"We'll clear out one of the apartments that overlook the area behind Howling Good Reads and A Little Bite. Less distraction than the apartments with windows overlooking Crowfield Avenue," Vlad said.

<Simon?> Henry asked. <Do you agree with this?> The Wolf seemed . . . twitchy.

<It's fine. We have to go to HGR. Some of the Elementals want to talk to the Business Association.>

Simon, Henry, and Tess stepped aside, giving Ruthie access to the door, which Vlad opened for her.

"You didn't tell her that Lieutenant Montgomery's kin may be bringing off-spring," Vlad said as the four of them left the social center and returned to Howl-ing Good Reads.

"I didn't think it would matter," Simon replied. He unlocked the front door of HGR and went inside.

Not good, Henry thought as Earth, Air, Fire, and Water turned to face all of them but focused on Simon.

"Ocean has a question and would like you to help find the answer."

"Girl talk," Meg told Nathan before she closed the Private door. Since he didn't do anything but yawn at her, she wondered if he already knew what the girls needed to discuss.

After Ruth told them about her meeting with the Business Association, Meg looked at the expressions on her friends' faces.

"Studying in the summertime is strange?" she asked. Unless a girl was truly ill, the *cassandra sangue* had had lessons every day.

"There's usually a break in the summer, but I understand the Others wanting the children corralled for part of each day," Eve said. "And while I want my kids to be safe, and would prefer more snarl and less teeth, I appreciate that the whole pack raises, and disciplines, the pups, and they see our children as two-legged puppies."

"They would see them that way because *their* pups run around on two legs part of the time," Meg said.

"It's not the studying during summer that I find troubling. It's the Business Association wanting me to order all the coursework for all the grades," Ruth said. "Is that their way of saying that human children connected to the Courtyard will *never* be able to go to school with the rest of the children in Lakeside?"

"Maybe. Or maybe there will be less paper available to print books and that will make it harder to buy schoolbooks." Merri Lee met Meg's eyes. "Or maybe the Others are saying something else. Meg?"

She hadn't intended to tell them. When she hesitated, Merri Lee added, "Girls only, need to know?" Meaning no sharing, not even with partners and husbands.

"Future undecided," Meg said quietly. "When I asked what would happen to Lakeside, I picked a card that had a big question mark and nothing else."

"Have you told Simon or Henry?" Ruth asked.

Meg shook her head. She'd have to tell Simon now that she'd told the girls. Then she told her friends about the other three cards—and watched them pale.

"Gods," Merri Lee said. "Captain Burke called a big meeting, all his officers, all shifts. Michael called to say he was going in and didn't know when he'd have a chance to swing by."

"Let's call Steve Ferryman." Meg turned toward the counter and the phone. "He can give us the name of someone who works at one of the schools in Ferryman's Landing. They'll already have the lists of books they use for each grade. And a teacher from that village will talk to us."

"Maybe we should ask about books that would be relevant for the kinds of things learned at the technical college too," Ruth said. "We should find out how people learn trades among the Intuits. Plumbers, electricians, that kind of work."

Meg made the call. Steve was helpful, but she could feel him thinking hard about what she was asking and *why* she would be asking. After all, the Courtyard wasn't the only place that would need schoolbooks. So would the five young *cassandra sangue* who were living on Great Island. So would any children in the new River Road Community, even if they were meant to attend schools in Ferryman's Landing.

He gave her phone numbers and e-mail addresses for the principals of each school in Ferryman's Landing and promised to call them immediately so they would be expecting her request.

"Meg, I can stay here and watch for deliveries while you and Ruth run up to the Business Association's room and send the e-mails," Merri Lee said.

"Anything you want me to do?" Eve asked. "Until the Others take possession of the apartment buildings—or until they clear out the furniture and that efficiency apartment is ready for a good scrub—there's not a lot for me to do. I was going to go up to the Green Complex and check the garden, see if it needed any weeding or watering while Pete watched the kids, but that can wait."

"I think we're covered," Merri Lee said.

Brittle cheerfulness, but Meg thought they all felt better about being able to do *something*.

Monty had expected all the patrol officers under Burke's command to show up whether it was their shift or not, and he wasn't surprised to see Commander Louis Gresh and his bomb squad in attendance, but he was surprised to see the other captains who worked at the Chestnut Street station file in to hear . . . whatever this was.

"Make a little room?"

Startled by the voice, Monty took a step to the side to make room. Apparently, even the station's chief was attending—and looking apprehensive.

Burke stood behind the podium. "I appreciate you all responding so quickly. I'll be brief so you can get back to your duties."

Burke hesitated, and Monty felt a cold knot in his belly. Douglas Burke didn't hesitate.

"As most of you know, I have a pretty good grapevine when it comes to getting information." Nervous laughter followed Burke's statement. "This is a best guess based on the photos news reporters took when they went back to some of the towns in the Midwest and Northwest for a follow-up story, as well as reports from police officers who drove to towns where they couldn't raise anyone from the police station or government building." He scanned the room. "Based on those sources, I would say the *terra indigene* retaliated against every town or ranch that had some residents who killed the Wolfgard. They gutted those towns—in some cases, literally. The *terra indigene* slaughtered the humans in the same way the Wolves were slaughtered. In some cases that meant they killed everything that was human, whether it was a man, woman, or child. In other places, a phone call was made to the nearest surviving human place. The people who answered that call found all the young children in the community together in a building at the edge of the town. Those children were unharmed, so I'm speculating that the Wolfgard young had also escaped the slaughter of the adults."

Burke waited a moment, letting all the men consider that. "Gentlemen, I've seen a few of the photos taken of the people who died as retaliation. These killings weren't done by the shifters humans usually have contact with. They weren't done by any kind of shifter most of us have seen—or will ever see while we have any chance of staying alive. The denizens of the true wild country—those parts of Thaisia that have *never* been touched by anything human—are no longer willing to let shifters like the Wolfgard act as a buffer between them and us, because we've just shown them that we can, and will, kill the *terra indigene* who were dealing with us. So now other kinds of earth natives are on our doorstep. They had already declared a breach of trust and had limited the use of the right-of-ways that run through their land and connect human populations. I think from now on, we should assume there is no right-of-way. Not for vehicles traveling on the roads; not for the trains. Certainly not for any vessel traveling on the lakes or rivers."

Burke gripped the podium. "This next part has to stay with the people in this room. You'll be tempted to tell other family members and friends and your next-door neighbors. If you do, you'll only cause panic over something I hope will never happen."

Extinction, Monty thought, feeling cold as he recalled Simon's comment about not fearing humans because most of them would be extinct.

"Every family member should have a go bag," Burke said. "A couple of changes of clothes, toiletries specific to each person, including any prescription medications that person needs to carry. Have a separate bag for general medications and first aid supplies, or put essentials in the bags for the adults. Include a list of bank account numbers as well as any important papers you don't keep in a safe-deposit box. Put the go bags someplace where they can be grabbed by people scrambling to find them. You want your families to be out of the house in a couple of minutes."

Silence. Uneasy looks.

Louis Gresh cleared his throat. "Having go bags is fine, but if they're needed, where are our families supposed to go? If the *terra indigene* are going to attack us for what was done in another part of Thaisia, and if your point about there no longer being a right-of-way through the wild country means the Others are going to attack anyone who tries to leave the city, where can we go?"

"Here." Burke sounded grim. "We've been working with the Lakeside Court-yard and have gained the trust of the leaders. I think if this is put the right way to Simon Wolfgard, he might know how to prevent a direct attack on this building and its personnel. He might be willing to help us."

"Captain?" Kowalski raised a couple of fingers. "Why now?"

"Some of you met my cousin Shamus Burke, who was visiting from Brittania. I received a cable from him this morning, which is the second reason I called this meeting." Burke glanced at the station chief. "I don't know how far this news has traveled through official channels, but the Cel-Romano Alliance of Nations attacked the *terra indigene* all along their border. They have new kinds of weapons—airplanes—that can fly over a long distance and drop bombs that can destroy buildings and kill a lot of people, no matter their shape. They bombed *terra indigene* settlements situated between Cel-Romano and the wild country. Troops followed and killed the Others who survived the bombing. The Alliance of Nations has expanded its borders by miles in one collected attack."

"What have the *terra indigene* done in response?" the station chief asked.

"They've done nothing." Burke looked grimmer, if that was possible, and pale. "They've done nothing. If you read Thaisia's history—or the speculations that have been written about conflicts in the past between humans and the *terra indi-gene* throughout the world—you'll see they do nothing while they consider the actions and behaviors of the predators attempting to take their territory. Those hours or days are usually the calm that precedes a catastrophic counterattack. I have no doubt the *terra indigene* are going to strike Cel-Romano. Maybe, if we're lucky, the Others from the wild country won't understand that the Humans First and Last movement is the common factor between the attacks on the Wolfgard in Thaisia and Cel-Romano's grab for land that resulted in an unknown number of *terra indigene* deaths." He paused. "That's it."

Monty filed out with the rest of the men. There was no answer at his sister's apartment, no communication at all since his mother's last message. They could be anywhere at this point—and nowhere was safe.

"Should I bring the car around, Lieutenant?" Kowalski asked.

Monty nodded. "I'll take a minute to check my messages; then I'll be ready to go."

At the trailing end of dusk, Simon trotted over to the part of the Courtyard where the Elementals resided.

They were all there, except for Autumn and Winter.

"Wolf?" Air said. "You have an answer?"

<Perhaps.>

He'd talked it over with Blair and Nathan, with Henry, with Vlad and Nyx. He'd even talked with Tess in order to shape an answer to the question of why humans would have killed the Wolfgard in two regions of Thaisia when they should have known their so-called victory would be nothing more than a short-lived illusion.

<Sometimes a pack tests a herd to see which animal would be the best prey. But if the prey has been chosen already, some of the pack will go after another animal, splitting the herd so that the true prey is in a smaller group. We go after one in order to successfully bring down another.> Simon looked at the Elementals but wasn't sure if he'd provided them with an answer that made any sense to their form of *terra indigene*.

"Go after one in order to bring down another," Water said thoughtfully. "Attack in one place to distract anyone from seeing the beginning of the true attack."

<Yes.> Simon tried to stay still. He felt surrounded by a dangerous charge, like a storm that hadn't given a single rumble of warning thunder before it struck.

"We will give your words to Ocean," Water said.

Dismissed. Simon trotted back to the Green Complex, moving as if he didn't have a care. He didn't think the Courtyard would be in danger from whatever was coming as long as he was sure that anyone within its boundaries wouldn't be considered an enemy. He would have to think about how he could split the police pack to herd those he trusted into the Courtyard, where they would have as much protection as the *terra indigene* who lived here.

When he reached the Green Complex, Meg stepped out of the summer room.

"Simon? We need to talk. You don't have to shift. I just need you to listen."

He wasn't sure he liked this arrangement of not being able to voice an opinion she could understand, but he could listen this time. He followed her into the summer room. When she sat on a lounge chair, he sat in front of her, his front paws on either side of her feet, bringing him so close her knees brushed his chest.

She told him about the cards she'd drawn when she wondered what would happen because of the death of the Wolves. She told him about the question mark after she asked about Lakeside.

"It wasn't really a prophecy, but I thought you should know."

He thought it was a pretty accurate prophecy. Jean had seen a vision of Lakeside being one of the few human places that survived. Now Meg saw an undecided future. After meeting with the Elementals this evening, he would agree with that. Whatever actions and decisions were made by humans and Others in the days ahead would decide Lakeside's future.

He didn't want Meg to feel unhappy, so he licked her nose and made her laugh. She stretched out on the lounge chair. He stretched out beside it and thought about human males and females and how females on TV often complained that the male didn't talk to them, didn't know how to communicate.

Even when he was in Wolf form, he and Meg communicated just fine. Maybe they communicated better than two humans because she *didn't* expect him to talk.

That was an entertaining thing to think about, so he thought and dozed and, when she fell asleep, gave her hand a couple of friendly licks.

CHAPTER 43

Words became thoughts conveyed as a wind that riffled the surface of lakes; as a taste in grass; as the smoke rising from a short-lived natural fire. Those thoughts, those ideas, moved swiftly to the north, the south, the west, the east.

Tasting the thoughts when they reached the surf, Alantea spun them back into words.

Distraction. Diversion. Attack in one place in order to destroy the true prey that lived in another place.

I can create distraction. Alantea sent that thought back to kiss Thaisia's shore.

We can be a diversion, offered other Elementals.

They waited for Namid's teeth and claws to reply.

For two days the Elementals, from the smallest to the most powerful, waited for an answer.

Then, for just a moment, an odd and terrible silence formed a skin over the whole world. Then it was gone, leaving behind the answer.

Distraction.

Diversion.

Destruction of the true prey.

Thin the herds.

A wind began to blow from the northernmost part of Thaisia.

A wind began to blow from the south, teasing the water Elementals who lived around the gulf until they slapped at the wind, creating surges that slipped over the retainer walls that humans had built to protect their cities.

One of the Elementals known as Earth pretended to pick a quarrel with Pacifikus, the Elemental who ruled the Pacifik Ocean. Earth stamped her foot, then leaped onto Tsunami's back and raced for the West Coast of Thaisia. Pacifikus laughed, mounted Typhoon, and gave chase, still undecided if he would steer the coming storm away from most of the coastline or run with Earth and feed the storm until it reached its full potential.

And off the coast of the eastern Storm Islands, Alantea mounted Hurricane and began to limber up her steed.

CHAPTER 44

Watersday, Juin 30

Hope frowned at her half-finished drawing. The Wolfgard cabin looked fine. So did the trees and grass. But the *real* sky was a clear, deep blue, and the sky she'd drawn was dark, ominous. The storm clouds had shadows in them that almost formed shapes—creatures with teeth and claws.

She tore the drawing out of her sketch pad and turned the paper over to the clean side. She wasn't going to finish that drawing, but Jackson had told her that paper might be harder to come by, so she wasn't going to waste what she had.

She slapped a hand in front of the nose of the juvenile Wolf who was sneaking up on her colored pencils. "Those aren't twigs to chew on."

The culprit made a sound like a guilty grumble. Another juvenile made a sound that could only be laughter. The next thing she knew, all the young Wolves had abandoned her and were engaged in a mock battle—lots of snarls and body bumps as they chased one another.

Tension eased from her shoulders as she picked up a black pencil. Ever since her hysterical warning had thwarted an attack on the Wolves, there were always a couple of juvenile Wolves keeping her company. More to the point, they were watching intently for any sign that she was going to do the crazy thing again. The youngsters weren't sure what had happened or why; they just knew that the adults had responded to a threat they couldn't see—and their Hope had given the warning howl in her own way.

So they watched her. So did the juvenile Hawks, Eagles, and Ravens. She'd even spotted one of the big golden Panthers watching her from a distance.

Maybe she should go inside and compose a letter to Meg Corbyn. Or ask Grace if she could go down to the communications cabin and send a short e-mail. She wasn't sure what she would say, but it seemed important all of a sudden.

"Hope? What's that?"

Hope blinked as she focused on Jackson, who was crouched beside her. Why did the sun look so bright? Had she fallen asleep? "What is what?"

He pointed to the paper. "That."

She felt a little sick as she looked at the simple, almost childish drawing she didn't remember creating.

An outline of Thaisia, with inverted Vs to indicate mountain ranges. Heavier lines marked the boundaries of the regions, although there was a heavier line dividing the Midwest Region into a north and south. Over one of those lines, she'd drawn a magnifying glass that revealed the poles and wires for the telephone and telegraph lines that ran along the shoulders of the roads. But there were no lines connecting the poles on either side of the regional boundary. Instead there were human skulls piled beside the road like a cairn, and the poles had deep claw marks.

Jackson took the paper, turned it over, and studied the half-finished drawing that showed a storm.

"Could I send an e-mail to Meg Corbyn?" Hope asked.

Those amber Wolf eyes studied her now. "Is there something you need to tell her?"

"I don't know. I just wanted to send one . . ." *While I could,* she finished silently.

"I have to contact Simon Wolfgard. I can tell him you asked about Meg."

She heard a growl beneath his words. "Did I cause trouble again?"

"Warning us of trouble isn't the same as causing it." Jackson stood. "But don't give peanut butter and bread to the pups. That's food for you."

"I didn't *give* it to them," she grumbled. She just wanted to keep her fingers more than she wanted to keep the treat. Of course, watching them try to tongue the peanut butter stuck to the roofs of their mouths *was* pretty funny.

Jackson sighed and walked away, carrying her drawing.

She gathered up her supplies, checking the area to make sure she had all her pencils. She would sit on the porch and read for a while, or help Grace with chores.

Anything that would keep her occupied so that she wouldn't see the moment when the sky changed from a deep, clear blue to the storm clouds that were coming.

After putting Hope's drawing in a cardboard mailing tube, Jackson jogged down the road to the communications cabin. A century ago the *terra indigene* had little knowledge or use for the wires and poles humans used for communication. They just tended their part of the land and were aware of neighboring groups of earth natives. That was good and necessary, especially for young Wolves who needed to leave their home packs in order to find mates. And some of the more adventurous Wolves had traveled a long way simply to learn about other pieces of Thaisia and the *terra indigene* who lived there. Somewhere along the way, some of them began to understand what the wires and poles meant to the clever monkeys, who had encroached on a little more land every year until the Elders lashed out and refused to give up any more of the wild country to the two-legged predators.

The wires and poles made it possible for humans to talk to one another over long distances. That had been fine, even beneficial for the Others as well as humans, when the talking had been about moving food from one place to another, or selling blankets where they would be needed. But the humans had used the wires and poles to plan attacks on the *terra indigene*, and, right now, he was the only one who knew what the Elders intended to do because of it.

"Jackson?"

He turned away from the communications cabin and waited for the Intuit men to reach him.

"Are the prophet pups all right?" he asked.

"Fine. A bit restless today, but they're fine." They looked at one another, then back at him. "Have you listened to the news today? No? Strange weather on the West Coast. A tsunami and a typhoon collided, breaking up both storms before they made landfall. But now, instead of being focused, those storms have spread their force in a way that they are going to hit most of the West Coast. The people who study weather can't explain it any more than they can explain why there's suddenly cold air coming down from the north and hot air coming up from the south. And there's a hurricane gathering force as it moves up the East Coast. We aren't sure if we're going to be dealing with weather coming over the mountains from the west or coming down from the north. We just have a feeling that it's going to get rough these next few days."

He saw them glancing at the mailing tube, and he thought about the storm clouds Hope had drawn. More than one kind of storm was coming.

"It's going to get rough," he agreed.

"Thing is, the fire that turned against the men who tried to burn us out didn't take the whole of Endurance. And we figure not everyone who lives there was in favor of the Humans First and Last movement or what they were going to do."

"That's probably true."

"Several of us had a feeling that we should go down there and make sure those folks have enough provisions to last through the storm. It's not right to stand by and let them suffer."

If it had been you, or us, they would have done exactly that. But maybe not. All humans might be the enemy, but not all of them were bad.

"Why are you telling me?" he asked.

A hesitation. "We wanted your permission. Maybe you could let other . . . folks . . . know we're going down to Endurance on your say-so."

"You have a feeling that you need my say-so?"

"Oh yes, Jackson. We are *certain* we need it."

No more buffers. Even the land used by humans for crops or pastures would feel the Elders' presence now. And any human who was out there might not return home.

He looked up and spotted the Eagle overhead. <Eagle? Can you provide watch and escort for these Intuits? If the Elders ask, tell them I gave these humans permission to visit the other village.>

A moment of startled silence. <I will watch. If asked, I will repeat your words.>

"Go soon," he told the men. "Get back to your own village before nightfall." He hesitated, his instinctive distrust of humans warring with his choice to work with the Intuits who lived in Sweetwater. "When you get back, you should inform your Intuit contacts that lines of communication may be severed between regions. I *think* we'll be able to use telephones and send telegrams within each region, but we're going to be isolated."

"For how long?"

Forever? "I don't know."

"In that case, one of us will stay behind and start sending out the alert."

Nodding to the men, Jackson walked into the communications cabin and greeted the Crow on duty. Maybe Simon already knew, or knew even more, and was already making plans for the Lakeside Courtyard. But the Wolfgard youngsters in Prairie Gold were vulnerable. And the Intuit village there was much like the one here—a small community that might not survive long if it was cut off from everyone else.

He removed the drawing from the mailing tube and studied the storm clouds in the half-finished drawing. Then he rolled it back up and reached for the phone. He would try calling Simon first, then Jesse Walker and Tolya Sanguinati. If he understood the Hope pup's vision drawing, it wasn't just the Elementals who were going to rip Thaisia apart.

To: All Intuit Villages and Settlements

Oncoming storms may sever lines of communication for an indeterminate time. Recommend that three or four villages with the best chance of surviving the storms become message hubs for their region. Also recommend that each village send a *brief* report to its designated hub daily to confirm status.

Protect your supplies and livestock as best you can. May the gods watch over all of us.

—Dispatcher at Sweetwater, Northwest Region

To: Pater

Hurricane coming up the East Coast. Support of HFL rapidly diminishing. Taking the last ocean greyhound leaving Toland this evening. Will be with you soon to celebrate Cel-Romano's victory.

—NS

CHAPTER 45

Watersday, Juin 30

Simon barely had time to finish the phone call with Jackson and relay the information to Vlad before Steve Ferryman rushed in from the stock room of Howling Good Reads, dodging Vlad when the Sanguinati tried to block him.

"Have you seen this?" Steve set a piece of paper on the checkout counter.

Simon read the warning, then pushed the paper toward Vlad. "Haven't seen this, exactly, but I just talked to Jackson Wolfgard, and he basically said the same thing."

Steve blew out a breath. "Penny Sledgeman has appointed herself dispatch coordinator for our area."

"As the mayor of Ferryman's Landing, aren't you supposed to make such appointments?" Vlad asked.

"Penny and my mom have been helping me deal with the deluge of requests for information about the *cassandra sangue*. This is going to be even more work. My mom and dad are working the barge to bring supplies to the island side of the village; my brother is moving as much as he can on the ferry. So if Penny wants to take this on, may the river bless her. I'm trying to get everyone warned in time to prepare." Steve paused. "You think we're going to lose power lines as well as phone? Well, no way for you to tell, is there? Uprooted trees can take down lines and knock out power in a whole area."

Thinking about the cards Meg had selected in answer to a question, Simon looked at Vlad. To some degree, they would all feel the storms, but he had no reason to believe that the Intuit villages would face Namid's teeth and claws, so why frighten Steve with too much truth?

<We should tell him something,> Simon said.

Vlad leaned on the counter. "It's possible that power lines will come down if the storms become severe. But those can be fixed. The loss of communication between regions should be thought of as long-term, and the Intuits and *terra indigene* should consider how to compensate for that."

They watched Steve consider the implications, and saw the moment when he understood, as they did, that the shape of Thaisia was about to change.

"What about radio?" Steve asked. "What about television? Those are forms of communication."

<Do you think the Elders considered those?> Vlad asked Simon.

<No,> he replied. <And there's no reason they will. It's easy enough for the Elementals to silence those things if they become troublesome.>

"If used with care, those forms of communication probably will remain intact," Vlad said.

"All right." Steve rubbed the back of his neck. "I'll head to the River Road Community now and make sure all the people working on the houses get everything closed down and secure. We're using the old industrial building to store supplies except for food. Oh, and a couple of the new residents arrived yesterday. A Roy Panthergard? I gather he's an enforcer for the community?"

"He'll deal with problems if any come up," Simon said vaguely. Steve could figure out for himself the end result of a problem meeting Roy's claws. "Who else arrived?"

"Two pairs. They both said they were Lynxgard, but then one pair said they were Bobcats and the other said they were Lynxes."

"A gard name can be specific to one form, but sometimes it serves as an umbrella for *terra indigene* who took their forms from related animals," Vlad explained. "Beargard includes all kinds of bear forms. Panthergard includes what humans would call panthers, cougars, mountain lions, jaguars, leopards, and probably a few more names."

"Good to know." Steve stepped away from the counter. "I'll be in touch."

They waited until they heard the back door close.

"First come the storms," Simon said. "Then come the Elders."

"Then comes death," Vlad finished. "There won't be much mercy, if any."

"How much mercy did the humans show when they killed so many of the

Wolfgard in the Midwest and Northwest? How much mercy did they show when they attacked us here? Or when they dropped bombs on the *terra indigene* who watched the borders of Cel-Romano?"

"And that's how we should behave?"

He shook his head. "I don't want to be that human. We can't protect everyone in Lakeside from the storms or the Elders, but we can try to protect the human pack. If we bring them into the Courtyard, the Elders might leave them alone."

"Some members of that pack have connections with humans who want nothing to do with us. Do we let in a potential enemy in order to protect a friend?"

"No. If anyone in the human pack can't accept that, then that's their choice." The phone rang. Simon growled at it.

"The call might be about an order. We still get orders from the *terra indigene*."

Good point. He picked up the phone. "Howling Good Reads. Yes, I am. Yes, I remember who you are." He must have started growling, because Vlad poked him. "Stay there. We'll come and get you." He hung up and turned on his friend. "Don't poke me."

"Just trying to help." Vlad tapped the phone. "Who wants a ride?"

"Agent Greg O'Sullivan. And Lieutenant Montgomery's pack. I'll go with Blair and pick them up at the train station."

"I'll call the lieutenant—and ask Captain Burke to drop by for a quiet word." Vlad started toward the stock room and the stairs, then stopped. "Do you know where Michael Debany is now?"

"He was working at the Green Complex's garden. Might still be there or heading this way to get ready for work." Simon tried to stifle excitement as he added, "He is riding a bicycle to and from the garden."

He had no interest in learning to ride a bicycle, but he really wanted to chase one. On foot, humans weren't fast enough to be fun play-prey. Except Meg, but that was a different kind of chase game. But the bicycle . . .

That game would have to wait.

"Why do you want him?"

"I have something to discuss with him on Tolya's behalf," Vlad replied.

They walked out the back door together, stopping long enough to tell Merri Lee that she was minding the store for a while. Then Vlad shifted to smoke and headed for the Green Complex while Simon waited for Blair to bring a van around.

When a pack got too big, it was hard to bring down enough game to feed everyone. Problem was, their numbers were swelling with two-legged predators who wouldn't be much good at bringing down meat.

They would have to earn their keep, just like everyone else in the Courtyard. This not working in the summer was a strange idea. You had to eat in the summer, same as in every other season. That required work.

Couldn't tell yet if the storm that would hit Lakeside would come across the Great Lakes or swing in from the storm coming up the East Coast—or both. No way to tell how much time they had left to bring in supplies.

While he waited for Blair, he dashed into the Liaison's Office to tell Meg that she and the female pack needed to order the schoolbooks today. With a bit of luck, they would receive some of them before the storms—and the Elders—arrived.

Vlad shifted to human form and waited for Michael Debany to notice him before approaching the garden.

There was that delicious moment when both hearts beat faster, and prey and predator recognized each other for what they were. But with the human pack, it really was just a moment before recent experience quieted generations of instinct.

"Hi," Debany said. "It's looking good, don't you think?"

Vlad didn't see anything different from yesterday in terms of edible food, but he nodded. "It is, yes. Do you have a minute?"

"Sure." Debany pulled a towel and water bottle out of a small pack. He drank deep, then poured some water over his face and wiped it off. "What's up?"

Casual. Trusting. At least trying to be those things.

"You have a sister."

"Yes, I do." The voice was still casual, but the eyes were wary.

"She likes animals."

"She does. She has enough schooling to qualify as a veterinarian's assistant. The family couldn't afford to pay for more schooling, so she came home to find some work and save up to continue later. She was looking to work with animals as a job. Practical experience and a paycheck, you know?"

The same could be said for younger members of a Courtyard. "Has she ever considered living out west?"

"Don't think she's ever said, but with all that's happened, I wouldn't want her to go out there."

"Even if her safety was assured as best it could be?"

"Meaning?"

"We can't be responsible if she sticks her hand in a hole and is bitten by a rattlesnake. But the not-edible rule would apply." Vlad studied Debany's face. Police stance. Listening but no longer reacting. "Tolya Sanguinati is now in charge of a town called Bennett."

"I've heard of it." Flat voice.

"Then you also know there are no longer any human residents."

A nod.

"There are, however, surviving house animals that need care, as well as the other animals that were left behind. Sanguinati and Wolfgard are on their way to Bennett, as well as some other forms of *terra indigene*. Some Intuits are also on their way to help run the businesses that are needed to support that train station. There wouldn't be many humans like herself there, at least not in the beginning, but it would be an opportunity to do the kind of work you say she wants to do."

"Who's looking after the animals now?"

"I don't know. Whoever is in town that day, I think."

Debany rubbed the towel over his face. "I'll tell her about it. Has to be her choice."

A reminder to me or you? Vlad thought. "Well, we don't need an answer until we get through these storms." *And find out what's left of Thaisia when they're done.*

"Thanks for coming to get us," Greg O'Sullivan said when Simon walked over to the chairs at the train station where the ITF agent guarded four females.

Simon almost told him that Blair needed to come to the station anyway to pick up some things they had ordered for the Courtyard, but that might make it sound like the humans were extra luggage, so he said, "It's fine."

The oldest female stood. She was short and thin, with brown skin and brown eyes, and her short curly hair was more tarnished silver than black. The other adult female was younger, and had black hair and brown skin, but her eyes were a clear, startling green.

O'Sullivan made the introductions. "This is Twyla Montgomery, her daughter, Sierra, and the girls are Carrie and Bonnie. Ladies, this is Simon Wolfgard, leader of the Lakeside Courtyard."

"Can we call you Wolfie?" the girl with the missing front tooth asked.

"You can call him Mr. Wolfgard or Mr. Simon, same as you would any other grown-up," Twyla said.

She didn't raise her voice or threaten, but she subdued the pup and left no doubt that question wouldn't be asked again.

Simon was impressed—and hopeful there was now someone who could keep the human puppies in line without biting them. "What should we call you?"

"Twyla will do."

Maybe. He'd see what Lieutenant Montgomery said about that.

Humans were starting to notice them, and it wasn't smart to linger. Simon grabbed a couple of the carryalls piled around the females and tried to remember the things humans asked about travel. "Did you have a good trip?"

"It was just fine once we got seats," Twyla replied. "We'd probably still be sitting in the station at Hubbney if Agent O'Sullivan hadn't stepped in."

"Oh?" Simon looked at O'Sullivan, who was also carrying a couple of bags that weren't his own. Simon knew this because one carryall was black; the other two were bright pink and smelled like the little females.

"There has been some trouble with trains running out of Toland, so everyone is being funneled through Hubb NE," O'Sullivan replied in a quiet voice. "Now that trains aren't running after dark, to avoid incidents, there is a backlog of passengers, and those who could afford to 'upgrade' their ticket were being given the seats. Ms. Montgomery and her family had already been sitting at the Hubbney station for a full day when I arrived to catch the train to Lakeside. When I heard her son was a police officer, I stepped in and gave the railway a choice of putting us in the executive car or having me shut down the station while the ITF investigated the preferential treatment of some passengers over others."

Simon smiled. "You have teeth, O'Sullivan, even if you are human."

"Thanks."

They packed the van with cargo and carryalls and humans. As he settled into the front passenger seat, Simon heard the distant sound of thunder.

Meg opened the gate and slipped inside Henry's yard. Nathan was still in the Liaison's Office, and Jake was perched on the wall between the delivery area and the yard, so she'd have plenty of warning if a truck pulled in.

She hurried up to the studio door and tapped on the frame. "Henry? Can I come in?"

The Grizzly stepped away from one of his sculptures and gave her a quizzical look. "When have you needed to ask?"

She went in and sat on the bench where she could watch him work without getting in the way.

"I'm glad you came. I wanted to show you this." Henry picked up a piece of wood and came over to sit beside her. "What do you think?"

Not finished yet, but she could make out a tree in the center. In each corner of the box, touching some of the branches, was something that represented each of the seasons. "It's wonderful. This is the lid for the box to hold the prophecy cards?"

He nodded. "When it's time, you can help me stain the pieces. That way the wood will get to know you."

She ran her fingers gently over the wood. "I'd like that."

He took the lid and set it aside. "What's on your mind, Meg?" He waved aside her excuse before she made one. "You wouldn't come to visit during your work time if you didn't want to talk while everyone else was occupied—and with the new visitors, everyone *is* occupied."

"Henry? How much human is too human?"

In human form, Henry was a big man with shaggy brown hair and brown eyes, but he didn't *feel* human. At least, not when she'd first met him. Now? Was it just that she'd gotten used to him, or had he lost some of the wildness in these past few months?

"That depends on who you ask," he replied.

"The *terra indigene* who no one talks about. The really dangerous ones. Well, you're dangerous too, but . . ." She stopped, afraid she'd insulted him. Then she pressed on, because she had to know. "Simon has brought more humans to the Courtyard. It's Lieutenant Montgomery's family, so it's a kind thing to do, but will *they* think he's becoming too human because he's spending so much time with humans? Are *you* at risk? Did I cause this?"

Henry leaned forward and rested his forearms on his thighs. His expression went from puzzlement to amusement as he slowly shook his head. "Have you been saving up these questions, Meg?"

"You think it's funny?"

"Funny? No. Amusing?" He tipped a hand back and forth. "There is always a danger of taking too much from a form, but I imagine that's been true since the first *terra indigene* took the form of another predator in order to study its way of hunting and become an even better hunter than the original animal. But humans are an odd kind of predator, and most of what they fight over among themselves . . ." He shrugged. "Yes, we've become more entangled with humans, and not just in Lakeside. Yes, there's a risk that we'll become too involved in their concerns and forget who we are and what our own kind need. But I don't think Simon will become *too* human, not in any bad way. You know why?"

Meg shook her head.

Henry smiled. "Because you won't let him."

She sat back and sighed. "Tess is kind of cranky."

"Tess is Tess."

"Do you think the Courtyard will still be able to buy those apartment buildings across the street?"

"We have bought them. The humans have to do their paperwork, but that's a formality and should be completed anytime now."

"Until then, where do we put everyone?" In the compound where she had been raised, every girl had her own cell. She didn't have a training image that would help her visualize many people crammed into a room to sleep, even temporarily.

"Meg? You take your quiet time whenever you need it. You're not responsible for Lieutenant Montgomery's pack; he is."

"Well, I'm not going to make the mistake of showing them the ponies!"

Henry's booming laugh rang out. "As if Jester would let you near the Pony Barn with small humans after the last time."

She'd made mistakes when she'd taken Lizzy to see the ponies. She had no reason to believe the other little girls would react the same way and want to *ride* the Elementals' steeds, but she wasn't going to take that chance.

They heard Jake cawing.

"Sounds like I have a delivery." Meg stood. "Thanks, Henry. I like the box."

She hurried out of the studio, ran the length of the yard, dashed out the gate, and rushed into the back room of the Liaison's Office. She reached the front counter in time to see the deliveryman getting back into his truck. The packages and her clipboard, with the information filled in, were on the counter.

She took the packages into the sorting room, then turned on the radio. She wasn't sure how long she'd been listening to the weather report when she realized that Tess had come in.

Meg tipped her head to indicate Tess's coiling green and red hair. "You're feeling tense."

"So are you." Tess looked pointedly at Meg's arm, where her fingers were digging into skin. "Are you feeling prickles?"

More than that. Worse than that. "I haven't made a cut in a few days."

"It won't tell us anything."

"It could tell us if we'll survive."

Tess gave her a long look. "No, I don't think it will this time."

Simon led Captain Burke and Agent O'Sullivan upstairs to HGR's second floor. "Vlad is checking e-mails, so we'll talk in the office where he can hear us. Unless we should wait for Lieutenant Montgomery?" He felt restless and didn't want to wait. You could dig a den in the earth to escape a bad storm or hide from fire if you couldn't outrun it. But you could drown in that same den if the storm brought a flood or if the packed earth collapsed and trapped you inside. Shifters like him weren't the target of the storms, but they were going to get hit just the same.

"No, the lieutenant needs some time with his family," Burke replied. "I'll relay the information to him once he gets everyone settled in the duplex."

How could he tell these humans that he would try to save some but he couldn't risk trying to save others who belonged to the same pack?

<The Sanguinati and Wolfgard arrived in Bennett,> Vlad said.

<Any word from Stavros?> Simon asked.

<No.> Vlad closed down the e-mail program.

Simon studied Burke. "The Courtyard will be a safe place during the storms. If Lieutenant Montgomery's pack is denning too far away, he might not be able to bring them here in time."

"My duplex isn't that far away. Besides, you've already taken in more people than you can comfortably fit," Burke said.

"There aren't enough individual dens for the newcomers to have their own place here," Simon agreed. "But there are beds above the social center that could be used for sleeping and temporary shelter. And humans sleep on the floor sometimes. Kowalski has a puffy blanket for sleeping on the ground."

"You're pussyfooting around."

Simon stepped back, insulted. "I'm a Wolf. I do not have pussy feet!"

O'Sullivan laughed.

Burke smiled, but the smile quickly faded. "You're offering shelter to humans? Why?"

"Not just any humans," Simon said at the same time Vlad said, "Because there's a storm coming."

"Yes, there is," Burke agreed. "The only question is which direction it's coming from, because, right now, there are multiple possibilities."

"Captain, the storm you can see isn't the one that is going to kill your people," Vlad said.

"If Jean's prophecy about Thaisia is correct, Lakeside is one of the human-controlled cities that will survive." Simon didn't mention that Meg had seen Lakeside's future as being undecided. He looked at O'Sullivan. "Hubb NE is another."

"Toland?" O'Sullivan asked.

"Yes, but the light was dim." He didn't want to be responsible for humans he didn't know, but he believed this gesture of friendship would help decide Lakeside's future, one way or the other. "The police we know and their kin can hide here. We don't think Namid's teeth and claws will harm any humans who are with us in the Courtyard."

"That's a generous offer," Burke said.

"If there are enemies of the *terra indigene* among those humans, we may not be able to protect any of you." Simon looked at Burke, willing him to understand. "Choose carefully."

"I've been making provisions for families of officers to take refuge at the Chestnut Street station. Being able to send some of them here . . . I appreciate it." Burke appeared to be thinking hard for a moment. "You think this will happen soon?"

"As soon as one of the storms hits Lakeside."

"I take it I shouldn't plan to get back to Hubb NE before things happen," O'Sullivan said.

Simon shook his head. "I'll talk to Elliot about letting you work out of the consulate for now. Then you can call Governor Hannigan."

O'Sullivan looked at Simon. "He's already mustering all the manpower he can in the Northeast to respond to the storms. Is there anything in particular he should prepare for?"

Hatred was now a taste in the water, rage a scent in the air. "He should prepare for a lot of humans dying."

Sitting in A Little Bite, Monty drank coffee and listened to his mother's quiet, no-nonsense recitation of the trouble they'd had getting seats on a train. Noting the strain on Sierra's face, he figured it had been a lot more trouble than Twyla would acknowledge.

He smiled at his nieces and wished he could seat them at another table—or better yet, scoot them into Howling Good Reads and out of earshot so that he could really talk to his mother and sister. "You all had quite an adventure."

Catching some movement, he turned his head and watched Captain Burke and Agent O'Sullivan approach their table.

"Ladies." Burke tipped his head slightly. "I am very pleased you're here."

"Would you be needing a word with Crispin?" Twyla asked.

"Actually, I need a word with most of you."

Nicely worded, Monty thought. Burke didn't say he wanted the girls to leave—which would have made them want to stay—but he was quite clear.

"John Wolfgard is working in the bookstore," Burke said. "I asked him to show the girls around the store. He's right over there." A gesture toward the archway that connected the two stores.

Since John was the friendliest Wolf in the Courtyard, Monty didn't think the girls would provoke him into biting if left in his care for just a few minutes.

He smiled at Carrie and Bonnie. "You could each choose a book to read. A present from me."

Carrie slid off her chair. "Can we have—"

"A book?" Sierra smiled at her daughters. "Yes, you can each have a book since that was the treat that Uncle CJ offered."

Sierra's firmness was a veneer that was wearing thin, and the girls could have broken it with whines and pouts. But Twyla's firmness ran to the core, and one look at their grandmother had the girls heading for the archway and the Wolf waiting there.

"You're Mr. John?" Twyla asked.

"Yes," John replied warily.

"They're allowed a book apiece, not anything else you might sell in your store."

John scratched behind one ear. Monty felt relieved that the ears weren't pointed or furry.

"Only sell books," John said. "And a few magazines. And some maps."

"That's fine, then."

John hesitated, then led the girls into the bookstore.

Nadine approached their table and looked at Burke. "Can I get you anything?"

"A few minutes of your time. Have a seat, Ms. Fallacaro," Burke replied.

"I have cookies baking."

"This will just take a few minutes, and it's important."

Nadine took a seat. Burke took another while O'Sullivan grabbed a chair from another table.

"I offered the other side of my duplex for your use." Burke looked at Twyla. "But I've been told that, under the current circumstances, it would be wiser if you stayed here. It will be cramped, especially since Simon Wolfgard has offered sanctuary to a few police families when this coming storm hits Lakeside. However, this is the one place where you should be protected—and there will be people here who can help you." Now he looked at Nadine. "You have a room here. What about Chris?"

"He's bunking in one of the rooms above the social center. He comes up to my room for a shower."

"Impress upon him that he needs to stay here until this storm passes."

Nadine smiled bitterly. "He has a broken hand, Captain, and he's been branded a Wolf lover. He's too vulnerable right now to go out among the humans."

Monty winced at the way she said "humans," but he couldn't blame her for feeling that way. The HFL had burned down her shop and home and would have killed her and Chris. No matter what Simon thought about getting more tangled up in human concerns, the Wolf had stepped up and offered Nadine and Chris shelter and protection.

Twyla studied the men, her eyes lingering on Monty. "This storm is part of the trouble that had you asking me to get to Lakeside as quick as I could?"

"Yes, Mama."

Now Twyla looked at Burke. "How bad is the bad going to be?"

Burke studied Twyla in turn. "Here in Lakeside? I don't know. When it comes time for the reckoning, I hope our efforts to work with the *terra indigene* will count for something. Across Thaisia? We just hope for the best now."

A kitchen timer dinged. Nadine jumped up. "I have to get those cookies out of the oven."

"Miss Nadine?" Twyla said with quiet courtesy, stopping the other woman. "You run this shop?"

"Working here. Tess runs it. I don't know where she is right now."

"I think the three of us should talk soon."

Nadine nodded and rushed into the back.

"And I'm thinking that Mr. Simon and I should talk soon too," Twyla continued.

Monty laid his hand over hers. "Mama?"

"Whatever provisions they have here for humans living or even staying overnight isn't going to fit the number of people they're going to take in and shelter. Doesn't matter how you wiggle things; they're going to need help. I've got two good hands and I know how to work. So does Sierra. And the children can do what they're able. You asked me to come and help you with Lizzy, and I will. But right now there's a lot to do and not much time to be doing, so I'm not going to sit by, Crispin. That's not my way."

"I know, Mama, but—"

"What can you do?" Simon asked, walking over to their table.

Monty wondered how long the Wolf had been standing in the archway listening.

"You tell me what needs to be done, and I'll tell you if I can do it," Twyla replied. "One thing I know right off. You're going to be feeding more people than you're used to, and that might not be easy in this coffee shop."

"We have Meat-n-Greens in the Market Square."

"I'd like to take a look at it, offer an idea or two after I speak with Miss Nadine and Miss Tess."

Those amber Wolf eyes studied Twyla with too much interest.

"If the human pups misbehave, we'll bite them," Simon said.

"If I had your teeth instead of these dentures, I'd be inclined to do the same."

Simon cocked his head. "What are dentures?"

"Perhaps a discussion for another time?" Burke suggested.

"Now," Twyla said, looking at Monty, then at Burke and O'Sullivan, and finally at Simon. "We're here and we're fine. Sierra and I are grown women who are capable of sorting out who is staying where. You men have your own work to do, and you don't need to be fussing about us."

"Ruthie, Merri Lee, and Eve Denby are the females in the pack who already have dens here," Simon said. "They can help with this sorting." He went back to Howling Good Reads.

"You sure you'll be all right?" Monty asked. He addressed the question to his mother, but they both knew it had more to do with Sierra and the girls than Twyla.

"We'll be fine, Crispin." Twyla patted his hand. "You go about your business."

Burke and O'Sullivan stood and said the appropriate things. Monty kissed Twyla's cheek and whispered, "I'm glad you're here." Then the three men went out the back way.

"We'll walk over to the consulate with you," Burke said.

"What should I tell the governor?" O'Sullivan asked.

Monty glanced at the back of the Liaison's Office. He caught the faint sound of music coming from the open windows, but Meg wasn't playing it loud enough for him to determine if it was earth native music or popular music. He needed to talk to his mother and sister before they met Meg Corbyn and saw the scars that were now visible since she'd begun wearing summer clothes.

"You ever watch nature programs?" Burke said. "You ever see one of those anteaters with the big claws breaking open the ant hills in order to get at the ants?"

"I vaguely recall seeing something like that," O'Sullivan replied.

Burke nodded. "Then you tell the governor that the storms heading our way are the claws of the beast that will break open our cities in order to get to the meat."

"Can we take a walk?" Meg asked.

Simon paused, the T-shirt halfway raised. He finished pulling it off, dunked it in the water trough in the Green Complex's open communal area, then, with a happy sigh, put it back on.

"That's better. Sure, we can. Do you need to rub bug spray on your skin?"

If she did, he'd stay so far away she'd have to shout instead of having a very quiet talk. "No, I'll be all right."

"Then dunk your shirt like I did so you stay cool."

She looked around, not sure who else was home right now. "Girls aren't supposed to take off their tops."

"That's a stupid human rule," Simon growled. "*We* don't care."

She couldn't argue that one way or the other, and the air had become close and viciously muggy in the face of the oncoming storm. The weather forecasters couldn't decide whether Lakeside was going to be hit by the storm coming up from the south or the one swinging over the Great Lakes from the north. They were cautiously optimistic that the rain and damaging winds from the hurricane that was leisurely pummeling the East Coast wouldn't reach Lakeside. The hurricane hadn't stalled; it just seemed to pause at certain cities to inflict the most damage before continuing north.

After dunking her shirt in the trough, Meg put it back on and sucked in a breath when the cool, wet fabric touched her skin.

"Isn't that better?" Simon asked, taking her hand.

"Much better."

They walked over to the road, then paused.

"Which way?" Simon asked.

Good question. If they headed toward the Market Square, they would pass the kitchen garden. It was dark now, so it wasn't likely that anyone would be working there, but there was always a chance, and she didn't want to see her human friends right now.

Meg turned in the other direction, which would take them up to the Utilities Complex if they stayed on the Courtyard's main road.

"Are we walking so you don't itch?" Simon asked after a minute.

Should have known he would notice. "Too much that's new and unsettled." She hadn't met Lieutenant Montgomery's mother or the other members of his family, but just their presence in the Courtyard had caused twitches and prickles and buzzes on her arms and legs. Those potential prophecies could have been caused by Agent O'Sullivan just as easily. After all, *he* would have more influence on whatever might happen, wouldn't he?

In the end, she'd closed the Liaison's Office early and gone home—and wasn't surprised to find Nathan waiting on her porch by the time she'd put her BOW in the garage and connected it to its charger. Until Simon got home, the watch Wolf was on duty.

She wasn't sure if it was being home, or doing some of the moves she'd learned in the Quiet Mind class, or her amusement at Nathan, in Wolf form, doing some of the moves with her, but the prickles faded. And yet the unease had lingered through the rest of the afternoon.

"Simon, what's going to happen?"

He didn't answer. Then: "I don't know. A lot of things broke at the same time. A lot of the Wolfgard died. In the past, trouble boiled up in one place. One form of *terra indigene* or other would deal with it, the humans who caused the trouble would be gone, and some—or all—of the land would be reclaimed and become part of the wild country again."

"The *terra indigene* who none of you will talk about."

"The Elders."

Meg nodded. "The Elders. Are they going to reclaim all of Thaisia? What's going to happen to people like the Intuits at Ferryman's Landing? They aren't the *terra indigene*'s enemy."

They walked in silence. Finally Simon stopped and looked around. Meg wondered how much more he could see than was apparent to her.

"Do you know why Wolves howl?" he asked.

"To say, 'We are here.'"

He looked at her and smiled. "Yes. We are here, keeping watch. We are here, thinning the weak from the elk and deer herds, from the bison. We are here to defend the wild country that borders on the human places." The smile faded. "But the *terra indigene* who are Namid's teeth and claws are coming to deal with the invasive predators, and where there are no Wolves to sing to the night sky . . . I don't know what's going to happen in the places that are filled with silence."

"It won't be silent in Lakeside. You'll tell them you are here and you're still keeping watch." Meg thought a moment. "What about Ferryman's Landing or the River Road Community? None of the Wolfgard live there."

"The Coyote and the Fox live there. And there are a few of the Beargard on the island, and now there are Bobcats and Lynxes and a Panther at the River Road Community, as well as the juvenile Sanguinati. Different songs but the same message."

He stepped closer and put his arms around her in a tentative hug.

Meg tensed, not sure what to do. The assault of male hands. Her body still reacted to the memory of her life in the compound. But this was Simon, and Wolves just liked contact with members of their pack.

She put her arms around his waist and allowed her body to relax against his.

"We were attacked here too, so I don't know how much of Lakeside will be standing when this is done, but I think our pack will be all right," Simon said quietly. "I don't think the girls at the lake will let things get too bad in the Courtyard."

"When?"

"At least one of the storms will reach us by tomorrow." His arms tightened around her as he rested his cheek against her fuzz of hair. "You'll be all right, Meg."

"*We'll* be all right." She wanted to believe that, but would believing it be enough to make it true?

CHAPTER 46

Watersday, Juin 30

Jesse Walker opened the general store's door, glad to have even that much relief from feeling closed in. She'd pulled the shutters over the store's windows just before the storm hit. Prairie Gold hadn't lost electric power—yet—but the lights kept flickering and annoyed her enough that she'd shut the damn things off, preferring the twilight and the reassuring hum of the refrigerated units to the constant reminder of how much food they could lose if the power went out in town.

"*Arroo!*"

"Rachel, honey, that's enough. Come in now."

The juvenile Wolf had shown up shortly before the storm hit and had stood outside the general store howling and howling. And her howls had been answered by two Wolves who had arrived in Bennett the day before—the new leader and dominant enforcer of the Prairie Gold pack. Jesse had expected them to continue on to the *terra indigene* settlement once they reached Prairie Gold. Instead, they had taken one of the rooms at the truck stop motel.

The howling of the wind and the howling of the Wolves started at pretty much the same time.

"Rachel?"

The Wolf looked at Jesse, then resumed her howling.

Jesse stayed in the doorway to keep Rachel company and because she had a feeling she would learn something important if she did. Besides, the wind had finally quieted and the rain was more a drizzle.

Gods above and below, no one would be able to travel on the dirt roads until they dried out some—assuming that the roads hadn't washed out completely. At least the storm had passed over them quick enough. She saw some trash that had blown into the street, and a few shops had a shutter or two missing, but it didn't look like too much damage.

"*Arroo!*"

A shimmer in the rain was the only warning that something moved out there. More than one. Intelligence and power. She'd felt that when she'd taken the human children and *terra indigene* youngsters to the hiding place in the hills. That same sense of something out there, thinking. Judging.

They moved on past the town. Jesse sagged against the doorframe, realizing only then how much they frightened her.

"We are here," Rachel said, now a naked, shivering teenager. "That's what we told the Elders. We are here to take care of the land, and you're helping us."

So they passed us by, let us live, Jesse thought. "Honey, either put your fur back on or come inside and dry off before you catch a chill."

"Do you have warm milk?"

The girl sounded so hopeful, Jesse had to smile. "I can warm some up for both of us."

Rachel followed her into the store, full of curiosity and questions about the unfamiliar human things piled on the shelves. The danger had passed, and the fear was shaken off like water shaken off fur.

As Jesse warmed up milk for them, she thought the Intuits would be wise to learn that skill, because she had a feeling that the Elders would never again be a danger seen from a safe distance.

CHAPTER 47

Watersday, Juin 30

S tavros watched the passengers boarding the ocean greyhound. So many of the wealthy HFL supporters were taking the last ship leaving Toland before the storm descended on that part of the coast. They were going to Cel-Romano to see for themselves the triumph their money helped bring about.

Fools.

And there was Nicholas Scratch in a "disguise" that wouldn't fool a human, let alone one of the *terra indigene*. Of course, most of the people coming aboard had talked to Scratch—or at least seen him enough times that he couldn't really believe a disguise would work for the length of the voyage. He had probably told the elite that this was a ruse to escape his "enemies."

Scratch did have enemies now among the humans. Toland's elite might still support him, or still believe there would be some reward for that support once they reached Cel-Romano, but those who understood the connection between the human places that were disappearing and the HFL movement were now pointing fingers and calling Scratch a charlatan who had deceived them.

Stavros had found this epiphany quite entertaining since it came in the wake of Scratch's final speech, in which the man stated he could not be held responsible for actions other people took because they misinterpreted his motivational speeches as a call to commit violence against the *terra indigene*. Every man should be held accountable for his own actions.

Scratch had slipped away before the stunned crowd could react.

Stavros smiled. Now Nicholas Scratch was here, and so was he. And somewhere in the waters just beyond sight of land, the Sharkgard waited.

Stavros flowed from one shadowy place to another, observing, waiting—and wishing he'd fed before coming on board. Was there no one on this ship who wasn't inebriated? There was the captain, but the water had turned rough— Ocean's version of foreplay—and he didn't want to weaken the man. And he didn't want to dull his own senses by consuming alcohol thinly disguised as blood.

He'd overheard enough throughout the evening to realize the HFL supporters had some wildly romantic ideas of being hailed as heroes for providing food and steel and whatever else they'd helped Cel-Romano acquire under the table. But now, with a bounty of land newly won by the Cel-Romano armies, those supporters were no longer needed. There was only one human on this ship who *would* be welcome in Cel-Romano.

Stavros idly watched a few people come out on deck.

<Vampire? Do you have something for us?>

<Not yet,> Stavros told the Sharkgard. That gard had been following the ship for hours in a relay, waiting for him to deliver the promised special meat. He needed to strike soon. He had no intention of going all the way to Cel-Romano, and even in smoke form, he didn't want to travel too far over open water.

Finally, he heard the hated, familiar voice.

"Today we have conquered the land," Nicholas Scratch said as he stepped onto the lower deck with two other men. "Soon the human race will conquer this too." He waved a hand to indicate the ocean.

You think so? Stavros calculated the distance between them.

<Shark?> he called. <Are you ready?>

<Ready.>

Stavros watched the other two men. The ocean at night held no appeal to them, and rubbing elbows with Scratch was no longer a novelty. They wouldn't linger outside.

"You going to join us for cards, Nicholas?" one man asked a minute later.

"Go on without me," Scratch replied.

"Nothing to see out here."

"That makes it a good place to think."

The men nodded wisely and went inside.

Shifting to human form, Stavros wandered over to the railing and smiled at Nicholas Scratch.

"You must be glad to be heading home," Stavros said pleasantly.

Scratch gave him a look that sharpened when he took in the quality of the suit and black shirt. Stavros could almost hear him wondering how to play this new fish to get a fat donation for the cause.

"I don't think we've met," Scratch said.

"We haven't, but I've listened to your speeches with sharp attention," Stavros replied, extending his hand. "You're of great interest to many of us, Mr. Scratch."

Scratch's hand gripped his. "You belong to a group?"

"More of a fellowship of like-minded groups."

"What's your group?"

Stavros tightened his hold on Scratch's hand and smiled, revealing his fangs. "The Sanguinati."

That instant of shock, of fear. That's all it took to pull Scratch close and slash the man's neck—not to feed but to wound.

Still holding Scratch's hand, Stavros took a fistful of the man's coat in the other hand. In smoke form, there wasn't much that could harm the Sanguinati. In a tangible form, they had the strength of the *terra indigene*. Before Scratch had a chance to scream for help, Stavros stepped up on the railing, hauled Scratch over the top, and jumped.

Shifting to smoke as he fell, Stavros flowed down to the surface as Scratch hit the water and went under. Spotting a hand, Stavros shifted to human above the waist and pulled the man up.

Wild-eyed, Scratch coughed and batted at Stavros. Then he screamed and went under again as one of the Sharkgard took a playful bite.

Stavros hauled Scratch up again and stared at this enemy who had been responsible for killing so many and hadn't faced any of the *terra indigene*.

"We're going to destroy Cel-Romano. I wanted you to know that before you die," Stavros said. "You upstart infestation. You thought you could wipe out the *terra indigene*? It's your species that is going to wither—and you will be one of the things the survivors, if there are any, can thank for that."

He released Scratch and floated a safe distance away as dozens of the Sharkgard rushed in to strike the enemy, consuming the human piece by piece. A foot. A hand. A forearm. A thigh.

How long before Scratch is missed? Stavros wondered as he drifted above the waves. *If I can't get home, how long before I'm missed?*

<Vampire.> A fin sliced the water nearby. <Do you see the light?>

Stavros rose to a column of smoke and turned slowly. Yes, there, going in the opposite direction of the ocean greyhound.

<Intuit fishing boat,> the Shark said. <They were told to wait for you. Can you get to them?>

<I can.>

<Then, go. They will take you to their homeport. You are going to resettle near the Five Sisters?>

<Yes. A place called Talulah Falls.>

<Not our territory, but we will remember you if you travel here again.>

Stavros looked around. He smelled blood on the water, but there was no sign of Nicholas Scratch. <Not much of a meal for the effort.>

<There will be more. Do you know what the Sharkgard call humans on a ship?>

<No, what?>

<Meat in a can.>

Alone again, Stavros flowed above the water at his swiftest pace. Shifting to human form, he hailed the fishing boat as soon as he was close enough to be heard. They brought him on board, and a couple of them, swearing they were healthy and sober, offered to let him feed. He declined the meal he would have preferred but accepted a plate of meatloaf and mashed potatoes and listened as the men talked about the catch and the seas and their hopes that their town would be spared some of Ocean's wrath.

He offered no comment but thought Ocean would be inclined to spare their homes and families. A favor for a favor.

After the meal, he found a quiet place to rest. He'd enjoyed the work he'd done in Toland, but being dominant in Talulah Falls would be new and exciting. He would miss Tolya's company, but he would be nearer to Grandfather and Vlad . . . and Nyx.

Yes, he was ready for some changes.

Stavros laughed silently. Meat in a can. He would have to remember to tell that one to Grandfather Erebus when he reached Lakeside.

CHAPTER 48

Alantea held Hurricane to a canter as they moved up Thaisia's East Coast, followed by Air riding Twister. Waves that could swallow buildings and winds that could shred anything in their path kept the humans hurrying and scurrying—too busy trying to save themselves to think of anything else.

But there were places where other Elementals made their presence felt to soften the punishment, and that was right and proper. After all, it wasn't *her* job to thin the herds who clung to the land. That was the task of other forms of *terra indigene*. Her task . . .

<Are we agreed?> Air asked.

<We are agreed,> Alantea replied. The Intuit fishing boat was snug in its harbor, and the Sanguinati who had helped the Sharkgard silence the voice of the enemy was safely on land that would feel only a kiss from the storm.

She aimed Hurricane at the city of Toland.

Air let out a triumphant scream as waves rose high enough to turn city roads into rivers.

Distraction. Diversion. This wasn't the real battle.

Alantea turned Hurricane away from Thaisia, leaving Toland to the sharp mercy of Air and Twister. Giving her steed his head to run and run, she gathered the waters of her domain and aimed her fury straight at Cel-Romano.

To: Simon Wolfgard

Can't reach anyone in the Midwest and haven't received any phone calls or e-mails from anyone there. Suspect phone lines and telegraph lines are down. We're still connected with other Intuit communities in the Northeast. Contact with the Southeast Region is erratic. No information about human-controlled cities and towns along the coast in that region.

Some Midwest radio stations are still broadcasting, and Intuit towns near the border between the Midwest and Northeast have passed along news. The first news indicated that the storm damage would, as one announcer put it, huddle the herd. Later reports talked about entire groups of people disappearing—and officials used the word "slaughterhouse" to describe the scenes.

Will keep sending news as long as I can. Black clouds on the horizon. Storm is moving toward us fast.

—Steve Ferryman

CHAPTER 49

Earthday, Sumor 1

"**F**lood warnings and high-wind warnings in effect until further notice. A travel ban is already in effect in anticipation of flooded roads or streets dammed with debris, including downed power lines. City officials are recommending that families fill jugs with drinking water and prepare for power outages. This is Ann Hergott at WZAS."

Every new human entering the Courtyard made Meg's skin prickle and buzz in a different place. Those people needed to be here; they were the families of trusted police officers, many of whom were her friends. She'd never forgive herself if any of them were sent away because of her and then something happened to them.

Everyone was busy, scurrying to get beds made and food prepared. Either the storm would be vicious but brief and everyone would feel like fools for closing down the city, or the flooding and damage would make the blizzard in Febros look like a weather hiccup.

Either way, today the Courtyard was crowded with strangers whose future was in question. And the answers were buzzing under her skin as prophecies screaming for the razor to release them.

She dropped the silverware on one of the tables in Meat-n-Greens, oblivious to the noise it made. Turning blindly, she rushed for the door, barely hearing Merri Lee calling to her.

"Meg!"

A hand on her arm. "I have to go. Too many prickles. Too much buzzing under the skin."

"Go where?" Merri Lee asked. "The storm is going to hit any minute now."

"To the Liaison's Office. I can sort something. Mail. Packages. Anything. Need . . . routine."

"There isn't going to be routine today, Meg. And there's no one else at the office. Nathan isn't going to be there. We've been told to keep the doors locked so they don't get caught by the wind."

Meg pulled away from her friend. "Can't stay here." She ran to the archway in the Market Square that provided access to the employee parking lot and, beyond that, the back door of the Liaison's Office. She didn't realize Merri Lee had come with her until the other girl said, "Hurry up, then, so we can get inside."

A gust of wind hit them and the door just as Meg turned the lock, and they almost fell into the back room. It took both of them to push the door closed.

"Gods," Merri Lee muttered. She checked the under-the-counter fridge, then the cupboards. "If we're really going to stay in here, we should have a few more supplies."

"You don't need to stay. I'll be all right on my own." *Better,* Meg added silently. Even now, as she tried to stay focused on the friend who was with her, her skin still prickled and buzzed in a couple of places.

"Please, Merri. Please. I need to be alone or I'll have to cut."

They both knew what would happen if she made a cut now. Simon, Vlad, and who knew how many other *terra indigene* would lash out at the humans who had come here for shelter and protection.

"You have your mobile phone?" Merri Lee finally said.

Meg nodded. "And I know the phone numbers for A Little Bite and Meat-n-Greens. I'll stay in touch."

"You're sure?"

"Yes. Please." There had been this many people working in the compounds. There had been all the girls. Maybe it was because the girls had been cut on a regular schedule that they didn't experience any prickles about one another. Or maybe they had been exposed to one another so much they stopped feeling the possibilities.

Or maybe they had felt no prickles about one another because none of them had had a real future.

Once Merri Lee left, Meg felt a moment's relief. No prickles, no buzzing. She walked into the sorting room, not sure what she could find to do, especially if she ended up stuck there for a few hours.

She looked at the five CDs she'd been playing that week, but none of that music appealed to her right now. No mail, no packages, no deliveries bringing anything new today.

She opened the drawer that held the prophecy cards.

The room did one slow spin.

Meg slammed the drawer shut and held on to the counter. She gritted her teeth, craving the silver razor as her skin buzzed and crawled.

She was alone but she was still too close to too many strangers. The humans would remain within the Courtyard's business district. *She* had to get away from it—and them.

She ran out the back door, then crossed the paved area between her office and the garages that held a couple of BOWs.

Had to get away before someone saw her and tried to argue.

Once she was on the road that would take her back to the Green Complex, she sighed with relief and trepidation. There would be such snarling when Simon found out she had bolted.

He wouldn't be able to snarl at her for hours and hours since he had to protect the Courtyard. Maybe by the time the storm ended, he would be too tired to snarl.

Maybe pigs would learn to fly.

Entertained by the image of piglets with wings, she almost relaxed her death grip on the steering wheel, when a gust of wind lifted the passenger-side wheels off the road for one heart-hammering moment.

Meg looked around. Straight ahead would take her to the Green Complex— where she would be totally alone because everyone who lived there would be in the Market Square or with their own gards.

If she went to her apartment, her friends would fight against the storm to reach her. If something happened to her or Simon because of her need for solitude, what would happen to Sam?

"Sam," she whispered. She needed a kind of quiet but not necessarily isolation.

Then she couldn't see a thing. She rolled down a window, hoping it wasn't her vision that had gone wacky. She stuck her head out, and her fuzz of hair was playfully lipped. Pulling back, she stared at the gray muzzle of the steed. "Fog?"

"Meg?" Air leaned close to Fog's neck. "You shouldn't be outside now."

"I couldn't stay with all those other humans. They're nice people, but . . . my skin. Too many prophecies." Behind Air, she could see tree branches bending, almost breaking, but around the BOW there was no wind. "I was hoping Jester would let me stay with him at the Pony Barn."

Air studied her. "You want to stay with our ponies?"

"Yes."

The Elemental smiled. "Follow us."

Meg turned on the BOW's lights and followed in Fog's wake. That was easy enough to do since the fog made by the steed swirled around her, but she had no trouble seeing him.

She pulled up at the Pony Barn, thankful that Air was still sheltering her from the wind. One of the barn doors opened. Jester ran out and helped her out of the BOW. Then they both yelped as the first fat raindrops changed to hail.

"Do you have a change of clothes in there?" Jester asked.

"No." She hadn't thought about that.

"Then get inside before you get soaked." He gave her a push toward the barn door.

Hearing a familiar *arroo*, she turned toward the road instead. "Sam?"

Sam and Skippy ran toward her.

"Well, chew my tail and spit out the fur," Jester snapped. "Get inside, all of you."

"The BOW," Meg said, finally realizing the little vehicle could be seriously damaged.

"I'll deal with it. And the Wolfgard," Jester muttered as he got in the BOW.

"Get inside, Meg," Air said. "What is coming does not like humans. But you'll be safe with our ponies."

"Thank you. Come on, Sam. Come on, Skippy. Let's get inside."

She rushed into the barn, the two Wolves right behind her.

Jester returned a minute later and scowled at her. "I know you're human, but I would swear you have some Coyote blood. Only one of my kind could cause this much trouble so easily."

Before she could apologize or explain, Jester was conferring with Mist and fetching a harness that had baskets with flaps that kept mail dry in bad weather. As soon as the pony was fitted out, he trotted off, heading toward the Market Square.

"That stall has fresh straw," Jester said. "We can all curl up there and keep an eye on things."

"Okay. Jester . . ."

The Coyote waved off her apology before she could say it. He glanced at Sam and Skippy, then at her. "Good thing Simon is going to be busy most of the day. I don't imagine Blair will be able to get here either for at least a few hours."

Meg spread blankets over the straw, then sat down with Sam while Skippy explored the Pony Barn.

"Did you run away too?" she asked Sam.

Sam looked up at her. *"Arroo."*

She sighed. "We're going to be in soooo much trouble."

"Roo."

As she put an arm around Sam, she realized all the prickles and buzzes beneath her skin had stopped.

For now, at least, everyone around her was where they were supposed to be.

"Stay, Daddy. Please stay."

Monty hugged his daughter. "I can't, Lizzy girl. The police have to help the people who might be in trouble during the storm."

"We'll be fine." Twyla put her hands on Lizzy's shoulders. "We're as ready as anyone can be, and we'll be just fine."

"Have you told Simon Wolfgard he's not in charge anymore?" Monty asked.

"Huh." Twyla smiled. "Eve Denby and I told him the women had things in hand to look after the people coming here for shelter, and he had the sense to go off and take care of his own business."

It felt a little forced, but Monty returned the smile. "Yes, ma'am. Message received."

Her smile faded. "We'll be fine here, Crispin."

He touched Lizzy's hair. "You mind Grandma Twyla, you hear?"

"Yes, Daddy. I hear."

Being the newest members of the female pack, Twyla and Sierra were assigned the care of the children—a practical choice since three of the five were family. They were tucked in the efficiency apartment that would be turned into the school. It had drinking water and plumbing, was easily reached by the adults, both human and *terra indigene*, who would be looking after the Courtyard's businesses, and had a television, a movie disc player, and a sufficient supply of movies to keep the youngsters occupied, not to mention the games, books, and changes of clothing. The kitchen was packed with food. Everything that could be done to protect the young had been done.

As he hurried down the stairs and turned toward the back door of Howling Good Reads, where his team was meeting Burke to receive their orders, he wondered where Sam Wolfgard and Meg Corbyn were going to wait out the storm.

Gods, Monty thought as lightning scarred a dark sky and the wind knocked him sideways a step. This area behind the stores was sheltered on all sides. If wind gusts were this bad here, what were they going to be like out in the open?

As he fought with the wind for possession of the door and finally got it closed, he heard Kowalski's voice coming from the stacks on his left.

"Dad, I know what they're saying on the radio. I've been listening to the freaking weather reports too. But I'm telling you, this is going to be a bad storm. Bad enough that the families of police officers are being offered shelter at the stations. You, Mom, and Tim can . . . Gods above and below! Those people are *finished*. Can't you see that? Let me talk to Mom. Dad? Dad!"

A defeated sigh and a soft, "Fuck." Then Kowalski squeezed through the stacks of books and other supplies, blushing when he saw Monty.

"Is your family going to take shelter at the station?" Monty asked quietly.

Kowalski shook his head. "'I lived through the storm of blah-di-blah-blah, and I'm not leaving.' He still believes the HFL movement is going to 'sort those creatures out.' And I can't tell him the real reason this storm is going to be so bad, can I?"

"No, you can't." It wasn't the storm itself that was going to devastate the city; it was what was coming in hidden by the storm.

Burke had had a quiet word with Captain Zajac and Captain Wheatley, two patrol captains in other precincts who recognized that the *terra indigene* held the key to Lakeside's survival. He'd told all the police stations that they should offer shelter for their officers' families, but the men working out of the Chestnut Street station were the only ones who really took the warning seriously enough.

"What about Ruth's parents?" Monty asked. Looking at Kowalski's bitter smile made his heart ache.

"When she called them, her mother said, 'My daughter is dead,' and hung up."

Kowalski squared his shoulders. "But the MacDonalds are on their way to the Courtyard. So is Michael Debany's family. They're bringing the perishable foods from their fridge and any other supplies that might be useful."

Monty didn't know if Merri Lee's family lived in Lakeside, and he didn't ask.

The back door blew open and Michael Debany stumbled into the stock room.

"Whoo! That's a mean bitch out there!" Debany said, not seeing Simon Wolfgard coming in right behind him until he turned to close the door. "Ah . . . Sorry. That just slipped out. Is it anyone we know?"

"No. And she is a mean bitch." Simon closed the door, then looked at the three men. "You want to wait for Captain Burke in the front of the store? There's more room. I don't know who's working at A Little Bite right now, but there might be coffee."

In other words, you're in the way, Monty thought. "We'll do that."

His mobile phone rang at the same time Simon's rang, so he hurried toward the front of the store, stopping near the archway that connected HGR with A Little Bite. "Montgomery."

"Lieutenant," Burke said. "Let someone there know that Commander Gresh is bringing his family to the Courtyard. I'll be along shortly."

"Yes, sir." Monty ended the call. Seeing Simon coming toward him, Monty started to speak. But Simon rushed past him, checked the coffee shop, then turned around and ran for the inside staircase that led to HGR's second floor. Judging by the look on the Wolf's face, Simon had his own problems right now.

As Debany and Kowalski answered their mobile phones, the looks on their faces told him that Simon's problem would be his too.

Ready to snarl and howl about idiot puppies, Simon rushed into the office, startling Vlad, who was monitoring e-mail and marking up a map to indicate the towns that were still out there.

Blessed Thaisia! Why would Sam go running off just as a storm was about to hit? And why take Skippy with him?

"Simon, what . . . ?" The phone rang. Vlad answered it. After a moment, he said, "Yes, I'll tell him."

Vlad hung up the phone, but Simon didn't give him time to say anything. "Sam ran away from the Wolfgard Complex. You'll have to deal with the humans until I find him." Assuming he *would* find the pup. He'd been trying to reach Sam through the *terra indigene* form of communication but hadn't received any response. That was bad. Very bad.

"Sam is fine," Vlad said. "So is Skippy. So is Meg."

"*Meg?* But Meg is . . ." Not in A Little Bite, where he had expected to find her. His fangs lengthened to Wolf size. "Where are they?"

"With the ponies and Jester in the Pony Barn. Jester thinks Meg was overwhelmed and too close to cutting, so she ran away from the other humans."

"The pack's nanny thinks that Sam ran off because he wanted to be with Meg during the storm." Simon scratched behind one ear, then made an effort to shift the ear—and his teeth—back to human form. "She almost died the last time a storm hit Lakeside."

"I remember," Vlad said softly. "But, Simon, except for staying with Grandfather Erebus, I can't think of a safer place for the three of them to be than in the Pony Barn with the Elementals' steeds."

Tense muscles began to relax, and he began thinking past finding Sam. "Did Meg pack anything?"

"No. Mist is on his way to the Market Square. Jester doesn't have enough food for the four of them—and certainly not enough human food. We can ask the female pack if Meg kept any spare clothes at the office."

He could sniff out any clothes that belonged to Meg. But if there weren't any, the females would be better at guessing what to pick up from the Market Square stores. And Meg and the brainless Wolves would need something to do, especially if Sam shifted to human form. Which meant packing shirts and shorts for Sam too.

As if I don't have enough to do, Simon thought as he bounded down the stairs. Someone was going to get a sharp nip for the worry those three had caused—even if the worry hadn't lasted more than a few minutes.

Turning toward the stock room, he almost slammed into a human male he didn't know. He bared his teeth and snarled a challenge before realizing there were two females with the male—one of an age to be the mate and the other a grown pup.

"You must be Mr. Wolfgard," the man said with a smile that wobbled. "Michael told us to come through the back door of the coffee shop, but there's a pony blocking that door, and he didn't seem inclined to get out of the way."

"Michael . . . ?"

"Debany. I'm Michael's dad. This is his mom and his sister."

Simon gave the younger female a quick but thorough look. This was the sister who wanted to work with animals—the sister who might be suitable to go to Bennett and work with Tolya.

Wishing he hadn't been quite so quick to snarl, he ran a tongue over his teeth before he tried a smile. "Sorry I snarled." He wasn't, but that seemed like the right thing to say.

"You've got a lot on your mind," Mr. Debany said.

"You can come this way to reach A Little Bite." He led them to the archway that connected the two stores and almost ran into Officer Debany.

"Dad. Why did you . . . ?"

"Mist is in the way," Simon said, figuring he could distill an entire conversation with those few words. "Where are Ruthie and Merri Lee?"

"They're here. Any word from Meg? Karl and I were about to go out and help you look for her."

Touched that Meg would matter to them enough that they would leave their own pack, Simon felt easier about having Debany's family in the Courtyard. "She's with Jester at the Pony Barn. Sam and Skippy are with her. Mist is here to bring supplies."

Debany turned and raised his voice enough to be heard over a buzz of human voices. "Karl! Lieutenant! They found Meg. She's okay."

Now Merri Lee and Ruthie rushed toward him. "She's okay? You're sure? Does she need anything?"

"Change of clothes. Clothes for Sam. Books. Food for Meg. Boone Hawkgard will make up a package of meat for Sam and Skippy. Mist will deliver it."

They stared at him for a moment, blinking. Maybe thinking. Then they both rushed past him, calling out greetings to Debany's family and leaving him feeling less sure of who was in charge. At some point, he was going to have to take the time to establish dominance.

First he would see just how big a human pack he was dealing with now.

<Boone?> he called to the Hawk who ran the butcher shop. <I need some meat for Sam and Skippy. They're at the Pony Barn. Mist is waiting at A Little Bite.>

<Give me a couple of minutes. I'll bring it over.>

The sky darkened. Wind tossed a fistful of hail against the coffee shop's windows.

Vlad walked into the shop leading Commander Gresh and what Simon assumed were the man's mate and offspring. Behind them were Captain Burke and Agent O'Sullivan.

And pushing past them came Merri Lee and Ruthie. They dodged everyone else crowded into the coffee shop, had a hurried discussion with Nadine Fallacaro, who was behind the counter, then headed for the back door, where Mist waited.

"Arroo!" Even from a human throat, a Wolf howl silenced humans quite satisfactorily. "There is food here and at Meat-n-Greens. There are books in the library, and you can read anything in the store." Simon gestured toward the archway to indicate Howling Good Reads. "Pups are staying in one of the efficiency apartments with Miss Twyla and the Sierra. They have books and movies and food up there. You humans need to pick a place where you're going to wait out the storm *and then stay there.* When the storm arrives, we'll be locking the doors because anything in the open is prey."

Silence.

Burke stepped forward. "I appreciate you offering shelter to some of our families. Lieutenant Montgomery will remain here with his team to give you whatever assistance they can, and to respond to any calls in the area. I'm going back to the station. The rest of my men are there."

Simon looked into Burke's eyes. The man knew—or knew enough—of what was coming with the storm.

"Stay inside until it's done," Simon said. "That won't guarantee your safety, but you'll have no chance in the open."

You're going to have to let some humans die if you want to survive and save the rest. That was the real message.

Burke nodded. "I'd better be on my way."

Louis Gresh looked at his mate. "I'm going to the station too. You and the children will be safe here."

His mate didn't look sure of that, but she nodded.

"Elliot Wolfgard gave me permission to remain in the consulate and maintain contact with Governor Hannigan," Greg O'Sullivan said. "He suggested that I pick up food and drink before the storm hits."

"Do that now," Simon said.

"People." Burke's voice boomed in the coffee shop. "While there is comfort in numbers, you need to consider what has been said. Two places are stocked with provisions and other supplies. You need to split up between them so that one place doesn't run out of food while the other place has food spoiling."

The older Debany male looked around. "The captain has a good point. So where can we be the most use?"

Simon stared at the humans who seemed to be waiting for him to issue instructions.

Where can the humans be of use? He hadn't anticipated any of them wanting to be useful, just wanting a safe place to shelter.

"I'm working with Nadine here," Merri Lee said. "Ruth and Eve Denby are dealing with the food at Meat-n-Greens." She looked at Simon. "We filled the baskets and tied on a carry sack with things for Meg. Mist is on his way back to the Pony Barn."

"How long do you think the storm will last?" Kowalski asked.

He looked at the humans crowded into the coffee shop. They were there because they, or their mates, understood the need to work with the *terra indigene*. They deserved honesty.

"How long the storm lasts will depend on how much hatred Namid's teeth and claws hold for the humans in Lakeside," he replied. "A lot of human places in Thaisia will be gone when this is done. A lot of them are already gone." He looked at Vlad, who nodded grimly. "Like fire that destroys in order to make room for new growth, the earth natives who are coming in with this storm come to destroy. Hopefully we'll be among the survivors who will make something new."

"I'll go with Captain Burke," Nathan said from the archway leading into HGR. "They might leave the police station alone if one of the Wolfgard is there."

<Are you sure?> Simon asked.

<Meg is safe, and you and Blair need to stay here and protect the Courtyard. I have been to the police station before.>

None of the humans spoke. Then Burke said, "Thank you. I hadn't expected any of you to . . ." He stopped, then continued brusquely, "Lieutenant, with me a moment."

Burke walked out of the coffee shop, followed by Louis Gresh and Lieutenant Montgomery.

The humans huddled together, the females talking with Nadine and Merri Lee, the males talking with the police, and the juveniles huddled together looking lost.

Simon joined Vlad, who said, "You're staying here?"

He nodded. "John is at Meat-n-Greens to help with the humans. Blair is guarding the Utilities Complex. Henry is staying at his studio, so he'll be nearby if there is any trouble. Jenni, Starr, and Jake are at Sparkles and Junk. Julia and Marie Hawkgard and Allison Owlgard are keeping watch in the Market Square Library."

Vlad looked around, frowning. "Has anyone seen Tess?"

"Wait for me at the car," Burke told Louis Gresh and Nathan Wolfgard. Then he looked at Monty. "I want you and your team here. Could be some looting in the stores around this area, and there are bound to be some disturbances and requests for assistance. But wait for Wolfgard to give you the all clear before you venture out for anything. You understand me?"

Monty studied his captain. "You know what's going to happen?"

"I saw something like it once. It's bloody and terrible, and it gives a man a reason to do just about anything to stop it from happening again. And I do not want to bring any of my men to the morgue looking . . ." Burke stopped.

"I should be at the station with you."

"Your team is working here, and it's important that you stay with them."

Something else under the words. "You don't expect to come through this."

Burke hesitated. "Our odds have greatly improved with Nathan Wolfgard being with us at the station. And I wouldn't have told men to bring their families to a place I thought would be destroyed. But if something should happen and I'm no longer fit for duty, I want a ranking officer who the Others trust to be able to step up and take command."

"The station's chief isn't going to promote me over men who have been working here longer," Monty protested.

"This isn't about seniority, Monty. It's about survival."

A crack of thunder made them jump.

Burke held out his hand. "Good luck, Lieutenant."

Monty took Burke's hand and held on tight for a moment. "Good luck, sir."

He stood in the doorway and watched Burke lumber across the paved area and disappear around the corner to the employee parking lot, where he must have left his car. Then Monty forced the door closed and leaned against it. If he dashed over to the efficiency apartments to look in on Lizzy, would he stir up the children when his mother would have them settled?

He heard footsteps and voices and the rustle of raingear.

The Gresh family smiled at him. "We're on the Meat-n-Greens team," Mrs. Gresh said.

"Better hurry." Monty held the door for them and noticed Kowalski hurrying to catch up.

"Any orders, Lieutenant?" Kowalski asked.

"Stay in touch and keep everyone inside. Wait for the all clear before you go out."

"Yes, sir. You'll be staying here?"

"Yes." Having contact with Simon and Vlad was prudent. And if Lizzy did need him, he'd have a better chance of reaching the apartments from the back door of A Little Bite than from the Market Square.

"Michael is staying here. So is Pete Denby."

"We're covered. Now, get going."

Kowalski ran.

Bloody and terrible, Burke had said. He would pray none of the men he knew would face the bloody and terrible—but he didn't think that particular prayer would be answered today.

Tess watched the black sedan drive out of the Courtyard and waited a minute before she unlocked the front door of the Liaison's Office and stepped outside, pulling up the tight-fitting hood that hid her face and all but two coils of black hair.

"Not a day to be outside," Nyx said.

Tess turned to her left but kept her eyes directed at the pavement. The human mask was now a transparent veneer that muted the effect of looking at her. Oh, her preys' organs would blacken and their brains would bleed, but not as fast as when she revealed her true form with no veil to soften it. Too sick to cause trouble, the prey would flee and die elsewhere—which suited her just fine since she would have supped on the best of the life energy.

"Are you out here for a reason?" Nyx persisted.

"To make sure nothing comes here to cause harm," Tess replied, watching the people hurrying toward the Stag and Hare. It was as good a place as any to wait out this storm since it had plentiful food and drink, but she didn't think the clientele were the kind of humans who held a neighborly opinion of the Courtyard or its residents.

"You're talking about humans?"

"They're included." She felt Nyx move closer.

"Even your form of *terra indigene* couldn't take on one of *them*."

"Harvesting that much life, I wouldn't need to feed for a year," Tess said dreamily. How long had it been since she'd felt fully sated?

"Not feed for a year?" Nyx sounded disgusted. "What if you got a sour one and then had to wait so long to be hungry again?"

The thought made Tess laugh, and red threads appeared in the black hair. "You should get inside."

"I'm safe enough from Namid's teeth and claws. Smoke would just catch in their throats and make them cough. Didn't you know?" A light touch on Tess's back as Nyx said more seriously, "Today you aren't going to hunt humans alone. I'll keep watch from the back door of the efficiency apartments. That way I can also check the stairs that open on Crowfield Avenue."

As Nyx flowed along the access way, Tess heard her tell someone to hurry. Looking toward the consulate, she spotted Elliot Wolfgard and looked away quickly when she realized there was a human with him.

"No," Elliot snapped. "Don't look. Just get inside."

<Wolf,> Tess said. <That is good advice. If I were you, I would close the blinds on the windows that look out on the delivery area. I wouldn't want any harm to come to you unintentionally.>

<I'll pass that advice on to Henry,> Elliot said.

A gust of wind tugged at the hood, almost revealing her face.

Tess went inside the Liaison's Office and turned the simple lock to keep the door securely closed.

There were plenty of HFL supporters in the city. Once they had drunk enough courage, a few of them would come here looking for trouble, so she would make herself easy to find.

Alone in HGR's office, Simon looked at his mobile phone and almost played the message that he had saved just to hear Meg's voice. Instead he called the Pony Barn.

"Pony Barn. Meg speaking."

Hearing her voice delighted him, relieved some unhappiness he hadn't known he'd felt until it faded. That's why he growled, "I am going to bite you so hard."

"No, you're not." Her voice sounded prim. He suspected she was laughing at him. "You're going to give me a large bonus in my next paycheck for not only realizing I needed to get away from all the people who were making my skin prickle but for going to a quiet place where I wouldn't be alone and you wouldn't have to worry about me. And if I hadn't done that, I wouldn't have found Sam and Skippy."

He couldn't argue with any of that, but . . .

"I wish you were here too," Meg said quietly. "I wish we were all curled up in the straw watching the storm. Then you would be safe too."

"I'm safe." Somehow, knowing he couldn't just run out and join her made it feel like she was too far away.

Rain mixed with hail lashed the windows. Damn! Had he remembered to close the apartment windows this morning? Had she? He wasn't going to ask. This would be a new thing for her and she would fret.

He sighed. "It's started. I'd better go. You stay with Jester."

"I will."

"And don't let Sam go out, not even to pee."

"I won't."

"And if Skippy rushes out, don't you follow him."

"I *won't*. Geez, Simon, are you becoming a micromanager?"

He didn't know what that was, but it sounded like an insult—and it sounded like something he should bite.

He grunted and hung up. As he went downstairs, it occurred to him that feeling a little insulted by Meg's teasing had cheered him up.

To: Douglas Burke

I hope this gets to you. Reliable sources say the Cel-Romano troops stationed in the land taken from the *terra indigene* have disappeared. Lots of blood and smashed equipment; some body parts—and indications that at least some of the men died from an unknown kind of plague. Some speculation that soldiers from "provincial" areas deserted and are making their way home, but it's assumed that most of the men stationed in the wild country are dead.

Fishermen from mainland villages situated on *terra indigene* land warned Brittanian fishermen that Cel-Romano is "about to get some weather" and advised the men to stay close to home.

—Shady Burke

CHAPTER 50

Earthday, Sumor 1

In Lakeside, lightning struck any moving vehicle with uncanny precision while rain rushing in house gutters roared like Talulah Falls. Streets became swift-flowing rivers. Roofs leaked. Basements took in water. And everyone prayed to the gods and their personal guardian spirits that the rain would stop before the creeks overflowed their banks too far.

Then a fierce north wind blew the rain south, and a dense fog covered the city of Lakeside with an odd silence.

And then *they* entered Lakeside to roam the streets for prey, and the worst of them walked on two legs.

Douglas Burke grabbed Louis Gresh the moment the rain lightened to drizzle and that damn fog covered the city.

"Take your men and hold the back door," Burke said with quiet urgency. "Keep it locked. Keep everyone in, and I do mean everyone."

"Storm's over," Gresh protested. "We should get out there now."

"Louis, the storm hasn't started yet." The men were restless, coiled to get out there and *help*. Gods above and below! Did his men think he felt any different? But if they went out too soon, they would be among the victims instead of being the rescuers.

"Hold that door, Commander."

Louis studied Burke's face, then nodded and went off to set up a barricade at the station's back door.

Satisfied that Gresh would stand with him, Burke hurried into his office. He wasn't sure if Police Commissioner Kurt Wallace had landed at the Chestnut Street station by chance when the storm hit or if the man had thought hiding among officers who had been labeled Wolf lovers would keep him safe. But Wallace was still a vocal HFL supporter, and having him here at the same time as Nathan Wolfgard was creating a dangerous kind of uneasiness among some of the civilians and cops who weren't quite convinced that the HFL movement was about to become as extinct as the dinosaurs.

After checking to make sure a round was chambered in his service weapon, Burke took two more loaded magazines from a desk drawer and slipped them in his suit coat pocket.

As he strode for the door, he stopped and turned around. "Nathan?" The Wolf had spent the past couple of hours in here—and forced the station's chief to host Wallace in order to keep the two apart. Now the visitor's chair held the clothes that Nathan had worn, but there was no sign of the Wolf.

Hoping Nathan wasn't in danger inside the station—or about to attack anyone he considered an enemy—Burke strode through the building, pushing past a group of people heading for the station's front door. He locked the door, stood in front of it, and drew his weapon.

"No one is leaving yet," he said in a voice that allowed no discussion or challenge—at least not until the chief or Wallace confronted him.

He would deal with them if and when the time came.

Something moved outside the Pony Barn. Meg couldn't hear it, but she knew it was there, felt the weight of its presence on her skin.

She tightened her grip on Sam, not that he seemed inclined to leave any space between them. Skippy, for once showing sense, had burrowed in the straw at the back of the stall. Jester stared at the barn doors as if that alone would keep them closed and keep everyone safe.

All the ponies who weren't out with the Elementals poked their heads out of their stalls, but Tornado and Quicksand came out and faced the doors.

Jester glanced at Meg, then focused on the doors again.

She felt nothing like prophecy under her skin. No pins and needles, no prickles or buzzing. Because none of them had a future? Or because she should already know the choice she should make?

We are here, still keeping watch. Still protecting the world.

Meg raised her head. "Arroo!"

"Shhhh," Jester whispered.

"They need to know we're here. Arroo!"

"Arroo!" Sam howled.

Something pulled one of the barn doors open an inch or two.

"Arroo!" Meg howled. Now Sam *and* Skippy howled with her.

More howls now from the Wolves keeping watch in various parts of the Courtyard.

We are here. Wasn't that the message that had been silenced in other parts of Thaisia? But not in Lakeside. The Wolfgard was still here.

"Arroo!"

A snuff. A huff. A . . . laugh?

The barn door closed—and something moved away, leaving behind an odd silence.

Meg blinked. "Was it . . . were they laughing at us?"

Grinning, Jester collapsed in the straw beside her. "They had never heard the howl of a not-Wolf, and they were curious."

"They were laughing at us."

"That too," Jester agreed cheerfully. He sprang up. "Want some food, Meg?"

"Is it done? The storm and . . . after?"

"For us it is."

He seemed sure of that.

She stood and brushed off her backside. "I'm going to wash my hands first."

"Don't use too much of the toilet paper. I wasn't planning on having a female here when I brought in supplies."

Grabbing the carry sack that held her personal items, Meg went to the toilet in the back of the barn. She closed the door, opened the sack, and smiled. There, on top, was a roll of toilet paper that Merri Lee or Ruth had packed.

"Ha!" Meg said, setting the roll on the toilet tank.

As she took care of business, she wondered if her little "arroo" would become another story that traveled to other Wolf packs.

———

Nathan shouldered his way through the crowd of humans who were between him and the front door, careful to avoid the shoed feet that could stomp on his paws.

"No one is going anywhere yet." Even with the mutters and mumbles and, in a few cases, loud curses, Burke's voice boomed, making it easy to locate the man.

Gresh had his pack to help him guard the back door, but Burke was facing down these humans alone. He pictured Burke with fur and decided he would have made an acceptable Grizzly.

Reaching the front door—and Burke—Nathan looked out the glass at the fog. The Elders were out there, thinning the herd. He could feel them. If he could convince Burke to open the door just an inch, he could sniff the outside air and get a sense of how close they were to this police den. Since he didn't think Burke would open the door, he'd do his job another way.

"*Arroo!*" Nathan howled. "*Arroo!*" He continued howling to the other *terra indigene*.

"Burke!" a human shouted. It sounded like that Wallace man. "Make that . . . creature . . . stop that racket."

"I think he's trying to save the lives of everyone here by warning off the other predators," Burke replied. "Do you really want me to tell him to stop?"

Nathan, and Burke, waited for an answer. Met with silence, Nathan resumed his "I am here" howl.

<Wolf.> A voice, deep and powerful—and too nearby. <Are you trapped in this human place, Wolf?>

<No. This police pack works with the Courtyard and with the Wolves. Some of this pack is helping Simon, so I'm here to help the ones who are protecting mates and puppies.>

Something came close to the glass door. Something on two legs that towered over Burke, who was a large human. Couldn't really see the shape—it seemed clothed in the fog—but the claws that suddenly raked the glass, scoring it, were clear enough.

Humans gasped. Some fell in an effort to move away from the door. The police in uniform stared at him, at Burke, at the glass—and finally, maybe, understood.

"Captain?" one officer said. "When . . . ?"

Burke looked at Nathan, who thought for a moment. The Elders were moving away from this den, but they weren't far enough away yet that they wouldn't return if prey suddenly began pouring out the doors.

He took up guard position in front of the door and returned Burke's look.

"Not yet," Burke said. "But soon. Patrol officers, work with dispatch and start prioritizing the calls so we can move as soon as we get the all clear."

Burke holstered his weapon and studied Nathan. "I need to make some calls. Will you be all right here?"

"Arroo," Nathan replied softly. He didn't think any humans would bother him while he was between them and the *terra indigene* who were hunting on the streets.

Tess walked out of the Liaison's Office, took two steps away from the building, and stopped. She couldn't see a damn thing in this fog, and she didn't want the embarrassment of tripping over something—or someone.

Taking a step back, she held one hand behind her and felt the reassuring metal handle on the door.

Main Street should be directly in front of her, just beyond the delivery area and the sidewalk. But she didn't hear the sound of cars; she heard fast-running water.

Meg would be disappointed if the young plants in the kitchen garden drowned or were smashed beyond recovering by the hail and pounding rain. The rest of the human pack would be disappointed too, but they didn't quite belong with the *terra indigene* in the same way that Meg did, and *their* disappointment wouldn't ripple through the Courtyard.

Nothing she, or anyone else, could do about saturated ground and runoff and streets turned into streams.

Whispers. Muffled curses. The splash of an animal fording water. The yelp as one of them lost his footing and was swept away.

Tess pushed the hood off her head. No need to maintain a veneer over her true form in order to lessen the impact of looking at her; the fog would serve that purpose now. After all, she wanted to harvest enough life from her prey to make them fatally ill but not immediately. Let them scurry back to the cars parked across the street or their companions in the Stag and Hare who probably had cheered them on when they proposed striking at the *terra indigene* under the cover of the storm. Too bad they hadn't realized that the storm had been shaped for the benefit of the other predators who moved through the city now.

Clear stripes in the fog, as if something had raked claws over a gray blanket. Tess saw figures approaching. Four, five, six. Did they have weapons? She had to assume they did, and even one of Namid's most ferocious predators couldn't afford to be careless about weapons like guns.

<Nyx, six monkeys are in the delivery area. Can you block the access way in case any of them get past me?>

<I'll help if you agree to let two get past you,> Nyx replied. <I'm hungry.>

<They're full of liquid courage.>

Nyx sighed. <I don't want to get drunk on a meal. One, then.>

<One.>

Six flashlights turned on, beacons that said, *We're here, come eat us!*

Seeing no reason not to oblige, Tess moved swiftly, heading in the direction of the man who was closest to the shoulder-high brick wall between the delivery area and Henry's yard. Her shoulder hit an arm. The man swore and looked directly at her as he tried to grab her.

She pulled away from his weakened grasp, relishing the kind of sustenance she rarely allowed herself to consume since coming to Lakeside. Moving away from him, she heard him stumble toward the street.

The other five turned toward her, flashlights aimed so the light would hit her face and blind her. But she kept moving, looking into their eyes and then looking away from the blinding light. Fatal sips. But the one who swung a piece of chain and managed to hit her leg . . . Tess held his gaze long enough to make it rain inside his skull.

<Tess!> Nyx shouted. <Get inside!>

She had a moment to understand the quality of the sudden silence before two of Namid's teeth and claws rushed out of the access way and went straight for the illuminated prey.

It was like the fog had turned into huge furred shapes that defied description or naming.

Tess turned to dash into the Liaison's Office, but the one leg wasn't working right. She stumbled and hit the brick wall. She reached up, felt air. There was nothing graceful about her scramble over the wall, but she heard claws scrape the bricks as she fell into Henry's yard and pressed herself against the wall in an effort to hide.

A little too close, she thought. But not a serious attempt to catch her. <Nyx? You okay?>

<Meg left the little window in the bathroom open partway. That was the fastest way into the office. I'm going to have to talk to her about keeping the toilet lid down. I came too close to landing in the bowl.>

Tess clamped a hand over her mouth. <Don't make me laugh. I'm hiding in Henry's yard, so I'm not technically inside, and my leg is banged up enough that I'm not going to be able to run for cover.>

<You shouldn't let humans get close enough to hurt you,> Nyx scolded.

<I miscalculated.> Tess tried to breathe very quietly. There were sounds on the other side of the wall—not exactly feeding sounds, but definitely nothing that came from the humans. In fact, she hadn't heard one human scream, which told her a lot about the speed of these earth natives.

The quiet scrape of claws on the bricks above her head. The smell of something earthy and so very wild leaning over the wall to sniff her.

Did she dare move enough to meet its eyes? And if she couldn't harvest enough life from an Elder, could she weaken it enough to get away before it tore her open?

It suddenly occurred to her that her form of *terra indigene* was one of Namid's most ferocious predators *until* you crossed into the true wild country and met the earth natives who lived there.

The Elder withdrew.

More sounds. It took the second splash for Tess to identify that the Elders were batting human remains into the water-filled street. She would try to warn Montgomery and his men before they went out and found . . . whatever they would find.

Then she heard another sound that had her struggling to stand up. They were going into the Liaison's Office? *Why?*

<Nyx!>

<I know. Another one came in through the back door and is sniffing around.>

<Can you get out?>

<Smoke isn't tasty, so I'm not that worried.> A pause. <I think a couple of them are in the sorting room now.>

One of Meg's constant places that helped her deal with all the things in the Courtyard that changed. Well, she and Nyx would have to put it back together before they let Meg see it.

Assuming the Elders weren't caching special meat in the cupboards.

Tess tested the sore leg. Hurt but not broken, and not bleeding.

<Tess, get down,> Henry said.

Her hair had changed to more green than black, so she dared glance in the direction of the studio, confident that a look wouldn't harm the Grizzly. He stood at the studio door, watching the Liaison's Office.

She caught a whiff of that wild scent that had never been touched by anything human—until now. Then it was gone without so much as a splash, and the oppressive silence, like the fog, lifted.

Henry stepped out of his studio and approached Tess. "Foolish to take on six enemies when they couldn't see you well enough to die."

She shrugged. "Wasn't going to let them into the Courtyard."

A light came on in the sorting room, and the window cranked open a bit.

Tess limped to the window with Henry politely following.

"Nyx?"

A sigh before the Sanguinati said, "Come to the back door."

Henry didn't wait for Tess this time. He was out of his yard and entering the office before she reached the wooden gate.

When she limped into the Liaison's Office, a hurried look around the back room didn't reveal any obvious damage—more like things had been shoved out of place by something large sniffing around.

Nothing torn up in the sorting room either, but . . .

"I heard one of them growl something about the howling not-Wolf and how this place smelled like one of her dens," Nyx said.

"Meg's scent is strong here," Henry said. "Maybe they liked it." He didn't sound pleased about that.

Tess wasn't pleased either. The Elders were already sufficiently intrigued by Meg's relationships with the Others in the Courtyard without giving them more reasons to be curious about her and Simon.

"That's not all they liked." Nyx dropped two clawed and mangled plastic containers on the sorting room table. "They ate all the Wolf cookies."

Simon opened Howling Good Reads' back door an inch and sniffed the air. The Elders' primal tang drifted around the area behind the stores, but they had moved away from the Courtyard. Were they heading back to the wild country, or were the Elders gathering in another part of the city for a massive hunt?

He poked his head out the door, ready to duck back inside.

"Simon!" Henry called at the same time Simon heard the phone in HGR's office ring. Well, Vlad was working upstairs and could take the call.

The Grizzly's voice wasn't coming from the studio or yard; it came from behind the Liaison's Office.

<Simon!>

The tension in Vlad's voice had Simon running up the stairs to the office.

Vlad held out the phone. Simon's heart raced and his body trembled. He'd seen that look on Vlad's face once before.

Taking the receiver, he said, "This is Simon."

"The metal snake stays in its burrow, or we will kill it." It wasn't a voice meant for human speech, and even over a phone line, it scraped against Simon's bones.

"Forever?"

Silence. Had they taken the question as a challenge?

"The trains bring some of the human foods we use in the Courtyard," he added.

"You do not need *human* food, Wolf."

"The sweet blood needs human food." By this time, Henry, Tess, and Nyx had entered the office. They looked alarmed when he mentioned Meg. All right, there weren't many things that couldn't come by truck or ship if they were supplying only the Courtyard, but it would be good to know if trains were no longer a means of transportation.

"Day dweller," was the snarled final answer. "It travels with the sun now."

Meaning trains, and any cargo, could no longer travel through the wild country between sundown and sunrise—a rule that was already in place but hadn't been strictly enforced. Simon wondered how many trains would be destroyed and how many passengers killed before humans believed the access through the wild country was really limited.

But not completely denied—yet.

"The sweet blood is the howling not-Wolf?"

"She sings with the Wolfgard," he replied warily.

A huff. A snuff. A . . . laugh? Then the buzz in his ear of a disconnected call.

<Wolf.>

<Air?>

<The Elders are returning to the wild country, but we think some of them are curious about our Meg and will visit again.>

He whimpered. Couldn't help it. He put the receiver back in the cradle and noticed Lieutenant Montgomery had joined the group in the office.

"We'll need to talk to Captain Burke and Agent O'Sullivan to convey a message."

"Can the police get out there now?" Montgomery asked, gesturing toward the windows to indicate the city.

"Some humans tried to invade the Courtyard," Tess said. "The Elders killed them. I couldn't see what was done, but the police should be prepared for something bad."

"How many bodies?"

"Six."

"There will be more," Simon said, then added, "but not so many." Because Meg, the not-Wolf, had amused some of the Elders.

"If you have no objections, I'd like the families of police officers to remain here a while longer," Montgomery said. "The fewer people on the streets, the better."

"The Denbys will want to go across the street and check on the house." Vlad went to the windows that looked out on Crowfield Avenue and the buildings the Courtyard had acquired. "Make sure the curtains or blinds stay drawn on any windows that overlook the streets. And don't let anyone go out there who doesn't have to."

Montgomery moved to the window and looked out. His brown skin turned gray and he braced a hand on the window frame for support.

"What is it?" Tess asked.

"I'm not sure what's on the lawns of the two apartment buildings," Vlad said with forced calm, "but there are intestines hanging from the branches of the trees like some strange moss."

"Lieutenant?" Simon said softly. The humans couldn't be pragmatic about the available meat—and with so many human strangers in the Courtyard right now, the Others couldn't take advantage of the abandoned kills either.

When Montgomery turned and looked at him, he felt pity for the man. This was a hard truth about who guarded the continent of Thaisia, but Simon thought the other part of the truth would hit humans like Montgomery even harder.

"In Wolf form, we could help you find all the parts." He would have to choose Wolves who dealt with humans enough to understand why they couldn't snack on what they found.

"I need to call Captain Burke," Montgomery said.

"The Business Association's room is empty," Henry said.

They waited until Montgomery went across the hall.

"When do you want to meet the humans to tell them the rest?" Vlad asked.

"In an hour, if Captain Burke can get here by then. I want Nathan back here too," Simon said.

"Tess needs to tend to her leg, but I will fetch Merri Lee, and she will help Nyx and me put Meg's office back in order," Henry said.

"As much as we can." Nyx gave Simon a fanged smile. "The Elders ate all the Wolf cookies."

He just sighed. What else was there to do?

After the rest of them went downstairs to deal with humans and sort out what needed to be done, Simon called the Pony Barn and felt relieved when he heard Meg's voice.

"Simon? Is that you? Are you all right?"

"It's me. I'm fine. Are you?"

"Yes. Something thought about entering the Pony Barn and . . . they laughed at us."

They weren't laughing at all of you. "They ate all the Wolf cookies in the sorting room too."

"They . . . Well! Can you bite them for doing that?"

Even the thought made him want to hide under the desk. "No. But . . . they might have jumbled things up a bit when they were looking around. Henry, Nyx, and Merri Lee will straighten up the office, but I wanted you to know in case something wasn't exactly right."

"Then I'll be prepared if something is different." Meg didn't say anything else for a moment. "I'll check with Eamer's Bakery and see when they can send more cookies."

"You're all right?" Her voice sounded tired.

"Jester, Sam, and I have been reading a Wolf Team story aloud for Skippy and the ponies. I'm the narrator and the human female who faints a lot."

Meg sounded sour about that. Maybe he should invite some of the Wolf Team writers to spend a few days in the Courtyard. He'd bet a month's worth of cookies that there wouldn't be human females fainting in future stories if they did visit.

"Jester reads the parts of the bad humans and the Wolf Team leader, and we're both helping Sam read the Wolf Team bits," she continued. "We were just taking a break for drinks and snacks when you called."

That explained her tired voice. "Stay there a couple more hours. Then I'll pick you up and we can check out the Green Complex and the garden."

"Okay. Do you need to talk to Jester? He says you probably already know what you need to."

"I don't need to talk to him, but I do have other calls to make."

He hung up, wishing he could be reading the Wolf Team with her. But the sooner he dealt with the human things, the sooner he could take care of the things that really mattered to him.

"Henry?"

Henry stopped wiping off the table in the back room of the Liaison's Office and considered the tone of Merri Lee's voice. Not, *Help, help, I've seen a mouse.* More like, *I made a rattlesnake angry. What should I do?*

Dropping the rag on the table, he strode into the sorting room at the same time Nyx flowed in from the front room.

"What's wrong?" Nyx said.

Merri Lee pointed at the two cards on the counter above the drawer that held Meg's prophecy cards.

The first card was a beautifully rendered but terrifying representation of what Henry guessed was one of the Elders' forms. Next was half a Wolf cookie. Last was a card that had a simple drawing of a smiley face.

"That is sooooo wrong," Merri Lee said, shuddering.

"Yes, it is." Henry picked up the cookie. "Leaving food on the counter will attract mice."

She gave him a look that told him he'd missed the point.

"And the Elders shouldn't have been playing with Meg's cards." Nyx opened the drawer and used the tip of her finger to nudge the cards inside. "It might interfere with her reading a prophecy."

Now Merri Lee looked at Nyx. "I'm going outside for a minute to get some air." They watched her leave.

"She seems disturbed," Henry said.

"Of course she is," Nyx snapped. "Don't *you* find that smiley-face card disturbing?"

Nathan watched the fog lift to reveal a blue summer sky.

<Nathan!>

<Marie?> If the Hawk was flying, did that mean it was safe to go out?

<Simon says you should come home now. The Elders have left the city.>

He howled out of happiness and scattered the humans who were clustered near the door as he dashed for Captain Burke's den. The big human looked at him when he entered the room and shifted to pull on his clothes, but Burke kept talking on the phone.

"Looks like he got the news. If I'm delayed, I'll let you know. Otherwise, expect us in an hour." Burke hung up, walked to the doorway, and boomed, "We received the all clear. Go, go, go!"

Nathan watched the police officers moving out for their own kind of hunt.

Burke returned to his desk. "I'm expected at the Courtyard in an hour; I can give you a lift home." Then he held out a piece of paper he'd taken from his desk. "What do you make of this?"

A message from the Shady Burke. Nathan read it, then handed it back with a shrug. "The humans weren't going to hold any part of the wild country for long."

"It's the phrase 'about to get some weather' that interests me. Did we get some weather, Nathan?"

The question had a bit of Foxgard slyness. "We had wind, lots of rain." Not to mention Namid's teeth and claws roaming the streets.

"Have you ever seen a human doing magic tricks?" Burke dipped his hand into his pocket, took out a quarter, and held it up for Nathan to see. "Like making coins disappear or pulling rabbits out of a hat?"

When he was a juvenile, he had seen a magic act. He'd wanted to find a bunny-filled hat like the magician's, but all the trading post had was a hat made of bunny fur. "That was a trick? The hat didn't really hold a bunny?" How disappointing, but not unexpected from humans.

"Getting hungry?" Burke asked dryly.

"Yes." Hopefully the humans hadn't eaten all the meat in the Courtyard. He was bound to have work to do for the pack, and he wouldn't have time to chase down a meal.

Burke moved his hands and the quarter disappeared. "Sleight of hand. Distracting the attention from one thing by drawing attention to something else."

Burke turned his hand and revealed the coin again. "We didn't get anything like the weather that's heading for Cel-Romano, did we?"

"Ask Simon. He might know."

"Yes, most likely, he does know." Burke looked at the quarter. "He has said more than once that the *terra indigene* learn from other predators. He wasn't just talking about hunting techniques, was he?"

It didn't sound like a question that needed an answer, so Nathan said nothing.

Burke pocketed the coin. "Well, I expect Commissioner Wallace wants to yell at me for being an alarmist and a pain in his ass, not to mention holding an entire police station hostage—more or less." He walked to his office door.

Simon was the Courtyard's leader and would tell the humans what he wanted them to know. But Nathan felt *he* should say something to Burke about keeping the police pack denned.

"Captain? You're not an alarmist."

Burke looked back at him and smiled tightly. "I know."

CHAPTER 51

Earthday, Sumor 1

"*. . .* M*ajor flooding in Toland, along with power outages and damage to roads and railways. In a bizarre twist to the storm, a severed head was found on the steps of one of the television stations. It is rumored to be the head of Nicholas Scratch, the motivational speaker for the Humans First and Last movement. It is also rumored that Scratch had taken a ship bound for Cel-Romano before the hurricane reached the Northeast Region of Thaisia. Initial examination by police medical officers confirm there are signs that Scratch had been in salt water at some point, but they refused to comment about whether the head had been severed by tools or teeth.*"

Vlad took a seat at the big table in the consulate's meeting room. After hearing the report about Nicholas Scratch, he understood why Stavros Sanguinati had lingered around Toland instead of coming here to assume his position as *terra indigene* leader of Talulah Falls.

It also explained the backhanded slap Ocean had given Toland. She had been hunting specific prey, and, with Stavros's help, she had silenced the enemy's voice.

Now Stavros was on his way to Lakeside, riding in earth native or Intuit trucks that were going in the right direction. It would take a little longer for him to get to Lakeside, but until they were sure the "metal snakes" really would be allowed to run through the wild country during the daylight hours, it was better for the *terra indigene* to use other means of travel.

Vlad nodded to Agent Greg O'Sullivan, who looked pasty and trembled slightly. Taking a seat, O'Sullivan dropped a folder on the table and muttered, "Gods above and below."

"Problems?" Vlad asked.

"Plenty to go around."

Simon, Henry, Lieutenant Montgomery, and Captain Burke walked in, followed by Elliot Wolfgard. The humans took seats on one side of the table; the *terra indigene* took seats on the other side, with Simon at the head of the table.

"We have to stop meeting like this," Burke said to O'Sullivan.

"I'd rather not consider the alternative to these discussions," O'Sullivan said grimly. He spoke quietly, but he wasn't trying to hide his words from all the sharp ears in the room.

Vlad wondered what O'Sullivan had heard—and how he'd heard it.

"I've been on the phone for the past hour and have so much information, I'm not sure where to start," Simon said.

"There is a saying: all roads travel through the woods," Burke said. "Let's start there."

"All right. Trains will be allowed to travel in the Northeast Region, but only during daylight hours."

"We've already put that policy into place. For the most part, the railways have followed it, at least for the passenger trains," O'Sullivan said. "How is this different?"

"From now on, there is no safety in the dark. The earth natives in the wild country will destroy anything that moves through their territory after dark."

O'Sullivan frowned. "No safety in the dark. Does that apply to vehicles on the roads?"

Simon nodded.

"So we're back to closing the stockade gates." O'Sullivan sighed. "Can people go about their business after dark within the boundaries of land leased to humans?"

Simon hesitated. "Maybe. But humans invaded the wild country and erased the boundaries, so now there are . . . gaps . . . in your stockades that you can't mend, and I don't think some kinds of Elders are going to stay away from the human cities anymore."

"Sounds like cities are going to have to establish, and enforce, curfews," Burke said.

Vlad noticed that neither Burke nor Montgomery mentioned that police officers, of necessity, would be out after dark to enforce the curfews and other human laws. What about the humans who drove ambulances or put out fires?

No way to tell. Not yet. But Vlad *was* sure of one thing: no matter how hard or terrifying life would be for humans in Thaisia from now on, it was going to be much, much worse for the people living in the Cel-Romano Alliance of Nations after Namid's teeth and claws retaliated for the deaths of the shifters as well as the humans' attempt to claim a part of the wild country.

"What about travel between regions?" Montgomery asked.

Simon shrugged. "I only know the new rules for the Northeast."

That wasn't quite true, Vlad thought. *Because of the drawing Hope made, Simon and I—and Jackson—know more about what will happen between regions than anyone else.* "You already know that lines of communication between regions have been severed," he told O'Sullivan. "You can no longer call, send an e-mail, or even send a telegram to a person or business in another region. But there has been no sign of train tracks or roads being destroyed at regional boundaries that would deny travel or the flow of mail and merchandise between regions. I'm guessing that travel is still possible but will be difficult, especially if any form of transportation that is hauling freight has to be off the roads or at a train depot by dark. Or docked at a harbor if the cargo is going by boat."

"No sign of tracks or roads being destroyed *yet*," O'Sullivan said. "I heard the word you didn't say, Mr. Sanguinati." He paused. "The governor's office is working on a list of towns and cities in the Northeast that are still accessible to humans."

"Has anyone heard from the people in Toland?" Montgomery asked.

"Radio stations indicate the damage to the city is serious, and the death toll is rising," O'Sullivan said. "Telephone and telegraph lines are down. Could be days before they're reconnected."

"Could be months, could be never," Simon said. "Thin the herds, then isolate the herds."

Silence. "We could be cut off completely from the other cities?" Burke finally asked.

"The HFL caused trouble throughout Thaisia," Simon said. "Even though a breach of trust had been declared, and you all knew it would get bad if you broke that trust further, you did it anyway."

"Not all of us, Simon," Montgomery said.

"Not all of you," Simon agreed. "But the monkeys chattered over the telephone wires to plot against us. So the wires will not be allowed to stretch between regions anymore. Maybe not even between cities."

"Mobile phones might still work," Vlad said. "Radio and television can still convey information over a distance."

"The Elders broke the link they could see," Henry said. "And they will keep it broken since those wires were strung across the wild country with their permission, which they no longer give. But the Elementals know how to silence radio and television if humans try to use them against us."

"Steve Ferryman says the Intuits had already built communications cabins at two settlements near the tip of Lake Superior," Simon said. "One is in the Northeast, the other in the northern Midwest Region. The operators are using citizens band radios to talk to each other and convey messages between regions. Each cabin also has telegraph and telephone wires, so the Intuits can make phone calls and also use e-mail, but only within their own region. They feel that, if they use the radios carefully, the *terra indigene* in the wild country will not be provoked into destroying the cabins and that means of communication between the two regions."

"They will send and receive messages for a fee?" O'Sullivan asked.

"Of course—but they haven't worked that part out yet. For now, they're only taking messages for Intuits and *terra indigene*."

And probably will continue to do so, Vlad thought.

Simon handed Vlad a folded half sheet of paper. "Ferryman received this for us."

Vlad opened the paper. *We're safe at Prairie Gold and Bennett. Heard from Jackson Wolfgard. Everyone at Sweetwater also survived. Tolya.*

He handed the paper back to Simon, a little surprised by the depth of his relief. He had expected Tolya to survive. What surprised him was how much the confirmation meant to him.

"A lot of humans—and a lot of human places—are gone," Simon said. "We don't know how many. It's not the Lakeside Courtyard's job to know. Our job is to watch over *this* city, but from now on, we won't be the only ones who are watching." He looked at Burke. "The wild country begins right on your doorstep now. It will prowl your streets in ways we never did. The next time the humans in Thaisia turn against us will be the last time."

"Understood," Burke said roughly. He brushed his elbow against O'Sullivan's arm. "You have any questions?"

"Do any of you have a suggestion for where I could set up a small office for the ITF? I'll talk to Governor Hannigan about it, but I think it would be wise to have an ITF agent stationed here in Lakeside."

"There are desks here in the consulate going unused," Elliot said. "You could make use of one of them for the time being."

"Thanks."

"Just don't expect any clerical help. It's in short supply."

"Understood."

Vlad watched everyone but Simon leave the room. Resting his chin in his hand, he studied the Courtyard's leader. "Think O'Sullivan and the other humans really understood?"

"How much human do the *terra indigene* want to keep?" Simon countered. "Or more to the point, how *many* humans do we want to keep? The ones we let in. We're stuck with them now."

He couldn't disagree with that. "We have a Courtyard, a village, a city, and a community to work with, including the land that supports them."

"We can't feed all of Lakeside."

"We're not supposed to. Predators gather when there is a bounty of food and stay until the food source crashes and they begin to starve. Then some stay but more leave to find another place to hunt. There are empty places now, Simon. They're not human controlled anymore, but there is work, and where there is work, there will, most likely, also be food."

"Tolya and Jackson are all right. So is the Hope pup."

"And Stavros is on his way to Lakeside to talk to Grandfather before going on to Talulah Falls." Vlad pushed his chair back. "Go find Meg. Check out the garden and let her see if the green things survived."

"They're probably floating, with the ground being so soggy."

Simon was a friend, but every once in a while Vlad couldn't resist pulling the Wolf's tail. "If you don't want to be out there trying to mop up the water to *unsoggy* the ground, I suggest you sound more optimistic."

"Meg wouldn't want to do the mopping thing."

"Are you sure?"

Simon just growled and walked out of the room.

Vlad smiled. None of them were sure what the female pack would think was a reasonable thing to do, but the one thing he *was* sure of was that the Others weren't going to ask those females what should be done for baby plants stuck in soggy ground. They might think mopping the garden was a fine idea.

Amused—and wondering if he should mention the garden to Jester and let the Coyote be the one to start a little trouble—Vlad returned to Howling Good Reads to deal with humans who hadn't been harmed but still had good reason to be terrified.

CHAPTER 52

Cel-Romano

I n villages all along the Cel-Romano border, people regarded their restless, fearful animals and, remembering stories passed down through generations, knew what was coming.

After sundown, when soldiers bivouacked around the villages wouldn't see and report them to the Important People, they placed bowls of sweetened milk on their back doorsteps, or a slice of bread with a bit of oil or butter, or a slice of cake that had used up precious rations. They placed their gifts and whispered, "For our friends," before they gathered their children close and prayed they would see the dawn.

They heard the *rat-tat-tat* of gunfire and the truncated screams of the soldiers who had laughed at the villagers for their superstitions about the creatures that lived in—and guarded—the wild country. They heard things bump against their doors, sniffing around the gifts. And they held their loved ones tight as a terrible silence brushed against their homes and continued on its way to the Big Cities where the Important People lived.

Elementals rode their steeds through the cities on the western half of the Mediterran Sea, tearing through factories and warehouses, leaving nothing but rubble and fire in their wake.

Elementals rode their steeds through the cities on the eastern half of the

Mediterran Sea, the pounding hooves shaking buildings into pieces, or cracking the land to swallow buildings whole.

And the leaders of the Humans First and Last movement, fleeing their cities, saw a truth about the world just before Namid's teeth and claws tore them apart.

Alantea rode Hurricane across the waters of her domain, gathering a storm full of fury and vengeance—a storm unlike anything that had been seen in a very long time. She caught small ships and snapped them in half, driving the debris and toxins inland for miles as she struck her enemies' shores.

On the eastern side of Afrikah, Indeus rode Tsunami, heading for the strait that Earth and Earthshaker had expanded to accommodate the monstrous waves that struck that part of Cel-Romano minutes after Alantea and Hurricane galloped onto the western side of those lands.

And on her island in the Mediterran Sea, ancient Tethys summoned the waters to rise and reclaim the land she had once, long ago, ceded to Earth.

As the waters of the Mediterran receded and the surviving humans stumbled around the ruins of their cities, looking for the living and mounding the dead, the Plague Riders came down from their isolated lairs to feast and breed and establish new territories within the broken cities.

CHAPTER 53

Thaisia

Drops became a trickle, which became a stream, which became a raging flood of failures as the structure connecting the human places in Thaisia broke.

While roads between some cities remained untouched, other roads became asphalt-littered mounds of earth—or disappeared into sinkholes that would expand and deepen if more than a loaded pickup, or a loaded wagon pulled by horses, tried to get around the hole in order to transfer crops or goods and send them on to people hoping to buy them.

Trains were allowed two passenger cars—one for humans and one for the Intuits and *terra indigene*—and no more than two dozen freight and livestock cars. If some of the cars held goods destined for Intuit villages or *terra indigene* settlements, all of the freight was usually allowed to migrate across regional borders, but passengers had to disembark unless they had a letter from a *terra indigene* leader stating that the person had permission to travel to a specified destination.

At first, the railroads defied the restriction about the number of cars they could hook up to an engine, and the first few trains did reach their destinations. After that, no one had to ask why the tracks were destroyed halfway between two stations, stranding passengers and crew too far from any human habitation. And no one asked about what police officers had seen when they finally found what was left of those trains.

There was no mercy in the wild country, and no safety in the dark.

As letters traveled slowly across the continent, humans learned, piece by piece, what the Humans First and Last movement had cost the people of Thaisia.

To: Douglas Burke

For all intents and purposes, the Cel-Romano Alliance of Nations is gone.

—Shady

CHAPTER 54

Moonsday, Sumor 9

Tolya Sanguinati waited at the Bennett train station for the town's new arrivals.

He had argued for days that phone lines connecting Bennett and Prairie Gold to Sweetwater were necessary, that the sweet blood living with Jackson Wolfgard should not be cut off completely from the beings who would help her stay alive.

At first, the Elders had ignored his arguments as well as Jackson's pleas because Prairie Gold and Bennett were Midwest towns and Sweetwater was located in the Northwest, and all the wires humans used for their talking had been torn down along every regional border—and no one who tried to repair the lines survived the wrath of Namid's teeth and claws.

Then came a question: this sweet blood was a howling not-Wolf?

After careful consideration of what that might mean, Tolya told the Elders that the Hope pup was a friend of Meg Corbyn, who was friend to Simon Wolfgard, leader of the Lakeside Courtyard.

The next day, work crews were permitted to repair the phone lines that crossed the regional borders and connected Bennett and Prairie Gold with Sweetwater. And although they were watched every moment, the men on those crews survived.

Tolya wasn't sure who was on the train. Some Intuits, upon arriving, had taken one look at the town and said they would stay a week to help clean up and clear out the houses, but they had a feeling this wasn't the place for them to settle and asked for an assignment in another town. Some didn't even leave the train station before asking for a return ticket home.

It wasn't an easy place for any kind of human. One of the Intuits said the town felt like it was filled with ghosts. Tolya didn't tell the young man that it wasn't human spirits that were spooking him; it was the more primal earth natives who continued to prowl around and through the town—and the most terrifying among them were the ones who shifted to a clawed, furred form that walked on two legs.

The train pulled in. A few passengers got out.

Tolya was a mature, adult Sanguinati in his prime. He certainly wasn't *old*. But he looked at the fresh-faced humans getting off the train and felt like a pack's nanny. It made sense that adults who hadn't found a mate yet would be the most likely to travel to a new place like Bennett, but did they all have to be so young?

The four males—he guessed they were Intuits by the way they looked around—saw him and kept their distance. They knew he was Sanguinati and he was in charge of this town; they couldn't have come here without receiving that information. But they weren't used to having contact with his kind, if any of them had had actual contact with any of the *terra indigene*.

The female, on the other hand, gave him a bright smile and walked up to him, her hand extended. "I'm Barb Debany. My family calls me Bee because my name is Barbara Ellen, which makes my initials B.E., so . . . Bee. But, new place and all, I would rather be called Barb."

Wondering why she told him about a name she didn't want to use, Tolya shook her hand, shifting his palm to smoke for just long enough to get a taste of her blood and know if the chatter was natural or induced by some chemical.

He sensed nothing but the adrenaline made by nerves and excitement.

"Do you have papers, Barb Debany?"

"Oh. Yes." She opened one of those sacks human females carried, dug around a bit, and finally, looking flushed, produced the letter.

Tolya scanned the document signed by Vlad and Simon Wolfgard. "You're the one who is going to look after the animals and figure out what to do with them." He'd flowed through keyholes to unlock doors and release the dogs and cats—animals he'd been told could live outdoors, at least for the summer. Billy Rider, who divided his worktime between Prairie Gold's ranch and the town's livery stable, and Tobias Walker had set up areas in the town where they put out food for the dogs and a couple of different spots for the cats' vittles. The chirpy caged birds were all moved to one house to make it easier to feed them until the "pet person" arrived.

He'd thought the fish in the aquariums were live food for the cats and hadn't mentioned the creatures to Billy or Tobias, so most of them, by the time someone checked those houses, were floating belly up.

All in all, except for the fish, Tolya thought he'd dealt with the pet problem rather well over the past couple of weeks.

"They told you I'm not a fully qualified vet, didn't they?" Barb asked, sounding a bit anxious. "I'm just an assistant."

"You're more qualified than anyone else here, so now you're the vet."

She gulped and turned a little pale, making the freckles across her nose and cheeks stand out.

"For now, we're providing food and lodging at the town's hotel and boarding-house as part of your wages. I believe there is still a room available at the board-inghouse, so you have a choice—if you decide quickly," he added, seeing the four young men approaching.

Barb glanced over her shoulder. "Any other girls at the boardinghouse?"

"Not another human girl like you. There aren't many females of any species here yet."

She gulped again. Then she smiled. "Part of the adventure, right? And some-thing I can tell my family. My brother is a police officer in Lakeside. He handed me a package of labels, already addressed to him and our folks, as well as a variety of stamps, and said, 'Write once a week or else.' I don't think the 'or else' is much of a threat, do you, not when I'm all the way out west?"

Tolya smiled. "I believe I met your brother when I visited Lakeside. I know I met a Lieutenant Montgomery. Doesn't your brother know him?"

"Oh, *forelock*! The long arm of the law is really long, isn't it?"

He laughed because she sounded so annoyed and because her version of a swearword amused him. He hoped this human female stayed around for a while.

He led his new residents to the pickup truck, where Tobias Walker waited to take them to their designated living quarters. He watched them drive away, Barb and one of the males in the cab with Tobias while the other three males rode in the bed with the baggage.

He looked at the station, considering his duties. Then he headed toward the center of the town. Other Sanguinati, as well as a couple of Wolves and Eagles, would deal with the train's personnel and any deliveries. He wanted to see how Jesse Walker and her gaggle of volunteers were doing with the inventories of several of Bennett's stores, as well as collecting all the perishables from all the houses. They needed to know what they already had in order to figure out what the town's new residents would need. Until they hired shopkeepers for the stores that would reopen, Jesse was coming up from Prairie Gold two days a week, leaving her own general store in the paws of the inquisitive Rachel Wolfgard.

As he reached the building that would become Bennett's general store and carry everything except groceries, he saw an unfamiliar truck driving in from the north. After it parked in a space near him, a Wolf and a human male got out.

"Howdy," the man said, brushing the brim of his hat. He looked haggard, but his voice was firm—and familiar.

"I remember you," Tolya said. "You and your men helped Joe Wolfgard load the bison into a livestock car."

"We did, yes. I was sorry to hear . . ." He shook his head. "That was a bad day. I'm Stewart Dixon."

"Tolya Sanguinati."

"Tolya is the leader of this town now," the Wolf said, sniffing the air and scanning the town square for what wouldn't be seen.

Tolya studied the Wolf. <Are you alone?> Some Wolf packs had been wiped out completely, but in other places, a few of the Wolves survived.

The Wolf slanted a glance at Stewart Dixon. <The ranchers who live around us don't like those HFL humans, so my pack wasn't attacked. Besides, the Wolves sometimes hunt elk with Stewart Dixon to bring down enough meat to feed both our packs. He is not an enemy.>

So there were some alliances between Others and humans. Perhaps those alliances could be expanded. After all, the ranches between Bennett and Prairie Gold still had animals but no humans, and Tobias Walker and the hands at the Prairie Gold ranch couldn't deal with so much on their own. But if the work—and the profits—could be split with ranchers who were already trusted by *terra indigene*, they might be able to tend all the herds and keep the cattle alive until they were needed for meat.

Tolya looked at Stewart Dixon. "You have come to town for supplies?"

"I was hoping to get some of what's available."

"Jesse Walker is handling the stores today." Tolya offered a smile. "Some of us are wearing many hats right now. That is the phrase?" He knew quite well it was the proper phrase, but the question put the man at ease.

"That's the phrase." Stewart rubbed the back of his neck. "Well, I'm looking for gas and grub. Those are the immediate needs." A blush stained his cheeks. "And some female things for the wife and daughters."

Tolya wondered if the man was usually uncomfortable speaking of such things or if it was something that wasn't talked about with strangers. Interesting. He would ask Jesse Walker. "I think we can accommodate all of those needs. Follow me."

As he led Stewart Dixon and the Wolf into the store, a howl rose from the train station—and was answered by Stewart's companion.

We are here, keeping watch. We are here.

As the Wolves' reassurance filled the air, the earthy tang and odd silence that had filled the town square faded away and headed for the untouched land beyond the town.

To: Vladimir Sanguinati

Barb Debany arrived in Bennett and is settling in. Her brother supplied labels and stamps. We supplied postcards and stationary as a welcome gift. She was more excited about being given the use of a horse than she was about the postcards.

—Tolya

Dear Michael,

I've been working all the daylight hours since I arrived because so many small animals need care until I find new homes for them. I'm living at a boardinghouse, see address below. Will write more later. Love to Mom and Dad. Barb.

P.S. They gave me a horse!

CHAPTER 55

Sunday, Sumor 17

Meg smiled at Simon and Vlad.

"There is something behind that smile," Vlad said.

"Like the first time you see a striped pretty and don't learn what it is until you poke it with a paw and it sprays you," Simon said.

She wasn't smiling now. "Did you just compare me to a skunk?"

Now *they* smiled.

"To be fair, you don't smell like one anymore," Simon said.

"What?"

"Why did you want to see us, Meg?" Vlad asked.

Having witnessed a scene with Twyla Montgomery and some of the children earlier this morning, it was clear to Meg that throwing what Merri Lee called a hissy fit didn't get you what you wanted. And if doing that didn't work with Twyla, it certainly wouldn't work with Simon and Vlad—especially if they didn't understand what she was doing and she had to explain it. Which would be embarrassing. And not mature.

Amused at herself, which made her feel steadier, Meg laid some cards on the table.

"Meg?" Sharpness in Simon's voice. Sharpness in Vlad's eyes.

"I'm not drawing cards for a vision," she explained. "I'd like a favor. Two favors, actually."

"That must be why you asked for two of us to come here," Vlad said.

She pointed to the cards she had taken out of a deck on the sorting room table. One card was a smiley face. Another was a sad face. The third was the question mark she'd drawn once before when she asked about Lakeside's future. "These cards are from a game. Some of them got mixed up with the prophecy cards."

"How did that happen?" Simon asked.

She shook her head. She wasn't going to be a tattletale. She knew that Merri Lee and Ruth had already talked to Eve Denby and Twyla and Sierra Montgomery about the importance of the children not going into the Liaison's Office unsupervised and, especially, not playing with the cards.

"That's not important. The *important* thing is that I think these actually are useful for revealing prophecies without me making a cut."

She had their complete attention now.

"But these particular cards . . ." She went to the drawer and randomly pulled five cards that had different backs, which meant they were from different decks. She turned them over and lined them up above the first three cards. "Do you see? These are from different decks of cards—some reveal the natural world and some are illustrations of human or urban things. Even though they're different, they complement each other. Do you see?"

Vlad came around to her side of the table. He picked up the deck of game cards and fanned them to see more of the images. "So you want a deck of cards with these images but done in a style that would fit in with the rest of the decks you're currently using?"

"Yes." Eventually she would have to pare down the number of cards that would become the Trailblazer deck of prophecy cards, but for now she didn't want to limit possibilities while she was still exploring what the *cassandra sangue* might be able to do with this way of seeing visions.

"Could the Hope pup draw those?" Simon asked, cocking his head.

Meg felt something run over her skin. Not strong enough to be pins and needles or prickles, but definitely a response to the question. "I don't know. Could we ask her?"

"We can get a message to Jackson."

"Could you purchase another deck of these?" Vlad asked, waggling the fanned cards. "Hope would need the images for reference."

Meg said she would see about getting another deck. She didn't mention that she was going to ask Eve Denby where to buy one.

"That was an easy favor," Simon said.

Of course, there was no guarantee that the cards would be available. With people now considering what they needed instead of what they would like to have, a children's card game wouldn't be a high priority when companies had to choose what to ship by truck or train.

"What's the second favor?" Simon asked.

"Could you find a job for Harry, the deliveryman? He quit his job at Everywhere Delivery because the company became Everywhere Human Delivery. But he still needs to work." Sensing resistance, Meg hurried on. "You wouldn't have to find a place for Harry and his wife to live. If he could use one of our vans, he could be the Courtyard's deliveryman and pick up orders we place with companies in Lakeside. Or maybe you could talk to Jerry Sledgeman about hiring Harry to work for him and make deliveries between Lakeside and the River Road Community."

"Meg . . ." Simon sighed. "We can't keep taking in strays. On top of the human pack, we're already letting Officer Debany's parents shop in the Market Square. Same with Officer MacDonald's parents. And Captain Burke. And Commander Gresh and his mate and young. When a pack gets too big, it needs to split so that part of it finds new territory and new prey. We're looking after a lot of humans now. And Merri Lee and Ruthie will have pups, and they'll need food too, after they're weaned."

"They're not having pups yet," Meg muttered. But Simon had a point. After promising to give her a daily summary of what was happening in Lakeside and the rest of Thaisia, her friends urged her to avoid the news and the newspaper until things calmed down. Since just looking out the front windows and watching the cars drive by on Main Street made her skin buzz viciously, she didn't think she would be able to resist the razor if she had more contact with the world outside of the Courtyard.

"Just two more?" she pleaded. "Just Harry and his wife?"

Simon and Vlad looked at each other.

"Everyone has to earn their part of the meat," Simon finally said. "Everyone in a pack has a job, and that has to include any humans who want part of the food we have here or can bring in."

"Harry and his wife, but no more," Vlad said. "We're helping to support the River Road Community too. Don't forget that."

They wouldn't be trying to support *any* of those humans if they hadn't taken her in and accepted her as one of them. "No more." She hesitated, and wondered if it was cowardly not to give the message directly. "Could you tell Captain Burke something?"

Vlad nodded.

Meg tapped the question-mark card on the table. "This card came up once before, when I wondered about Lakeside's future."

"I remember," Simon said. "Future undecided."

"I overheard Agent O'Sullivan say he and Captain Burke had an appointment with the mayor, and I asked myself what Captain Burke should tell the mayor about Lakeside."

Vlad drew in a slow breath. "Future undecided?"

She nodded.

"You should make the call," Simon told Vlad. "Burke owes you one or two favors."

"He owes you too, but I'll call him."

After Vlad left, Simon rested his forearms on the table, his arm lightly brushing against hers.

"Talk to the human pack about paper for writing letters," he said. "Not just paper the females like, but paper that won't cause the males to cough up hairballs if they have to use it."

"People don't write that many letters. They use e-mail . . . Oh. Electronic mail stays within a region now."

"There are ways to send messages between the regions, like we're going to do to send a message to Jackson, but those messages aren't private anymore. The Intuits or *terra indigene* manning the communications cabins will see them. Humans aren't going to be able to attack again like they did under the HFL."

"Simon? Did a lot of places disappear?"

"Here in Thaisia? I don't know. It's hard to tell right now if the places—and the humans who lived there—are gone, or if a place isn't under human control anymore and that's why it's not being counted among the human places." He thought for a moment. "You gave Vlad a message for Captain Burke. Anything I should tell Lieutenant Montgomery?"

Scooping up the cards that were on the table, Meg returned them to the drawer that held the prophecy cards.

What should Simon tell Lieutenant Montgomery about Lakeside?

At first there was nothing. Then the prickles began. Meg closed her eyes and let her fingers search for the answer. When she chose three cards that produced the strongest prickles, she brought them back to the table and turned them over.

Wolf card. The telephone/telegraph key card. And a card that showed heavy surf striking the shore.

"I don't know what this means," Meg said. Then Water walked in from the back room, leaving wet footsteps on the floor.

The Elemental said, "I have a message for the Wolfgard."

"Give me a minute," Simon replied.

Water nodded and left.

"I guess Water is supposed to give you the message," Meg said.

"Huh." Simon studied the cards. "You're getting pretty good with those things. Do the prickles go away after you choose the ones that answer a question?"

She nodded. "Unless there is more that can't be seen with the cards."

"So you don't have to cut anymore."

If he believed that, he would be more upset when she *did* cut. "Using the cards doesn't produce the euphoria."

"They also don't cause pain or leave a scar," he countered.

The new scar along her jaw bothered all of the *terra indigene* more than the other scars she'd added since living in the Courtyard. The cards released prophecies but did nothing for the craving that was entwined with the addiction to cut. Still, she had resisted using the razor for almost four weeks.

"Don't keep Water waiting," she said.

When he went outside to talk to the Elemental, Meg returned the cards to the drawer.

No, the cards didn't help with the craving for the euphoria. Nothing but cutting could satisfy that.

Prickles filled her fingers. She ran her hands over the cards in the drawer until she found the one she needed to see.

She studied the card. Studied it and studied it.

A man and woman, standing close together in a garden under a full moon. Except the moon was shaped like the symbol for a heart.

Uneasy, Meg put the card back in the drawer. Romance? No. Men . . . Bad things had happened in the compound, things that were veiled in her memory but remembered by her body. So *that* couldn't produce anything like the euphoria.

Could it?

She closed the drawer and tried to ignore the light prickles that felt more like fingertips brushing the skin on the inside of her thighs.

Simon carefully slit open the box of books, pulled out the packing slip, and checked off the copies of each book before putting them on the shelves in the stock room. Everything he'd ordered before the storm suddenly showed up, making him wonder if railcars that were carrying merchandise for the *terra indigene* had been left on a siding somewhere. Now it was advantageous to ship merchandise to the Others because any properly sized train that had an earth native freight car had a better chance of safely passing through the wild country. "All freight or no freight" seemed to be the new motto.

Fine by him. Blair and Henry were taking two of the Courtyard's vehicles to make a second cargo run, which made him think Meg might be right about hiring the Harry to pick up deliveries.

The back door opened. Michael Debany eased around the boxes piled willy-nilly.

"You want me to break down the empty boxes?" Debany asked.

"Break down?"

"Slit them at the seams and flatten the cardboard."

Simon pondered that for a moment. Did the Others have a use for flat cardboard? "No. We can use the boxes to ship the books we're sending to other places."

Debany lifted a handful of books out of the top box and handed them to Simon without marking the packing slip. It reminded him of Sam offering toys in an effort to engage an adult because he was unhappy about something. Since Simon didn't know why Debany was unhappy, he placed the books together on a shelf instead of where they were supposed to go. He would mark the packing slip after the human went away.

"I heard from Bee. Barb. My sister?"

Wondering why that would make the man unhappy, Simon said, "Isn't that good?"

"It is, yes. She's settling in and busy." Debany's laugh sounded forced. "They gave her a horse. She'll never come back."

Simon stopped trying to work and studied the police officer. "Some young stay with their pack, but others have to leave their home territory to find a place in a new pack or to find a mate. Humans travel for those reasons too."

"You found a place where she can do the kind of work she wanted to do. I appreciate it."

"No, you don't."

This laugh sounded more natural. "I do, but I don't." Debany sighed. "It's so far away now, you know? A couple of months ago, Bennett would have been just as far away, but Mom and Dad would have been talking about making a visit to see Barb's new home. They would have sent an e-mail a couple of times a week to keep in touch and make sure she was doing okay. But now, they can't call to say hello or receive a quick response that would reassure them. It's different now."

"Yes, it's different now." Debany was thinking about quick communication, but Simon was thinking about Joe Wolfgard, whose howl wouldn't be heard again. "But you gave your sister labels and stamps, and Tolya and Jesse Walker gave her postcards and paper to write letters." And knowing the girl's connection to the Lakeside Courtyard, Tolya would keep an eye on her. Not sure if that would be a comfort, he didn't mention it.

"Merri says if I want to receive letters, I'd better start writing letters."

This he would mention. "Postcards are better unless you're writing a long letter or it's something private. There are Crows and Ravens helping to sort mail now in places like Bennett, and they like looking at the pictures and reading the messages." Seeing the look on Debany's face, he shrugged. "There's more than one kind of shiny."

A bump and a mutter had them looking toward the front of the stock room.

"Lieutenant," Debany said.

"Michael." Montgomery looked around at all the boxes. "Back orders?"

"Orders and back orders," Simon replied. "And two more vans full of boxes coming in."

"Guess I'll get ready for work," Debany said.

"This afternoon we're finally signing the papers and handing over the money for the two apartment buildings. By tomorrow, Merri Lee can choose her den, and Eve Denby will help her clean it and paint it." Since Montgomery was listening, Simon resisted the urge to ask about mating customs and if Debany would be moving into the den too. The sex part of mating and the living in the same den were different things for humans. He and Meg spent as much time living in the same place—and sleeping in the same bed—as Debany and Merri Lee, but Meg was still more like a maiden female who wasn't ready for the sex part of mating.

But she was very good at play.

Shaking off those thoughts—and admitting he wanted to postpone giving Montgomery the message he'd been asked to deliver—he realized Debany had slipped out and now it was Montgomery who was handing him books.

The man looked older and weighed down by some hard truths.

"Miss Twyla nipped the pups this morning," he offered.

Montgomery smiled at that. "My mama doesn't take back talk from anyone. Lizzy should have known better."

"She will the next time."

"We always think there will be enough time, but that's not always true, is it?"

Simon waited, but when Montgomery just held the books, he reached over and took them. "Sometimes a pack doesn't catch meat in time to save all its members if they've been hungry for too long, but you'll bring back food in time." Wasn't that the most important consideration right now? The farms that belonged to the *terra indigene* and were worked by Intuits in exchange for part of the bounty hadn't suffered much from the storms and the Elders' sweep through human places, and the Courtyard's gardens had survived and were growing quickly during these warm, sunny days. While the Others could easily adapt to eating whatever the current season would provide, he and the rest of the Business Association were aware that humans weren't used to thinking in those terms.

"The reports coming from Brittania and the west coast of Afrikah . . ." Montgomery reached for more books but didn't pick up any. "Cel-Romano is really gone. All those cities, all those people. Millions of people dead. Whole cities turned into charnel houses. Whole cultures destroyed beyond recovery. No survivors." The last words were barely a whisper.

"There are always survivors, Lieutenant," Simon snapped. Didn't mean there would be enough survivors for the species to continue, but he wasn't going to share that with Montgomery. Not when he had a message to deliver.

"What will happen to the survivors?"

Wondering if the man was concerned about humans on the other side of the Atlantik or if he was thinking of something—or someone—else, Simon said, "They'll get up in the morning and work in their fields, tend their animals, drive their carts to the marketplace in their village, gossip with their friends, take out a boat and bring back fish to eat and sell. There may be things that will be hard to buy, at least for a while, but the humans who kept their bargain with the *terra indigene* will get by. Even in Cel-Romano. And so will we. Your pup may not get all the treats she wants, and there will be some days when none of us have a completely full belly, but we'll have enough."

"In the Courtyard."

Since Montgomery had stopped helping with the books, Simon retrieved the packing list and checked off the books in one box before he opened the next one.

"We're not here to take care of you humans," he said. "We never were. We're here to take care of the world." He set the packing slips aside. "Tell Captain Burke and Agent O'Sullivan that tomorrow morning the three of you will meet some of us at the consulate."

"Why?"

A shiver went through Simon. "Because Ocean is coming to Lakeside, and she wants to talk to you."

"Gods above and below," O'Sullivan said. "Was Wolfgard serious?"

Standing in Burke's office with the door closed, Monty wished he could deny it. "He's serious."

"The Great Lakes are the largest source of fresh water on the continent," O'Sullivan continued. "What will happen to Etu and Tahki if the *ocean* flows in?"

"I imagine some . . . accommodation . . . has been made," Burke said.

Like what? Monty thought. "What happened at your meeting with the mayor?"

Burke's blue eyes were filled with sharp amusement.

"Governor Hannigan has requested that any public official who supported the HFL resign immediately so that human governments in the Northeast can try to reestablish a working relationship with the *terra indigene*," O'Sullivan said. "He feels that the Others aren't going to be sympathetic to any request humans make if they're represented by a human they consider an enemy."

"I agree with that," Burke said. "When Mayor Rogers began to bluster, I felt obliged to remind him that, by being a member of the HFL, he broke his promise to work with the *terra indigene*—a promise he made after the death of his predecessor, who also supported the Humans First and Last movement."

"And I felt compelled to remind him that he was the *acting* mayor, not an elected official," O'Sullivan said. "I encouraged him to resign before he was fired."

"Or eaten," Burke added.

"That seemed to be the incentive he needed to write his resignation then and there," O'Sullivan continued. "So Captain Burke and I helped His Honor clear out his desk, and we made sure we had all the keys to the government building and the mayor's office before we said good-bye."

Monty stared at them. "What happens now? Do we have a government?"

Burke gave them one of his fierce-friendly smiles. "I'm in favor of asking Elliot Wolfgard to act as interim mayor until the fall elections or until the governor appoints another person as acting mayor. At least Elliot understands the workings of human government, being the consul for the Courtyard."

"Do you really think he would argue on behalf of humans if what the citizens want or feel they need conflicts with what the Courtyard wants?" O'Sullivan asked.

Burke sighed. "No, I don't. At least, not now. As I've said before, Simon Wolfgard is the most progressive *terra indigene* leader I've come across, and we need people who will work *with* him, now more than ever. Especially when you consider that, of the four places around here that have human inhabitants—Lakeside, Ferryman's Landing, Talulah Falls, and that new community on River Road—Lakeside is the *only* one that is human controlled and has a government that answers to the regional governor and not to the *terra indigene*."

O'Sullivan sat on the edge of Burke's desk. "I'll deny saying this, but Governor Hannigan thinks there may not be any human-controlled towns left between here and Hubb NE. And communication with Toland has been . . . erratic. A couple of the other ITF agents are driving down to assess the situation. A couple more are hoping for answers about the condition of the small towns that were around the Finger Lakes."

Monty noticed the slight tremble in Burke's hands—a reminder that even his captain's previous experience with the Others didn't always prepare him for the things happening now.

Burke said, "Before we start making plans for Lakeside, let's go to that meeting tomorrow and find out if we even have a future."

CHAPTER 56

Windsday, Sumor 18

Standing in the consulate's meeting room, Monty heard seagulls and the surf before he caught the briny smell of the female who walked into the room, flanked by the Lakeside Elementals, Water and Air.

The shape was female, but she never would have passed for human. Her hair was kelp, and snails and small crabs moved about in it. Her body was fluid and blue-gray, covered by a gown that moved continuously, like waves coming to shore—and was the source of the sounds of surf and gulls.

He had taken Lizzy to the shore a few times to look for shells. He had found the Atlantik alluring, but he had never wanted to bet his life by going out on that water—and that was before he had learned there was something sentient that could command that water.

"Ocean," Simon said. "Welcome to the Lakeside Courtyard."

He's not comfortable with her being here, Monty thought, watching the Wolf struggle to maintain a sufficiently non-furry human shape. *Or maybe he doesn't want to look human in the presence of such a dangerous form of* terra indigene.

"The Sharkgard, Orcasgard, and I have enjoyed the stories that have flowed from this place in recent times," Ocean said. Although quiet, the voice held depth and the memory of the storms just past.

Simon's ears suddenly shifted to Wolf, and he made a frustrated sound as he struggled to get his ears back to human shape.

She smiled at Simon, and the sound in the room became the soft murmur of gentle waves kissing sand. Then she looked at the three humans, and the smile faded and the sound of storm surge returned.

Stepping up to the table, Vlad unfolded a large map. "As you requested. I hope it's adequate."

Ocean nodded but she continued to look at the three men standing tensely on the other side of the table.

"This I command," she said. "No ship that sails from Thaisia will touch Cel-Romano. That place is closed to the humans here. Defy me, and *no* ship from this land will survive me."

Captain Burke quietly cleared his throat. "What about other places? Brittania, for example."

Ocean turned her attention to Simon. "Wolf?"

"Captain Burke's kin from Brittania helped us when we asked," Simon replied. "We have no quarrel with the humans who live there."

"Then I will permit ships to sail between Thaisia and Brittania. And Felidae and Afrikah since they did not spawn enemies of our land kin."

"What about Tokhar-Chin?" Monty asked, wondering if a Wolf would be considered "land kin" to something like her.

"It does not touch my domain. You would have to ask the guardian of the Pacifik about that place," she replied.

Had he really wanted confirmation that there was more than one of these creatures? Well, now they all knew.

Ocean studied the map of Namid, paying particular attention to her own domain. She brushed a finger over the Fingerbone Islands, leaving a wet line on the paper. "My home. The place where I keep the treasures that the water, the Sharkgard, and the Orcasgard retrieve for my pleasure. I have many things. Old things. Old maps. I enjoy looking at the way you humans think I have changed. I am not the one who changed." Her smile was savage and primal and terrifying.

"On the old maps, you used to put the words 'Here Be Monsters.'" Her finger traced a wet curve in front of the strait that provided entrance to the Mediterran Sea. She looked at Burke and O'Sullivan, and the punch of that look made Monty feel weak, even though it wasn't directed at him. She bared teeth that might have been made of coral. "You should put those words on the maps again."

She walked out of the room, followed by Air and Water.

Monty braced a hand on a chair.

"So," O'Sullivan said. "No trade with Cel-Romano. I'm not sure how we'll enforce that."

"You won't have to," Simon said, touching his ears as if to reassure himself that they had returned to human shape.

"But if Thaisian ships disobey that command, Ocean will destroy *all* the ships sailing from this land, and that would include fishing vessels," Vlad said. "Can your people afford to lose the food that comes from the sea?"

"We'll spread the word," Burke said after a tense silence.

Simon nodded. "We'll let the *terra indigene* know as well."

As they left the consulate, Monty realized that he'd stopped thinking of Simon Wolfgard as a predator. Faced with the truth of what else was out there, the Courtyard's residents didn't seem like much of a threat anymore.

He opened the back door of Burke's sedan but didn't get in. "Here be monsters. Do you think she was referring to the *terra indigene* or to humans?"

Burke looked at him over the roof of the car. "At this point, Lieutenant, does it really matter?"

CHAPTER 57

Thaisday, Sumor 19

Meg wasn't sure how long she'd been staring at the three-ring binder that held the names and contact information for Intuit companies. But when she became aware of the sorting room again, she was startled to see Twyla Montgomery standing on the other side of the table.

"Miss Twyla. What . . . ?"

"Didn't want to disturb you while your mind was wandering," Twyla said gently.

"Arroo?" The click of nails on the floor in the front room as Nathan hustled to find out what was going on in the sorting room.

"It's all right," Meg said, looking at the watch Wolf, who had his front legs braced on the counter.

"I know this is an off-limits place," Twyla began.

"For the children," Meg said hurriedly.

"You got reasons for your rules, and those reasons should be respected." Seeing Meg's scars, Twyla's dark eyes held neither pity nor discomfort. "But I believe in earning my keep. The folks running the Courtyard are looking at what skills are available to them, and they'll sort out the work as soon as they can. In the meantime, I can help with the dusting and mopping if that would be of use to you. I noticed the back room could use a bit of shine. And there's bound to be plenty of loose hairs coating the floor in that front room." She winked at Meg.

Nathan growled and went back to his Wolf bed.

"Thank you," Meg said. "I haven't kept up with cleaning."

"Mind if I ask what you're doing?"

"This binder holds the names of companies owned or run by the Intuits. I'm supposed to order as much as I can from them from now on so that the people in Lakeside can't complain that we're taking rationed goods away from them. And I have lists of things people would like to buy in the Market Square grocery store. But some things . . . People have listed a dozen different kinds of cereal, and I don't know how to choose."

"How many kinds of cereal does that store have now?"

"I'm not sure. The Others eat a lot more meat than cereal."

Moving slowly, Twyla eased around the table until she stood beside Meg and could look at the lists.

"Which of these do you think something like himself would eat?" Twyla tipped her head to indicate Nathan. "Or those Crows?"

"Sierra gave me this list of cereals the children would want. . . ."

Twyla shook her head. "Children will pester and pester for something until you buy it, and then they won't want it anymore. Don't you be thinking about that. You just think about what's useful to the most residents." She tapped a list. "Oatmeal is a winter cereal that can be fancied up with berries and nuts and a bit of sweetening. If you can get them, order a cereal made from corn and another made of oats—things you can eat by the handful if you need something quick. Those who want something different can buy it at another store or do without."

"Tess said something like that." Actually Tess had said if humans didn't want to eat what was offered in the Courtyard they could feast on their stubbornness and starve.

Twyla gave Meg's hand a little pat. "Don't you let everybody else's wants get you flustered. Whether it has two legs or four, just because a pup yaps at you doesn't mean you have to pay it any mind. Now, I'll let you get back to your work while I put a bit of shine to the back room."

Listening to Twyla singing in the back room, Meg put aside the binder and the lists. Yes, she felt flustered, but it wasn't really about the foods and merchandise people wanted. Worrying about things like cereal was a way to avoid the question that had been in her thoughts ever since she pulled that "romance" card from the drawer.

How much human did *she* want? In many ways, she counted on Simon not thinking like a human, not acting like a human. She *trusted* him because he wasn't human. Could she count on him not slipping too far into being human if she wanted to explore just a little bit, just enough to see if romance might provide a different kind of euphoria?

She frittered away the afternoon, signing for a couple of deliveries, but mostly shuffling the lists without doing anything with them.

Just how human could Simon be without giving up what he was? Was there a way to find an answer without either of them getting hurt?

Nathan had left for the day, and she was closing up the office when Simon walked in, looking hot and ready to bite.

"I want to go swimming tonight," Meg said, not sure if she was making a suggestion or issuing a challenge.

"With the female pack?"

Understandable assumption. The female pack would need permission to go to the swimming hole in the Corvine part of the Courtyard. "No, with you. Just us. Not even Sam."

Simon cocked his head. "Not with Sam? Why?"

She swallowed hard. "I want to try skinny-dipping."

He was so still, she wasn't sure he was even breathing.

"That's swimming without clothes," he finally said.

"Yes."

"Both of us swimming without clothes. In human form."

"Yes. But . . . that's as much as I want to try."

"After dark?"

She couldn't imagine doing it when she could be *seen*. "Yes."

Simon scratched behind one ear. "All right. Are we going home now?"

He didn't sound angry or upset that she didn't want to do more. He sounded . . . baffled.

They finished closing up the office and loaded the BOW with her carry sack and whatever he was bringing back to the apartments. As they drove away, it occurred to her that she was just as relieved to leave the humans behind as he was.

"Meg wants to go skinny-dipping?"

That Vlad sounded as baffled as he felt made Simon feel better. At least he wasn't the only one who was confused. "That's what she said. With me. After dark. With both of us in human form."

"None of us wear clothes when we play in the water unless we're giving the clothes a quick rinse without removing them."

"I *know* that. But this is important to Meg. I just don't know why." Simon growled in frustration. She'd been upset the last time she saw him as a naked human. Why was *this* time different?

Vlad took a restless turn around Simon's living room. "I read a couple of those kissy books before I sent them on to Prairie Gold."

"Really? Why?"

Vlad shrugged.

"Did the books mention skinny-dipping?" Simon thought for a moment. "Do you think Meg read those books?"

"Don't know, but I'm wondering if this is a step in human courtship, another kind of play before the female is ready to mate."

"Ruthie and Kowalski weren't skinny-dipping in the winter before they mated," Simon argued.

"But showering together is considered pre-mating play."

Simon threw himself on the sofa. "This isn't helping."

Vlad sat beside him. "How much human is the *terra indigene* going to keep?" He paused, then added quietly, "How much human are you going to absorb?"

The possibility of losing the Wolf, the essential part of his nature, scared him. But Meg didn't want, didn't trust, a male who was a *human* human. She *needed* him to retain the Wolf.

What did the Elders need and want from the Others living in the Lakeside Courtyard? There hadn't been a new form of *terra indigene* in a very long time.

He wasn't ready to shoulder the weight of that possibility. And Meg certainly wasn't ready. But play would be good.

"Are you going to tell Meg that the Elders are curious enough about the howling not-Wolf that they're going to return to the Courtyard?" Vlad asked.

"No. I think the skinny-dipping will be enough excitement for one night."

They drove to the swimming hole. Since Vlad hadn't been much help, Simon had considered asking one of the human pack about human courtship, but he decided against it. Meg was no more knowledgeable than he, so this was just another thing they would figure out together.

Her mood had changed as the sun went down. She seemed small and timid, as if she had already used up her allotment of courage for the day.

"We don't have to do the skinny-dipping thing," he said, trying to understand her mood. "We can paddle around wearing clothes. We'll feel just as cool."

"No. I want to do this."

You want to do this as much as I want to be stepped on by a bison. But he parked the BOW and pulled the blanket out of the back. Someone had thoughtfully set some of the solar-powered lights around the water, creating enough illumination that Meg wouldn't be stumbling around in the dark.

She removed her sandals, then stood at the edge of the swimming hole, looking so unhappy.

He wondered how to back out of this adventure when Meg suddenly pulled off her clothes and jumped into the water. She went under, then surfaced, squeaking from the shock of water so much cooler than the air.

He stripped off his clothes and jumped in. Yes, the water shocked the human form more than it did the Wolf, but only for a moment.

"You okay, Meg?"

She paddled to the edge and grabbed handfuls of grass to anchor herself, her legs rising to float behind her. "I'm okay." She floated for a minute before saying softly, "I'm okay."

He joined her at the edge. "The water feels good after a sticky day."

She nodded.

Fragile, complicated Meg. What did she want him to do?

She turned her head away from him just enough for light to shine on the new scar along the right side of her jaw. Winter or summer, she wouldn't be able to hide *that* one. And he wouldn't forget why she'd made that cut.

He gently kissed that scar and felt something changing inside him—just a flutter of change, there and gone, but leaving its mark.

She looked at him, her eyes wide with uncertainty. If he kissed her again, she would flee like a bunny.

So he licked her nose and made her laugh before he lunged for the center of the pool, making as big a splash as he could. A moment later, she leaped on top of him with a joyful yelp that was cut off when they both went under. Sputtering, he pulled her to the surface.

For several minutes they splashed around, their bodies brushing and bumping like two Wolves at play. Then they climbed out and collapsed on the blanket—she on her back and he stretched out on his belly.

He looked at her and grinned. She looked at him and laughed.

Simon listened while Meg's breathing quieted as she drifted closer to sleep. Propped up on his forearms, he watched her for a moment before he shifted to Wolf and eased closer to her, letting out a happy sigh when she buried her fingers in his fur.

How much human was left in Thaisia? How much would the *terra indigene* keep? He didn't have answers, but he and Meg would figure out a way to look after their pack, and they would be all right.

Simon gave her shoulder a couple of licks. Sleepy now, he laid his head on his paws, still aware of Meg's fingers in his fur.

Yes, they would be all right.

GOOCH

www.transworldireland.ie

www.penguin.co.uk

GOOCH

The Autobiography

COLM COOPER

with

VINCENT HOGAN

TRANSWORLD IRELAND

TRANSWORLD IRELAND PUBLISHERS
Penguin Random House Ireland, Morrison Chambers,
32 Nassau Street, Dublin 2, Ireland
www.transworldireland.ie

Transworld Ireland is part of the Penguin Random House group of companies
whose addresses can be found at global.penguinrandomhouse.com

Penguin
Random House
UK

First published in the UK and Ireland in 2017
by Transworld Ireland
an imprint of Transworld Publishers

A CIP catalogue record for this book
is available from the British Library.

ISBN 9781848272187

Typeset in 12.5/15.5 pt Ehrhardt MT by Jouve (UK), Milton Keynes
Printed and bound in Great Britain by Clays Ltd, Bungay, Suffolk

Penguin Random House is committed to a sustainable
future for our business, our readers and our planet. This book
is made from Forest Stewardship Council® certified paper.

MIX
Paper from
responsible sources
FSC® C018179

1 3 5 7 9 10 8 6 4 2